VISIONS OF SARAH

VISIONS OF SARAH

By Kelly A. Zarembski

Writer's Showcase
San Jose New York Lincoln Shanghai

Visions of Sarah

Writer's Showcase
an imprint of iUniverse, Inc.

For information address:
iUniverse, Inc.
5220 S. 16th St., Suite 200
Lincoln, NE 68512
www.iuniverse.com

ISBN: 0-595-21962-4

Printed in the United States of America

CHAPTER 1

❀

*T*he day was cold and the wind sharp, with the smell of roses in the air. After all they were her favorite, the yellow ones of course. Standing there I couldn't move the simple thought of leaving was more than I could bear. Taking a deep breath I closed my eyes and exhaled slowly, feeling the cold air pierce my lungs. It hurt and I wanted it to. For some strange reason I wanted to experience nothing but pain today.

Opening my eyes I picked up one of her roses and let my forefinger slowly yet painfully push its way on the tip of a pointy thorn. Watching a small trickle of blood fall between my fingers my heart hurt and my knees felt weak. I fell back down in the chair directly in front of her.

After the crowd left it was just me, alone with my thoughts, my memories, and my dreams. Dreams I know will never come true, dreams that ended this twelfth day of October.

Sitting with my head in my hands I separated my fingers to stare at her coffin and was blinded by the brightness of the sun shining down on it. I used my fingers to shield my eyes from the bright light. If only the same would be possible for my heart, all I wanted to do was shield it from all of this pain.

I couldn't believe she was gone. With one hand I wiped away my tears while I stared at her coffin, knowing she was inside and I couldn't leave her. I couldn't leave knowing the minute I did she would be lowered into the ground and she would be so cold. I just wanted to keep her warm forever. I knew I couldn't. I guess the only comfort I had was that I knew she was no longer in pain.

My head lowered and my hands flew to my face while my eyes burned from all the tears. I looked up and grabbed hold of her coffin to help me stand then laid my hand gently resting on the cool metal of her final resting place.

I set the rose down in place of my hand and at that moment I knew it was true, the horrible fact was that I was now alone and she was gone forever.

Closing my eyes to force the tears from them, I looked up to the sky. "Sarah, what do I do now? How do I go on? I know that people deal with this everyday, but right now it's me Sarah, and I am devastated.

Oh Sarah, I can't even think of going on without you."

Standing there with both hands resting on top of her coffin I gently began rubbing it watching my tears slowly roll down my cheek and hit the top of her coffin splattering into little droplets everywhere.

I stood, quiet, just listening to the wind and the rustling leaves, then smiled because the smell of the leaves brought back a strong memory of Sarah raking them in the backyard. She stood holding a rake in her hands while she looked up at me. I was watching her from inside our back porch. She always was the outdoorsy one. She was amazing.

"Melissa, you can't stay here all day it's not good for you, besides people are waiting to say goodbye."

I felt my sister standing behind me and I just couldn't turn around, I was still in my dream world, it's where I wanted to stay.

She yelled. "Mel did you hear me? Are you okay?"

I turned with tears running down my face. "Yeah Kimmie, I'm fine."

She looked at the ground and put her hands in her pockets. "Mel I'm sorry." She looked up in my eyes. "There's just people waiting to see you and say goodbye."

"I know, I know, just one more minute." I flashed her a small smile giving her all I had in me.

I turned to wipe my tears away and a split second later felt her arms slipping around me. My hands flew to grab her arms that were gently placed around my neck and I laid my head back on her shoulder to look up at the sky.

Still my tears were falling. "Kimmie I think she'll like it here, don't you?"

She squeezed me tight. "Yeah Mel, she'll love it here."

We both stood quietly looking around at how beautiful and peaceful it was. The wind gently blew the leaves that were scattered about and the sound was...well peaceful.

After several minutes of quiet Kimmie kissed my cheek and raised her hand to rub my tears away. "Take your time Mel I'll be at the car."

I turned to her. "Thanks."

"You know I love you and I just worry about you that's all."

"I know." I turned staring straight ahead, again at the leaves.

I felt her kiss the back of my head, then I listened as she walked away until I heard nothing but the wind twisting the autumn leaves still clinging to life on the trees. Standing there I let that same wind rustle my hair and gently kiss the back of my neck.

Sitting down my head fell into my open hands, and then slowly it rose. "Well honey, I guess this is goodbye for now. You know I'll always love you and in spite of anything and everything that's going to happen to me, you will always be in my thoughts as well as my heart."

I stood and lightly touched the single rose that lay on her coffin letting all the feelings of anxiety and loneliness rush through me. I knew this day was coming, I just couldn't believe it was finally here.

What on earth am I going to do without her? She was my lover, my best friend; she was the rock in our little family. Now there's just me, lonely, heartbroken and I don't have a clue how to go on by myself.

Stepping away from her coffin I had a funny feeling of entering into a new life, a new destiny, a whole new world. Before I walked away I kissed my fingers and ran them along the side of her final resting place then turned away and did just that, I entered the world of my family and friends with all their good intentions. Although it was no consolation for what just happened to my world and me, as I had always known it to be.

As I walked away I felt like I was somehow abandoning Sarah in some way. I kept turning around, looking back at her there, alone, beneath a single Maple tree and felt a horrible emptiness in my stomach and soul.

I approached everyone, hugged, kissed and said my goodbyes and just when I thought I was finally alone I felt a hand on my shoulder, my whole body jumped as I gasped for air. Then I whipped around only to see my sister.

"Jeez Kim you scared the hell out of me!"

She stood sadly smiling at me. "I'm sorry. I waited around to see if you wanted to come home with Dave, the kids and myself for a few days? The kids would love to see you. You know you're their favorite aunt." She playfully tugged at my arm. "Besides I don't think you should be alone right now."

"Thanks for the offer really, but I think I'll just go home. What I really need now is to be alone."

"I know that you do, but I'm concerned about you, and being around family might be good for you."

"No Kimmie, I'm going to go home." I looked past her and saw Dave leaning against his car with his hands in his pants pockets. Then I looked back at Kim.

She smiled and tucked my hair behind my ear. "Okay, but if you need anything at all you just call me." She turned to walk away, then turned back. "Mel are you going to be okay?"

I lowered my head then looked back into her eyes. "I know what I had with Sarah wasn't everyone's dream but it was my dream, it was my life and now…I'll be okay. I just need some time to myself. Don't worry."

I saw worry and concern in her eyes. "Mel, I love you."

"Yeah, me too. Now go home to your family."

I pulled her close and hugged her tight, then told her I'd call her in a few days. Standing there I watched her walk away and at that moment I think it finally hit me as to how different we really are. Oh, we're sisters and as many things that we have in common and as many ways that we're alike, we're also different. Watching her walk I saw our similarities, both tall and thin, with light brown hair, yet she walked into the arms of her husband. That's where all our differences begin. I felt a slight smile come over my face knowing how happy she is in her life. Then I turned and walked straight ahead, down the hill and through the trees for what seemed like the longest walk of my life. Somehow I felt that by leaving, I was leaving Sarah as well. I knew deep down that wasn't true, but yet deep down I knew that it was. That scared the hell out of me.

I turned to see Sarah's coffin sitting high on the hill. I felt sad, but I continued on.

Getting in my car I rested my head on the steering wheel because I knew this was just the beginning of me being alone. My life with Sarah was all planned out, our home, our talks of a family, our future. Now I have to start all over again, and not only don't I want to do that, but I have no idea how to do that.

I raised my head, staring out at nothing.

I never realized that when her pain ended mine would just begin. She was my first true love. We both knew it the first time we saw each other, and we've been together ever since. This would have been 11 years that we were together. I met her when I was nineteen, she was a couple of years older than me but we grew together. She was my life and now I'm scared to death to go on without her.

I wiped the tears from my eyes and face, I knew I had to leave before my emotions took over and I would be unable to drive.

As I pulled up in front of our house I realized that I would never be able to stay here. After all this is where we both lived and dreamed. The memories would be too much for me, I knew that, and yet I still went in through the front door.

I walked through the house as I've done a million times before but this time I knew that Sarah wouldn't be following behind me. I laid my keys on the kitchen table and just walked through the house knowing how painful it would be but yet somehow feeling that it may help me in some way. Like as if remembering every little detail of where she walked, and where she sat down or rested her head would help ease my pain. Well it didn't ease my pain, in fact it made it worse because I now felt that someday I might forget these little memories that I had always taken for granted. With that in mind I walked through the house, top to bottom trying to remember everything, and not forget anything. When I was done and thoroughly exhausted, I sat and cried for what seemed like hours, and probably was.

I just started to fall into a much-needed sleep when the phone started ringing. On the tenth ring, it finally stopped.

Now I'll never be able to fall asleep, so I'm forced to lay here and have my mind wander. Remembering and thinking of all the things that Sarah and I used to do in and out of this house, everywhere I looked I saw her. I just couldn't stand sitting here anymore so I went to the backyard.

Sitting in the yard was worse than being in the house because I think we spent more quality time in the yard. We would always barbecue, swim, do yard work and just sit around talking, drinking beer and playing games. Games were Sarah's favorite; she would absolutely love playing all sorts of games. Sitting at the patio table with a large fire burning in our outdoor fireplace, music playing and the two of us battling over a game of Monopoly was probably my strongest memory of her right now. I could almost smell the fire burning.

Tightly wrapping my arms around myself I shivered. "God, I can't stand this. Why? Why her?"

I felt myself beginning to cry again so I went back inside to try and get some sleep. As I walked through the house, I grabbed a bottle of vodka from the freezer and made a quick martini. My favorite, I think it all has to do with the olive. Anyway, I figured that it would help me sleep. As I sat and drank I came to the quick realization that work was all I had left, so I should just throw myself into it.

Stretching out on the couch I covered myself with an old afghan, and to take my mind off of Sarah I began to think about work.

I work in an art gallery and love my work. Windy Berrington is the owner of the gallery and has really taught me a lot about the business. She is also a strikingly beautiful and generous woman. Windy is very tall with long dark hair, amazing almond shaped green eyes with skin like milk, and an absolutely beautiful personality. Sarah didn't like her very much for the simple fact that she thought I did, more than I should have anyway. While Sarah was so very sick I turned to Windy a lot for friendship, just for someone to talk to and help me through the rough spots. I really came to depend on her a great deal. After awhile though I started to have feelings for Windy and felt very confused, not to mention very guilty. Although I knew nothing would ever come of it, I wouldn't let it, and Windy certainly wouldn't have. She never really talked about her personal life except for one man that she brought up in more than one conversation. So I assumed she was straight, but that didn't stop me from staring at her. Every once in awhile I would catch myself and wonder what the hell I was doing. While Sarah was home so sick in bed and I was staring, and daydreaming about Windy. The guilt was eating me alive.

I was constantly at her bedside; I did everything and more for her. But when I was with Windy just talking to her seemed to help me. I was actually glad that Windy wasn't gay because that helped with my confusion greatly, besides I never wanted to lose her friendship.

Right now thoughts of work were somewhat of a comfort to me, and the feeling of comfort helped me relax. My mind wandered from thoughts of work to thoughts of whether I'm going to move from this house or not, it just seems too creepy being here by myself.

After my second martini, and all of the tears I cried, and all of my thinking, I finally started feeling tired and fell quickly asleep.

CHAPTER 2

When I awoke I reached over and touched Sarah's pillow, then it hit me, she is no longer with me. I cried until I fell asleep again.

Opening my eyes again I grabbed Sarah's pillow, then just held it and cried some more. After what seemed like hours I got out of bed only to realize I had Sarah's pajamas on. Sometime in the middle of the night I must have crawled into bed and without realizing it, put Sarah's pajamas on. Looking down and feeling the softness of the flannel I fell back into bed curling up with her pillow lost in my memories, realizing this is the first time in 11 years that I'm in bed and in this house alone. It's been so long since I've slept alone, I'm afraid that I'll never get used to it.

The night was long and restless and the memories of us kept rushing through my mind like a cool wind that precedes a thunderstorm.

I'm not looking forward to this day because I know what it brings, loneliness.

I looked up at the ceiling. "Oh God, Sarah without you here to guide me and accompany me through my days I feel like a puppet with no one to hold my strings. I guess I never really understood the kind of impact you had on, and over my life. Well if I didn't then, I do now, and I miss it. I miss you already."

Wiping my face in her pillow I decided to just lay here and dream.

❧   ❧   ❧

After getting up for the third time I went straight into the bath-room to take a shower, after all I still didn't wash any of the make-up or hairspray off from the funeral.

I washed, and then sat in the bottom of the bathtub with my head in my hands, weeping uncontrollably, and remembering vividly.

When the water turned from hot to ice cold I got out of the tub and wrapped myself in my warmest L.L. Bean flannel robe then went into the kitchen to make a pot of coffee. Opening the refrigerator to get out the milk for my coffee, I saw her grapefruit juice. Sarah drank grapefruit juice religiously every morning. I wanted to cry, but couldn't, I just couldn't. I had no more tears left.

I fixed myself a cup of coffee and listened to what seemed like endless messages on my answering machine. I could feel myself hesi-tating because I really didn't want to listen, let alone talk to anyone right now, but I did anyway. The messages were all family and friends concerned about me, although it did feel good, it really didn't make me feel any better, if that makes any sense. I love that everyone worries and cares about me, but this is something that I have to get through alone. Sarah and I both knew for a long time she was dying, the doctors told both of us the cancer was terminal. We were some-what prepared, if anyone could be prepared for something like this. It's just the final realization of it all that's hitting me so hard. I guess a lot of it is guilt I'm feeling because I almost feel relieved after Sarah's death. She was in a hell of a lot of pain and quite frankly she really didn't want to go on any longer. Her whole body was riddled with cancer and I really hated watching her everyday try to deal with the pain, for my sake. I felt so much guilt and pain every time I looked at her, knowing she was hurting, and dying, and there wasn't a damn thing I could do about it. If it was up to me I would have held on to her forever, but I do feel some comfort in the fact that she is no longer in pain. Just watching her lay there and slowly being eaten away by the disease was actually more than I could bear. I guess it's for the best and I'm just being selfish wallowing in my pain, but I can't help what I feel.

With my coffee in hand I walked into the downstairs bedroom where Sarah stayed when she was too sick to go to our own bedroom upstairs. It was in this room where she died. I crawled in the bed just as I did when we both knew that the end was near.

Lying there I looked around the room at all the hospital equipment, and the fresh flowers that I always made sure she had. She loved wild flowers, but yellow roses were her favorite. I lay staring at the flowers and all their beauty. Wiping a tear away, I pulled a rose out of one of the many vases surrounding her bed. I held it in my fingers, smelling it, and rubbing it along my cheek, feeling its soft and silky petals on my skin. It's so beautiful and soft, it reminds me so much of Sarah.

When I remember back to the night before her death, everything is still so vivid. I was sitting in the chair next to her bed holding her hand, studying her fingers, her nails and her delicate wrists. That night I noticed everything about her I might have taken for granted before.

I rolled over and stared at the other side of the room.

Then I lay next to her in bed holding her tight, matching my breath for every one of hers. I wanted to feel her pain, and experience everything that she was going through, hoping that I somehow could take the pain away if only for a little while.

The next morning the sun woke me, I was in the chair next to her bed, and I must have dozed off for a while. Sarah's eyes were open; she was lying there, watching me.

I smiled and knelt next to her bed straightening her covers, and kissed her good morning. "Honey did you sleep well?" My lips moved to her forehead.

Her eyes closed halfway and she swallowed hard while she licked her lips. "No, I didn't sleep at all. All I wanted to do was watch you."

I moved to look in her eyes. "Watch me? That's silly you know you need your rest."

I started to giggle nervously because somehow I knew what she knew. I began to straighten her pillows when I looked in her eyes. I knew, and crawled into bed with her holding her, with my face nestled in her neck. I just couldn't look in her eyes because I didn't want to believe this was actually happening. I repeated over, and over how much I loved her, and how everything was going to be all right

I tasted my own tears as they rolled down her neck. I squeezed and held her as tight as I could while I rubbed my face in her neck kissing her lightly on her throat.

I could feel her body weakening and struggling for every breath.

She then reached over with her hand and touched my face, lifting my head so I could look in her eyes. My face wet from my own tears, I just couldn't stop them, they wouldn't stop. I know she didn't need to see them, but I couldn't stop them. She had a far away look in her eyes, and it scared me.

Her eyes closed half way, then opened again to look in mine. "Melissa I loved you with my body, my heart and my soul. I know what you have to offer. I want you to love for a second time." She struggled for a breath. "Don't cry for me I'll always be here for you, I promise you that. A love like ours will never die. It can't possibly."

I kissed her on the mouth. "Sarah I'll always love you."

"I know Mel…" She struggled for air. "I know." She smiled a half smile.

We lay there quietly for a few minutes and all I thought about was that I couldn't believe this was happening. I couldn't believe that she was going to leave me and I'll never see, or hold her again.

I rubbed her arm feeling her skin, burning this memory in my head, trying to remember every detail of her, then I felt her take a deep breath, and exhale slowly. I actually felt her body release her from all of her pain. I closed my eyes knowing what just happened, but I still couldn't release my grip on her. I lay there holding her, crying and telling her over and over again how everything was going to be all right. I told her stories and memories of the times we shared. I couldn't believe how fast her body got so cold.

Getting out of bed I went into the hall closet to get her another blanket. Standing there I held the blanket up to my face and wiped my tears away, then I reached for the phone to call my sister, as I grabbed the receiver my hand was shaking so badly I dropped it, then fell to my knees. Doubled over, my head fell on the blanket and I reached for the receiver while tears rolled down my face, I dialed my sister's number and I told Kimmie what had happened, then went to cover Sarah with the blanket and crawled back into bed with her.

All of the memories of that night brought back all of my tears, and I realized I had to get out of this bed. I climbed out and dropped the rose I was holding on Sarah's pillow.

With my hand on the door handle I turned, and I swore I saw Sarah sitting there on the edge of the bed. She looked so real I almost lost my breath. She was smiling at me. She looked like her old self. Her hair was full, shiny and perfect. Her face had its old glow about it. Her eyes dazzled, and her lips were full and red. Looking at her I could see her weight was back as well. She simply looked wonderful, and tears started rolling down my face.

Her smile took over her face. "Mel don't cry for me I'm no longer in pain."

I let go of the door handle and turned to stand in front of the bed. "Sarah!" I screamed and went to her.

"Mel I love you so much." Her hand stretched out to me. "But I have to go."

I tried to grab her, but she was starting to fade away. Her voice was still so clear though. "Mel you have to let me go. Remember I'll always be here for you."

Then nothing. I stood in front of the bed where she was sitting, and I felt a cold chill run down my spine, then I turned and ran out of the room.

I banged my head and my fists on the closed door wondering if I was going crazy then slumped to the floor crying hysterically and uncontrollably, sitting there in my own thoughts until it was dark.

I started feeling uneasy and scared after seeing Sarah, and the darkness only intensified this feeling, so I decided to go upstairs to bed.

        ❧   ❧   ❧

Waking up I felt refreshed. All night I dreamt of Sarah coming home to me. Jumping out of bed I threw on a pair of sweats and a long sleeved t-shirt. I could feel myself almost running downstairs as I headed straight for the bedroom, throwing the door open I ran inside. My heart was beating so hard I thought it was going to burst out of my chest. I really don't know what I thought I would find. Maybe I thought Sarah would still be there, but she wasn't. Thinking that maybe she would appear to me again I made myself comfortable in the chair next to her bed and sat there falling in and out of sleep until the next morning, dreaming of Sarah.

When I awoke I looked around, then realized where I was. Sitting with my head in my hands I wondered what was happening to me. With tears rolling down the palms of my hands and wrists, I watched as they hit the floor hard, splattering in a little puddle. It was then I knew I had to get out of this house for a while.

I finally tore myself away and went upstairs to take a shower and change my clothes. On my way back downstairs I looked at Sarah's door, standing there I wondered if I open it, would she be there. Instead of opening the door I turned and grabbed my shoes. Putting them on I couldn't help but stare at that door. Jumping up I ran over to it throwing it open. Nothing. Nothing was there. I knew nothing would be.

Taking my keys, I left the house and slammed the door behind me.

I thought a bike ride with the cool October air hitting my face might clear my head. Climbing on, I rode about 10 miles then stopped by a creek grabbing for my water bottle as I fell into the grass.

Stretching out on the grass with my arms reaching behind my head I stared at the clouds above me and had a flash back to when I was a kid. My sister and I would always try to make objects or people out of the cloud shapes. Lying there I picked out Elmo from Sesame Street, and a giant waffle iron. Silly I guess, but I did notice that it was the first time in months I didn't think about anything, all I did was lay there picking out cloud shapes. Then the clouds started getting darker and darker until I figured I better start heading back before the rain hit. October is always an unpredictable month in Ohio.

Pulling up to my garage I put my bike away and ran into the house just as it started raining. Cold and damp I decided to take a long hot bath.

On my way upstairs I stopped in front of Sarah's door staring at it. I hesitated as I raised my hand and let my fingers gently touch the cool wood softly laying my head against it; my other hand touched the door handle. Tears started to form in my eyes and I ran upstairs.

As I sat in the tub I realized how very lonely I am. I miss her so much I just can't believe she's no longer with me. I wondered if I should call my mother, or sister, then thought against it, I'm not one to reach out to people. Sarah and I never really did have a whole lot of friends we didn't need any. We had each other.

I continued to lay back relaxing, letting the warm water roll over my shoulders while I made some sort of mental list of things to keep me occupied.

All I could think of doing was sleeping.

CHAPTER 3

Finally I woke and crawled out of bed, but thoughts of Sarah were still in my head. I still don't know how I'm going to shake this. How am I going to go on with my life? Oh, I know people do and I know what she would say, that I was whining too much…maybe I am, but how could I not.

Coming out of the bathroom I did everything I could not to crawl back in that bed and dream of her.

Lately all I've done is lay on the couch, staring at her door. I flip through photo albums and watch home videos, every once in a while I would go for a bike ride, but more and more all I did was sit in Sarah's room, or lay in bed dreaming of her. I didn't know if I sat there waiting for her to appear to me again, or if I somehow felt close to her being in her bed.

After hours turned into weeks I knew I couldn't keep this up. I never answer the phone or the door; I really haven't talked to anyone since Sarah's death. Well except for Sarah.

It's been weeks and I've been laying in her room and my bed too long. I have to get up and face life and everything around me…without her. So I came to the decision that it's about time for me to go back to work. I've got to start getting my life back.

I picked up the phone.

"Berrington Gallery!"

"Windy, hi it's Mel. Are you busy right now?"

"No, I'm not. Mel how are you? I've been trying to get in touch with you for days. Are you okay? You've had me worried sick."

"I'm fine. It just took me awhile that's all. So how are things at work?"

"Well the truth is it's very busy and I could use your help if you feel up to it."

"That's why I'm calling. How about if I come in tomorrow?"

"That would be great!"

"Okay I'll see you tomorrow then."

"I'll be looking forward to it."

"Me too."

I hung up the phone, made a grocery list then went to the store. I figured I'd come home; clean house and that should pretty much occupy most of my day.

I never looked forward to work so much in my life.

CHAPTER 4

Getting through the holidays was probably the hardest thing I ever had to do, but with the help of my family and friends I did just fine. It's been six months now since Sarah's death and going to work has been the happiest time of day for me. I have to start doing more with my life though because I'm starting to realize that I'm becoming more and more dependent on Windy, and as a result I'm becoming more and more attracted to her. So with that in mind I decided to go out tonight with some old friends I haven't seen in a long time.

Donna Clark is probably my oldest friend; we met in college and have been close ever since. It was actually because of her that I met Sarah. She played on a softball team that was short handed so I filled in, and Sarah played on the opposite team. The minute I saw her I was immediately attracted to her, her medium built fit her small frame perfectly, and the way she tossed her blond hair around made her look unbelievably sexy. Her hair was a shoulder length blunt cut that fit her oval face perfectly, and made her big brown eyes almost jump off her face. I just thought everything about her was perfect and I had to meet her, when I did I knew that I was going to spend the rest of my life with her. She was everything I always wanted, beautiful, smart, funny and extremely sexy. I remember the first time

I ever talked with her, all I wanted to do was grab her and kiss her passionately on the mouth, and I did.

Sarah and I were together from that day on.

Donna on the other hand was always in and out of relationships. Until she met Vicky, her and Vicky are great together.

When Sarah was alive, Donna and Vicky were our best friends. After Sarah's death that all changed. I really had a hard time being around them, because all I could think of was Sarah. When the three of us ever got together all we would end up talking about was Sarah, in some way or another. We would either talk about all the things we used to do together, or we would talk about how we all missed her. Anyway, it always came down to Sarah, it's not that I wanted to forget about her, but I just needed time to get over losing her.

By going out with Donna and Vicky I'm not saying I'm over Sarah, I don't think I'll ever be over Sarah, I just feel it's time for me to start living my life again.

Going out for a change will be a lot of fun, and the more I think about it, the more I'm looking forward to it. Because I'm so excited I decided to leave work early today so I could get ready. Yes I'm one of those women who have to make sure her hair, make-up, and clothes are perfect. My hair is long, one length, and wavy. I usually wear make-up when I go out or go to work, and dress up a little, but I like to be comfortable too.

It's funny because Donna is very butch looking and basically wears the same thing whenever you see her; which is either sweatpants or a pantsuit. She never wears make-up, but she's the type of person who doesn't need to, she looks great the way she is. We look so funny going out together, with Donna only being 5'3" and me 6'0" tall, and with me everything has to be perfect before I leave the house.

Walking down the hallway to Windy's office I passed a lot of the artwork that we're going to be showing next month, and it's absolutely fabulous. I also felt a sense of pride because I discovered the new artist, and I'm the one who decided to give him his own show. Windy's not too crazy about him, but I think he'll be good for the gallery. Anyway, as I approached Windy's office door I had a sudden sense of anxiety. I felt nervous telling her I was leaving early to go out drinking with my friends. Even though she made me a full partner, I still think of her as my boss, and I don't want her thinking I'm neglecting my job in anyway. Especially to go out partying, so maybe I'll just tell her I'm not feeling well, and want to go home, making a long weekend of it.

God I feel like I'm 12 years old trying to come up with a lie to tell my parents to get out of school.

As I got closer to her office I noticed that her door was slightly open, and I heard her talking on the phone. I tapped lightly on her door, and then slowly opened it a little further. She motioned for me to come in and have a seat. As I sat I noticed something different about her, I just couldn't place it. I didn't hear whom she was talking to, or what she was saying, I was just so focused on her, and couldn't get over how good she looked today. She always looks good, but something was different, I just couldn't figure it out and it was driving me crazy.

As she hung up the phone I realized she had gotten her hair cut, and it looks great. Well this just tells me I should get out of my office more frequently.

She smiled while hanging up the phone. "Mel, how are you doing today? I haven't seen you in a while, you've been hold up in your office for what seems like days."

I couldn't stop staring at her, I know she noticed, but I didn't care. "I know, I've been busy getting everything ready for the show next month."

"So how are things going? Do you need any extra help?"

"No, actually things are good."

"Alright, well if you need anything you just let me know."

I watched as she picked up her pen and wiggled it between her fingers, and then I looked up in her eyes. "I will. Hey, I just realized you got your hair cut, and it looks great. That cut really suits you."

She sat back in her chair. "Thanks, I was a little afraid to go short but I thought what the hell it can always grow back. Right?"

"Right, but I'll tell you, you certainly made the right choice, it looks great." I stared at her with my eyes slightly squinting because I didn't want to blink, I might miss something.

She raised her hand and uncomfortably rubbed the nap of her neck, I thought I was going to die. She looked sexy as hell. I had to look away, or else risk her discovering the secret crush I had on her.

I shuffled in my seat a little and decided to just tell her I wanted to leave. "Windy, I was wondering if you would mind if I took off a little early today."

She giggled. "No not at all, just take the rest of the day off. What makes you think I would mind?"

"Well I just thought since you never leave early, you might think I was taking advantage of my position."

She straightened up and rested her arms on her desk. "Mel, if you take a look at how many hours you've put in, in the last six months, you'd realize that you probably deserve a week off instead of an afternoon."

"Are you sure you don't mind?"

She laughed. "No I don't mind just go, no explanation needed. Okay!"

I still couldn't take my eyes off of her, the way she smiled when she talked, and her eyes…her eyes were just amazing the way they danced and dazzled whenever I would compliment her in some small way.

"Alright well I guess I'll see you on Monday then."

"Okay." She smiled. "You have a good weekend."

Sitting there I knew I was suppose to get up and leave, but I just couldn't take my eyes off of her.

As I walked out of her office I couldn't help but think what she would be doing this weekend. I almost turned around and asked her to come out with me, but quickly came to my senses. I went back to my office, grabbed my briefcase and headed out.

On the way out I looked over at Tara, our secretary, and told her to be careful this weekend. As usual she laughed at me.

"So Mel, where might you be going this weekend that you're leaving so early?" She spun around in her chair behind her desk as she crossed her legs and arms.

"Who me? I'm just going home to relax." I had to laugh at her.

"Yeah right. You forget who you're talking to." She pointed to her chest with her long nails.

I laughed and just kept walking. Tara's an original party girl, she goes out every night with a different guy, and most of them are pretty scary. Obviously she goes for the dangerous type, and these days that's just not very smart. I worry about her.

It felt like it took hours to get to my car, but once I got in, I suddenly got very excited about going out tonight.

I finally got home, ran through the house, tossed my keys on the kitchen table and headed upstairs to my closet to find something to wear.

Tearing through my closet I grabbed the phone and called Donna to find out what she was wearing, although I knew she was just going to laugh at me.

Well, the hell with it I dialed her anyway. "Hi Donna."

"No, it's Vicky…Mel?"

"Yeah. Hi Vicky, how are you doing?"

"I'm fine, how about yourself?"

"Great. Is Donna there? I want to find out where we're going, and what to wear."

"You know she's going to laugh at you."

"I know, I know."

"Okay, hold on."

I could hear her screaming for Donna. Vicky's really a nice person. Her and Donna have been together for a while now and they really compliment each other. When Donna graduated college she joined the police force and now has been promoted to detective. She really deserves it; she puts her whole heart into her job.

Donna met Vicky on the job. I don't remember how exactly, all I do know is that it must have had something to do with kids, because Vicky works with abused children so they really understand each other, and each other's jobs.

All of a sudden I could hear Donna mumbling as she came to the phone.

"Mel look, I don't care what you wear, as long as you don't back out on us this time."

I started laughing. "Oh come on now, that's not fair. I don't always back out on you guys."

Then I heard Donna talking to Vicky. "Vic does she, or doesn't she, always back out on us?"

I could hear Vicky screaming in the background. "Yes she does."

I was still laughing. "Well not always."

"Okay then, 99.9% of the time."

"Well see now, that's not always."

"Well it's damn close." She was laughing hysterically.

"Okay. Okay, but I'm not going to back out this time. I really need to know though what to wear tonight, what kind of place is this?"

"Mel I don't know, it's a gay bar. There's a restaurant in the back, but that's about it. I'm sure what ever you have in mind will be just fine. You always look great."

"Alright. Well you were no help what so ever. So what time are you guys coming to pick me up?"

"How about eight o'clock?"

"That's fine."

"Okay I'll see you then."

Well that did absolutely no good, I still don't know what I'm going to wear but at least I have about five hours to decide. First things first, I'll take a shower and maybe a quick nap, and then I'll decide what I'm going to wear.

Just as I was going to get in the shower the phone rang. I glanced at the caller I.D. and saw that it was my sister; I decided I would just call her back tomorrow, so I didn't answer. Boy, caller I.D.'s, how did we ever live without them. I shook my head and jumped into the shower.

Getting out of the shower I put my flannel robe on and curled up in bed, after I set my alarm so I would have plenty of time to get ready.

I fell asleep immediately; I must have been more tired than I thought.

When I woke up I brushed my teeth, washed my face and plugged my hot rollers in. I figured I might as well put a little curl in my hair tonight.

I walked through the house and poured myself a big glass of water, then went back upstairs to again tackle the project of finding something to wear. I flipped on the stereo to my favorite Blues station, and lay across my bed. I laid there listening to B.B. King while I finished my glass of water then ran back downstairs to grab a beer out of the refrigerator and a glass out of the freezer.

Going back upstairs I poured my Miller Lite into my frosted mug thinking to myself how I just love a cold beer in a frosted mug, then I stood staring at my clothes until I finished my beer. Still I had no clue. So I went back downstairs to get another beer and make a quick grilled cheese sandwich. While I was digging through the fridge I found a tomato and a jar of jalapeno peppers to put on my sandwich.

Sitting at the kitchen table I realized I forgot the ketchup, so I grabbed it out of the fridge then sat to enjoy my sandwich. After all who could eat a grilled cheese sandwich without ketchup to dip it in anyway.

Just as I finished the last bite I decided what the hell does it matter what I wear out anyway. So I washed up and started to roll my hair.

I don't know why I go through the pain of putting in hair curlers and putting on make-up, only to have an anxiety attack every time I look for something to wear. But I still do it, every time I go out.

So I pulled on my favorite pair of khaki cotton slacks, with a white vest. As I unrolled and brushed my hair I heard someone at the front door. Running downstairs I knew it was Donna and Vicky and laughed when I realized I timed everything just perfectly.

As I opened the front door I glanced at myself in the hallway mirror and was actually satisfied with the outcome.

"Hi, come on in." I stepped back while I held the door open.

When Donna stepped through the door she looked at me and said. "Is that what you're going to wear tonight?" She stopped and stared at me from head to toe.

I looked down at myself. "Yes I am, why what's wrong with it?"

Vicky then came pushing her way through. "Nothing Mel, you look great."

"Thanks Vicky, so do you. Come on in." Vicky always looks good. She's very pretty with short black hair that's always perfect looking. She's one of those people who probably looks great in the morning just after getting up.

Donna walked through the house and yelled back at me. "Hey Mel, got any beer in the fridge?"

I closed the door and started for the kitchen. "Now what do you think?"

She stood in the middle of the kitchen. "Yeah, I guess I should know better, does anyone else want one?"

I caught up with Donna in the kitchen. "Sure I'll have one how about you Vic?"

"Sure why not."

Vicky and I stood at the kitchen table when Donna walked over to us with our beers. I looked at her. "What no glass?"

She threw her arm in the air. "Oh, heaven forbid."

She reached in the freezer and handed me one, then looked at Vicky. "How about you?"

Vicky giggled. "No thanks."

While I started to pour my beer I heard Donna rummaging through my cabinets, I knew she was looking for an ashtray and I started laughing. "You still haven't given up that nasty habit yet?"

"No I haven't but I'm getting better." She turned to face me.

Vicky then walked up to her and slipped her arm around her waist. "Yeah she's getting better alright, she went from one and a half packs a day, to one pack a day." She rolled her eyes and laid her head on Donna's shoulder.

Donna giggled. "So that means I'm getting better." She took a drink of her beer.

I laughed while I sipped my beer then poured the rest of my can in my glass. "She's got you there Vic."

Donna then threw her head back. "Could someone please find me an ashtray?"

"Alright, alright calm down there's one under the sink." I walked over to the sink and bent down reaching for it, when I pulled it out Donna came running over, and not a minute too soon, her ash was just about ready to fall off the end of her cigarette.

She flicked her ash, and then smirked at me. "Who in their right mind keeps ashtrays under the sink?"

"Maybe people who don't smoke." While I was laughing with Donna in the kitchen I saw Vicky walking through the house, just what I didn't want.

I headed for the living room trying to get Vicky's attention but nothing worked.

"Mel why is this door still locked?" Her hand was on the door handle as she turned to look at me.

That got Donna's attention and she walked over by Vicky. She too then tried to open the downstairs bedroom door. Donna turned around and looked at me, and I could see the look of concern on her face.

I stopped in my tracks. "Look, I've been meaning to clear that room out I just haven't gotten around to it yet, but I will."

Donna was still staring at me as she stepped closer. "Oh yeah, when?"

I turned around and walked into the kitchen playing stupid. "When, what?"

She followed me into the kitchen. "Come on Mel this is not healthy. All you do is work anymore, you never talk to anyone, you never go out, and you still have all of Sarah's things in the house. Jeez, you wouldn't be coming with Vic and me today if I didn't twist your arm."

I stood in the middle of the kitchen not looking at her, not even facing her. "To tell you the truth Donna I can't bear to part with any of her things. Getting rid of her things would be like letting go of her, and I don't know if I'm ready for that yet."

Her voice softened with concern. "Mel it's been over six months, when do you think that you'll be ready?" She came even closer and I felt her standing right behind me.

Vicky then came into the kitchen. "Donna come on now, why don't you leave her alone. She'll know when she's ready."

I turned to look at the two of them.

Donna stood in front of me. "Mel I'm not trying to be mean, I'm just worried about you that's all." Then she walked over to Vicky and kissed her on the cheek. "I'm really not trying to be mean. I just care, is that so horrible?"

My eyes lowered, and then looked up again trying not to cry. I looked at Donna. "No it's not so horrible. The truth is that I'm look-ing for somewhere to move, and once I find the right place I'll take care of everything I've been neglecting up until now." I moved across the room to stand against the counter. "Now does that ease everyone's mind a little bit. You now don't have to think I'm some kind of wacko."

Donna looked at Vicky suspiciously, then they both turned to me and I immediately felt like I was being ambushed. "Hey guys would you mind telling me what's going on here please?"

Donna walked over to me. "Why, whatever do you mean?" She grinned. "Vicky go ahead and tell her."

"No you tell her honey."

I walked over to the fridge to grab another beer then turned around. "Will somebody tell me please?"

Donna moved over to the kitchen counter and set her beer down, then looked at me. What made me really nervous was that she was smiling. "What are you guys up to?" I grinned slightly watching Donna as she wiped a watery bead off her beer can. Then she came closer to me.

"Well, you know that huge barn we have in the back of our property?"

I looked at both of them. "Yeah, so?" And I laughed having no idea what they were up to.

"Well Vicky and I just finished remodeling it."

"I didn't know the two of you even started remodeling it."

Vicky then came walking over by the two of us and set her empty beer can on the counter. "Mel it really came out very nice. We added two huge bay windows and an upstairs loft, which made the downstairs one big flat. It even has a great fireplace. We're looking to rent it out, and it would be absolutely perfect for you. That's if you're interested. It could be just until you find something that suits you better." She rested her hand lightly on my forearm.

Donna grabbed Vicky from behind and at the same time they said. "So are you interested?"

I laughed then walked over to the table and set my beer down. "Okay well, I guess it won't hurt to take a look at it."

Donna put her empty can next to the rest of them on the counter. "Well what about now, after all it is right on the way."

"Guys, if this place that we're going to is right by your house, why didn't you just have me come by your place instead of your coming over here?" I folded my arms in front of me and smiled at the two of them.

Donna stepped forward and threw her arm around my shoulder. "Well we had an ulterior motive." She looked at Vicky smiling.

"What, you planned on getting me drunk didn't you?" I looked at Vicky who had her hand in front of her mouth as she laughed.

"Well we wanted you to have a good time and we didn't want you to worry about driving home." She winked at Vicky.

"Alright, let me lock up the place and we'll leave okay."

I walked past the two of them to make sure the back door was locked, and as I turned around I saw Donna and Vicky heading for the front door. "Mel we'll be waiting for you in the car, don't take all day okay." They were both laughing as they went out the front door. Watching them I knew that's what I wanted again, just someone to laugh with. I stood watching them for a minute, and then reached for my keys thinking to myself, what on earth am I doing? Well I guess it doesn't hurt to take a look at the place.

While I had the chance I did a quick check in the mirror. I sprayed my hair, did a few face touch-ups and decided I was satisfied with what I saw. I mean there's not much more I could do anyway. So I turned the lights out, locked the front door and hopped in the back of Donna's car. "Alright guys I'm ready let's be off." I smacked the back of Donna's head rest and leaned back in the car glancing back at my house wondering if this is really what I want.

"Well it's about time, Vicky and I both thought you changed your mind, you were in there so long."

"Not a chance I've been looking forward to this all day." I seen Donna rest her hand on top of Vicky's then she looked and smiled at her. "We're all going have a great time."

A great time, I don't even know what that is anymore; let alone how to have one. But I figure just being out with friends will be a nice change of pace. After all my weekends usually consist of renting a movie and sitting by myself until I fall asleep in front of the television.

I was so busy wondering to myself if I could actually do this that I didn't even realize we pulled up in front of Donna's house. Donna put her arm around Vicky's shoulder and turned to look at me.

"Here we are. See the barn's far enough away from the house that you'll have all the privacy you'll need. Now Vicky did all the painting and decorating so should there be any gripes they go to her." She looked at Vicky and giggled.

I crawled out of the car. "Vicky I'm sure you did a fine job."

"Thanks Mel." She turned and gave Donna a playful dirty look.

"Oh jeez, enough of the pleasantries let's go and take a look at it shall we?" Donna broke through the two of us and headed for the barn.

Walking up to it I must say it looked fantastic from the outside, two huge bay windows that went from the ground to the roof and I really like the big original double doors in the front. I also like the fact that they kept the barn it's original red color. "Donna, Vicky this place looks great."

Vicky slipped her hand in Donna's. "Thanks, let's go inside."

Vicky opened the doors and I stepped inside instantly falling in love with it. The downstairs had beautiful hardwood floors and a fireplace that had to be the biggest I've ever seen in my whole life, it was made with the big round sandstones and it went from the floor to the ceiling. The upstairs loft was huge with a skylight in the ceiling that let in great sunlight. "Guys this place is unbelievable." I walked into the bathroom flipping the light switch on.

They both followed me in and Donna stood next to me. "So does that mean you'll move in?"

I looked at her smiling, then turned to look around again. "This may be a bit impulsive on my part, but yes I'll take it. This is too great to pass up."

While Donna grabbed Vicky's hand she turned to me. "Okay now that all of this is out of the way why don't we get going? We could take care of all the details tomorrow."

Going back downstairs I stood in the middle of the floor looking around, smiling. The first thing that I thought of was that Sarah would absolutely love it here. I too was going to like living here, and having my friends so close. I just hope that I can actually go through with it.

Turning around I followed Donna and Vicky outside. "Alright so where are we going anyway?"

Vicky held the door for me. "It's called Flowers, Donna and I go there a lot. They have good food and a nice bar. I think you'll like it, a lot of nice people hang out there."

"Yeah, hell we do right Vic?" Donna locked the door and headed for the car.

"Well now you're making me rethink this whole thing." I laughed and looked at Vicky grabbing her arm.

"Ha, ha come on and pile in or else I'm going alone and you and Vic could hang out here all night."

Vicky leaned close to me hanging tightly on my arm. "Touchy isn't she." She held the car door open. "Come on Mel get in."

When I climbed in the car I glanced back and just knew this was going to be a good thing for me, even though it was going to probably be the hardest thing I ever did. I would be leaving a lot of memories when I leave my house for good. Sarah and I spent ten years in that house. But this might actually be what I need to get me living again.

I saw Donna look at Vicky then she yelled back to me as she looked at me in the mirror. "Are you okay back there? You've been pretty quiet."

"Yeah I'm fine, I was just thinking that's all."

"Well stop thinking, because we're here." She pulled into a parking lot that was relatively crowded.

Stepping out of the car I looked around and suddenly got very nervous. It's been a long time since I've been out, let alone out on my own.

I know that I'm not really alone; Donna and Vicky are here with me, but alone as far as having nobody by my side.

As we started walking to the front door I felt myself slowing down. Vicky looked at me and whispered. "Are you okay Mel?"

I was staring straight ahead, and then I turned to her. "Sure I'm fine, just a little nervous is all. I haven't been out in a long time."

Reaching for my arm she reassured me that everything will be fine, and actually I believed her. Walking through the front door I wondered what on earth I was nervous about. Once I got in the bar I felt at ease and more comfortable than I ever thought I would. It took us awhile to fight our way through the crowd to find a couple of barstools, but once we did Donna and I sat down quickly before someone else grabbed them. Donna ordered us a round of Miller Lites and I swung around on the barstool to take a look at the bar. To my surprise it was a very nice place and surprisingly crowded. The bar was very long and the whole place, restaurant included, was covered in dark Mahogany wood. It's really a gorgeous place. The solid glass wall behind the bar showed the reflection of everyone in the place. I really didn't think that people went to bars so much anymore. But this place sure proves me wrong.

When I turned around I saw that Vicky had her arms around Donna's shoulders only to reach down and grab a couple of quarters off the bar.

"Anyone up for a game of pool?" She giggled while she shook the quarters in her hand.

She looked directly at me and I thought now this is something that I could do; after all I was really pretty good at pool. Sarah and I used to be on a pool league when we first met. So you see I couldn't really help but get good at playing as often as we did. "Okay Vic I'll play why don't you rack."

The pool table was directly behind our seats so Donna turned around on her barstool and laughed at Vicky as she racked the balls. "Now you know Vic that she's going to kick your ass."

Vicky stood up from racking the balls and walked over by the both of us, then put her hand on Donna's shoulder, and her mouth close to her ear. "Jeez you could at least give me a chance here."

Donna laughed and kissed her on the cheek. "Oh I'm going to give you a chance."

"Well thank you honey." Then Vicky kissed her lightly on the mouth.

Donna looked up. "I'm going to give you a chance to get your ass kicked."

We all started laughing, then I got off my barstool and picked out a pool stick, as I chalked my stick I looked at Vicky. "Are you ready Vic?"

"You know I just might surprise the two of you smart asses." She turned to face the table and leaned against Donna's leg watching me.

I broke then proceeded to just about clear the table, I looked at Vicky smiling and noticed Donna was already laughing. I smiled. "Now Donna give her a break, she has a point, she might just surprise us."

Donna was still laughing. "Come on Mel you pretty much have the table cleared."

I walked back to the bar and picked up my beer. "Go ahead Vic show us what you've got."

Vicky grabbed her pool stick and walked over to the table, glaring at the both of us as she did. "You know, have I told the two of you lately that I hate both of you."

We just laughed at her and I called the bartender over to order all of us another round of beers. As I watched her walking towards us I noticed everyone that worked here wore the same white shirts and black pants.

She walked over smiling. I ordered, and then walked Vicky's beer over to her. "Here you go Vic this might help you relax a little bit more, you look kind of tense."

"Thanks Mel but I don't think that it's going to work. It's your turn already." Vicky took her beer and went over by Donna.

I set my beer on a table that was closest to me and picked up my pool stick. After sinking a ball I walked around the table and looked at Donna and Vicky who were talking very close to each other. Standing there watching them I smiled and thought how nice it would be to have someone who could captivate my attention like that.

I sunk the eight ball and walked over to the two of them. "Come on guys knock it off, and Vicky you owe me a drink." I climbed on my barstool next to Donna.

"Hey, I didn't know that we were playing for drinks." Vicky leaned against the bar and folded her arms in disgust.

I laughed. "Come on now quit trying to weasel out, you know very well that we always play for drinks. But we'll call this a warm up game, and I'll buy." Smiling I raised my hand for the bartender to come over.

Donna reached up and put her hand on my wrist. "No you don't Mel, I'll get this round."

I turned to her. "No that's okay this is a thank you shot anyway."

Donna looked confused. "What do you mean, a thank you shot." She looked at Vicky. "What the hell is a thank you shot?" Vicky shrugged her shoulders.

I was laughing. "It's a thank you shot for dragging me out of the house. In case you haven't noticed I'm having a great time."

The bartender walked over. "What can I get for you ladies?" She smiled as she looked at all of us.

I looked at her. "We'll have three tequila shooters." She smiled as she looked at all of us.

Donna turned around and looked at the table. "God Vic, she did kick your butt. Look at all the balls you have left on the table." Donna was poking my elbow with hers, and we were both giggling. Then she turned back to Vicky. "Why don't you practice on those before you play her again?"

Vicky took a step back and stared at Donna. "Who said that I was going to play again? Being humiliated once is enough. Besides, you have such a big mouth, why don't you play next game."

Donna faced her. "Maybe I will."

Just then the bartender came with our shots. "Come on guys quit arguing and let's drink these." I handed each of them a shot and we just looked at each other, and smiled.

We slammed our glasses on the bar and I turned to Donna. "Okay, let's go."

"What do you mean?" Her head snapped as she turned to me, her eyes as wide as quarters.

"Well didn't you say that you wanted to play?" I laughed.

"No, I'm fine just sitting here thank you." She turned to face the bar.

Vicky stepped away from Donna. "Oh come on I'll play again, she's a big baby." She walked to the table.

I grabbed my beer and walked over to Vicky, then I realized that I hadn't felt so comfortable and relaxed in a long time and being with the two of them only contributed to the way I felt.

Looking around the bar I felt happy thinking of Sarah because I was remembering all the good times that we used to have when we went out like this. I smiled to myself, and then I started feeling tears coming on when I realized I started missing her terribly. I suddenly felt so alone.

I think Donna sensed that I was thinking of Sarah because she came walking over with a beer in her hand. "Here you go I thought that you could use this, it looked like yours was getting pretty empty."

"Thanks, I am empty." That's exactly how I felt too...empty. I set my beer on the table and finished the game with Vicky. The three of us then walked back over to our barstools and sat down. Vicky moved her chair closer to Donna, and then called the bartender over.

"Being the good sport that I am, I'll buy the next round." She was giggling.

I sat my beer down on the bar. "That's okay I'm good. Besides you're suppose to buy the next round anyway." I looked at her and she laid her head down on the bar laughing. "Okay, okay so I'm suppose to buy. Enough already about that, but anyway you're going to have another so I don't have to hear about this me owing you a drink anymore."

I held my hands up. "No really I'm okay."

The bartender came to our side of the bar. "A couple more beers here ladies?"

Vicky set some money on the bar, and pointed to Donna. "She'll have another beer." Then she pointed to me. "And she'll have another shot."

The bartender looked at me. "Tequila right?"

"That's right." I turned to Vicky. "What are you trying to do get me drunk?"

"Oh come on Mel we all know exactly how much you can drink." She pushed my arm with her hand and I laughed.

I pushed her back. "And what about you?"

"Hey remember, I'm the designated driver." After we got our drinks Vicky gave her the money and ordered herself a Pepsi. The bartender gave her the pop and Vicky looked at her pointing to herself smiling and grinning at the same time. "See I'm the good one."

I looked at Donna. "Jeez how do you stand her, she's such a suck up." We laughed and Vicky just stared straight ahead.

"That's alright." The bartender said grinning and looking at me. "I like the bad ones." She then turned and walked away. As she walked away I noticed she was perfectly shaped with tight black jeans and a walk that could put you in a trance.

Donna looked at me. "I think that she was talking to you."

I smiled finally looking away from her and at Donna. "No, I don't think so."

"No Mel, I think that Donna's right. I think that she was talking to you."

I looked down at the bar then up again at the bartender who was glancing at me through the long ringlets of her curly hair, I giggled nervously and grabbed my shot glass. "Hey why is it that I'm the only one with a shot here?"

"Alright here." Both Donna and Vicky raised their glasses and toasted my shot.

I was laughing so hard I almost couldn't drink. "You guys are so queer." Just as I set my shot glass on the bar the bartender came walking back over. All of us looked up at her.

"Excuse me." She looked directly into my eyes. "There's a woman at the end of the bar that would like to buy you a drink."

I looked at the end of the bar and she was very attractive but I felt uncomfortable, I smiled looking up at the bartender knowing that I was flirting with my eyes. "Could you tell her thank you but no, I'm set right now." She smiled and turned around.

Donna was poking me in my side. "What's wrong with her?" She stretched her neck to look at the end of the bar. "She's exactly your type."

"I don't know, let's just forget it, okay." I pushed my hair back from my face.

The three of us then sat laughing so hard tears were running down my face, and I just knew that my mascara was running down my face as well, so I asked Donna where the restroom was.

As I stood up I was still laughing and wiping the tears from my eyes. "I'll be right back."

On my way out of the restroom I glanced around the restaurant thinking to myself that this really is a nice place. Then a table in the back of the restaurant caught my eye. There were two women sitting very close at a small table in the back. I stood there staring, for some reason the woman on the right caught my eye. She looked so familiar, but it was so dark I couldn't get a good look, so on my way back to the bar I walked the long way around. I just knew that the woman sitting at that table really looked familiar to me. Getting closer to the table I realized who exactly was sitting there and it totally freaked me out.

Putting one hand on the side of my face I almost ran back to the bar where Donna and Vicky were sitting. Sitting down I grabbed my beer, finished it and waved the bartender back over. I could feel my hand shaking when Donna looked at me.

"Mel what the hell is wrong with you? You look like you've seen a ghost."

Sitting there I was barely able to talk, all kind of visions were running through my head. "Donna this place is a gay bar isn't it?"

"Yeah, why?" She was looking strangely at me.

"I mean I'm sure that people probably come in here not knowing what kind of place this is, right?" I was looking straight ahead, but I also kept glancing back to the restaurant area.

"Well sure. Why? Mel what's going on?"

The bartender came walking over. "Are we ready ladies?"

I looked up. "Yes, can we get a couple of beers here?" I wasn't smiling or flirting this time, as a matter of fact I kept looking away from her stare. I turned to Vicky. "Do you need anything Vic?"

"No thanks I'm fine." She turned to Donna.

I finally looked at the bartender. "I guess that's it then." She turned and walked away with a somewhat confused look on her face, and then Donna turned my barstool around to face her.

"Okay Mel what the hell is going on here?" She stared hard in my eyes.

The bartender came over and set our beers on the bar. Without looking I said thank you. Donna forced me to look at her by turning my head to her.

"Mel quit stalling. What is going on?" She had a serious look of concern on her face. Her eyes followed mine, it was almost as if she was hurting as much as I was without even knowing why.

I stared at her. "Well I was walking out of the bathroom when I noticed a familiar face sitting in the restaurant, very close to another woman."

Vicky stood up and came around by Donna putting her arm around her chair. "Who was it? Did you see?"

I don't know what I felt really, I felt nervous for sure, although I don't know why. I know I felt scared, scared that what I was thinking was true. "Well it's Windy. She's having dinner with a woman in the restaurant. Sitting very close in the darkness, and candlelight." I ran my fingers through my hair, pulling it back from my face. I almost felt like crying. "I guess it could be totally innocent, I don't know why I'm so bothered by this." I giggled. "It's probably an innocent mistake that they ended up here. Right?" I nervously looked at the both of them searching their faces for an answer.

Donna turned to Vicky then to me. "You're right it probably is an innocent mistake. After all you said she's not gay, right?" She looked back at Vicky like she didn't really believe what she had just said.

"Well I never asked her but she's always telling me about this guy that she goes out with, so I'm just assuming that she's not."

As Vicky put her hand on Donna's shoulder she said. "Mel I wouldn't worry about it. It's like you said I'm sure that it's just an innocent mistake."

Sitting there I knew this shouldn't bother me but it did. After all it's not like there's anything between Windy and myself it's just that everyone that knows anything about me, knows that I've always had a crush on her ever since I met her. Even when it was wrong for me to have those feelings, I just couldn't push them away. It's as if I always knew there was going to be a bigger bond between us then a casual working relationship. Maybe I was wrong.

I picked my beer up off the bar and I felt Donna poking me in the side. I turned to her. "What are you doing?" She just pointed and I looked around to see that the woman who was sitting at the end of the bar and offered to buy me a drink was on her way over. "Donna what am I going to do. I don't feel up to this right now."

"You're going to do nothing, just sit there. Maybe it's what you need right now."

I grabbed Donna's elbow. "Donna." Before I could finish she came right up to us.

"Hi, the three of you look like you're having so much fun I was wondering if I could join you?" She looked at Donna and Vicky, and then turned to me. I smiled slightly and turned to pick up my beer.

Donna was the first to speak up. "Sure, here sit down."

Donna stood up and I looked over at her with a look like, what are you doing? "Go ahead sit down." I said as I moved the chair closer to her.

She sat down. "I hope that I'm not intruding."

Donna reached her hand out. "No, you're not intruding at all. My name's Donna, this is Vicky and this is Melissa everybody usually just calls her Mel though."

I smiled at her then she introduced herself as Linda. Looking at her I was taking her all in but my mind and focus was still on Windy. As I stared at Linda with her blonde hair and big brown eyes all I thought of was Windy. How could she be here, here with another woman? I guess I just thought that if she should be here, she should be here with me.

Donna could tell that I really wasn't interested, I mean after all I just found out that the woman I've had a crush on for three years is in the restaurant with another woman. I looked over at Linda. "Linda it's really nice to meet you."

All the time that I was talking to her I kept glancing into the restaurant area. I don't know what I was hoping to find out. I think I would rather not know if Windy lied to me all this time. Or even worse that she is gay and totally involved with someone else. With all this running through my mind I realized that I was being very rude to Linda, and she doesn't deserve it, it had to take a lot of guts to walk over here and introduced herself to us like that. I know that I couldn't do it. So I turned to Linda. "Linda do you like to shoot pool?" I smiled and as hard as I could I tried to be sincere.

"Sure why don't we shoot partners?" She looked over at Donna and Vicky. Donna looked like she was in absolute shock as she turned to Vicky.

"Sounds good to me. What about you Donna, are you up for it?" Vicky smiled smartly at Donna while she was poking her arm. She then jumped off her chair and stood behind Donna putting her arms around her neck, and looked up at us. "Donna's the shy one."

Donna grabbed her wrists with both of her hands as she leaned back into Vicky's chest looking up at her. "No I'm not I just don't really like to shoot pool that's all."

I stood up. "Well you're gonna now, like it or not." And I gave her a look like don't even try to back out. Then handed Vicky some change. "Here you go Vic."

Donna looked at Linda. "Are you sure that you want to hang out with someone so demanding?"

Linda laughed then walked over by Vicky to pick out a pool stick. I turned in my chair to face Donna as I was laughing and I realized I had forgotten all about Windy that is until I saw her walking into the bar. I couldn't believe it but she was, she was holding hands with the woman she was having dinner with in the restaurant. I couldn't help staring. Donna was trying to get my attention, but I couldn't look away. I was in absolute shock.

I felt almost scared like I should hide from her. I felt like I was invading her privacy. I watched carefully as they sat down at a table and the woman that Windy was with put her arm around her shoulder and pulled her close. Watching them I was afraid Windy would see me and think that I was spying on her but the more I watched the two of them together the angrier I became.

Finally I looked at Donna. "Donna look." I motioned my head for her to look over in Windy's direction. Then turned away in my chair as I grabbed my beer off the bar.

She looked back at me in disbelief. "Mel I don't know what to say. Are you going to go over and talk to her?"

"I honestly don't know. Right now I just can't help but stare at her. I just don't believe what I'm seeing."

I turned again glancing in her direction when Vicky came walking over. "Hey, are you guys going to play or what?"

I turned to Vicky. "Is it my turn already?"

"Yeah, it's you then Donna." She rested her hand on Donna's thigh.

I walked over to the table and when I looked up I saw Donna talking to Vicky. I knew what she was telling her because Vicky snapped her head around to look at me. I just couldn't concentrate on playing pool. All I thought of was Windy. I wondered whom she was with? Where she met her? Why didn't she ever tell me? I had all these questions and more running through my head and it showed because my turn was over before I knew it.

Linda turned to me. "Hey, are you sandbagging?" She rested her pool stick against her shoulder and her hands on her hips. "Vicky told me that you were a great pool player."

"I'm sorry." I shook my head as my hands leaned on the table. "My mind's just not on the game right now."

She started walking towards me. "That's alright I'm still really enjoying myself."

I stood up trying to get a better look at Windy as I talked to Linda. "So Linda are you here tonight all by yourself?"

"Well I'm suppose to meet some friends here, but they haven't showed up yet."

"Maybe they're just running late."

"I hope so, I just wonder if maybe something happened."

"I'm sure that they'll be walking in any minute." I still couldn't keep my eyes off Windy, the whole time I was talking with Linda I was maneuvering so I could keep an eye on her. "If you'll excuse me for one minute I'll be right back." I touched her arm lightly and walked back over to where Donna and Vicky were sitting. Standing behind Vicky's chair with my hands on her shoulders I asked. "So what's going on?"

Vicky turned her head slightly. "It doesn't look good Mel, they look pretty tight. But who knows maybe they just met and they're just starting to get acquainted."

I picked up my beer and looked at her rolling my eyes. "Yeah right." Vicky then went over to the pool table where Linda was. I turned to Donna. "I think that I'm going to go over there. What do you think?"

Donna looked at me with a totally surprised look on her face. "Mel I'm not sure that would be such a good idea."

"I don't care, I've got to know what's going on. If I don't it will just drive me crazy all night." I picked up my beer and finished it. "Well, here I go." I looked at Donna for some kind of reassurance.

"Good luck!"

I smiled and started my journey. Walking over there I had no idea what I was going to say, but I didn't let that stop me. About halfway there Windy finally looked up and noticed me and the closer I got the more she had a nervous look on her face. When I finally reached the table she was as white as a sheet. Even as I stood there I still had no idea what I was going to say.

"Windy, hi." I stood nervously with my hands folded in front of me.

"Mel!" She choked a little. "I didn't think that you came to this place."

I watched as she eased her hand out of her companion's hand then looked nervously into her friend's eyes, then quickly away. Finally she managed to meet my stare.

"I guess that you didn't or else you probably wouldn't have come here yourself. Right?" I looked at her friend then back at her. While I was staring at her she looked at her friend, then lowered her eyes as she turned back in my direction.

Looking back at her friend I could see she had no idea what was going on.

"Mel, I'm sure that you're confused, but you have to understand, this is really hard for me."

Windy's friend finally turned to her and asked her what the hell was going on. Windy looked up at me. "I'm sorry Mel." She made a motion with her hand. "This is Barb." I looked at her and smiled slightly. She then turned to Barb and lightly touched her forearm. "And Barb this is Mel, she's my business partner."

Barb looked at me. "Well it's a pleasure to meet you."

I smiled at her. "It's nice to meet you Barb." I reached for her hand and leaned in as she grabbed it. "Would it be totally rude of me to ask if I could speak with Windy in private. It's business, I promise I won't take long, then she'll be all yours."

She looked from me to Windy, and Windy put her hand once again on her arm. "It's okay I'll just be a minute."

She stared at Windy putting her hand on top of hers. "Okay I'll be at the bar, there's someone there that I haven't seen in a long time." She stood up. "Mel nice to meet you." She leaned over and kissed Windy on the mouth, then whispered in her ear. "I'll be right back."

Windy smiled at her as she walked away. I kept watching Windy then took it upon myself to take a seat next to her at the table.

She looked away from Barb, but she didn't look at me. She stared and played nervously with her beer bottle.

"So Windy what's going on here. Since when do you not only go to gay bars, but also kiss women? You told me that you were as straight as they come."

She finally looked up at me. "No Mel, I never said that. As a matter of fact, I never said anything. You always just assumed that I wasn't gay. It probably was easier for you that way."

"Well why didn't you ever tell me? Did you feel that you couldn't talk to me or something?"

She looked back down at her beer bottle and nervously picked at the label. "No Mel that's not it."

I kept watching her fingers picking at the label and balling the little pieces of paper up, and throwing them on the table. "Well then tell me Windy why didn't you ever tell me? I'm sure that you know how I feel about you, don't you?"

She looked up at me and I stared into her eyes. It was then that I remembered why I had secretly been in love with her this whole time. It was as if I could see straight into her soul, and what I saw now was pain.

"Mel that's the reason why I never told you."

Looking in her eyes I was so mad at her but at the same time my heart was breaking, because all I saw in her eyes was pain and I knew that I was the cause of it.

"Why, because you knew how I felt?"

"Yes, exactly." Still she avoided my eyes as she started picking up the little pieces of paper and putting them in an ashtray.

"Windy I don't understand. You could still have told me, all you had to do was say that you were involved with Barb and that would have been that. I would never have acted on my feelings for you. You know that I was with Sarah at the time. I just hate the fact that you felt you had to lie to me."

"Mel the truth is that I wanted to be with you since the first time you walked into my gallery. It's just that the timing was never right. First you were with Sarah, and I would never have come between that, because in spite of how you might have thought you felt about me, I knew just how deeply you loved her. After that it just never felt right. Then I met Barb and things are pretty good between us. So you see, it was all a matter of timing."

"Yeah, but that doesn't explain why you never told me the truth."

"Mel I just couldn't tell you." She looked straight in my eyes. "After Sarah's death you just weren't in any kind of shape to start a relationship. I know you, and if anything happened between us immediately before or after Sarah's death you would have been eaten alive with guilt."

"I guess you're right." I looked down and away, then almost with tears in my eyes, I looked back at her. "But still you just can't imagine the hurt I feel. After all of the personal things that I told you, you didn't feel like you could confide in me about something like this. Did you ever plan on telling me?"

"Eventually I did. When the time was right." She looked at me with her big green eyes and I saw the hurt that all of this was causing her.

"Mel you have to know that I would never intentionally hurt you."

"I know." I touched her arm. "Well I hope that you're happy with Barb. Are you?" She looked down and touched my hand that was resting on her arm. "Yes I am."

I tried to read her face, but it was hard when she wouldn't look at me. "Alright, well I guess that's that. Why don't the two of you come and join us at the bar?"

Before Windy could even answer I heard Barb behind me. "Thanks, but no. I want this woman all to myself tonight, but maybe some other time."

Windy then let go of my hand and I stood up. "Sure I understand. Windy I'll see you Monday at work, and Barb I hope to see you again soon." I stared at Windy and smiled, then turned to walk away.

I saw both Donna and Vicky staring at me as I walked back to the bar. As soon as I sat down they were all over me. Donna was first. "So what did she say? Mel you were over there for a pretty long time." Looking at her I asked where Linda was. "Her friends came by and she left. So come on what did she say?"

Sitting there I turned to look at Windy. "Well she's been with that woman it seems like quite a while. Her name's Barb, she seems nice. Windy said she didn't want to tell me because the time was never right." I still stared at her.

Vicky looked at Donna then over at me. "That's it, what else did she say?"

I threw my hands up. "I don't know, why don't we just forget about her and continue to have a good time, okay?"

Putting my head in my hands I almost wanted to cry, this started out to be such a great night. Now I'm devastated, I feel so hurt and even worse I feel like I hurt Windy.

Looking over at Windy and watching Barb put her arm around her pulling her close, I could feel myself getting mad and feeling betrayed, and I didn't want that. I didn't want to be mad at her; she had her right to privacy.

Vicky walked behind my chair. "Come on let's order a drink."

We all ordered a beer and sat there in uncomfortable silence. I couldn't help myself; I kept glancing in Windy's direction. Everything that I felt started to turn to jealousy as I continued to watch them.

Donna and Vicky were whispering amongst themselves when I heard Vicky ask the bartender for some darts. "Anybody up for a game of darts?"

Turning around I realized that playing darts was better than just sitting here staring. "Alright I'll play. How about you Donna?"

She stood up. "Okay I'm in."

We grabbed our drinks off the bar and walked over to the dartboard. Sitting down at a table I went back to the bar to order a couple of shots. "Hi, could I get a couple of shots of tequila?"

She stared smiling in my eyes. "Sure."

She walked away and I did everything I could not to look over in Windy's direction so I kept all my attention on the bartender, watching her walk and maneuver behind the bar. Finally she started back in my direction and set the shots on the bar.

"Here, these are on me."

I smiled at her. "Really, well thanks. You know it looks like there's enough people back there, why don't you come and play a game of darts with us." She stood there looking at me. "Come on. I'd like it if you were my partner." She was terribly cute; I don't know why I didn't notice before.

She giggled. "Sure I'll play, they can handle it back here for awhile."

She came walking over from behind the bar. As she walked past Windy's table I knew what I was doing. I was trying to make Windy jealous. I guess I wanted her to know how I felt.

Finally she reached me. "Hi, my name's Mel."

She reached her hand out. "Nice to meet you Mel, I'm Tulsa."

"Get outta here. That's such a cool name, it sounds like you should be a bartender." She laughed and I realized that I couldn't use her like this; she's been way too nice. "Look Tulsa I wanted to tell you something." I looked over in Windy's direction then back at her.

She put her hand on my back as we started walking over by Donna and Vicky. "No need Mel, I know what's going on." She looked at Windy, then back at me. "Standing behind that bar you really begin to catch on to everything."

I turned to her with a look of surprise on my face. "Really!"

"Really, and it's okay. I just want to have fun tonight and you and your friends seem like a lot of fun. So no, I don't mind."

I smiled, as I looked into her sexy brown eyes. "Come on let's play darts."

Reaching where Donna and Vicky were standing, we sat the shots on the table. Tulsa sat down and I sat next to her. "Hey guys I'd like you to meet Tulsa. Tulsa this is Donna and that's Vicky."

She turned to both of them. "Hi, hope you don't mind me barging in like this." She smiled and gave a slight wave.

Donna picked the darts up off the table. "No not at all. Tulsa, boy that's a great name."

"Thanks."

We began to play darts and actually we were all having a great time. The game ended and I couldn't even tell you who won, we were all too busy laughing and having fun to notice. Throughout the whole game I always had one eye on Windy. I guess I was looking to see if she was watching us.

I caught her a couple of times looking, but then she turned away fast. Donna and Vicky didn't catch on to what I was doing, but I know that Tulsa did. Sitting next to her I put my arm around her chair and leaned into her. "I'm sorry, I hope that you're having a good time?"

"Don't worry, I am." She looked over at Windy then she turned to me. "What about a dance?"

"I don't know. I'm not very good on the dance floor."

"Come on." Then she looked past me over in Windy's direction.

Smiling at her I leaned in so close I could feel her curls on my face. "Okay, let's go."

She stood up and grabbed for my hand, it was a slow dance thank God. We grabbed each other and began swaying to the music, when she looked into my eyes. "I know what's going on here but I want you to know that I'm still having a great time."

Looking at her I noticed how pretty she was. I smiled. "Thanks." I then held her tight and the soft curls of her hair tickled my cheek.

As we swayed to the song, I was lost in the music. Her perfume and the sweet smell of her hair had me captivated.

Towards the end of the song she pulled away and looked into my eyes. "Would you mind if I kissed you?"

Looking in her eyes I gently kissed her on the mouth. It was tender and slow at first, and then it became more passionate. We stopped dancing and just stood there lost in our emotions.

After the song was finished I pulled back smiling at her, and we walked off the dance floor hand in hand. Passing where Windy was sitting I glanced into her eyes and it seemed as if she didn't even notice. It was then that I knew it would be nothing more than a working relationship with Windy, and somehow I was okay with that.

When we reached the table Tulsa turned to me. "Well I better get back to work before I don't have a job." She stood. "Donna, Vicky it was very nice to meet you." She then looked to me. "Can I buy you a drink?"

I smiled at her. "Sure, why not." I followed closely behind her and sat at the end of the bar where she was standing.

"So Mel what'll it be? How about a beer?" She had her hands on the bar while she faced me smiling and throwing her head back.

"Sure, a beer will be great."

She turned and walked away and I looked over at Donna and Vicky to see them talking closely. They were probably relieved to get some time to themselves. I smiled inside knowing how happy they are, I was happy for them. Glancing around I saw that Windy was no longer sitting at her table, but Barb was still there. I searched the bar with my eyes looking for her then turned my attention back to Tulsa.

I watched her maneuver behind the bar and I could feel myself becoming more and more attracted to her. I knew that it was wrong, because all that I really had on my mind was Windy.

Tulsa came walking towards me with a smile on her face and a beer in her hand. "Here you go, anything else that I could get for you?"

I leaned forward. "Well now that's a dangerous question."

She rested her elbows on the bar and we both laughed. Then I heard a voice behind me ask for two more. Turning around I saw that it was Windy. I just stared at her smiling. "Hi Windy. I'm surprised to see you away from Barb."

"What's that suppose to mean?"

I raised my hand. "Calm down, I didn't mean anything by that, it's just that she barely lets you out of her sight." I moved my chair over so she could stand next to me.

"I'm sorry." She nervously looked around. "Mel I really am sorry how this all came about."

I looked at her and could only think of how great she looked. She had on a green blouse that set off the flecks of gold in her green eyes, as if they weren't amazing enough. I looked down at how well her tan pants fit, then my attention was drawn back to her beautiful face where I couldn't stop staring at her lips. After all the drinks that I had my head was pretty fuzzy and I wasn't thinking that clearly, so I didn't notice that I was staring.

She looked at me. "Mel is there something wrong?"

I looked nervously away to see what Tulsa was doing. She was all the way at the other end of the bar. "No, why?" Finally I looked in her eyes.

"You were just staring that's all." She looked back over at Barb, and then she settled in closer to me. "Mel, you're not mad are you?"

"No, not at all. I mean I'm a little bit hurt but I'll get over it. It's not like you have to tell me everything that's going on in your life."

"Mel it's not that I don't want you involved in my life because I do."

"But only as a friend, right?"

She was staring directly into my eyes and I could feel myself melting from her stare. God I could look into those eyes forever. Then she looked away in a hurry. When I turned I saw Barb standing behind me. She walked up to Windy and Tulsa came over with their drinks. Windy stood trying not to look at me. I nervously turned around and smiled at Barb. Then Windy said goodbye and they went back to their table.

I watched her walk away and thought, God we could have been good together. Tulsa was trying to get my attention and finally she did. "I'm sorry, I just drifted off for a moment but I'm back."

"I think your friends are looking for you."

Turning around I looked at Donna, waved, and then turned back to Tulsa. "Do you mind?"

"Not at all." She smiled, while not taking her eyes off of mine.

I smiled at her then winked and was on my way over to where Donna was sitting. "Hey guys how long did it take before you noticed that I was gone?"

Vicky stood up laughing. "Excuse me ladies while I go to the bathroom."

Donna quickly turned to me. "So tell me what is going on. First I see you kissing Tulsa then I see you talking closely with Windy. What's going on, and what did Barb have to say when she came over?"

I looked at her laughing and sat down next to her at the table. "Donna what did the two of you do watch me the whole time?"

"Well we just wanted to keep an eye on where you were. Come on, fill me in, what's going on?"

"Okay. Well let's see. First I was kissing Tulsa because I don't know I guess I just felt like it at the time."

"Did it maybe have something to do with the fact that Windy was staring holes through the two of you?"

I smiled. "Well maybe, but Tulsa is really a nice person."

"But she's not Windy, huh?"

"No, but nothing is ever going to happen between Windy and myself, she made that perfectly clear. She seems happy with Barb and I'm not going to come between that. So from this point on, we are just friends and that's all we'll ever be."

"You know Mel you might not want to hear this but it's probably for the best. The two of you work too closely together."

"Yeah I know." I looked down at my beer thinking how lonely I was.

Vicky then came sneaking up behind us. "So what did I miss?"

I laughed at her. "Nothing at all." I then stood up. "Hey how about a ride home?"

Vicky sat down. "Already? I thought you were a party animal."

"I might have been, but way too much has happened tonight, and I know that I had more than my limit to drink. Besides I have to get up early and start to pack things up."

Donna stood up and helped Vicky with her coat. "Yeah I think we all had enough fun for one night."

We all headed for the door when Tulsa came walking from behind the bar.

She grabbed my elbow. "Mel could I talk to you for a minute?"

I looked at Vicky. "Tell Donna that I'll meet you guys outside."

Tulsa tugged at my arm. "Follow me."

We walked to a hallway by the restrooms. I looked at her. "Where are we going?"

She stopped. "Right here. Mel I just wanted to tell you that I had a really great time tonight, and I know that you're going through a lot right now, but if you happen to straighten out your life, I want you to come back."

I smiled at her. I really liked this woman. "You got it." Then I raised my hand, lightly brushing a long strand of hair off her face. Her long curly black hair frames her face perfectly. I looked into her eyes and really was amazed at her height. It's unusual to find a woman as tall as I am.

With our eyes fixed on one another I kissed her lightly on the mouth. Then I pulled away, wrapping my arms around her and kissed her with such passion that I didn't even hear people going in and out of the bathroom.

Wrapping my hand in her hair I kissed down her neck and could feel her breathing increase, then she tossed her head back moaning softly, bringing her mouth back down to meet mine.

Our mouths met with such passion that I almost lost my balance. I stepped back. "Tulsa I really have to go now, because if I don't, I'm going to be leaving with you tonight."

"That wouldn't be so bad now, would it?" She smiled at me and twirled my hair in her fingers.

"No actually it wouldn't, but it would be for all the wrong reasons. You know that."

"I know. What if I said that it didn't matter?"

I touched her cheek softly with my fingertips. "I couldn't do that. I think that I'm beginning to like you too much."

"Damn, just my luck." She giggled.

I laughed at her. "I really have to get going." With my hand tangled in her hair I guided her mouth to mine and kissed her one more time before I left.

As we let go of our grip on each other I heard a soft. "Excuse me." Turning around I saw that it was Windy. She was coming from the bathroom so she had to have passed us and we never even noticed.

I stepped aside. "Sure."

Tulsa looked at me and we both laughed, then she took out a pen and wrote her phone number on the back of my hand. Smiling I kissed her cheek. "Goodbye Tulsa." She said nothing and I walked by Windy's table to say goodbye.

"Goodbye Windy. Nice to meet you Barb." I didn't wait for a reply all I wanted was to hit some fresh air.

Crawling in the back of Donna's car it didn't take her long to start drilling me on what went on. All I told her was that in spite of everything I had a great time. Thinking back on the night the only regret I had was seeing Windy and finding out she was in love with someone else.

I really wish things could have been different between us.

CHAPTER 5

Waking up I felt surprisingly good considering I haven't drank that much in a long time. I think the fact that I drank a ton of water when I got home before I went to bed had a lot to do with my waking up feeling semi-normal. On my way downstairs I glanced at the clock and to my surprise it was only 9:00. I made a pot of coffee and went outside to get the paper. I thought about calling Donna then decided to wait a little while, it was still probably too early for her yet.

Drinking my coffee I looked around the house and decided today was the day. Today was the day that I was going to finally pack things up and move on with my life. Everything that happened at the bar last night tells me I'm finally ready. It was the feelings of jealousy for Windy, and passion for Tulsa that convinced me.

With my coffee in hand I headed upstairs to take a shower. Maybe when I get out I'll give Donna a call to tell her I wanted to move in today.

Standing in the shower I started making a mental list of things I had to get done, I knew I had to call a realtor and standing there under the hot water I decided to give most of my stuff to Goodwill. Starting fresh just seemed like the best thing for me right now.

I threw on a pair of comfortable sweats and went back downstairs to finish off the rest of the coffee, and read the paper before I called Donna. An extra hour might be good for her.

I wasn't surprised when I called Donna that she was still sleeping so Vicky and I set everything up for me to move in today.

When I finished calling the realtor and Goodwill, I called some movers so they could get the stuff I decide to take with me over there tonight. Now that all the phone calls were out of the way, the hard part...packing.

Opening the garage door I knew why I couldn't fit my car in there lately, I have been collecting boxes for some months in anticipation of using them, but never really got around to it. Running inside with my boxes I stopped at the fridge to pour a big glass of water, then started upstairs. After emptying out my closets and dressers, I began throwing everything else into boxes for Goodwill to pick up.

Watching the clock I was happy with the time I was making. It's only been a couple of hours and I have most of the upstairs taken care of.

When I was through upstairs I decided to take a break. I refilled my water glass and sat down to relax for a while when the phone rang. Looking at the caller I.D. I saw that it was Donna and answered. "How do you feel?"

"Jeez, not even a hello first?"

"Okay, hello. So how do you feel?"

"Actually I don't feel that bad. Obviously you feel pretty good; Vicky said you're going to move in today. So do you think you could empty out that house by yourself?"

"Sure, why?"

"Well Vic and I could come over and help, you have a lot of things in that house."

"That's okay I already emptied out the upstairs. Besides I called Goodwill to come and pick most of the stuff up, the rest I'm just going to leave here. I'm buying all new furniture so there's not really much to do. Right now I'm going to tackle the kitchen, then all I have left is the downstairs bedroom."

"What about all the stuff in the basement and the garage?"

"The basement I'm just going to have my brother in law come by and take whatever he wants. He can clean out the garage too. You know that I have no idea what any of those tools are even used for. Sarah always collected them, not me."

While I was talking to Donna the doorbell rang. "Hold on Donna someone's at the door."

Opening the door I saw it was the Goodwill. "Donna let me call you back in a few minutes."

I hung up with her and directed the guys to all the boxes upstairs, then told them to take everything I had tagged as well. I stood back watching them carry all my possessions out of the house and the weird part was, it didn't seem to bother me. They took what they could then said they would be back for the rest.

After they left I called my sister to tell her I was moving, then told her to have Dave come by sometime to go through all the tools in the basement and the garage. She was actually very happy for me and said Dave would be by tomorrow. I gave her the realtor's number, because once I leave this house I'm not coming back, she knew that, and understood. It would just be too hard, that's why I'm doing everything so fast, before I have time to think and turn back. After talking with her for a while I hung up and finished everything else in the house, except for the downstairs bedroom.

The phone started ringing when I realized I never called Donna back, and sure enough it was her. "Hello."

"Well that's better. So how far along are you?"

"Actually I'm almost done. I'm taking a break now for something to eat, then I'm going to finish."

"So what time do you think you'll be here?"

"Oh jeez, I don't know. Hopefully not too much longer."

"Okay well, we'll have everything ready for you."

"I'll call when I'm on my way."

"I'll see you then."

We hung up and I went into the kitchen to see what was in the fridge. I made a salad then cleaned the refrigerator out and unplugged it. Goodwill came back and took just about everything else, I told them the rest of the stuff will·be in the garage. I poured another glass of water and walked over to Sarah's door. Standing there I knew that I had to do this sometime so I unlocked it and slowly went in.

I already had most of Sarah's clothes boxed up and sitting on the floor in a corner. I walked over and opened some of the boxes for what reason I have no idea. As I grabbed and went through some of Sarah's things I realized that it wasn't as hard as I thought it would be. I don't mean that it was necessarily easy, but I didn't cry, instead I really enjoyed myself. Every piece of clothing, or pair of shoes I touched brought back great memories flooding into my head. I noticed after a while I started to slow down and take my time, as if I was savoring every single memory. I would pick up a shoe and hold it until I had a memory of some sort, then I would pack it away again. I was in absolutely no hurry to go through this room. At times I felt myself getting choked up over certain things, it was like I was saying goodbye to her all over again.

I took my time on everything; the only break I took was to get some more water and to go to the bathroom. I was almost through when I picked up one of Sarah's sweaters and I started smelling it. I couldn't get over the fact that it still smelled like her. I held tight to that sweater only to be disturbed by the ringing doorbell. I quickly came out of my dream thinking that it had to be the movers. Jumping up I grabbed my glass of water and stumbled to answer the door.

Opening it I almost fell on my face, boy I never saw this one coming. It was Windy.

"Hi Mel, you look pretty good for drinking all night long."

I was laughing as I stepped aside. "Thanks, come on in. You'll have to excuse the mess I'm in the process of moving and selling this old house. Actually that's who I thought you were, the movers or my realtor coming back for some reason."

She walked through the door and looked around. "You're doing this all alone?"

"Yeah." I moved a couple of boxes so we could get by.

She stood looking around. "Would you like some help?"

"Windy really, thanks for the offer, but you don't have to bother." I nervously reached for my water.

"Oh come on I would really like to help."

I smiled at her as she stood in the middle of the room with her arms folded. "Are you sure?"

"Yeah, I am. But first I think that we need to clear some things up." With her arms still folded she walked closer to me.

I moved into the kitchen to get some more water. "Look Windy there's really no need. You want your private life to be private and that's understandable. I know that there will never be anything between us, and I accept that." I turned around to face her. "What I do want is for us to be good friends as well as partners. I want for us to be able to talk to each other, whether it is professional or private. I really want for nothing more than for us to be good friends." I smiled and stared in her big eyes.

"Mel that's exactly what I want. I know that I deceived you but I really thought it was for the best." She looked away from me. "Not for me, but for you. If I were just thinking of myself I would have acted on the attention that you had given me. But I really care for you, so I did what I thought was best. You might think it was wrong, and I'm really sorry for that, you've got to believe that I didn't want to hurt you. You also have to believe that I didn't want for you to find out the way that you did."

She stood next to me as I leaned against the counter drinking my water. "Please you don't need to worry about me. I know that you meant well, but at the time I was really hurt." I looked at her. "Windy all that I want is for you to be as happy as you deserve to be."

She lowered her head then looked up at me. "Thanks."

I tried to look into her eyes but she seemed to be avoiding my stare. "Windy, are you happy?"

Finally she looked at me. "Yeah, I think that I am."

"Well remember you don't have to hide anything from me anymore so when ever you need to talk you know where I am right."

She smiled and I turned to hug her. When we were holding each other it felt so right but I know that will never be, so I tried my hardest to make it only a friendly hug.

I pulled away first and turned around. "Say Win how about a beer?"

"Sure I'd love one." She pushed her hair back. "Don't tell me that you're going to drink after yesterday."

I pulled two beers out of the fridge. "Come on now I didn't drink all that much yesterday. Besides I feel as if we crossed a bridge here and I'm going to celebrate. Even though the beer might be a little warm because I unplugged the fridge earlier."

She was still leaning against the counter top watching me. "I'm sure it's fine. By the way, I don't mean to be nosy or anything but that bartender was pretty cute last night. Are you going to see her again?"

I fumbled around in the freezer for glasses then turned around. I couldn't believe she came right to the point like that. "Yeah, she was cute." I could feel myself turning red. "But no, I don't think that I'll be seeing her again. We just met under the wrong circumstances. She understands though, she's the type of person who will never have any trouble finding someone."

I handed her a beer and a glass.

"What are you saying, that you would?"

"Hey, enough about me. This milestone we crossed is so that you can talk about yourself freely, not me."

She poured her beer. "Well, one step at a time."

I laughed. "Come on let's get some work done."

We both started walking into the living room. Windy then turned to me. "Okay so what do you want me to do?"

I pointed to all the boxes that were lying around. "All of these boxes have to go into the garage for Goodwill to pick up tomorrow."

She looked around at all the boxes. "Jeez you're a slave driver."

"Well, you offered to help."

"So what are you going to be doing while I'm lifting all of these boxes?"

I pointed to Sarah's room. "I'll be in there boxing up some more stuff."

She looked around. "Mel do you know this is the first time I've ever been in your house. I don't understand why you would want to move, this place is so nice. It really has a comfortable feeling about it, yet it's so stylish."

"Things are different here now, and I think that it's time for me to move on with my life." I moved closer to the bedroom door, and then turned to her. "Here we go again talking about me. Are you trying to get out of carrying these boxes?"

She laughed. "No I'm not. As a matter of fact I'm on my way now."

She set her beer down and picked up a box. "See, here I go."

I started laughing as I walked into the bedroom. While I was in there I thought to myself, this was going to be good. I just had a good feeling about Windy being here.

I heard Windy traveling back and forth from the house to the garage, and here I stood still in the same spot since I came back into the bedroom. When I walked in I picked Sarah's sweater up and for some reason I just couldn't put it down, or move.

I felt someone behind me and I spun around to see that it was Windy. "Mel I'm done out here, do you need some help or would you just like me to leave?"

I began to fold her sweater. "No I don't want you to leave. This is just harder than I thought." I swallowed hard, not being able to look at her. "Some things are easy, but once in a while I pick something up and the memories just come flooding back into my head."

She knelt down beside me and lightly placed her hand on my shoulder. "Are you sure that you don't want me to leave?"

I didn't want to look at her because I didn't want her to see the tears in my eyes. "No stay please, I'm enjoying your company."

"Okay well how about another beer then?" She stood up.

"Okay." I wiped my tears from my chin.

When she walked out of the room. I started to stack a lot of the boxes against the wall that were all ready for the garage. She came back and handed me a beer.

"Thanks."

"So Mel do you want me to take these boxes to the garage?" She pointed to the boxes that I had stacked up against the wall.

"If you want, that would be great."

She walked over and picked up a box then walked out of the room. I watched her leave and didn't know exactly what I felt. I felt sadness for sure but I also felt love, and most definitely I felt friendship, it was just everything at one time. All of a sudden I also felt tears beginning to form in my eyes. I was just an uncontrollable ball of emotions.

Windy walked in just in time. "Here I'll help you with the rest of these boxes." I stood up.

"Are you all done in here?"

"No I just need a break that's all."

We both picked up a box and headed for the garage. I knew that I had to finish this today but it just kept getting harder. When we picked up the last two boxes and took them to the garage I told her we should take a break. She said it probably would be best if we just finished.

I knew she was right and I stood looking around. "Well the realtor told me that she would take care of the hospital bed, so I just have to finish packing up the rest of these clothes and whatever else is laying around here. After Sarah died I just took all of her things and threw them in here so that they were out of my sight."

"Well that's understandable."

"Yeah, I guess." I picked up that same sweater of Sarah's showing it to Windy. "See this tattered old sweater, this was Sarah's favorite. I used to tell her over and over to throw it away, but she never did." I sat down giggling.

Windy sat down on the floor next to me. "It is pretty old." She touched it.

We were both giggling. "Yeah it is. I remember one time I even threw it away in the garbage and she went down stairs in the middle of the night to dig it out of the trash."

"She really must have loved that sweater."

"Yeah she did. It was the first thing that I ever bought her. It was a surprise to tell her we were going on a ski trip. She wore it almost everyday on the trip and after that it was definitely her favorite thing to wear." I put the sweater up to my face. "It still smells like her too." I felt tears running down my face, and then I turned to Windy. "I'm sorry you must think I'm an idiot sitting in a bedroom smelling a sweater. I'll understand if you have something better to do. After all it is Saturday night, you must have plans with Barb. I don't want to keep you longer than you intended to stay."

She touched my arm. "Mel I'm not going anywhere. I think that you need someone to be with you now and I'm happy to be that person. So if you don't mind, I'd like to stay. Besides I have no plans tonight."

I smiled and leaned my head on her shoulder. "Thanks."

She grabbed Sarah's sweater from my hand. "I think the first thing that we should do is put this aside. You should keep it. Some memories you just shouldn't get rid of."

She was folding the sweater then set it on the floor next to where we were both sitting. At that moment I just wanted to hug her but decided that I better not.

I stood up. "Okay let's see what else is in this room."

"You look around, I'm going to run to the bathroom. Do you need a beer on my way back?"

I picked mine up and poured the rest into my glass. "Yeah, okay."

She walked off and as I watched her leave I thought to myself that being friends with her is going to be very hard for me, but I'm not going to let her down. If it's friendship she wants, then I'm going to be the best friend she has ever had.

The doorbell then rang and I jumped up to answer it.

Windy strolled into the bedroom carrying two beers. "So who was at the door?"

"It was just the realtor. I gave her the keys to the place and she said that she would have someone take care of everything we couldn't, or didn't want to finish today. She knows that once I leave, I'm not coming back in here again."

"So what else is left?" She handed me a beer.

"Just a few things in here that's all. Hey, I have a proposition for you." I grinned and pulled the tab on my beer.

"You do huh, and what might that be?"

"Well I was wondering, since you have no plans tonight if you wanted to help me move some of my things into my new place, I'll spring for dinner. How does that sound?" I leaned into her with my shoulder.

"Actually that sounds great." She fell back into me. "So let's finish up here, I want to see your new place. Where are you going to be moving anyway?"

"Well you know my friends Donna and Vicky?"

"Yeah."

"They have a barn that they renovated, and I'm going to move in there. I know that it sounds a bit weird, but it's really a great place, I'm going to stay there just until I decide what I really want to do."

"No, I don't think it sounds weird, but first things first, let's clean this place up and start loading up the cars."

She started walking around the room and I smiled happily in the fact that she was here with me. Of anybody, I'm glad it's her. "The movers should be here pretty soon. I'm not taking that much stuff so they should be quick."

We both grabbed our beers and started working. The rest of the packing seemed a lot easier for some reason; I think Windy had a lot to do with that. It only took us a couple of hours and we were done.

"Windy I'll be right back." I went to the bathroom, then called Donna and told her that we should be there pretty soon. She wanted to know who was helping me, because I said we. I just told her it was a surprise, and not to say anything when we got there.

I heard a knock at the door. Opening it I saw that it was the movers. I let them in and asked Windy if she wanted to go outside and get some air while they load up their truck. She agreed and we went out to the backyard to sit at the picnic table. After we sat for a while in silence I asked her if she wanted me to build a fire.

"Build a fire, really?" She looked at me laughing.

"Sure, I have this outdoor fireplace. Here let me show you."

I stood up and went into the garage to get the fireplace. It's basically a big round metal container that holds wood for a fire. There's a metal ring in the middle that separates the top from the bottom leaving the middle open.

On my way back I grabbed a couple of logs and some lighter fluid. Spraying the lighter fluid on the logs I looked at Windy. "Do you have any matches on you?"

"No, but I think that I seen a lighter in the house, hold on." She jumped up and ran inside.

I smiled at her running around so excited, and then she came back out and tossed me the lighter. "Here you go."

Lighting the fire I sat back and looked at her. "See I told you this would be great. One last fire out here before I leave." I bumped Windy's shoulder with mine. "Do you need another beer?"

"No I'm okay."

"Okay I'll be right back, I'm going to go and check on the movers." Jumping up I went inside and the movers had everything that I was taking packed up and put on the truck, I signed the work order, then grabbed a beer from the fridge and went back outside.

"The movers have everything handled and they're on the way over to the new place. I already called Donna so she knows to be expecting them. You don't mind sitting out here for a while do you?" I looked at her and she turned to me and smiled.

"No, not at all. Mel this is really great. I was a little skeptical when you first said an outdoor fireplace but this is really nice." She took a drink of her beer. "It looks like you and Sarah had a really good life here. It must have been great being so much in love."

I sat down and stared into the fire remembering just how great it was. "It was. I just really hope that I find something even similar to what I had with Sarah one day. You can't imagine how lonely it is when you're used to having someone be there all the time." I poured my beer into my glass and then leaned forward stirring the fire a little bit with a stick. I looked at Windy. "I'm really sorry about unloading a lot of this on you but it's just that I know I'm never coming back here again, and I guess that I'm getting a little emotional."

"Mel it's okay, I'm really enjoying myself. I've never had what you had with Sarah and it's nice to know that it's out there, it gives me hope."

I looked at her and she was staring straight ahead. "I can't believe that you have never been that much in love before. You're beautiful, smart." I touched her arm. "Windy you have so much to offer someone. Anyone would be lucky to have you."

"Thanks, I just wish it would happen soon." Her head shyly fell forward.

"I'm sure it will happen, just give it time. At least you have someone in your life that's more than I have right now."

We both sat quietly for a while. We finished our beers and I started to put the fire out. "We better get going, I still have a lot to get done." I turned to her smiling. "Right now is the perfect time to bail out if you want."

She stood up. "No I'm in it for the long haul. I'll be in the house. One last bathroom break before we leave."

She went inside and I finished putting out the fire.

While she was inside all I thought about was Sarah. Being out here I started feeling guilty about leaving. I sat looking up at the sky. "Sarah I know that you're up there watching me and I just hope that you think this is the right thing for me to do. This was our home; you must see why I have to leave. I just can't see myself being here without you and I could never feel comfortable bringing someone else into our home. You have to know that because I'm leaving I'm not trying to forget about you, you will always be a big part of me, but right now I just feel that it's the right time for me to move on. Before, I couldn't walk through the house without crying, but that's all changed now. Now I can look back, laugh and remember not the pain, but all the fun we had together. I remember everything Sarah, and I will never forget. That to me is my cue to move on with my life. Don't ever forget me Sarah because I will never forget you, you will always be in my heart. Just because I'm moving on with my life and leaving our home doesn't mean you will ever leave my heart. I love you so much and that will never change. You will always be my first true love." I felt tears in my eyes, but I also was smiling. I got up to go inside and saw that Windy was standing there in the doorway with tears rolling down her face. "Windy what's wrong?" I walked up to her and put my hand on her back.

"Mel I really wasn't trying to listen but I just couldn't help it. What you said was so beautiful. God I can't imagine being so in love with someone. I really envy what you had with Sarah."

I smiled at her and all I thought of doing was reaching up and wiping the tears from her face, but I didn't. Instead I stepped aside and held the door open for her. "What do you say we head out of here?"

She smiled while she wiped her face. "Okay."

She stood there for a minute looking around, I almost thought that she wanted me to reach out to her, and then she turned around and went back inside. I followed behind her and locked the back door as I shut it. I stood looking around the kitchen then shut the light out. I walked through the house one last time then looked at Windy. "Well I think that I'm finally ready to enter into my next chapter."

She smiled. "Well that's a positive way of looking at it."

We started walking towards the front door and I stopped in front of Sarah's door. I let my hand slide down the door as one last good-bye and continued walking out the door. I locked the front door, and then I turned around and looked at Windy. Watching her get into her car I thought to myself that it was fitting for her to be the first one that I'm with as I entered the next chapter of my life.

As I got into my car I looked back at the house and couldn't believe how hard it was to leave. I told Windy to follow me then pulled away. All the time I was driving away I watched the house getting smaller and smaller in the rear view mirror. After a while it didn't seem like sorrow that I was feeling, but anticipation.

I pulled into Donna's driveway and looked behind me to see Windy was still there. When I pulled in, Donna came running out of the house with Vicky following behind her. "I wondered how long it was going to take you. The movers have been here and gone already. What took you so long?"

I got out of my car. "Nothing, I was just making sure everything was locked up and I didn't leave anything behind."

Donna came closer to the car. "Is that Windy behind you?"

"Yeah, why?" I turned and watched her pull in, then looked back at Donna.

"I didn't mean anything by it. I know that you said there was someone helping you, but I never dreamed it would be her."

"She came by to explain about yesterday. Then decided to stay and help. We actually have had a good time."

Windy then came walking up the driveway. "Hi Donna."

"Hi Windy, I hear that you've been helping Mel pack up."

"We've had a good time. It's given us some time to resolve some things. It's been good." She smiled at me then Donna grabbed her arm pulling her away.

I watched as Donna pulled her towards the barn, then Vicky called me inside the house. We handled all the paperwork then went to go and find Donna and Windy.

We found them inside my new place and I walked up to Windy. "So what do you think?"

"Mel this place is perfect." Her eyes traveled the room.

I smiled. "It is, isn't it? I turned to Donna. "Why don't you and Vic help us, then we could make a party out of unpacking."

Donna walked over to Vicky and put her arm around her waist. "Oh no you don't I'm not getting stuck doing your work, I'll come by when everything's all finished. Besides we have to go by Vicky's parent's house for dinner. You know those family obligations." She rolled her eyes.

"Yeah I know." I laughed. "Could you believe that I actually miss those?"

"No I can't." She grabbed Vicky's arm. "Well have fun, we have to get going. We'll both stop by tomorrow, okay?"

"Sure." I turned to Windy. "I guess it's just you and me. Remember now's the time to back out if you want."

"No way, you're not getting out of buying me dinner that easy."

I laughed. "You're silly."

As I walked through the door I looked around and realized exactly how much work we had ahead of us. We started right away just putting the important stuff away, and then we arranged the little bit of furniture that I did bring.

After I flopped down on the floor I looked at Windy. "I think we did enough for a day, why don't we sit down and relax."

She flopped down next to me. "You don't have to tell me twice."

I rolled over on my stomach and looked at her. "How would you like me to make us a pitcher of martinis?"

"That actually sounds great." She rubbed her hands through her hair and I couldn't believe how incredibly sexy she looked. After all the packing and unpacking we did she still looked great and I couldn't take my eyes off of her.

"Okay, while I do that why don't you think of something for us to eat? You have your choice of going out to dinner, or take out. So think about it and I'll be right back."

I jumped up and started to walk into the kitchen, and then I yelled back to Windy. "We did pack the vodka didn't we?"

"Yeah I'm pretty sure we did."

There was one box unopened in the corner of the kitchen. "Never mind I found it." I stood up and she was standing right behind me. "Sorry for yelling I thought that you were still laying down. So did you decide what you wanted to do for dinner?"

"Why don't we just order some take out and build a fire? That fireplace is fantastic."

I turned to her. "That's fine with me, but are you opting to stay home because you don't want to be seen in public with me." I started laughing and walked around in the kitchen looking for the martini glasses.

"No, not at all. I just thought that since we had such a long day it would be more comfortable if we just stayed in. But if you want to go out, we can."

I turned around to face her. "Windy settle down! I'm just kidding, I would much rather eat in. Now to something more important, do you know where the glasses are?"

She laughed. "Yeah I unpacked them and put them right over here." She reached around in the cabinet and pulled them out. "Here you go. Anything else?"

I looked at her. "Yeah what kind of take out would you like? I'm starving."

She was digging around for the olives. When she found them she came over to where I was standing. "How about Chinese?"

"Great. I know that I packed my take out menus somewhere."

She handed me the jar of olives. "Here I'll get them, I put them over here by the phone." She started walking to the phone. "I can't believe the amount of menus you have."

"Well it's kind of hard to cook for one all the time."

"I know what you mean."

I poured our drinks. "Why don't I start a fire while we decide what we're going to order."

We both grabbed our glasses and I started a fire, then we got comfortable and went over the menu.

After ordering our food we decided to play a game.

Choosing Monopoly I laid a blanket on the floor with a bunch of oversized pillows, and we made ourselves comfortable. Half way through the game our food came and we stuffed ourselves.

Lying there stuffed and tired I looked at her and thought to myself, how on earth could someone like her not be busy on a Saturday night. I wondered what happened to Barb, but I wasn't going to ask because I was glad she was here, with me.

The rest of the evening we just laid around, playing Monopoly, talking, and slowly but surely getting drunk. After hours of talking I looked at Windy and she was half asleep so I grabbed a blanket to cover her. Then I threw a couple more logs on the fire and lay there very comfortable in my new home.

Slowly I fell asleep.

CHAPTER 6

❀

*W*aking up I looked around and a smile came over my face. I felt satisfaction and comfort, as I stretched my arms over my head and yawned. Then remembering that Windy was here somewhere amongst all of these blankets and pillows, made my smile grow even wider, and I quietly rose to go to the bathroom.

Looking around though I didn't see her anywhere. Checking the bathroom I figured she must have gotten up early and took off. It didn't matter though I still couldn't lose my smile. I giggled at her thoughtfulness when I saw she made a pot of coffee before she left, I grabbed a cup and ran upstairs to take a shower.

After getting dressed I went back downstairs to get another cup of coffee before I went for a bike ride. When I reached the bottom stair there she was, sitting in the kitchen with a cup of coffee and a box of donuts in front of her. I smiled because it felt great to see that she just didn't leave without saying something. Plus it didn't hurt that she was the first person I saw in the morning.

I stood behind her. "I thought that you left for good this morning. I didn't even hear you get up."

I grabbed a mug out of the cupboard and she walked over with the coffee pot in her hand. "I wouldn't have done that. I'm really sorry I fell asleep last night. But I want you to know that I had a great time. Actually, it was probably the best time I've had in a long time."

I smiled. "I'm glad, and don't be sorry for falling asleep, I'm glad you stayed. It felt good spending the evening with someone again for a change. Even though it was totally innocent." I laughed. "I think that this friendship thing is going to be good for us. I'm really happy how everything turned out yesterday. Thank you." I walked up to her and hugged her, and as I slid my arms around her waist I was thinking that this was the happiest I've been in a long time.

She pulled away after holding me tight. "You look like you're dressed to go workout or something."

I stepped back. "I thought I would go for a bike ride. It's such a beautiful day out. Do you ride?"

"I haven't in a long time and I would love to, but I really have to get home and take care of some things."

"Well maybe next time." I walked over to the table. "So what kind of donuts did you buy?"

We both sat drinking coffee and talking for a while, and then Windy stood up. "Well I hate to leave because I'm having such a good time, but I really have to get home, take a shower and get some work done."

I stood up and walked her to the door. "Alright well thanks for all of the help yesterday and all the company…oh, and don't let me forget the donuts."

"You're silly, and you're welcome. Like I said, I had a great time it didn't even feel like you were working me to death."

We were both laughing as I opened the door for her.

"Windy again thanks. Really I mean that, for everything and I guess I'll see you at the office tomorrow."

"Okay, you be careful on that bike of yours."

"Sure. Bye Windy."

I stood watching her drive away and I realized that I was lying right to her face when I told her this friendship thing will be good for both of us. Watching her pull out of the driveway was like watching my future drive away. Boy I sure hope this gets easier, because I can't keep pretending that all I want is a friendship with her.

Before I even walked back inside I saw Donna heading straight for me. I held my hand up. "Donna before you even say anything it was totally innocent. We just unpacked, played a game of Monopoly and ate Chinese food all night long."

"Okay, I wasn't even going to ask about that, but since you brought it up. She stayed here all night and you just talked?"

"Yes, is that so hard to believe." I giggled.

"No." She started laughing. "I'm just kidding, so are things better between the two of you?"

"Yeah, everything's great. It's going to be hard being friends with her, but I'm determined to make it work."

"That's good. So what are you doing now? Do you want to come by for some coffee or something?"

"No thanks, I'm headed out for a bike ride. Then I might swing by the office and finish some work I let go because I left early Friday."

"Oh yeah, you're one of those people who actually like exercising. Well anytime you feel like stopping by, the door's always open."

"Alright maybe I'll see you later."

She started to walk away and I headed inside to get my bike when she turned and yelled to me. "Hey be careful on that bike, there's a lot of people out there who don't keep an eye out for bike riders."

"Alright, don't worry. I'll see you later."

I rolled my bike outside then went back in to fill up my water bottle. I locked the place up and headed out.

Pedaling through the new neighborhood I was getting a great workout and at the same time I was able to collect my thoughts. While I was riding around I made a mental list of things I had to get done. First I had to get a hold of my parents and friends and tell them that I moved. I also have to get to the store and buy things to furnish my new place.

Realizing that I had a lot to do I started to go back.

I ran inside and put my bike away then went upstairs to take a shower. I dressed in a hurry so I could get to the office. I just wanted everything to be perfect for our showing of this new artist.

Jumping downstairs I grabbed my keys and ran out the door.

CHAPTER 7

❀

*A*fter being in my new place for a couple of weeks I finally have it exactly the way I want it. With my mind being occupied on furnishing my home, I really haven't thought much about Windy. Well that's not exactly true, but at least she hasn't been all that I've been thinking about. Between new furnishings and work, I've been keeping myself busy enough that I put Windy in the back of my mind.

Sitting behind my desk and leaning back in my chair I felt a sense of pride because the show I've been working on is finally finished, and the opening is tonight. Looking up from my desk I saw Windy standing in the doorway.

She leaned against the doorframe. "So Mel are you excited about tonight? You really worked hard on this."

I straightened up in my chair. "Actually I am a little nervous, but I'm also very excited."

"Well I want you to know that everything looks great."

She held her briefcase in both hands in front of her and I thought she looked so sexy. "I think this is really going to be good for us."

"Yeah I think it will be. I've seen your guest list and it's pretty amazing."

"Thanks, I just hope everyone shows."

"I'm sure they will. Well…" She looked down at her shoes then back up at me again. "I'm going to head home so I can get ready. I'll see you tonight."

"Okay." I could feel myself smiling like a fool.

She turned around and walked out of my office. Leaning back in my chair again I wondered if she was going to be bringing someone with her to the opening. Then I shook my head, I don't know what I'm thinking, because it's none of my business.

Well I better get going myself, for some reason it always takes me so long to get ready. Before I go home though, I have to make one stop.

❧   ❧   ❧

Standing at Sarah's grave I knelt down. The ground was so cold; slowly I reached up touching the letters of her stone with my finger-tips, watching them slide back and forth. "Oh how I miss you. Things are going so good for me now, and I just wish you were here to share it with me.

I'm now a full partner in the gallery and tonight is the first show I ever put together. Everyday that something wonderful happens to me, you're always on my mind. I still miss you so much." I felt tears in my eyes then looked up blinking and shook them off. "Oh, I forgot to tell you that I moved. I moved into Donna's old barn." I giggled. "Yeah I know it sounds terrible but it really is very nice. I finally have it the way I want it to look, I bought new furniture and I'm really happy with the way it turned out, it actually looks like a home. I'm sorry but I just couldn't stay in our house without you, because it's just that, our house. The memories were too strong. I know that you understand. You would really love the barn though; it reminds me of an old rustic cabin.

A very nice family bought our house I made sure of that. I made sure they had all the love we had, and of course I made sure they had a dog. I know how you loved animals. I just wanted to make sure our house was well taken care of." While I knelt there I picked the long pieces of grass around her stone.

"I really miss you Sarah, I know I said it before but I just can't tell you enough. I miss seeing you first thing in the morning, and I miss your being the first thing I see when I come home. I miss your voice and your laugh. I miss your face, especially the way you would squint your eyes and smile in your sleep. Sarah I just plain miss everything about you, I'm so lonely, All I do is work and if I'm not working I'm riding my bike. I tell you though, I have never been in better shape." I laughed and wiped the tears from my eyes.

"Well hon. I better get going, I have to get ready for the big show at the gallery I told you about." I leaned forward and kissed her stone, and then I stood up wiping my tears away. "I love you hon, I'll be back in a little while. Keep smiling down on me because I feel it everyday."

I then turned and walked back down to my car.

Starting my car I looked back over my shoulder and sadness filled my body…then I drove away. I drove in silence for a while; visiting Sarah always put me in a somber mood. All I could think of was walking into the gallery tonight and being able to have her proudly by my side. Before I even knew it I was pulling into my driveway.

Going into the house I threw my briefcase on the chair and went into the kitchen to pour myself a big glass of water. All I wanted to do was relax for a while because I knew tonight was going to take its toll on me. I'm not really good with people, and having to work the room as they say is really going to make for a long evening. So I flipped on the stereo and carried my water upstairs to take a long hot bath.

After my bath I laid out all of my clothes then went downstairs to make myself a sandwich before I got dressed. Looking in the fridge I was surprised to find I actually had all the ingredients to make my favorite sandwich. Vegetables and cheese on an onion roll with Italian dressing. I poured another glass of water then sat down.

I turned the television on when I was done eating and kicked my feet up to relax just a little bit more before I got dressed. Lying there I almost fell asleep I felt so comfortable, and then someone was knocking at the door.

Opening the door I saw that it was Vicky standing there. "Where's Donna, and by the way aren't you guys just a little early?"

"No I don't think we're early, are you sure you're not late?"

I looked at the clock. "No I'm not that late, but I better start to get ready"

I stepped aside and Vicky came walking in. "Donna ran back home to get a pop, she's not drinking tonight and she just remembered you don't drink pop."

"Why isn't she drinking tonight?"

"Something about this case she's working on, she might get called into work later on."

"Tonight, really?" I turned around and looked at her.

"Well she did tell them not to call her unless it was an absolute emergency."

"By the way you look great in that dress." Vicky was wearing a long midnight blue velvet dress. It really did look great on her.

"Thanks." She ran her hands down her dress then looked over my shoulder as Donna came running up.

She caught the door just as it started to close. "Jeez Mel is that what you're wearing?"

"Why is it that you are always so concerned about what I'm wearing?" I started to walk into the kitchen and they both followed behind me.

"Don't worry Mel, Donna's just jealous because she always wears the same thing where ever she goes. She only wears a little bit more fancier pantsuit to affairs like this."

Vicky and I started laughing.

"Hey if you guys don't like what I'm wearing I don't have to go." She folded her arms across her chest and leaned against the counter pouting.

Vicky came and stood by me and leaned her head close. "Don't you just love it when she gets mad."

We all started laughing. "You know Donna you don't have to bring your own stuff to drink, I do have things here."

She walked over and opened the refrigerator. "Well let's see what you have here. Juice, water and beer what a big selection."

"Are you making fun of what I drink?"

"Yes, you always drink and eat too healthy it's just not normal."

I cleaned up my plate and glass. "You're funny Donna." I wiped my hands on a towel. "Hey Vic since you're not on the wagon tonight how about if I make us a martini?"

She looked at Donna then back to me. "Sure."

Just then Donna opened up her can of Coke. When we heard the pop of the can we all started laughing. I went into the freezer and got the vodka out, then poured Vicky and myself a drink. "Now if you both will excuse me I'm going to go upstairs and change."

As I headed up the stairs I heard Donna yelling after me. "Hey by the way, why aren't you dressed yet anyway?"

"Because I didn't want to wrinkle." I heard her mumbling down there while I ran into the bathroom. I brushed my hair and teeth, and then started putting on my make-up. I looked at my hand and it was shaking, I then realized that I was starting to get very nervous.

Coming out of the bathroom I grabbed my nylons and pulled them up, threw my dress on and reached for my earrings. I then stood back and looked at myself in the mirror. I guess all the bike riding I did paid off. Turning around I looked at myself in the mirror. Six months ago I wouldn't have dared put such a short tight black dress on, but now I feel confident and sexy all at the same time. Still standing in front of the mirror looking at myself, I was happy with the way everything turned out and that seemed to make things a lot easier.

I heard Donna and Vicky getting restless downstairs so I reached for my shoes and ran down. Hitting the bottom stair I put my shoes on so I didn't get a runner and walked into the kitchen. "So what do you think?" I stood in the kitchen twirling around in nervous excitement.

Vicky was the first to say something. "I love that dress, Mel you always look so good."

"You do look great." Donna stared.

"So what were you guys down here laughing about?"

They both looked at each other. "Donna here was going through your kitchen cabinets looking for some chips or something and she was making fun of the fact that you have no junk food in your house."

"You guys really need to start eating better. Hey Vic do you think I need a necklace?" I looked at her touching my neck lightly with my fingertips.

"No I don't think so." She looked at Donna who was standing there shrugging her shoulders, like she didn't have a clue.

"Alright then well I guess I'm ready."

Donna grabbed my arm. "Hold on a minute before we leave." She went into the refrigerator and pulled out three glasses of champagne and handed one to each of us. "Here you go, we just wanted to toast you on your first show."

I smiled. "Where did you get this?"

"Well when you were upstairs I ran home to get the bottle."

"Donna this is so sweet, but you do know this isn't my show."

"Well you are the one who put it all together."

"Well, yeah."

"Okay so be quiet for a minute so I can do this okay."

We all stood in the kitchen and raised our glasses; Donna was the first one to speak. "Mel here's to your day. Vic and I have known you for a long time and we both know that you have been through a lot. We also know how much work, time, and how much of yourself you put into this. I think that I speak for Vicky when I say that we are both proud of you and we know that this night is going to be a smash hit."

"Thanks Donna, that was great."

We all drank from our glasses. Vicky then came forward. "Mel I haven't known you for as long as Donna but I do know that you of anybody deserves this, and I'm so very proud of you."

"Thanks Vic."

We all raised our glasses again and finished our champagne. I looked at the two of them. "You know guys I don't think that I could have any better friends then the two of you and there's no one else that I would rather share this day with then the two of you." We then set our glasses on the kitchen table and I hugged each one of them.

Donna then fished her keys out of her pocket. "So are we ready to go?"

"Sure just let me check myself in the mirror and I'll be right with you." I went into the bathroom and sprayed some perfume on, then touched up my lipstick. Looking in the mirror I decided that I did need a necklace, and I knew exactly which one I was going to wear. Running out of the bathroom I went upstairs. I heard Donna yelling after me.

"Mel you're going to be late if you don't hurry."

"I'll just be a minute, I forgot something." Hitting the top of the stairs I rushed to my jewelry box and pulled out the necklace Sarah gave me for our first Christmas together. As I put it on I looked in the mirror and realized it was not only the perfect touch, but I also felt Sarah was somehow with me. I let my fingers slide down the chain and touch the pearl that was set in a gold heart with diamonds around it, and then I smiled and ran back downstairs. "Okay I think I'm ready now."

Vicky walked over. "Mel that necklace is perfect. I guess I was wrong when I said you didn't need one, because that finishes off your outfit perfectly."

Touching the necklace again I looked at her. "Thanks, let me just lock up and we can get out of here."

Donna put her arm around Vicky. "Okay, well Vic and I will be waiting in the car."

Walking into the gallery I ran around making sure everything was just perfect. Strangely enough everything seemed fine and people were already starting to arrive. I grabbed a glass of wine and started to greet people. Looking around I saw that Donna and Vicky were busy looking at the artwork. I was really surprised that Windy still wasn't here.

I saw Mark the artist and his wife walking around proudly mingling with people. Making my way over to them I congratulated him and introduced him around a bit.

On my way over to get another glass of wine I saw Windy standing at the door with Barb at her side. She looked great and I realized I was jealous. She had on a white satin, form fitting dress that not only makes her look amazing, it left me speechless as I stared at her.

I headed straight for her. On my way I saw my sister and her husband coming in the door. By the time I reached Windy, she was standing with my sister. "So everyone looks great here. Dave, Kimmie it's nice to see that you made it." I went up to Kim and gave her a hug, then stepped back. "Kim you look great." I looked at Windy. "Windy." I took a deep breath. "You look." I paused. "Amazing."

"Thanks." She smiled nervously. "I'm going to show Barb around, I'll let you get caught up with your sister. By the way, everything looks fantastic Mel, and it seems like it's going to be a great turn out."

"Alright I'll catch up with the two of you later." I watched them walk away and I couldn't take my eyes off of her.

Then Kimmie grabbed my arm and leaned in close to me. "Well from what I see so far, it's great. Why don't you show me and Dave around, then maybe you can keep an eye on Windy."

"Kimmie there's nothing between Windy and myself we decided to stay good friends only."

"If that's what you want."

I took Dave's hand. "Come on you two, I'll give you the grand tour."

We walked around and they both seemed to be pretty impressed with the place. After a while I handed them both off to Donna and Vicky so I could mingle around a little bit more. Walking around and talking to people was a lot easier than I thought it would be, and I was becoming quite good at it.

When I was tired of socializing I headed back to find Donna and Kim. Making my way through the crowd I said my hellos to everyone in my path then I spotted one of my biggest buyers, so I had to stop and give him some personal attention.

"So Cliff I'm glad to see that you made it." I stretched out my hand to meet his.

"I'm very impressed with this new artist."

"Well I'm glad, if there's anything I can help you with let either me, or Windy know."

"Actually I've already spoke to Windy and she's taking care of things for me."

"Great." I couldn't help but notice the woman he was standing with. It's as if I've seen her before but I just couldn't place her. All I did know was that I found her strangely attractive.

"How rude of me, Melissa this is Lily Bromwell I'm sure that you've seen her before she's a big soap star." I watched as his hand rested on her forearm.

I turned to her as she giggled and smacked Cliff's hand. "That's where I've seen you before, I just couldn't place you. It's very nice to meet you Lily." I reached my hand out to meet hers.

"So Cliff tells me you're one of the gallery owners."

"Yes, I'm a partner with Windy. I don't know if you had a chance to meet her yet."

"Yes I have she seems like a delightful person."

"She is." I just kept staring at her, there was just something about her, maybe it was the way her dark hair matched her dark eyes, and her skin, she had skin like milk. Usually I find myself attracted to more physically fit women, but Lily had a very womanly shape that I found surprisingly attractive. For some reason I felt such sexual tension between us and looking at her I almost think she felt it too.

I stepped closer to her. "It was very nice to meet you Lily, if I could help you with anything, you just let me know."

It was as if she was staring right through me. "I will."

I smiled and said goodbye to Cliff, all the while not being able to take my eyes off of Lily. Walking away I couldn't help but think that I must have looked like an idiot back there.

Before I even reached my sister and Donna they came running up to me. My sister was the first one to reach me. "Mel you never told me that you knew Samantha."

"I don't really know her, I just met her."

"Do you think you could introduce us?"

"No, I told you that I just met her."

"What's she doing here anyway she's a big star? I just love her soap, Forever Love."

"Would you just calm down. Her actual name is Lily and she's here to buy some artwork."

Donna and Vicky were staring beyond me then said they were going to go and look for Windy, but I knew they were going over to check out Lily.

They started to walk away when my sister called after them because she wanted to tag along.

"You guys are something else." I laughed shaking my head.

While I was left alone I thought I'd take the opportunity to go and get another glass of wine.

While I stood relaxing at the bar I turned around and was surprised to see that Lily was standing next to me smiling. "So Melissa, when are we going to talk artwork?"

"You can call me Mel, and we can talk artwork anytime, after all you are the buyer." I nervously sipped my wine.

She giggled. "You seem sort of nervous."

"Well big crowds tend to make me a little nervous." I was lying through my teeth, and I knew that she knew.

She picked up her glass of wine. "Are you sure that it's the crowd making you nervous and nothing else." Her eyes smiled at me as she sipped from her glass.

"Sure what else would it be?" I looked away so she wouldn't be able to tell I was lying as I set my glass back down on the bar.

"Hmm, I don't know. Well I better get going, I'll be looking forward to talking to you later."

"Me too." My eyes met hers and no matter how hard I tried, I couldn't look away.

She then turned and walked back over to where Cliff was standing.

A large crowd surrounded her, but when she got into the middle of the crowd, she turned around to look at me. It was as if she wanted to make sure I was still watching her. I was.

After a while I started to mingle again, all the while keeping one eye focused on where Lily was and who she was talking to.

The night seemed to just fly by, before I knew it people started to leave. Donna got called away a while ago and it's a good thing because Vicky isn't much of a drinker and she had just a little too much fun tonight. Our artist also left a little bit ago to go and hit some parties with his friends. My sister and Dave left early but I really think they had a very good time. So basically all that was left were a few stragglers and Windy.

Most of the night I didn't even see Windy. It's not like I didn't try though, I think Barb kept her at arms reach all night long.

I didn't see Lily leave but she must have slipped out while I wasn't looking. So I stood for a minute then started telling everyone who was left that we were going to start locking up.

When everyone finally did leave I headed back into Windy's office. "So what do you think? I thought everything came together rather well." I sat down on a chair in front of her desk.

"Yes it did, we sold a lot of pieces." She didn't look up at me, she just kept her head down working on whatever paperwork she was working on.

"Great, why don't we go out for a drink and we'll deal with this mess and paperwork tomorrow morning."

"No thanks I'm going to get caught up here then Barb's coming back to pick me up. So why don't you go on ahead, I'll talk to you more tomorrow." She looked up for a minute then back down again.

"I'm sorry I thought that Barb left for some reason, and since everything went so well here tonight that…"

Her head rose slowly. "Mel I know that we had a fun and profitable evening but remember our deal, just friends right. Besides if anything ever did happen between us I want it to be because it was meant to be, not because of circumstances."

The way she looked at me I instantly felt like a little kid getting scolded. "I see."

"I hope that you do."

"I'll call you tomorrow."

I turned around to leave and I knew that she was lying to me, I found out that her and Barb broke up. She told my sister earlier this evening, I just couldn't understand why she didn't want me to know. I guess she just really wants to be friends, or maybe she's just upset over the break-up.

"Mel!"

I quickly turned thinking she had changed her mind and finally realized that we would be great together. "Yes?" I stepped back into her office smiling.

"Never mind it's not important, I'll see you tomorrow."

I gave her a little smile, then walked out the door closing it behind me and leaned against it shaking my head. I am no longer getting my hopes up, I'm tired of getting shot down all the time.

I let go of her door handle and when I was standing outside I remembered that I didn't have a car. I started to go back inside when a car pulled up to where I was standing. The window rolled down, and it was Lily.

I bent down to the window's level. "What on earth are you doing here? I thought that you left a long time ago."

"Well I did, it's strange though, something kept drawing me back to you. So I thought that maybe we could go get a drink somewhere and talk, that is if you have no other plans."

"No I don't, and yes that sounds like a great idea."

We decided to go to this nice little quiet bar I knew of, hoping that no one would recognize her and we could actually talk without people hovering over us. Besides this bar is right down the street so that there wouldn't be an uncomfortable silence in the car.

I told the driver where to go and before I knew it we were pulling up in front of the place. Going inside it was just as I thought; we were just about the only people in the place. I ordered us a couple of beers and we sat down at a table in the back, far enough away from everyone that no one could over hear any of our conversation.

I sat across from Lily with nothing to separate us but a candle in a small red glass. With the candle flickering lights and shadows on Lily's face, I don't know if it was the candle, all the wine I drank, the excitement of the night, or the hidden romance of a sexy stranger picking me up in a limousine taking me to a far out of the way quiet bar for a secret rendezvous. I giggled at the thought of it that sounded too much like a romance novel.

The simple fact was that I just found her attractive, funny and extremely sexy. "So tell me Lily what exactly was the reason that you came back to the gallery again?"

"Well I could tell you that I came back to talk about art, but that would be a lie. The truth is I came back to see you, do you feel uncomfortable with that?"

I stared in her eyes smiling. "No not at all. The truth is I find myself very attracted to you. I didn't know if I was your type or not though, if you know what I mean."

She looked at me smiling. "Yeah, I do." She then took a drink of her beer. "You know that I haven't sat in a quiet bar like this drinking beer from a bottle in a long time." She picked up her beer turning the bottle in her hand as she looked at it.

I stared, smiling like a fool. "Is that a good thing or a bad thing?"

Looking at me she took another drink. "That's a good thing, very good."

I stared at her smiling. I had no idea where this was going; all I did know was that I felt very comfortable with her like this.

We sat there talking until they threw us out, then crawled in the back of her limo and Lily drove me home. We talked the whole way in the car; I couldn't believe how good I felt with her.

We pulled up in front of my house and I turned to Lily. "Lily I want you to know that I really had a great time tonight. Really great." I rested my hand on hers. "There is one thing that I've been meaning to ask you though." I giggled. "How on earth did you even know that I was gay?"

"Cliff told me."

I just shook my head. "I should have figured that out." We sat there for a little bit not saying anything, then I looked down at my hand wondering if I should remove it or not, then decided against it. "So how long are you in town for?"

"A couple of weeks."

"Could I see you tomorrow?"

"I was hoping that you would ask."

I looked in her eyes then reached over, touched her face and gave her a slight but meaningful kiss on the mouth. With my hand still on her face I tucked her hair behind her ear.

"Mel, wow." Her hand slid from behind my neck down my arm, only to land inside my hand.

I looked down at our hands then into her eyes. "Lily I better get going, I will see you tomorrow though…right?"

"Of course. I'll stop by the gallery if that's okay with you."

"That sounds great." I kissed her cheek. "Goodnight Lily."

With her eyes closed she smiled and I got out of the car.

Going inside my head was fuzzy from all I had to drink so instead of taking a shower, I tossed my dress on the chair and hit the bed falling right to sleep.

CHAPTER 8

❀

Rolling over I saw the sun coming through the bedroom window so I stretched to look at the clock and it was almost 9:30. I crawled out of bed and hit the shower so I could get into the office before noon.

On the drive there all I could think of was Lily. I know she said she would come by the gallery, but I thought I'd give her a call at the hotel anyway once I reached the office. Pulling in the parking lot I saw Windy's car was already there.

Going inside I headed straight for her office. I knocked on the door, and then opened it slowly. "Hi! I thought that I would be the first one here this morning."

"Well I had a lot of work I didn't get to finish last night."

"Alright I'll let you get to it, I've got some things I need to get caught up with myself so I'll be in my office." I turned to walk out then turned back. "By the way what time are you going to stay till?"

"I don't know probably 1:00 or so."

"Alright well let me know when you leave I'll probably still be here."

"Okay I will."

As I shut the door I grabbed some coffee and decided to get started on some much needed paperwork of my own. I made some phone calls and got caught up with a lot of things that I've been neglecting lately.

I thought about calling Lily but decided I would wait a little bit longer. I got up to stretch and get a glass of water when I heard a slight knock at my door. Right away I thought it was Windy coming in to say that she was leaving.

"Come on in Windy."

The door opened and to my surprise it wasn't Windy but it was Lily. "Hi! Am I disturbing you?"

I felt my whole body light up. "No not at all come on in."

Lily came through the door then closed it behind her and sat in the chair opposite my desk. I walked over and sat on my desk in front of her. Looking at her she looked great. "You look great today."

"Really, thanks." She smiled as she looked down at her dress while she smoothed it with her hands.

It was a gorgeous spring day and she had on one of those sun-dresses that are so popular with a pair of sandals. I was sitting directly across from her and noticed that I couldn't stop staring at her. But just as I was staring at her, she was staring back.

After a few minutes of silence Lily stood up and came close to me standing in-between my legs then put her arms around my neck. She whispered in my ear. "You look great in jeans."

I slipped my arms around her waist pulling her closer to me. She then kissed my ear softly and started kissing my neck.

Kissing my ear again she whispered. "I had a very erotic dream about you last night."

Wrapping my arms tightly around her I couldn't say anything, all I could do is think of how good she feels. I looked up at her and started to kiss her.

She played with the back of my hair as I rubbed up and down her back until I reached her hips. She felt as good as she looked. I moved my hands to her sides then I rubbed her thighs, making my way slowly up the front of her. All the while we were kissing so passionately I didn't even hear my door open.

I felt someone standing there so I opened my eyes and it was Windy. Nervously Lily stepped back and I hopped off the desk, wiping my mouth as I walked around and sat down in my chair.

"Windy, I didn't hear you come in. You remember Lily from last night don't you?" I motioned to her with my hand then looked directly at Lily, not being able to look at Windy. Lily kept her head down as she nervously played with her dress.

Windy turned to Lily. "Yes, Lily how are you?"

"Fine thank you." She lifted her head but didn't make eye contact.

Windy turned back to me. "Mel I just came by to tell you that I was leaving for the day and I'll see you on Monday."

I stared at Windy, slightly nervous but more importantly I wondered if it bothered her any. By looking at her though it really didn't seem to. I guess that bothered me more than anything. "Yeah okay, I'm going to be here a few hours longer so if you need anything just give me a call."

"No I don't think that I'll be needing anything so have a good weekend." She turned around and walked out the door.

As far as I was concerned though she might as well have been walking out of my life. When she walked out that door not showing any kind of emotion at all, I knew there was absolutely no hope for any kind of relationship between us.

I stood up and walked over to Lily stretching my hand out to hers and pulled her in front of me as I leaned on my desk.

Looking into her eyes I now knew that what ever is going to happen between us, I can give it an honest chance. "So do you feel like a kid with your hand caught in the cookie jar?"

She laughed. "Yeah kind of."

"So." I slipped my hands around her waist as she wrapped her arms around my neck. "Do you have any plans for tonight?"

"No I don't, what did you have in mind?"

"Well how does an early dinner sound, followed by excellent seats to the new play downtown?"

"Sounds great, but I better get going if we have early plans."

"Alright I'm going to finish up here then head home to get ready. I'll pick you up around 6:00, is that okay?"

"That would be great."

I kissed her gently on the mouth and she turned walking to the door, while I sat and watched her.

❧   ❧   ❧

Riding my bike has always been a way for me to think things through while getting some exercise. After riding for a while I dropped my bike, reached for my water bottle and stretched out on the grass.

Sitting there with my legs crossed I stared up at the sky and thought back to what a great time I've had this past week with Lily. I missed a lot of work but it was well worth it. We really got to know each other and have become very comfortable being together. I don't believe I've laughed so much with anyone in my whole life. We spent our whole week going out to great dinners, fantastic plays; I even dragged her to an art museum.

Tonight's her last night in town so I asked her to come over and I would make her a special dinner. Even though I feel so comfortable with her I can't help but feel nervous. It's been a long time since I've been with anyone and visions of Sarah keep popping in my head. I know it's ridiculous but I somehow feel like I'm cheating on her. I've really got to get past this, but it's just so hard.

I guess I'll just have to see how the evening goes, after all I told Lily everything about Sarah so she knows exactly how I feel. The feelings that I have for her though are so strong; you could just feel the sexual tension in the air when we're together.

Glancing at my watch I realized I didn't have much time to get things prepared, so I jumped back on my bike and headed for home.

Pedaling up my driveway I saw that Donna was sitting on her back porch, I yelled to her. "Hey, are you enjoying the day?"

"Sure am. It's a perfect day out isn't it?"

I reached her porch and steadied myself on her railing. "Yeah it is a great day. So what do you and Vicky have planned for tonight?"

"Just a relaxing evening at home. What about you?" She kicked her feet up on a small plastic table in front of her chair.

"Lily's coming over for dinner. It's her last night in town so we're going to spend it alone."

"Alone huh." She let her feet fall in front of her. "Are you ready for that?" She looked at me as she put her cigarette out in an ashtray next to her chair.

As I watched her I thought how funny it was that I never really noticed her smoking before. Oh I knew she did and I always teased her about it, but I just never noticed. Weird. I guess I was always too occupied worrying about Windy, work, or thinking about Sarah.

Lily has brought joy and laughter back into my life, and I guess it's opened my eyes up to a lot of things I've been missing for a long time.

I smiled as I rolled back and forth on my bike while I held onto the railing looking straight ahead. "Yeah, I think I am ready. So do you want to come by for a beer?" I looked at her.

"No, I think that I'm just going to sit out here and relax for a while. Why don't you come back out after you get things ready for tonight?"

"Well if you're still out here, maybe I will."

"Good."

I pushed myself away from the railing and went inside to take a much-needed shower.

After my shower and when I had dinner pretty much taken care of, I grabbed a couple of beers and went outside to visit with Donna.

Walking outside I saw she was still sitting on the porch. "Hey are you ready for that beer yet?" I walked over to her holding the beers up in the air.

"You have perfect timing I was just going inside to get a beer thinking you were never coming out."

I laughed and handed her a beer. "Here you go."

"Thanks, so are you all ready for tonight?"

I sat down on the chair next to Donna. "I think so I've got dinner almost done and the place all cleaned up."

She cracked her beer open and looked at me. "You're not making her anything weird are you?"

I laughed. "No I'm not, I happen to have a great menu planned." I pushed her arm off the chair.

"Does she know that you're a vegetarian and she's probably going to be eating something weird?"

"Actually I don't think that she does know." I took a drink of my beer. "Well yeah she probably does, I mean every time we went out I never ordered anything with meat in it, but it never really came up in conversation."

"So what did the two of you talk about?"

"Jeez everything really, well except the fact that I'm a vegetarian." I laughed looking at her. "We talked about every aspect of our lives. I told her all about Sarah and our life together. I talked about you and Vicky."

"So what did she talk about?"

"Well, she talked about her work a lot. She said that being in the public eye is hard for her so she mostly just works all the time."

"That's all she told you about herself?" She turned her head and looked at me.

"No, we talked a lot about everything. I like her Donna; I've never laughed so much in my life. I can't tell you how great I've felt this past week. I feel like a new person."

She put her hand on mine and looked at me. "I'm glad you're happy Mel you deserve it."

I smiled at her. "Thanks."

She stood up. "Are you ready for another beer yet?"

"Sure." I handed her my empty bottle as she walked through the back door.

Vicky came walking out shortly after and stood with one foot on the porch and the other on the top stair shuffling her keys and money in her hands. "So Donna says you have a big date tonight. I guess that means everything is going good between the two of you."

"Yeah it is. Real good."

"I'm so happy for you Mel. Hey I'm going to the store do you need anything?"

"No I don't think so."

"Alright, I hope you have fun tonight." She turned and walked down the remaining stairs."

"Thanks."

She walked to her car and pulled away. I watched her until Donna came walking back out on the porch. "Here you go. Hey did Vicky leave already?" She looked down the driveway.

"Yeah she just pulled away."

"So what time is Lily coming over?" Donna sat down.

I opened my beer. "She should be here in a couple of hours."

We sat quietly for a minute or so. "Mel you know I don't know if I should bring this up or not, or even if the two of you have discussed it but…"

I looked at her. "What, the fact that she lives in New York, or the fact that she's a high profile person and wants to keep her sexuality a secret?"

"Well both actually."

"We've discussed both and we decided to take things as they come."

"Do you think that's smart?"

"I don't know really. I just want to get through tonight."

"I hope that everything turns out okay for your sake."

I smiled. "Hey, thanks for the talk but I've got to get inside and finish preparing dinner." I stood up and put my hand on Donna's arm. "I'll call you tomorrow."

"Have fun."

I turned, smiled at her and walked inside carrying the rest of my beer with me. When I finished making the salad I put it in the fridge to get cold then stood there wondering if I forgot anything.

I made the dressing for the salad, and then started the mushroom paprika. I think I had everything basically ready all I'm waiting for now is Lily. So while I was waiting I positioned all the candles I had in the house around. Then started a fire, tossed some big pillows around on the floor, turned the stereo on and took the wine out of the refrigerator. I stood back and just before my nerves took over there was a knock at the door.

I opened the door and she looked absolutely great in shorts and a sporty top with little white tennis shoes on. I stared at her smiling. "Boy you look great. Come on in" I stepped aside.

"Mel the place looks great but aren't you afraid of starting a fire with all the candles?"

I laughed at her as I shut the door and followed her in. "Don't you like candles?"

"No, I love candles."

I laughed. "How about a glass of wine?" I walked past her and into the kitchen as she sat down on the couch.

"Sure I'd love a glass of wine."

I poured the wine, stirred my paprika and went to sit down by Lily. "Here you go."

As she took the glass from me I leaned in and kissed her. "I'm really glad you're here."

"Me too."

She stroked the back of my head then grabbed the glass from my hand and set it on the table. She stared in my eyes then leaned in to kiss me. Just when things started to heat up my timer went off in the kitchen. Lily looked at me as she fell back on the couch. "Does that mean you have to get up?"

"Unfortunately it does."

I held her face in my hands then kissed her gently on the mouth. Standing up I stretched my hand out. "Come on you can help me in the kitchen."

"Are you kidding, look at me I eat I don't cook."

I pulled her up and wrapped my arms around her. "You look absolutely beautiful. If you really don't want to cook though you can pour the wine for dinner."

"I could do that."

We went into the kitchen, Lily poured the wine and I stirred the sauce. I put a little bit on a spoon and called her over. "Here have a taste."

"Umm, this is great Mel what is it?"

"You know I never bothered to ask you if you liked mushrooms or not."

"Well I love them. So what is this?" She wiped the corners of her mouth.

"We are having mushroom paprika with potato dumplings, fresh green beans and a tossed salad with my home made dressing."

"That's different isn't it usually chicken paprika?"

"Usually but I don't eat meat."

"You don't really? All that we've talked about and I never knew that. I hope it doesn't bother you that I do."

I laughed. "No I don't mind. So are you hungry?"

"Always."

I turned around and hugged her. "You know that you're really great. Now let's eat I'm starved."

We sat down and finished just about everything. I just love cooking for someone who enjoys eating. I sat there watching her, listening to her, and taking her all in.

After we ate I picked up the table and got us another bottle of wine. We sat there talking and laughing until the bottle was empty. I watched her sitting there across from me and it seemed as if I knew her my whole life. I studied everything she did when she talked or laughed. The way her eyes would squint and water when she laughed uncontrollably. Or the way her upper lip would raise high above her teeth when she was being serious.

I watched her sipping her wine and after each drink she would lick her lip slowly with her tongue always starting from the left side.

I was infatuated with her every move.

"Mel that meal was fabulous you can cook for me anytime."

I leaned in and kissed her on the mouth just after she took a drink of wine and before she could lick her lip so gently with her tongue. "Hey, why don't we take our wine and go sit by the fire?" I was still leaning into her watching her lips as she talked.

"You read my mind."

I stood up, looked at the table then figured I would clean the rest of the dishes tomorrow.

Lily followed me into the living room with a bottle of wine in her hand. "This will save us from having to keep getting up."

"You thought right as usual."

We laid in front of the fire listening to an old Natalie Cole C.D. and talked for hours. Actually she did most of the talking, I just watched.

After pouring the end of the wine I looked at Lily. "I've got to tell you I can't remember when I've had such a pleasant evening. Well except for the last time I was with you that is." With my hand I lightly rubbed her arm.

"I know me too, I feel so good when I'm with you."

Then I kissed her, between the two of us you could just feel the passion and desire in the room. I couldn't stop my hands I had to feel every inch of her body.

When her hand slid under my sweater and rubbed my stomach it felt like a wave of electricity shot through my body. I never felt such a thing. Her touch alone drove me crazy. Lily stood up and slowly took her clothes off as she watched my face. I watched her every move with great anticipation, I couldn't take my eyes off of her. When she was finished I stood up and did the same. Then with her hand she invited me to lie down next to her. We laid together, our bodies touching and warm from the fire. With one hand I rubbed her arm from the top of her shoulder to the tip of her fingers, then I looked at her. "You're absolutely beautiful." Her eyes lowered and I gently touched her breast and kissed her passionately. I rubbed, touched and became intimate with every part and inch of her body.

With Lily moaning and wildly moving her hips underneath me I slowly kissed my way down her body, teasing her and driving her wild until she tangled her hands in my hair and pulled me to her. "Ohhh Mel I can't wait, don't make me wait." I followed, and then teased her even more.

Her arms flew over her head and her hips rose, she moaned and I slipped two fingers inside her making her grab my head while her body shuddered and stiffened beneath me. She immediately raised my head to her mouth and breathlessly whispered. "I can't remember the last time someone made me feel that incredible."

I smiled at her. "I'm glad."

She then attacked my body with such intensity, she took me to heights that I haven't been to in years. I was moaning and thrashing about so loudly I thought Donna would come knocking on my door.

We then lay holding each other not saying a word, just feeling good being in each other's arms. We enjoyed each other and the fire until we both fell asleep.

❦   ❦   ❦

Waking up I found Lily watching over me. I grabbed her around the waist and nestled my head in her breast. "It feels so good to be waking up with you. Last night was perfect." I rubbed my hands along her still naked body. "How long have you been awake?"

"Oh I don't know a while I guess. I think I'm too happy right now to sleep."

"I'm just happy that I can finally sleep. How about some coffee?"

She rubbed my hair. "Sounds great. I was going to make some but I didn't want to leave you."

I kissed her on the neck then stood grabbing my sweater and shorts. I started the coffee then ran back to Lily. "Come on let's go brush our teeth, then I can kiss you properly."

"Great. Mel I could really get used to this. To you, I'm really very happy right now."

We stood together holding each other. "Lily I want you to know that when our eyes met there were parts of me that finally came alive, parts of me that haven't been alive in years. Does that scare you?"

"Not at all. I feel happier than I have in a long time." Then she tickled me and ran upstairs while I chased after her.

I fixed our coffee and the rest of the morning we laid around reading the paper and watching the news until Lily had to leave. I laid with my head in her lap. "Do you really have to leave?" I reached up and put my hand around her neck.

"Yes I do I have to start taping first thing in the morning. I haven't even studied my lines yet." She pushed the hair out of my eyes then rolled me off of her while she laughed.

She stood up and started to gather up all of her things. I could do nothing but lay and watch her because I really didn't want her to go. She walked over to me and reached for my hand. I just laid there. "I don't want you to go. I know that you have to, but I don't want you to." I stood up reluctantly.

"I know I don't want to leave either, but we both know that I have to."

We stood holding and kissing each other then walked out to my car. Getting in I saw Vicky outside in her garden. She waved to us as we got in the car.

The drive to her hotel was pretty quiet and when we pulled up in front I smiled at her. "You will stop by before you leave won't you?"

"Of course I will."

I winked at her then watched her walk all the way to the hotel door before I left.

All the way home all I could think of was Lily and last night. I really haven't felt this way about someone, well since Sarah. Instead of going home I found myself driving to the cemetery. As I pulled up I thought it kind of strange, but I always talk to Sarah about everything in my life, so why should this be any different.

I walked up the hill and finally stopped where she rested.

Kneeling down I rubbed my fingers along her stone. "Hi baby. So much has been happening in my life I just need to talk to you right now." I sat down and rubbed my hand through my hair. "I think that I finally met someone. It's so hard for me to talk to you about this, but I really need to because talking to you always makes me feel better. It not only makes me feel better but it also helps me make sense of things." I sat and pulled my knees into my chest and hugged them. "I haven't felt this way about someone since you and it scares me a little. Her name is Lily and she's an actress. She's such a caring, honest, funny and incredible person. She just feels comfortable by my side. I know you know that feeling." I crossed my legs again. "She's everything that I'm looking for Sarah. I just need to know that it's okay. I need to know that she's not going to leave me. I know that you can't really help me with any of these decisions but just being here talking to you helps me." I sat there quietly for a minute like she was going to give me some sign that this is right.

"Well I've got to get going but I'll be seeing you soon." I crawled over and pulled some stray pieces of grass from around her stone while tears fell soaking the ground. "Goodbye honey."

I stood up and lowered my head over her stone, and then kissing my fingers I rubbed her stone. Walking back to my car I really felt better about things. On the drive home I did nothing but listen to the radio.

Pulling in the driveway I saw Donna and Vicky both in the garden. I walked towards them swinging my keys in my hand and they both stood up, reaching for their coffee cups. Vicky started heading for the house. "Hey Mel do you want a cup of coffee?"

"Sure, thanks Vic." I walked over by Donna in the garden laughing. "So how's the planting going?"

"Long, and don't laugh I don't think we'll ever finish." She stood up and wiped her forehead. "So did you get Lily off alright?"

I sat down on a bench at the edge of the garden. "Well I just drove her to the hotel she's suppose to stop back before she actually leaves."

She smiled and sat down next to me. "Did everything turn out the way you expected it to last night?"

I smiled and looked down at the ground. Then I heard Vicky from behind me. "Mel don't you dare answer that it's none of her business what happened between the two of you last night. Here you go." She handed me a cup of coffee and tapped Donna in the back of the head.

"Thanks Vic. I really don't mind answering at all, we had a great time and a fantastic dinner."

Donna crossed her legs and leaned into me. "So when are you going to see her again?"

"Well probably in a couple of hours." I looked at my watch.

"Come on you know what I mean." She bumped my shoulder with hers.

"Yeah I know we haven't really discussed it. We'll just have to play it by ear and see what happens."

"So do you want to help us dig in the garden?" She stood up and brushed off her pants.

"No!"

Vicky started laughing. "Jeez that was just a little too quick."

"Really…" I laughed. "I'd love to but I'm going to go for a bike ride." I stood up and rested my coffee cup on the bench. "Thanks again for the coffee Vic."

"Sure."

Donna turned and walked back into the garden. "Hey didn't you get enough exercise last night?"

I laughed. "You're so funny." And I continued walking right into the house. I cleaned up the kitchen then went upstairs to change. Grabbing my bike I rushed off so I could get a good ride in before Lily stopped by.

When I got back from my ride Donna and Vicky were still in the garden. I laughed shaking my head as I pulled up to them on my bike. "Hey, did Lily come by?"

Donna lifted her head. "No, nobody came by."

"I can't believe the two of you are still out here." I reached for my water bottle and squeezed a healthy drink into my mouth.

Donna looked over at Vicky. "Believe it. She's a slave driver."

Vicky stood up. "I am not." She brushed off her knees with her gloved hands.

"Well if the two of you are going to argue I'm going inside to take a shower."

Donna fell back as she stretched her legs out. "Go ahead abandon me in my time of need. Some kind of friend you turned out to be."

Vicky smacked her on the arm. I laughed at the two of them and rested my bike by the door then went inside. I ran upstairs to take a shower but I had to hurry, I didn't want to miss Lily. So I started taking my clothes off as I went up the stairs.

I threw on a pair of shorts and a t-shirt then headed to the kitchen to pour a big glass of water. I flopped on the couch to relax a little and just as I closed my eyes I heard a car pull up in the driveway. Glancing out the window I saw that it was Lily coming out of a taxi. Getting up I went and opened the door. She stood leaning in the doorway. "Boy you look good."

I smiled. "So do you, come on in."

She stepped in. "I really can't stay Mel my taxi's waiting outside, I just wanted to give you one last kiss goodbye. Well and to give you my phone number and my work schedule."

She walked towards me closing the door with her foot, then threw her arms around me and started to kiss me. I felt her hands wrapping around my bare waist and a wave of excitement rushed through me. I felt chills going up and down my spine. I then began kissing her more passionately and we both fell back against the door.

She started kissing my neck when I heard her say she really had to go. Her hands moved up my back and it was then that she realized all I had on was a t-shirt. Her mouth came back up searching for mine as her hands traveled my body.

"Oh Lily I don't want you to go."

"I know."

I started kissing and biting her neck wildly when my hands reached down to unbutton her pants. I heard her moan softly. "We don't have the time."

But that didn't stop me. My hand slipped in her pants, my fingers feverishly searching, when I finally entered her she moaned with a huge sigh of delight. She couldn't stop moaning. She grabbed my head and pulled it to her mouth, throwing her head back. I began kissing her neck when she pulled my head back so that I could watch her have an incredible orgasm.

At the same time the taxi driver began beeping his horn.

She collapsed her head on my shoulder. "Boy Mel this isn't fair. How on earth do you expect me to leave now?" She bit my shoulder softly.

"I just don't want you to forget how good I make you feel."

"Never."

I kissed her. "You better get going."

"Yeah, I know."

The taxi was still beeping outside. Lily started to fix herself up and I kissed her one more time then opened the door. "You better call me as soon as you land."

"You know I will."

We both stared at each other for a minute then she turned around and got into the cab. I waved, and then closed the door.

CHAPTER 9

❀

This was the longest week of my life but it was finally Friday and Lily will be here tonight. I wanted to leave early and I didn't think Windy would mind because I've been here early and stayed late everyday, after all what else did I have to do.

So I walked down to her office, knocked and opened her door. "Windy, would it be okay if I took off the rest of the day?"

She looked up from her paperwork. "Sure, you got plans for the weekend?"

I stepped into her office. "Yeah I do. Lily's coming in town for the weekend and I'm going home to get dinner ready for her."

Windy stood up and walked around her desk leaning on the front of it to face me. "So you're pretty serious about her, do you think this is wise?"

"Why not?" I sat down in the chair directly in front of her.

She shuffled her legs uncomfortably. "Well all I mean is that long distance relationships are hard. Not to mention the fact that she is some what of a celebrity."

"I think that we'll be just fine." I looked up in her face searching for what ever brought this on.

"I just worry that's all, I know what you've been through and I don't want you to be hurt again."

She hopped off her desk and I got up to hug her. "Thanks for caring so much."

"Well I do, I hope that doesn't bother you."

"No not at all, but there's really no need, I'm fine."

"Okay, I believe you."

As I looked at her there was a strange look on her face. It was as if she was jealous, but I knew that couldn't be. She was the one who made it perfectly clear she wanted to be nothing more than just friends. It must just be concern that's on her face. Before I left I asked her if maybe her and Barb would like to go out and do something tomorrow.

"Sure that would be great, I'll give you a call." She didn't look at me she just turned and walked behind her desk sitting down.

"Okay I'll look forward to hearing from you." I left a bit confused but happy.

I ran to my car and as I was driving I decided to pick up some Chinese food instead of cooking tonight.

I went inside with armloads of take out and put it in the fridge. After straightening up the house I went upstairs to take a hot relaxing bath. When my fingers started to wrinkle I thought it was time to get out. Coming out of the bath I went to change in my room and to my surprise I found Lily lying across my bed. I looked at her and dropped my towel. "Boy this is a surprise!"

She said nothing; she just threw back the covers on the bed.

"God, I missed you."

"I missed you too." Then she kissed me.

*   *   *

After several hours in bed I rolled over. "You're insatiable."

"Should I take that as a compliment?"

"Absolutely." I put my arms around her pulling her close. "Hey, not to change the subject but are you hungry because I'm starved." I kissed her cheek then her lips.

"I wasn't when I came in, but you sure know how to work up an appetite in me."

"How about some heated up Chinese?" I kissed her forehead.

"Sounds great, I'll help."

"Oh, so you can heat things up?"

She rolled on top of me and started to tickle me. "Yes I can heat things up, thank you very much."

I tickled her until she rolled off of me. "Okay well then prove it."

We both started laughing then we threw some clothes on and went down stairs. When we reached the kitchen Lily stood in the middle turning in circles. "Now which one of these big white things is the stove?"

I grabbed her from behind. "Oh you're so funny."

Going to the fridge I took out the food and grabbed a couple of beers and handed one to Lily. "Beer?"

"Sure."

The rest of the evening we ate, drank and talked until we could barely keep our eyes open. So we went up to bed and fell asleep in each other's arms.

When I woke up I looked over at Lily and smiled as I kissed her gently on the head. I lay there watching her, stroking her hair gently so I didn't wake her. Lying there I felt such comfort and pleasure. Then I quietly got out of bed so I didn't wake her taking some clothes with me. As I stood in the doorway I turned, looked at her and smiled. I just couldn't believe how happy she made me feel.

I poured a glass of juice then decided to get a bike ride in before Lily woke up.

I rode about five miles then turned around to head home. When I got inside Lily was in the kitchen making coffee. I went up behind her grabbing her around the waist. "Good morning." I kissed the back of her neck.

She cringed and giggled. "Good morning yourself, where on earth did you go so early?"

"I went for a bike ride. Do you want some breakfast?"

"No thanks I'm going to go and take a shower if you don't mind." She turned to me.

"No I don't mind if I could come and join you?"

"Absolutely!"

I chased her upstairs racing to the bathroom. When we were through with our shower we both laid in bed.

After hours of lovemaking I held her from behind. "Hey why don't I pack a great picnic lunch and we go to the park and relax in the sun for awhile."

"That sounds absolutely fantastic. Just give me a minute to get ready." She rolled over and faced me, kissing me on my nose.

"Alright I'll be downstairs." I kissed her then crawled out of bed.

I grabbed my picnic basket and started filling it with cheese and fruit from the fridge, then looked upstairs and yelled. "Hey are you ready yet?"

"I'll be down in a minute."

"Okay I'm going to go out to the car."

"I'll be right there."

Smiling I couldn't believe how happy I was. I gathered everything in my arms and went to the car, then Lily came down and she looked great. "Well it certainly was worth the wait." I stood looking at her and she had on a warm-up suit with shorts instead of pants. Her hair looked different though, she didn't have it curled or pulled back it just was, and it looked great, but what I focused on most of all and I always have, was her incredible mouth. Her lips looked fantastic in their cocoa colored lipstick.

"I'm glad that you think so."

I grabbed her around the waist. "Oh, I do." Then I kissed her on her neck not wanting to damage those incredible lips. I ran in the house to grab a couple of blankets then locked up. "I think that we have everything, are you ready?"

She started getting in the car. "Okay let's go."

I walked around the car and got inside. Pulling out of the driveway Donna was pulling in. I veered to the side and rolled down my window. "Are you just getting home?"

"Yeah I'm beat, I got called in late last night. So where are the two of you headed?"

"We're going out for a picnic to enjoy the day." I turned to Lily and put my hand on her leg. "Do you and Vicky have plans for tonight?"

"I don't think so, but I don't know. Why?"

"I thought that maybe we could get together and go out. Windy might come too."

She leaned forward a little bit. "By the way, hi Lily."

"Hi Donna, nice to see you again." She leaned forward looking at Donna as she rubbed her hand up and down my thigh.

Donna smiled. "Why don't you let me check with Vicky and I'll get back to you. Right now I'm going straight to bed."

I was giggling because Lily was playing with my leg. "Alright, go and get some sleep."

She waved to Lily and then pulled up in the driveway.

Looking at Lily I smiled. "You're bad." And pulled away.

We drove the whole way in a very comfortable silence just listening to the radio. Then I put in an Elton John C.D. and we sang the rest of the way.

I knew of a perfect spot for us to go, it was a little bit of a drive but well worth it. With my jeep it was easy to get to. It was a very private spot by a secluded lake with a little beach. We pulled up as far as I could get then we had to walk the rest of the way, but it wasn't very far.

Reaching the perfect spot I laid the blanket on the ground and Lily stood looking around. "Mel this is perfect."

"I thought that you would like it."

Lying on the blanket, the sun was surprisingly hot so I poured us some iced tea and we just laid back listening to an old radio that I happened to throw in the car.

I rolled on my stomach as Lily lay on her back telling me all about her role on the soap she's in. Laying there watching her talk and laugh I felt so comfortable and content. I watched her talking and getting excited about everything she said. I laughed to myself as she waved her arms when she talked. I touched and rubbed her hand while she told me about her future role in her soap. I watched her stomach rise and fall when she laughed, and I knew that this is how I wanted to feel the rest of my life.

The rest of the day we laid eating everything that I packed and laughed until our sides hurt.

I rubbed my fingers gently up and down her arm. "Are you ready to head back yet?"

She rolled on her side to face me. "Yeah I'm starting to get a little cold." She put her hand on my hip. "This was a perfect day Mel. Thanks." She touched my cheek.

"Why you're very welcome." I took her hand and kissed it. "Come on now when we get home I'll fix you a nice hot bath to warm you up. How does that sound?"

"Great. What on earth did I ever do to deserve you?"

I smiled as I stood up and stretched my hand out to hers. "Here let me help you up."

She grabbed for my hand and we packed everything up then walked back to the car. The drive home was pleasant and quiet. Before we knew it we were pulling in the driveway. We unloaded the car, and I was unlocking the door when I heard Donna on the porch. I turned my head around. "So you're awake already?"

"Yeah, a couple of hours can do wonders. So did the two of you have fun?"

Lily was hugging me from behind. "We had a wonderful time."

I smiled grabbing her hands. "Yeah we did. So are you guys on for tonight?' I continued to unlock the door.

"Actually yes that's why I came out here."

"Good, I figure that we'll go to the bar and have some drinks, is that okay?"

"Yeah, how about 8:00?"

"Sounds good, stop by later." Lily was squeezing me tightly from behind and I started laughing.

"Alright I'm going in to eat now I'll talk to you later."

"Okay." Finally I opened the door.

We managed to get inside and Lily started right away cleaning up the house, I grabbed her hand. "No you don't why don't you get upstairs and get ready for your bath. I'm going up right now to start your water"

"You really don't have to do this."

"I know but I really want to." I smacked her lightly on the butt and went upstairs pushing her from behind. Running her water I poured what else but Calgon in the tub, then Lily came walking in. She was carrying her script so she could read in the tub. I kissed her on the cheek and she crawled in. "God this feels great."

"Good now relax, I'll be right back."

I ran downstairs grabbed a couple of candles and poured a glass of wine. Then went back up and into the bathroom. I set the candles around the tub, lit them and handed her the glass of wine.

"You are too good to me." She reached up and grabbed the wine glass.

"Okay I'll leave you alone now so that you could get some work done. If you need anything just yell I'll be right downstairs."

"I do need one thing." She tilted her head up for a kiss.

I went back downstairs and started to clean the house, then looked for something to make for dinner. Opening all of the cabinets I decided to make some macaroni and cheese with jalapeno peppers and tomatoes mixed in. After everything was clean and dinner was in the oven I went upstairs to check on Lily.

"So how's everything going?" I walked over and sat on the edge of the tub putting my hand in the water to rub her thigh.

"Great. I was just ready to get out."

"Come on I'll help you." I helped her climb out of the tub and wrapped her in a big fluffy towel. "There you go. Now why don't you go get dressed while I jump in the shower."

"Okay."

She kissed me on the cheek and I started getting undressed, I was in and out of the shower fast so I could check on dinner. Running into the bedroom I threw on some clothes and went downstairs. Lily was in the kitchen pouring us both a glass of wine. She handed me a glass. "Something smells wonderful. What do you have cooking now?"

"I just threw together some macaroni and cheese."

"Really, homemade?"

After taking a sip of wine I set my glass on the table and opened the oven door. "Of course. I hope you don't mind but I also put some hot peppers and tomatoes in there."

"Not at all that sounds great." She rubbed my back as I was bent over checking dinner in the oven. Then I stood up putting my arm around her waist walking her into the living room.

"How about if I build a fire?"

"Alright I'll help, what can I do?"

"Why don't you go get some wood outside."

She went outside and I pulled dinner out of the oven. It actually looked and smelled great. We laid in front of the fire and ate dinner watching television.

Lily laid her head on my stomach. "I'm having such a wonderful time Mel, it makes me want to never leave."

I kissed her on the head. "I wish you didn't have to."

She hugged me and we rolled on the floor kissing passionately when I heard a knock at the door. Getting up slowly I answered it and it was Donna and Vicky. I looked at my watch and I couldn't believe what time it was. "Hi guys. I guess we lost track of the time.

Come on in." I looked over at Lily and she was straightening herself up as she climbed on the couch.

I moved over and they stepped inside. "You know why don't we just go ahead and the two of you could catch up with us later." Vicky grabbed Donna's hand and tugged her arm.

I looked and Lily was just starting to get up. "Are you sure? We won't be long."

Donna turned to me grinning. "No we'll go on ahead. Just don't be all night okay."

I started laughing. "Alright we'll hurry. I'll give Windy a call too."

They both started walking out the door. I yelled. "We're right behind you."

Donna turned around laughing. "Yeah right."

Closing the door I looked at Lily and laughed. "How on earth did it get so late?"

"You know, time flies." She walked over to me laughing as she put her arms around my waist kissing me lightly on the mouth.

"Well I believe that now, why don't you start to get ready I'm going to give Windy a call." I squeezed her hand and she headed upstairs as I watched, then I picked up the phone. After talking Windy into coming with us I went upstairs to get ready myself.

Walking into the bedroom Lily was sitting in front of the mirror putting her make-up on. "So is Windy coming along?" She kept looking straight ahead as she applied her mascara. I walked behind her placing my hands on her shoulders.

"Yeah I had to talk her into it though. Her and her girlfriend are on their way there now. It just happens that they were sitting around trying to decide what to do tonight."

She looked at me in the mirror as she paused and dipped her mascara applicator in the bottle. "I thought you said that you asked her about tonight a couple of days ago."

"I did, that's what is so weird. Well anyway they're both on the way up to the bar now."

I bent down and kissed her neck then turned to change, I threw on a pair of shorts and a vest then went in the bathroom to fix my hair and my face. Going back into the bedroom Lily was sitting on the bed putting on her shoes. She looked up at me. "Boy you clean up pretty good."

"Oh jeez thanks." I jumped on the bed next to her and pulled her to me. "Get over here." I hugged her and fell back on the bed. "Do we really have to go?"

"Now this was all your idea."

"I know I just wanted to show you off. Now I've changed my mind and I want to keep you all to myself."

We started to kiss when she sat up. "Come on now we can't start this because then we really won't go."

I tried to pull her back to me but she stood up and started pulling me up by my hands as I laid back on the bed. I reluctantly stood up. "Okay well if I go we have to agree to come home early. I want to spend as much time with you as possible." I threw my arms around her.

"Deal." She kissed me. "Now let's go."

"Okay, okay."

I slipped my moccasins on and we were out the door. On the way to the car I asked her if she wanted to do something special tomorrow.

"Sure what did you have in mind?"

"Well I thought that maybe we could go for a bike ride in the morning or something."

We got into the car and she was laughing hysterically. "Now would you take a good look at me, does it look like I exercise?"

I laughed and before we knew it we were pulling into the parking lot. "Well here we are."

Lily walked up to me and took my hand in hers. "I want everyone to know that you're with me."

I smiled then kissed her lightly on the mouth. When we walked in I looked around and saw Donna sitting at a table, then I noticed that Windy was there also. We waved and headed their way. "Hi, sorry we're late."

Donna stood up. "Yeah I informed them that you would be late." She looked at me grinning. "A couple of beers guys?"

I laughed. "Sure." Then looked at Lily.

She was nodding her head. "Okay."

Vicky kicked a couple of chairs. "Come on and sit down."

I pulled out a chair for Lily then myself. As I sat down I looked over at Windy. "Windy I'm glad to see that you made it."

She smiled as she rubbed the rim of her beer bottle. "So am I, Barb's in the bathroom she'll be right back and very happy to see you."

Just then Donna came with our beers. "Thanks Donna."

Barb came walking towards the table and I looked up at her. "Hi Barb how are you doing?"

She headed straight for Windy to kiss her and Windy offered her, her cheek, which I found strange. Barb looked at us. "Hi guys glad to see that you made it."

I put my arm around Lily. "Barb I'm not sure if you know Lily?"

Barb stretched her hand across the table. "No we never met but I'm glad I've got the chance."

Lily smiled. "Thanks. It's nice to meet you also."

I stood up. "Okay I'm going to the bar to get shots. Are there any particulars, or is it my call?"

Everyone shouted that it was my call. "I'm glad to know that all of you trust me so much."

I turned and walked up to the bar. Standing there I had a flash-back memory of the last time that I was here. The little escapade I had with the bartender. I looked around and didn't see her anywhere so I felt a little bit more comfortable. As I stood there waiting I felt a hand on my back. "Hi, I thought that you could use some extra hands."

I turned around. "Thanks Windy."

As I glanced at Windy I also looked around to check on Lily and saw that she was just talking away with everyone. Windy then caught me. "Mel don't worry she'll be alright for two minutes by herself." She looked from the table back to me.

I smiled. "I'm not worried. Hey how are things going with you and Barb? Everything okay?"

"Why do you ask that?"

Just then the bartender came walking over and asked us what we wanted.

I looked at Windy. "What do you say, tequila okay?"

"Sounds good."

"Okay then, we'll have six tequila shooters."

The bartender walked away. "So answer my question, is everything okay?"

She looked down at the bar rubbing her fingers along the grain of the wood. I stretched my neck to try and look in her eyes.

"I suppose it's okay. I guess I'm just not very happy that's all." She still didn't look up at me.

"What do you mean not happy. It seemed like you and Barb were getting along just fine." I watched her face wondering if she was going to tell me the truth. I knew that her and Barb broke up at the gallery show a few weeks ago. I just wonder why she keeps pretending to still be with her.

The bartender came by with our shots. I paid her and Windy didn't move from the bar.

"Mel I've got to tell you, Barb and I have been on and off again for a while now."

"Really, what's going on?"

"Well I just don't think that Barb's the one I want to be with, but she keeps wanting me to give it another chance, even though I do, it still doesn't feel right."

"So what are you going to do about it?"

"I'm just going to have to tell her I guess."

"I know that you'll figure it out, but if you need anything at all you know where I am, right?"

"I know, I'm glad I have you Mel." She finally looked at me.

I hugged her. "Come on now before everyone wonders what happened to us."

I grabbed the tray of shots and Windy picked up the limes and the salt. Setting the tray on the table Lily leaned in. "What took you so long?"

"I'll explain later." I then continued to hand everyone a shot and a lime. After everyone was set up I picked up my shot glass. "Here's to good friends."

We sat around talking for a while. I just watched Lily she really looked like she was having a good time. She glanced at me and I smiled back at her.

Looking around I was glad we did this, then I looked at Windy and she looked absolutely miserable. She caught me looking at her and I winked. She smiled then got up to go to the bathroom. I watched her walk away then looked at Barb and she got up to get everyone more beers.

I pulled a bunch of change out of my pocket and asked if anyone wanted to bowl on the machine. Everyone said yes.

Walking over to the bowling machine I wondered why I came up with this bright idea. Bowling was never my thing especially bowling on a machine.

Donna came walking over carrying her beer. "Hey we all decided at the table that the loser of each frame does a shot." She was laughing out loud as she put her cigarette out in an ashtray on a nearby table.

My head jerked up to look at her. "No way, you know that I suck at this."

"I know that's why I brought it up."

"Donna have I told you lately that I hate you?"

She just laughed at me and walked away. Walking back to the table I knew this was very bad. I also knew one thing that I was not going to be the one to go first. I'd rather play catch up. "I put the money in so I'm choosing to go last." I slumped down in a chair at the closest table.

Donna came walking back with ten shots of kamikazes on a tray. She set the tray in front of me. Her and Vicky were busting up laughing.

"You guys think you're so funny, well I might surprise all of you."

Lily looked at me. "Mel you're not really that bad are you?"

I looked at her shaking my head. "Yes I am. The bad thing is they both know it."

She laughed throwing her arms around my neck as I sat there. Hugging my neck and kissing my ear she whispered. "Don't worry baby I'm here to lean on if you feel like you can't stand."

I laughed and tilted my head back kissing her.

I lost the first two frames, but then I started to play surprisingly well. I put my arm around Lily pulling her close. "See everyone thought they were going to put me under the table with these shots, but I'm actually doing better."

Donna looked at me. "Quiet and bowl huh."

The next four frames were split between Donna and Windy. At the end of the game it pretty much was a tie between the three of us as to who drank the most. We sat back down at the table and I turned to Donna. "Let's not do that again."

"Don't worry we won't."

We laughed and I went up to the bar to get a couple glasses of water. I came back to the table and handed one to Donna, she turned to me. "How did you know that's just what I needed?"

"Don't you know that I'm psychic?"

"Oh yeah, that's right."

We both leaned into each other laughing and I watched as Lily came walking back from the bathroom. On her way she stopped to talk to a couple of people who probably recognized her.

When she sat down she turned to me. "You're drinking water?" She giggled.

"Oh stop it. By the way." I put my arm around her chair as she sat next to me. "You weren't picking up any strangers on your way over here were you?"

She laughed as she grabbed my face in her hands and kissed me on the mouth. "You're so silly."

"I know. That's why you're so crazy about me."

"You're right."

I swung one of my legs over hers and played with her hands as we sat there giggling and laughing. Vicky shouted at us. "Hey guys did you hear me?"

I turned to her. "No I'm sorry Vic what did you say?"

"I asked if either one of you would like to shoot pool?"

I looked at Lily. "So what do you say, do you want to play?"

"Sure, I'd love to, I'm actually very good."

"Great so am I, let's kick their butt."

Vicky came walking over. "What are you two whispering about?"

We both laughed and looked up at Vicky. "Nothing why?"

She looked down at us suspiciously.

I smiled. "Why don't we play partners for a drink?"

"Yeah, okay." She looked at Donna.

Donna stood up. "No you don't, I know how Mel plays and I'm not going to lose."

Windy stood up. "Come on Vicky I'll play."

I looked at Windy, then I looked to see where Barb was and she was off in a corner talking to someone. "Windy you're full of surprises I didn't know that you shoot pool."

"Well I don't really, but I thought it would be fun."

I asked Lily if she wanted another beer before we started, but she didn't so I asked everyone else. Donna was the only one who did. I turned and walked up to the bar when I heard a voice behind me. "I changed my mind I'll take a beer."

Windy was standing behind me.

"Alright." The bartender came over and I ordered, then I turned to Windy. "So are you having a good time?"

"Yeah I am." She smiled strangely at me, and then looked back at the table. "Mel you and Lily seem to be getting along really great."

"We are."

She just stared at me.

"Windy, is something wrong?"

"Well I guess I'm just thinking about some things that I should have done differently."

"What do you mean?"

The bartender came back with our beers and I turned back to look at her. "So Windy talk to me."

She looked up at me and stared into my eyes. Then I felt arms wrap around my waist. Turning around I looked at Lily, then I turned back to Windy. "I'm gone for two minutes and look how she misses me." I tilted my head back and kissed her.

Windy stared at us. "Yeah you're lucky." She then grabbed her beer and walked over by Vicky.

Lily picked my beer up from the bar and took a drink. "What's wrong with her?" She leaned against the bar.

"I think her and Barb broke up."

"It's a shame she can't be as happy as we are." She put my beer down and hugged me.

"Yeah I know she really deserves to be happy." I looked at her standing by the pool table and then back at Lily.

"Mel, what's going on between the two of you?"

I giggled. "What do you mean?" And I picked up my beer.

"I don't know it seems like there's a past between the two of you."

"No there's not, we're just really good friends that's all. She helped me a lot after Sarah died. I just want the best for her, is that so bad?"

"No it's not, as long as what's best for her isn't you."

I hugged her and kissed her neck. "You have nothing to worry about."

She smiled at me and I picked my beer up off the bar. "Now come on let's show these women how to shoot pool."

She grabbed for my hand and we walked over by Vicky.

Lily and I won the first game but Vicky and Windy wanted to play again.

I was sitting on a barstool and Lily was on my lap when she whispered in my ear. "Why don't we leave pretty soon?"

"I thought you would never ask." I kissed her on the cheek. Then she crawled off my lap to go shoot and Windy came walking over.

I motioned for her to sit down. "Windy you're impressing me with your talent."

She laughed then sat down on the stool next to me.

We both sat there making fun of Vicky when Lily finished the game. I turned to Windy. "Well you guys owe us a round."

"Somehow I knew it was going to turn out like this."

Vicky came walking over. "Alright what will it be?"

Lily came and put her arms around my shoulders. "Something quick because we're going to take off pretty soon."

I looked up at her. "How about a shot?"

"No you go ahead because I'm the one that's going to be driving home. It seems like you had just a little bit too much fun tonight."

I didn't want to drink alone so Windy did one with me then we went back to the table to sit down. All of us sat there talking and laughing for a little while longer then I looked at Lily and I didn't have to say anything. I turned to Donna, then Windy and said we were going to take off.

Of course they gave me a hard time, then everyone else decided to leave as well. Lily said goodbye to everyone, then told me she was going to get the car while I waited to make sure everyone was okay to drive. Vicky wasn't drinking that much so she drove Donna as well as Windy because Barb left.

Vicky went with Lily to get the car while Donna went to the bathroom before leaving.

I turned to Windy. "Are you going to be okay?"

"Sure, Vicky's going to give me a lift." She stood up.

"No I mean about Barb." I walked over to her and we started walking to the door, then she stopped and turned to me.

She shook her head yes, then I hugged her. "Well if you need anything you know my number."

She smiled and I could tell that she really had a lot to drink. I held her hands in front of me. "Well Lily's probably outside waiting for me so I'm going to go okay?"

"Okay."

I started to leave then she grabbed my hand. "Mel wait a minute."

I turned to her and she kissed me on the mouth. At first I wanted to kiss her back because after all this is what I've been waiting for, but I pulled away. It was then that I knew Lily meant a lot to me. I just stood there staring at her when I heard a horn beeping outside. "That's probably Lily, I better go."

She kept holding my hand and her eyes wouldn't look away from mine. "Windy I've got to go."

"Okay."

I turned around and walked to the door. Before I walked out I looked back at her and she just stood there, watching me leave. I got out to the car and Lily asked me what took me so long. I thought about telling her then decided against it. It wouldn't accomplish anything and it would only cause hard feelings. Besides, Windy was pretty drunk and she might not even remember what happened the next day.

After getting home we raced into bed and held each other. I brushed Lily's hair from her face. "Now this is what I've been looking forward to all evening."

"Me too."

The next morning I rolled over and thought my head was going to explode. I stretched my arm across the bed and realized that Lily wasn't next to me. I crawled out and went into the bathroom to brush my teeth.

Afterward I flopped on the bed wondering if I was going to die. A few minutes later Lily came up the stairs with a big glass of water and some aspirin. She sat on the edge of the bed. "So how do you feel this morning?" She put her hand on my head.

"Oh just dandy, how long have you been up?"

"I don't know a couple of hours I guess." She crawled in bed next to me.

"Really, what time is it anyway?"

"It's 11:30."

I rubbed my head. "Wow I'm sorry, why didn't you wake me?"

"Because you needed your rest. Besides while you were sleeping I managed to pack all my bags." She kissed me on the forehead. "Now that you're up, I'll fix us both a big breakfast. How does that sound?" She kissed the side of my head.

"You're going to cook?"

She stood up. "Yes, I'm going to cook. I think that I can manage eggs, I mean how hard could it be?"

I started to stand up. "Why don't you let me help?"

She pushed me back down on the bed and sat on top of me. "No you don't you just lay here and rest."

I must have dozed off for a little while because I opened my eyes to Lily sitting next to me in bed with a breakfast tray full of food.

"You really did cook?"

"Yes I did. So do you feel any better?"

I sat up. "Yeah I do. The aspirin and the little extra sleep must have done the trick."

"Well good because I made tons of food and I want you to eat every bite."

We both laid in bed eating and reading the paper until Lily jumped up. "Well I really hate to do this, but I better get going."

I pulled her hand. "Come on, can't you stay just a little longer?"

"I really wish that I could but I've got a plane to catch, you know that."

"I know, well give me a couple of minutes to change and I'll drive you to the airport."

She pulled me up by my hands and hugged me. "Actually I called early this morning and reserved a cab."

I pulled back. "Well call and cancel."

"I really hate airport goodbyes. Besides people seem to always recognize me in the airport and I don't think either of us need to deal with that."

"What do you mean, are you ashamed to be seen with me?"

"Come on now…you know better than that."

"I know." I hugged her tight.

We went downstairs and a few minutes later the cab pulled up in front of the house. I kissed her goodbye and walked her to the cab. As she got in I winked at her, then waved goodbye.

The phone was ringing, when I went back inside to see who was calling it was Windy. I really didn't feel like dealing with what happened last night, so I just didn't answer.

I spent the rest of the day cleaning and touching base with my sister on the phone.

CHAPTER 10

I woke up to the ringing of my alarm. Rolling over I smacked the snooze button thinking how badly I didn't want to go to work today. I lay there until my alarm went off again, then I shut it off again.

Finally I got up went into the bathroom and looked in the mirror thinking how I really didn't feel like dealing with Windy today. This is just one conversation that I wasn't prepared to have yet. So I decided to call off for the day. I called hoping Tara would answer the phone.

My heart pounded harder with each ring. "Tara hi." I sighed. "It's Mel, could you relay a message to Windy for me?"

"Do you want to talk to her, she's in."

"No, just tell her that I won't be in today."

"Are you sick?"

"No I'm not sick, I'm just going to take the day off."

"Okay, I'll give her the message."

"Thanks, bye."

I lazed around the house for the morning then I thought I would go for a bike ride. I changed, grabbed my bike then went outside. After locking up I turned to get on my bike and Windy was pulling in the driveway.

Somehow I just knew that I wasn't going to get away clean the whole day. I stood there while she got out of the car. I watched as she walked up to me.

"Hi Mel, I think that we have to talk."

"I know, lets go inside."

I unlocked my door, tossed my keys on the table, and then turned around to face her. "Do you want anything to drink?"

"No thanks." She walked closer to me. "I tried calling you all day yesterday but you weren't home or you didn't answer."

I stood leaning against my kitchen counter. "Windy the truth is I wasn't answering, I guess I just needed time to deal with what had happened. I'm sorry."

"There's no need for you to be sorry, what I did was totally out of line."

I walked over and sat down on the couch. Windy followed me. "Windy." I turned to her. "Why did you kiss me like that?"

"Mel the absolute truth is I regret everything that's happened between us."

I looked at her. "I don't understand what you mean."

She looked down at her hands. "Boy you're not going to make this easy on me are you?"

"I'm not trying to make things difficult for you Windy, I just want to be clear on what you're trying to say." I looked at her while she studied her hands.

"What I regret Mel, is not telling you that I've always been in love with you. Although that doesn't excuse what I've done, I know that you're with Lily now, and that's probably what made me realize, or face my feelings for you."

I stood up and went into the kitchen to get a glass of water. I couldn't believe what I was hearing. I waited for over a year to hear this and now when I'm finally in a relationship she tells me this. Now. I wiped my forehead.

"Mel please, say something." She didn't move from the couch.

"Windy I don't know exactly what you want me to say. I waited for you for so long, and now that I've finally found someone you come to me with this." I threw my arms in the air and turned around.

I just stood in the living room looking out the window. I could feel her standing behind me.

"Mel I would understand if you hate me right now."

"Windy I don't hate you. I could never hate you. My God, I've been in love with you since the day I met you. Right now though, I don't know what I feel. I do feel very confused."

She came closer to me, so close that I could feel her breath on my neck. "Windy please don't do this to me. Lily just left. I found that I have very deep feelings for her."

She came to my face. "But do you love her?"

I looked in her eyes. Staring in those eyes I felt like I was melting. This is the moment I've been waiting for, for so long. But even wanting this to happen I felt incredibly guilty. How could I do this to Lily?

I ran my fingers down her bare arm and couldn't look away from those eyes. She reached up and touched my cheek lightly.

I lowered my eyes and with her hand she raised my head. "Mel I want you to look at me."

I raised my eyes to look at her. She then leaned in and kissed me so passionately my knees felt weak. I wrapped my arms tightly around her neck and kissed her the way I had been dreaming of kissing her for years.

We stood there hugging each other and she spoke softly into my ear. "Mel do you feel the chemistry we have? Tell me that you don't feel it and I'll leave right now and never look back."

I ran my fingers over her lips. "Windy this isn't fair. You know that I've been dreaming of this day for a long time, but I have to think of Lily."

I hugged her again. As I was holding her I could smell her hair and her skin. She smelled so good. I rubbed my hands down her back and she felt incredible. I stepped back and looked into her eyes. "Windy I need some time."

"I know that you do. Take as much time as you need." She looked down at the floor then back at me. "If you need to go to Lily and explore your feelings for her I understand."

"I think maybe I will. I at least owe her that."

"Okay, well when would you leave?"

"I want to do this as soon as possible. So if it's okay with you I'm going to take a couple of weeks off work so I could leave for New York right away."

"Sure I understand. Well I'll let you go and make plans, just stop by and let me know when you're leaving and if there's anything I can help you with."

"Thanks." We continued to hug each other, and then I walked her to the door.

She took my hand in hers and she didn't say anything. After all what else was there to say. She smiled at me then walked to her car. I stood there and watched her pull away then went inside and fell on the couch. I covered my face with my hands and lay there trying to think of what to do. Although I knew what I had to do, I had to go to New York and see Lily. But what should I say to her. I didn't know if I should tell her why I was there, or just see how things go between us. Well what ever I decided to do I had to make flight arrangements, so I picked up the phone.

I booked a flight and made hotel arrangements then went upstairs to pack. My flight wasn't until tomorrow morning but I wanted to get everything ready early. As I packed I wondered if I should call Lily, but decided against it, I thought it might be better to surprise her. Just knowing her the small amount of time that I have, I knew she would rather be surprised. After I packed, I grabbed my bike and headed out for a long ride thinking that it might clear my head.

When I got home my head was no more cleared out now, then when I left. Going inside I ran a bath and lay there until there was no more hot water left. I changed and went into the kitchen to make myself a salad and pour myself a glass of wine.

When I was through eating I took the bottle of wine and sat on the couch just thinking of everything, and yet nothing at all. I finished the bottle of wine and went up to bed.

CHAPTER 11

❀

*F*inishing my coffee I picked up my bags and carried them to my car. I wrote Donna a short note telling her what I was doing and where I was going, then taped it to her door and drove away.

Before I went to the airport I stopped by the gallery to talk to Windy. Walking into the gallery Tara looked at me. "I wish that someone would tell me what's going on here?"

"What do you mean?"

"It's just that everyone is acting so weird around here anymore."

I laughed. "By the way I'm going to be out of town for a while so could you take all my messages. I'll call in every now and then. If it really sounds important though give it directly to Windy, okay."

She walked around and sat down behind her desk. "Okay, but could someone please let me in on what's going on at some point."

I started walking down to Windy's office and yelled back to Tara. "At some point." I laughed and kept walking.

I stood outside Windy's door almost frightened to go inside, but I quickly knocked and opened the door.

Windy turned around in her chair. "Hi Mel I guess you're here to tell me that you're on your way to New York." She kept swiveling nervously in her chair.

I gave her a half smile. "Yes I am." I handed her all my flight information and the hotel that I would be staying at. "Here's all the information you'll need." She reached for the paper then glanced at it and set it down on her desk.

She stood up, walked around her desk and leaned against it folding her hands in front of her. "Do you need a ride to the airport?"

"No, I'm going to drive."

"Are you sure?"

"Yeah." I played with my keys nervously. "Windy you know that I have to do this."

"I know. I told you that it wouldn't bother me, but I guess I lied. It bothers me a lot."

"I know it does. It would bother me too."

I stepped closer and hugged her. I pulled away then kissed her gently on the mouth. Without saying a word I turned around to leave. With my hand on the doorknob I turned around to look at her again before I left. I saw her leaning on her desk with her fingertips lightly touching her lips and her head down. I stepped through the doorway and closed the door behind me.

I stood there for a minute until Tara came by. "Mel is everything okay?"

"Sure. Tara take care of Windy okay."

"Of course, Mel what's going on?"

You could see she was concerned. "Maybe I'll fill you in when I get back."

She folded her arms around her chest. "And when will that be?"

"I don't know exactly. I'll keep in touch."

"Well be careful okay."

I smiled at her. "Always."

Walking to my car I knew that whatever happened, someone was going to get hurt. I think that's what bothered me most.

The plane ride was pure hell. Not only do I hate flying but all I thought of was this situation that I got myself in.

Standing outside the airport I finally managed to get a cab. Once inside I had the driver take me to my hotel. It was still early and I didn't know if Lily was at work or if she was already home, so I ordered something to eat from room service, then laid in the tub thinking of what I was going to say to Lily.

I had Lily's address on a shipping receipt from when she bought some artwork at the gallery. Pulling it from my briefcase I reached for the phone and called a cab. I finished getting dressed then went downstairs.

I was so nervous the whole cab ride I could barely swallow, and when I finally reached her building, I still couldn't believe how nervous I was.

I went inside and knocked at her door. I stood there for a couple of minutes and just when I thought no one was home, I heard the door start to open. Before the door even opened I smiled. "Hi Lil..." Then I stopped. A middle aged very distinguished looking man answered the door, I immediately stepped back. "I'm sorry I was looking for Lily Bromwell." Just as I finished I heard Lily in the background.

"Who is it honey?" And she came to the door.

"I don't know, she asked for you."

She stood there looking at me and she turned as white as a ghost. "Mel what are you doing here?"

The man turned to Lily. "So the two of you know each other?" He opened the door all the way.

I was too shocked to even speak.

Lily looked at him. "Yes this is Melissa Hadley, she owns the gallery where I purchased this great painting." She turned around and pointed somewhere in the apartment.

He reached his hand out. "It's nice to meet you Melissa. I'm Richard, Lily's husband." He then turned to Lily. "I'll let the two of you visit while I go jump in the shower." He turned back to me. "Again, nice to meet you Melissa."

I just smiled at him as he walked away, then I turned to Lily. Looking at her I didn't even know what I felt, hate, shock, I have no idea. I turned around and just walked away. She closed the door and came running after me. When she reached me she grabbed for my arm. Pulling away from her I just stared into her eyes. Then I began laughing. "Boy what a fool I am."

"Mel you're not a fool. Let me explain." She grabbed for me again as I turned. "Please! Let me explain."

I spun around. "Lily what on earth is there to explain? You're married." I rubbed my hand through my hair, and then I threw my arm down in disgust. "At least tell me that there's no kids."

"No, there are no kids. Mel I had to get married. It was a career move."

"Does he know that?"

"Well not really. I mean he does know I have been in relationships with women, but that's it." She came closer to me. "Mel I'm just not happy in this marriage. I would much rather be with you but that's just not possible, not now anyway."

"So what you're saying is that you choose your career over your happiness." I looked up at he ceiling trying to prevent the tears from rolling down my face.

She didn't say anything. She just looked down at the ground. At that moment I felt sorry for her because I knew that she will probably be unhappy for the rest of her life.

I grabbed for her hand. "Look at me Lil." She looked up into my eyes. "I really hope for your sake that you made the right decision, for you." I kissed her on the cheek. "Goodbye Lily."

I turned and walked out the door without even looking back. Reaching the street I took a deep breath and exhaled slowly. I had so many thoughts rushing through my head I couldn't separate them all.

A cab finally pulled up and I got in. I had him take me back to the hotel. The whole ride I sat thinking of Lily and how on earth I couldn't have known that she was married. Getting back to the hotel I went directly to the bar. As I sat sipping on a vodka martini I couldn't get the face of her husband out of my mind. Well I knew that someone was going to get hurt here, I just had no idea that it would be me. I thought about calling Windy but decided against that. What I really need is time to myself. I need to make sure if I get involved with Windy that it's the right thing for me to do. After my fourth drink I went upstairs to my room and crashed on the bed.

Waking up I still couldn't believe what had happened. I immediately picked up the phone and called the airlines. Hanging up I thanked God I was able to get a flight out of here this afternoon. After a shower I started packing.

When I was boarding the plane I did come to one realization and that was I needed to get away by myself for a while. I just needed to clear my head and find out exactly where I belong. I really just need to hide and think things through, and I know exactly where to go to do that.

Walking in my house I couldn't believe I was finally home. Although all I was going to do was repack and get the hell out of here. Racing around trying to do everything as fast as possible I heard a knock at the door. I didn't want to open it because I didn't want who was on the other side to hold me back.

But I did answer and it was Donna. "Mel you're back already?"

"Donna I'm in a real hurry so if you can talk while I run around here trying to pack all over again you can come in." I walked away leaving the door open.

Donna walked through shutting the door behind her. "What do you mean, you're packing again?"

"Well I'm taking off for a while to straighten some things out. I just need time to myself." I picked up my bags and pulled out things that I didn't need.

"What the hell happened in New York?" She sat down on the couch next to my bags.

"Well let me try and put it as concisely as possible." I still kept walking through the house putting things away and packing other things. "I knocked on Lily's door and her husband answered. That's about it." I turned and looked at her as she sat on the couch.

"Are you serious?" She stood up and walked over to me.

"Does it look like I'm serious?" I ran my hand through my hair.

"What did she say?" She stood in front of me with her arms folded.

"What it boils down to is that she would rather have a career than a relationship."

"So, she's married just for show?"

"That's not what her husband thinks." I walked away running upstairs.

Donna was one step behind and stood at the bottom leaning on the railing. "Well all I can say is that it's better you found out now, rather than later."

"You're right about that." I yelled to Donna, and then came down with armloads of clothes.

"So now where are you going in such a hurry?" She reached up and grabbed some things out of my arms and followed me to my bags.

"Well like I said I'm going away to sort out my feelings."

"Are you going to tell Windy?"

"Yeah, I'm going to stop by the office after I leave here."

"How do you think she's going to take it?"

"I would rather take some time now and make sure I'm making the right decision, rather than jump into something that I'm not ready for. That wouldn't be fair to either of us."

"Well you're absolutely right about that. I'm going to go so if you need anything you let me know okay."

I walked to the door and I hugged her.

"Mel just be careful."

"I will." I watched her walk home then I closed the door. Looking around I don't think that I forgot anything. So I picked up my bags and locked the door behind me.

Sitting in my car I called my sister to tell her I was going to our family condo in North Carolina. As I drove I confirmed with her that no one else was there and I also told her not to give absolutely anyone the number. Before I went to the gallery I stopped at the store to get some munchies for the ride. I got a bag of fruit, some bottled water and a couple bags of these already peeled baby carrots.

Reaching the gallery I took a deep breath and went in. I was glad to see Windy's car in the parking lot because I didn't even think of calling ahead.

Walking in Tara saw me first. "Didn't you just leave?" She walked around and sat behind her desk.

"Yeah I did, is Windy around?"

"She's in the back."

I smiled at her and went straight to the storeroom. Walking through the door she saw me right away and jumped off the ladder running up to me. "I didn't think you would be back this soon."

She hugged me, and then I pulled away. "Windy I'm not really back."

"I don't understand."

"Sit down and let me explain." She sat down and I sat next to her. "First of all, it's over between Lily and myself. But it's not because of why I went down there."

"Hold on I'm confused." She shook her head while she was squinting her eyes looking at me.

"I'm not really doing this right." I rubbed my hands through my hair as I scratched my head. "But I feel like such a fool."

She grabbed for my hand. "Mel you're not a fool."

"After you hear what I have to say, you might want to change your mind." I shuffled my feet then I looked at her. "Well here it goes. She's married."

I looked in her eyes and there was a hint of disbelief. "I know, I had that same look. But it's true. She said she did it for her career, and at this point in her life she would rather have a career, than a relationship."

"Mel that doesn't make you a fool, not at all. All you did was believe and put your trust in someone. That's not foolish. Hey, if that makes you a fool than we are all fools because we all believed her."

"Thanks Windy, that makes me feel a little bit better."

She looked at me still holding my hand. "So."

"Windy there's something else. I'm still going to take some time off. I just need to make sure that the two of us aren't making a mistake. I need to know that being here with you is where I'm supposed to be. Everything is just happening so fast."

"Okay, I understand."

I held her hands in mine. "So you're okay with this?"

"Of course. I understand how hard this is for you."

I stood up still holding her hands. "Okay I'll see you in a couple of weeks then."

"You're leaving right now?"

"Yeah, I'm all packed and ready to go."

She stood up. "Boy you didn't waste any time. Where are you going?"

"To my parent's beach house. It's quiet there."

"I understand."

I hugged her. "Don't worry I'll call you when I get there." I let the back of my fingers slide down the side of her face, burning her features in my mind.

"Walk me to my car?"

As we stood outside I hugged her one more time. "I'll really miss you."

She smiled. "I'm glad, I'll miss you too."

Driving away I watched her getting smaller and smaller in my rear view mirror, until I could no longer see her. That's when I knew I was finally on my way. One thing that I always remembered about this trip was it was one hell of a ride. Once I was on my way though I wasn't stopping for anything but gas.

I talked on the phone most of the way with my sister. That helped pass the time a little bit. Then when I thought I would never get there I saw the coastline. The closer I got the more excited I got. I haven't been here since the last time I came here with Sarah. We would come here just about every other summer.

The house is great it's right on the beach. The back faces the ocean's sound while the front looks to the ocean. Although you have about a half-mile walk to the ocean it's really beautiful. The back of the house has stairs and platforms that go directly into the water. The only draw back is that the neighbors are a little bit too close for my taste. Usually everyone who owns houses on the strip rents them out for the summer so you never really know who's going to be there.

Without getting any of my bags out of the car I went up the stairs and unlocked the door. Walking in I remembered exactly how much I loved this place. I made it as far as the couch then fell down for a nap.

When I woke the sun was just starting to set. I went to the car and unloaded all my bags. Then I looked to see if there was anything to eat. Finding a can of clam chowder I heated it up while I grabbed a beer and went outside to watch the sun set. Just sitting there on the deck stairs I couldn't remember the last time I felt so content.

After eating I decided to go for a walk on the beach. I tied a sweat shirt around my waist, grabbed a flashlight and a bottle of water, and then headed out.

On such a beautiful night I was surprised there weren't more people on the beach. I did pass a couple of joggers and a group of people playing volleyball, but that was about it. I walked for about an hour on the beach then stopped and picked up a seashell from the sand.

Sitting down I gently rubbed the shell remembering when Sarah and I took walks on this beach. We always walked searching for shells. God, how I miss her if only she were here I wouldn't have any of these problems. We were together so long that I had forgotten how hard new relationships are, not to mention all the troubles and heart ache you have to go through to find the right person. If only things wouldn't have changed I would be sitting on this beach with Sarah instead of by myself.

Sitting with my legs crossed I threw the shell into the ocean and brushed my hands off on my shorts. I fell back onto my elbows, stretched my legs out and threw my head back looking up at the stars over the ocean.

Closing my eyes I remembered the last time Sarah and I were here walking this beach, her running ahead of me kicking her feet in the water. Then I started to laugh as I remembered her bending down picking up a minnow out of the water and chasing me with it.

I sat back up when I felt my self starting to cry, I didn't want to do that so I headed back.

I was about halfway back when I was glad I brought the flashlight. Sarah always loved the beach at night. She would always say that it looked like a whole different world. Shining the light on the ground you can see little crabs and creatures that only come out at night. Finally I made it back and I decided to give Windy a call, and then go directly to bed.

CHAPTER 12

*A*fter several days of sun and surf I was very tan, but that was about it. I really haven't thought about anything but if the weather was going to be good for windsurfing tomorrow. Since I've been here I haven't talked to anyone. Once in a while I see the people next door and wave slightly then duck inside before anyone strikes up a conversation.

I was dragging my windsurf in when I looked up and saw a woman sitting on the deck next door. She waved, so I waved back. I tied the board up to the deck then slopped some sunscreen on and laid back on the lower platform enjoying the sun.

It wasn't long before I heard someone walking through the water, when I looked up I saw that it was the woman from next door. I sat up with my feet dangling in the water. "Hi." I adjusted my sunglasses and ran my hand through my half wet hair as I looked up at her. She stood before me knee high in water with the sun starting to set behind her. All I could make out was a dark silhouette with the bright setting sun behind her.

"Hi, I've been watching you out there on the windsurf you're pretty good."

"Thanks."

"I thought you might be thirsty, I brought beers would you like one?" She held up two beers to show me. Still I could only make out her silhouette.

I reached my hand up. "Sure, thanks." She handed me a beer. "By the way my name's Mel."

"Mel that's unusual."

"Well actually it's Melissa, Melissa Hadley. Everyone just always calls me Mel though.

She stretched her hand out. "Nice to meet you Mel. My name's Ivy." She took my hand in hers then let go. "I hope you don't mind me intruding like this, but my friends left me alone today and I started to get really bored. I've noticed though you're here alone. Actually you can't help but notice these houses are pretty close."

"Yeah they are close, that's the only complaint I've always had about this place. But no, you're not intruding, the company is actually nice for a change."

"So where did you learn to windsurf like that?"

"I practically grew up here." I slid over a little bit. "Here have a seat." I patted the space next to me. Finally she broke from the sun and I couldn't get over how absolutely beautiful she was. Then I immediately thought of Windy and Lily and knew I didn't need any more trouble, so I put her looks in the back of my mind.

"Thanks." She sat down. "So you grew up here?"

"No I grew up in Ohio, but my parents own this house so we spent a lot of time here." We both sat staring out at the water.

"Wow, that's great. It must have been really fun as a kid to have a place like this to come to."

"Yeah it was, so who are you here with?" I looked at her.

"Just a couple of friends, my sister and her husband."

"Are you guys having a good time?"

"Yes we are it's so relaxing here." She turned to me.

"It is, the nights I especially love."

"Yeah the sunsets here are amazing. So how long are you here for?"

"I don't know I guess until I decide it's time for me to go back to the real world." I laughed as I looked at her.

"Boy that must be nice. We're here for a few weeks then it's time to go back to work." She sighed softly.

I touched her forearm lightly then pointed out at the water. "Look!" She turned her head. "Do you see them, dolphins, two of them?"

She lifted her sunglasses off her face. "Yeah, I do." She turned to me. "These are the first dolphins I've seen since I've been here." She looked back out at the water. "I guess I never really knew to look for them."

As I still watched the dolphins in the water I crossed my legs. "I never tire of watching them. I always have a pair of binoculars on hand to look and watch for them." I turned to look at her. "So Ivy not to turn the subject sour but what kind of work are you going to be going back to?"

She laughed. "I'm a doctor. A pediatrician."

"Really, well, that's impressive." I kicked the water with my feet. "Do you like working with kids?"

"Yeah I do."

"I guess that was a pretty stupid question."

We both laughed. "So how about another beer? With it being so hot they seem to go down a lot easier than usual." I held my bottle up and looked at it.

"Sure that would be great, and you're right they do." She handed me her empty bottle.

I stood up. "Why don't you come and sit up top. I have some chairs up there."

"Okay."

She stood up and I realized then exactly how tall she was. We both climbed the stairs and she sat down then stretched her feet out to let them rest on the railing.

I giggled as I watched her. "I'll be right back." I went inside and grabbed a couple of clean beach towels then a couple of beers and went back outside. I handed her a beer. "Here you go, and here's a towel to sit on so that you don't stick to the chair."

She stood up and I laid a towel on her chair. Then she sat back down. "Well, you are an experienced beach bum aren't you?"

"I suppose so." I laughed. "Although I haven't been here in years. I guess it just all comes back to you once you get here." I started laughing as I sat down.

She looked around. "If I had a place like this I'd be here all the time."

"Well circumstances stopped me from doing that." I looked out at the water and immediately felt an empty aching feeling in my soul as I thought of Sarah.

"I'm sorry I don't mean to pry. I should probably get going." She started to stand up.

I stretched my hand out and touched her arm. "No please stay, the truth is the conversation is nice for a change. When you're alone for a few days you forget how much you miss talking with someone." I turned from her, back to the water.

"How long have you been here?"

"Well I've only been here let's see, four days now and the drive up here took two days so you see I'm actually starved for company about now."

She laughed. "Yeah, I guess you would be. So what possessed you to come all the way here by yourself? Are things that bad that you came here to hide out forever?"

I could feel her looking at me. "Well not forever, just until I make certain life decisions." I smiled and looked at her.

"This is certainly the place to do that. It's so quiet and peaceful here." She looked around.

My attentions though turned back to the water. "That could also be a big drawback, because now I don't want to leave."

"So what else do you do besides hang out on the beach?"

I laughed. "I'm a partner in an art gallery."

"That sounds like such a fun job."

"It is, I really enjoy it a lot."

We sat there on the deck talking for hours. She told me about her job and I told her about mine, neither one of us got too personal. I felt comfortable with her.

Then her friends came home and she left, but I must say I had a fun afternoon. I gathered up all of the empty bottles lying around and went inside.

For the next few days Ivy came by either to talk, or to borrow the windsurf. I gave her a couple of quick lessons and she picked it up pretty fast. The time that we did spend together we both had so much fun. I think it was because neither one of us got too personal we just had fun.

Today though I spent the afternoon baking a pie because Ivy and her friends invited me over for a barbecue and I just hate going any-where empty handed.

After my shower I pulled my pie out of the oven and looked up to see Ivy knocking lightly at the door.

I waved her in. "Hi, what are you doing here?"

"Mel we have to talk." She looked nervous and scared all at the same time. She was playing with her watchband, and then she moved to twirling her hair.

I walked over to her. "What's the matter?"

She sat down on the couch and I sat down on a chair opposite her. "I've got to tell you something that's not very easy for me. But if I don't tell you I'm sure it will come out at dinner."

She kept looking at me then quickly she would look away. "Well just tell me. After all what could be that bad?"

She looked up at me. "I just really like being friends with you and I don't want that to change."

"Don't worry nothing you say could change that." I smiled at her.

"Well first of all my friends that are staying with us are two gay men that have been together for a couple of years."

"So what, that's what you have to tell me." I laughed and I stood up. "Hey, would you like a drink?"

"Okay."

"How's vodka and cranberry juice?"

"Great."

I walked into the kitchen and started making the drinks. When I went back into the living room I noticed that she was still acting very nervous. I handed her a drink. "Ivy is everything okay?" I looked at her and she nodded yes. "Well if you'll excuse me for one minute I'll be right back."

I went into the bedroom and threw on a pair of shorts and a tank top then went back out. "So what do you think? Do I look like I'm going to a barbecue or what?" I laughed.

She stood up and walked into the kitchen and sat down at the kitchen table. I followed her and set my drink on the table while I combed out my hair.

"Okay Ivy, now tell me what's going on here?"

I looked at her and she had such a look of concern on her face. I sat down opposite her at her table and sipped my drink. "So what else, you can tell me. We're friends right?"

She looked at me and giggled nervously. "You don't know how hard this is for me."

I just looked at her and remembered what she said about her friends, and then I knew exactly what she was trying to tell me. I reached over and put my hand on hers. "Ivy before you say anything there's something that I should probably tell you first."

She just looked at me; I knew she was probably trying to tell me she was gay. Or at least that's what I think she was trying to tell me anyway. I thought I would tell her first that way if it is the same thing she'll feel more comfortable and if not, then at least she'll know the truth.

I picked up my drink and walked to the other side of the kitchen. "I think that this is something you should probably know. I mean I don't see how it would make any kind of difference between us but, well…" I looked straight in her eyes. "I'm gay. Like I said I don't know why it would make a difference in our friendship, but some people get upset if they don't know the truth, they feel like they're being lied to from the beginning of the friendship." I took a big sip of my drink.

Just then she busted up laughing. "Yeah I know what you mean some people do get mad don't they, you see that's exactly what I was trying to tell you."

"The truth is, I already figured it out and thought that it would be more comfortable for you if I told you first, seeing as how you were having such a hard time."

We both started laughing and I walked over to the kitchen counter. "How about another drink?"

She smiled and played nervously with her hair. "Sure that would be great." She followed me in the kitchen.

As I made our drinks I started giggling. "So you thought that your family and friends would spill your secret?"

"Well it's not a secret, not to my family, friends or even work, and I'm sure they would never intentionally say anything but you never know. You see I'm not ashamed of who I am and never have been, but we just met and hit it off so well, I didn't want you to feel uncomfortable."

I walked over and sat down at the table. "Don't worry I didn't say anything to you for just about the same reasons. So are you here all alone?"

"Yes, actually I'm here to forget about her."

I laughed. "That's pretty much the same reason that I'm here. You see that's the life decision I was telling you about."

She stood up. "Well how about that barbecue, this is getting very intense all of a sudden."

"You're right about that, let's go and have some fun."

We downed our drinks and walked out the back way. As we stepped on the back deck her friends were sitting outside and yelled at us. "It's about time. We thought we would be eating alone."

We walked over and I introduced myself, then I asked Ivy where her sister and her husband were. She said they went out to dinner alone but that they would be back later on so they could meet me. The four of us sat around and had a great time. We talked and laughed; it was one of the more pleasant evenings that I've had in a long time. When her sister came home she was an absolute delight, and her husband was great. It was just a very enjoyable evening.

After a couple hours of talking, drinking and eating everything in sight, I excused myself and headed for home. Ivy walked me to the back door. "Thanks for coming Mel I think everyone had a good time."

"Well you're very welcome." I leaned against the railing folding my arms in front of me. "I don't know about everyone else but I know I did. Your friends and family are great."

She looked back into the house smiling. "Yeah they are."

I started walking down the stairs. "I better be going I'll see you tomorrow, I have some phone calls to make before I go to bed, and it's getting kind of late."

She walked me to the bottom stair. "Sure, I'll see you tomorrow."

I finally made it up to my deck, as I climbed the stairs I looked back at Ivy and waved, then went inside.

I right away picked up the phone to call Windy, and again there was no answer. Hanging up I wondered where she could be this late.

Oh well, she's probably either sleeping or she's out with her friends, anyway I'll try again tomorrow.

I changed and climbed immediately into bed.

❧   ❧   ❧

I woke up to the sun shining in my window and the smell of salt water in the air. Stretching my arms over my head I crawled out of bed thinking how great it would be to wake up like this everyday. I started a pot coffee and went to take a shower. I figured today I was going into town to buy some things for my nieces. They always love to get a present, who doesn't.

I changed, finished my coffee, and then grabbed for my keys. I went out the back door and saw that Ivy was sitting on her deck and I yelled over to her. "Haven't you had enough sun yet?"

She lifted her head laughing and threw her arms up in the air. "Everyone else deserted me and there's not much else for a person to do around here without a car?"

I dangled my keys in the air. "Well I have a car and I'm headed into town. Would you like to come along?"

She sat up in her chair. "Sure, I haven't been anywhere or seen anything since I've been here."

"Well we could change all that in one afternoon. So go on and get dressed. I'll be waiting for you inside, come on by when you're ready."

She jumped up. "Okay I'll just be a few minutes."

She went inside and I decided that I'd try and give Windy another call. I dialed her number then went into the kitchen to pour a glass of water. Still no answer, when I hung up Ivy was standing at the front door. I set the phone down a little disgusted, but also a little worried. Then I turned to her. "So are you ready?"

"Yeah, Mel this is really nice of you to let me tag along."

"It's always more fun to have someone to shop with." I walked to the door, picked my keys up off the table and we both went down to the car. "So is there anywhere in particular that you want to see?"

"No, what ever you want to do is fine with me."

We both crawled in my jeep. "Alrighty then, let's be off." I pulled away. "How about making our first stop the aquariums."

On the way there we had a little small talk, nothing that really added up to much, which made it a comfortable ride.

As we walked through the aquarium Ivy was like a little kid. I had to laugh at her pointing and fingering all the tanks. It was like she never saw a fish before. I just stood back and watched her, laughing inside at how she reminded me of a little kid. All she needed was an ice cream cone in her hand and my mental picture would be complete.

After the aquarium we drove straight to the old fort that was close to town. Walking through the fort it struck me, watching Ivy reminded me so much of Sarah. Absolutely every time we came here she would be so excited. She loved to go sight seeing and it didn't matter how many times she visited these places you could still see the excitement in her face. Just watching Ivy see these places for the first time flooded my head with memories of Sarah. I stood back watching her and all the excitement that flowed through her body. She hurried around trying to see everything at one time as I stared at her. The more I watched her the more she turned to Sarah in my mind. At the moment when she turned to Sarah she looked at me smiling and my heart skipped a beat. I felt a warmth through my whole body and tears in my eyes. I knew it was Ivy; I just wanted her to be Sarah with all my heart.

Ivy came walking up to me. "Is there something wrong Mel?"

I started blinking my eyes so the tears wouldn't fall out. "No not at all, come on let's finish the tour." I grabbed her hand.

When we finished the tour we walked back to the car and I asked Ivy if she was ready to go do some shopping. "Absolutely, I especially love going into the small interesting shops."

"Great, there's a lot of those here." We both climbed in the car.

Going into town we hit every gift shop there was. I was amazed at Ivy's shopping stamina. "Girl you can shop!" We both laughed. "So are you ready for something to eat. I know this great little bar that has amazing clam chowder."

She put her hand on her stomach. "Sounds great, I'm starved."

We walked down to the bar because it was close to where we had parked. But first we had to make a pit stop at the car to unload all of our packages.

When we reached the bar we sat down and ordered a couple of beers and two bowls of clam chowder. "So are you having a good time?"

"Are you kidding, I'm having a blast. Thanks so much Mel this is really nice of you to include me in your day."

The waitress came back with our beers and set them on the table. I started to pour mine. "You're welcome. I'm having fun just watching you see all of this for the first time. It brings back a lot of great memories." After I said it I realized what I said and I hoped that Ivy would leave it alone, I really didn't want to explain what I meant by 'great memories.' "There is one more thing for us to do and then we'll head back. You don't have to be back at any particular time do you?"

I watched her take a drink of her beer. "No, I left everyone a note as to where I would be."

"Good."

The waitress then brought our soup and set the bowls in front of us. After she left Ivy looked up at me while she tasted the soup. "Mel you're right this soup is fantastic." She picked up her beer.

"I thought you would like it." I tasted my soup and it was as good as I remembered.

She then looked up at me with her beer in her hand. "Are you sure everything's okay?"

"Yeah, why?" I lifted up my glass to take a drink.

"Well it's just that you seem kind of distant." She stared at me.

"I'm sorry I hope that I'm not ruining your day." I set my glass down.

"Not at all. As you can tell I love to shop. I just wanted you to know if you want to talk sometimes it's easier talking to a stranger."

"You're not a stranger." I laughed and folded my hands then rested my chin on the top of them.

"No, but I'm not your best friend either."

"True." I giggled.

We finished our soup then ordered a couple more beers and went to sit outside on the patio. Sitting there we basically just people watched and also watched all of the amazing ships that passed by.

While we were out there I went and bought tickets for the tour boat. Going on this boat was Sarah's absolute favorite thing to do when we came here. As I was walking back Ivy looked at me. "Where did you go?"

Is sat down taking a drink of my beer. "It's a surprise. We have just enough time to finish our beers then we have to leave."

"Okay, but where are we going?" She picked up her beer taking a drink.

"You'll see."

Sitting there we were laughing so much we almost missed the boat. We had to run to catch it. I was running in front of Ivy then I turned around and yelled for her to hurry up. We finally reached the boat and climbed aboard.

Ivy turned to me huffing and puffing. "So where does this boat take us?"

I was laughing at her. "It just tours around the island with wild horses, some famous houses things like that." I turned to her. "Want a beer?"

"They actually have beer on this boat?" She turned around.

I have to admit it wasn't the most attractive boat I've ever seen, but it was always a good time. They served beer from a Coleman cooler in the back, with chips, candy, and of course popcorn.

We got a couple of beers and I also bought some popcorn to feed the birds. I gave the popcorn to Ivy and then handed her a beer. "What's the popcorn for?" She looked at me questionably.

"Here watch." I tossed some in the air and sea gulls came flying from everywhere. "You throw it up in the air and the sea gulls come by and eat it."

She was laughing as she grabbed the bag out of my hand. I watched her and laughed, because she was just as excited about doing this as Sarah used to be. I sat back and watched her with a smile on my face. Then I closed my eyes and saw Sarah standing there. Every once in a while Ivy would look back at me and smile, it was then that I was glad I asked her to come with me. Watching her feeding the birds I noticed again how attractive she was. I never really paid any attention since that first day I saw her and told myself to put it out of my mind. But with her long curly blonde hair blowing in the breeze of the ocean, and her green eyes as bright as emeralds she looked incredible. When she turned to me in the sun and the ocean water dancing behind her, her smile managed to light up the boat.

She came walking over to me holding her hand out. "Come on and join me Mel."

"No you go ahead I'm having fun just watching you." I smiled at her.

"Oh come on." She still had her arm stretched out and she was wiggling her fingers at me. I just smiled and she grinned. "Okay if you're sure, but you don't know what you're missing."

She put her hand back in the bag of popcorn and turned around smiling the whole time. She was wrong though I knew exactly what I was missing, and that was Sarah.

When we stepped off the boat Ivy jumped behind me and grabbed a hold of my shoulders. "Mel that was the best time I think I ever had."

"Oh I doubt that." I laughed at her.

"Well since I've been here anyway." She started skipping next to me.

"I'm glad, so are you ready to head home?" I looked over at her and she started to walk.

"Yeah everyone is probably wondering where I am by now, tonight is our get together night."

I looked at her as we started for the car. "A get together night, what's that?" We reached the car and climbed in.

"All of us set a day and time to go out to dinner together. We figured we would get together and go out at least one day while we were here. Seeing as we all have different interests."

"That's a good idea." I looked at her as I drove.

"Do you want to join us?"

I looked back at her. "No that's okay, beside you guys should all be together at least one day while you're here."

She turned to look straight ahead. "Yeah I guess."

We were almost back home, and when I glanced at her sitting next to me in the car, I knew I had to do some real soul searching. After all that is why I came down here. The whole time here i tried to decide what to do about Windy, but the honest truth is I haven't really thought about it. Every time I started to, I put it out of my mind.

Pulling into the driveway Ivy asked me again if I wanted to join them but I declined. I went inside and put away everything that I bought, and then tried to call Windy again. Still no answer, so I tried to call Donna and neither her nor Vicky were home, I just left a message that I'd try again later. I poured a big glass of water, and then put my suit on so I could hit the water.

I untied the windsurf and was about halfway out when I saw Ivy and her friends waving. Sitting there I waved back, they must be headed out for dinner together.

I let the sail fall and I laid back on the board. While I was out there I saw a couple dolphins swim by and a few people passed me in a boat, then after a while I pulled my sail up and started back.

Reaching the deck I tied the board up and stretched out on a towel to get some sun. As I lay there I thought about Windy. I wondered what she was doing all the time I couldn't get a hold of her. I also thought about what would happen if we did become involved with each other and it didn't work out, I don't want to lose her friendship. My head began to hurt and I closed my eyes.

I must have fell asleep in the hot sun because when I woke it was already starting to set. I stood up and went inside to fix myself something to eat. While I had some pasta cooking, I went to take a shower. After I ate I went outside to watch the sun set.

I sipped on a martini and relaxed still thinking about Windy. Realizing that if I didn't give it a try between Windy and myself I would probably regret it for the rest of my life. The only thing that held me back was the fact that my going to Windy seemed like such a betrayal to Sarah. After all she was a friend to both of us. Sitting here I tried to examine my feelings. I wondered if this is what I really want. I know I've always been in love with her, but now we've become good friends and I just don't know what's more important to me right now.

After a few more martinis the sun was totally down and it started to get a little cool outside so I went in.

I flipped on the stereo, poured another drink and laid on the couch letting my thoughts wander. I almost fell asleep when I heard a knock at the door; I raised my head to see it was Ivy.

Climbing off the couch I answered the door. "What are you doing here, I thought you would still be out."

She leaned against the doorway crossing her arms and legs, and tilting her head to the side. "Well I got kind of tired being the fifth wheel so I made it an early night."

I stepped aside. "Come on in."

She walked through the doorway. "Alright but just for a minute."

I walked past her into the kitchen. "I was just having a martini. Would you like one?"

She stood in the living room and turned to face me. "Alright sure." She walked closer to me and sat down at the breakfast bar while I poured her drink. "Mel I don't want you to be mad at me but I really stopped by to see if you were okay?"

I looked up. "Okay? What do you mean?"

She looked at me. "You could say it's non of my business, but it looked like all afternoon something was bothering you."

"Oh that. I just had a good day that brought back a lot of good memories." I handed her, her drink and walked over to the couch trying to avoid any more questions. "So did you have fun on your little dinner excursion?"

"Yeah it was okay." She sat down on the chair across from me. "I must say Mel you do make one hell of a martini."

We sat there talking about nothing really for a while until Ivy decided it was time for her to leave. I walked her to the door. "Hey what do you have planned for tomorrow?"

"Nothing. Why?"

"Why don't you just be ready for a day of fun."

"Okay, what time?"

"Early."

She laughed. "Goodnight Mel."

"Goodnight." She started to walk down the stairs. "Oh and Ivy." She turned around with one hand on the railing. "Thanks for the concern." She smiled and kept walking. I watched to make sure that she got home okay then I locked up and went to bed.

CHAPTER 13

✿

*A*fter being up for a while I had everything packed for my day with Ivy. I glanced out the back door and there was no sign of movement over there, so I went back inside and put my bathing suit on. I poured another cup of coffee then went to check on Ivy again, this time I saw her standing on the deck sipping from a mug. I waved her over and yelled to her to wear her bathing suit.

She came right over. "So what's this day of fun that you have planned?"

"Well first of all." I opened my bag. "Bottled water and beach toys."

She looked up at me laughing. "What on earth do you have planned?"

"Well I thought we would hit the beach early, I heard on the news that the waves were going to be amazing today." I closed my bag and set it down.

"Really, that sounds fun." She put her hands on her hips and crossed her legs as she stood in front of me.

"You don't sound too enthusiastic." I laughed at her.

"Well I don't think that I ever really played with beach toys in the ocean."

"Get outta here. Where on earth did you grow up?"

She looked down at her feet then back up at me laughing. "Idaho."

"Well I guess that explains it." I leaned up against the porch railing.

"But I live in Boston now and I still don't play in the waves." She unfolded her arms and let them fall to her side.

I picked up the bags and started walking inside. "Well today is going to be a first for you."

We filled our arms with stuff and headed to the beach. It was about a five-minute walk and we laughed the whole way. Ivy must have dropped her bags a million times. We finally got there and found the perfect spot, then laid down a big blanket. "Okay before you get too comfortable let's hit the waves." I grabbed for a couple of rafts. "Now don't go too far out on your first time. So stay close okay."

"Don't worry I'll be holding on to your suit." She slipped out of her shorts but left her beach shoes on.

I laughed, and we ran into the water. I caught the first wave and rode it all the way into the beach on my raft while Ivy watched. After she tried it a couple of times she was relentless. I couldn't get her out of the water.

I finally was beat and went back to our blanket. Sitting there I watched her and just laughed as she ran in and out of the water trying to get the perfect wave that would bring her all the way in to the beach. As I watched her playing in the water I realized I was becoming more and more attracted to her. I wasn't even looking on the outside, although she is amazingly beautiful. I was more attracted to her soul. She is unbelievably intelligent, extremely funny and I just find myself so comfortable with her. She really is amazing, her long beautiful curly hair, her long slim tan body and those amazing green eyes of hers. As I watched her jumping in and out of the water I couldn't believe how much she reminded me of Sarah. I know that I don't know her all that well and we never really talked about the personal aspects of our lives but I feel so close to her. I can feel her gentleness, her caring, and sensitivity. In short I know her for who she is now, not who she was, not even a month ago. It almost makes me wonder why I decided to come here; I haven't been here in so long, was it fate? What I do believe in is Sarah, and I only wonder if she had anything to do with this. We always had such a good time here and after she got sick I told myself that I would never come back here again. I didn't want all the memories or any of the pain that I knew would come with them. But the memories have been good and meeting Ivy has been a definite bonus.

As I watched her I saw her lips moving and knew that she was talking to me but I was stuck on her beauty. I was so consumed that I didn't even hear her. She came closer as I watched her walk towards me.

"Mel, did you hear me?" She tossed her raft down and reached for a towel.

"No, I'm sorry, what did you say?" I watched as she leaned over and dried her hair with the towel.

"I asked if you were all tired out?" She started to fold her towel in half.

"Yeah, I'm beat." I handed her a bottle of water, then she laid down next to me on the blanket.

"You were absolutely right this was great fun."

"So you're having fun?" I watched as she rubbed suntan lotion up and down her legs.

"Yeah I am, I never thought that playing in the waves could be so much fun."

I couldn't take my eyes off of her as she rubbed lotion all over her body. Finally I laid my head down. We laid around sunning until we finished all the water that I brought. I rolled over and looked at Ivy. "So are you going back into the water?"

She held her hand up to her eyes to shield them from the sun as she looked at me, "No, I think that I'm through."

"Me too. Why don't we go back and rinse off, then I'll make us something to eat." I rolled over on my stomach.

"Sounds good."

We gathered everything up and packed all the bags, then started our walk. I laughed at Ivy the whole way back as I followed behind her. She was picking seaweed from everywhere. It was in her hair as well as her suit. She turned around and threw a piece at me. "You failed to tell me this part of playing in the waves."

"Well there usually always is a drawback to anything. Don't worry you can jump in the shower when we get back."

We finally reached the house and as Ivy showered I fixed us a couple of vegetable sandwiches and a pitcher of iced tea. I sat waiting for her on the back deck.

"Boy I can't believe how much better I feel." She laid her towel down on the chair and sat down next to me.

I laughed. "Here have something to eat and when we're through do you want to take the windsurf out?"

"Alright just let me catch my breath here." She took a big drink of her iced tea.

We ate quietly then I went inside to clean up and grab the sunscreen. After slopping some on myself I handed it to Ivy. "So are you ready yet or are you whimping out on me?"

"Never, let's go." She stood up.

We must have been out there at least two hours when I turned to Ivy. "What do you say we head in, grab a couple of beers and just lay around the rest of the day? That is if you don't have any plans." I jumped off the board and started pulling it back in towards shore.

"No I don't have any plans and that sounds great." She walked beside me.

We tied the board off then climbed the stairs. Ivy flopped down on a lounge chair while I went inside to get some towels and beers. Then I laid down next to her. Ivy looked up at me as I handed her a beer. "This was probably the most exhausting day that I've had in a long time. But it was a good kind of exhaustion."

I smiled and lay back in the chair. After laying in silence for a while Ivy got up and I lifted my head up to look at her. "Where are you going?"

"Don't worry I'll be right back." She ran over to her beach house and I just laid my head back down. Looking up again I saw her running back with a big radio in her hands. She plugged it in and set it on the upper deck. I rested on my elbows watching her. "If you would have asked me I had a radio inside."

"I didn't want you to have to get up again." She was bent down next to the radio.

"You're silly." I laid my head back down and closed my eyes as she fiddled with the stations. She finally settled on a station then decided she didn't like it. I lifted my head. "Are you a little hungry?"

She turned around with her hand still on the radio. "Actually I am, I think it's all the water activity today."

"Okay I'll go make something real quick." I jumped off my chair and went inside. Looking around I decided on some cheese, fruit and vegetables. As I was chopping things up in the kitchen I watched Ivy outside. The more that I was with this woman the more confusing my life became.

She came running inside. "Mel you have to hear this." She turned on the stereo inside and played with the dial. When she turned it up I quickly raised my head.

She stood in the middle of the living room looking at me. "What's wrong, don't you like 70's music?"

"Yeah, I do." What I didn't tell her was that all Sarah ever listened to was 70's music. A sudden rush of sadness came over me, then I stopped what I was doing and just watched her, singing and dancing around. It was like she belonged here. Like we have been together for a lifetime. After a while I no longer felt sad I felt good, real good.

I made a pitcher of long island ice tea then carried everything outside. We laid the rest of the afternoon eating and soaking up the sun.

After a while I sat up. "I think I've had just about all the sun that I can take for the day."

She laughed. "Yeah I think I'm going to go and take a shower so that I can scrub off all of this sunscreen." She rested on her elbows.

"Now that sounds like a good idea." We gathered everything up from outside. Then I turned to Ivy. "Do you have any dinner plans for tonight?"

She looked up at me. "No, what did you have in mind?"

"Why don't you come back in a little bit and I'll make dinner then maybe we could watch a movie or something." I just wanted her to come back, I didn't care if we just sat and didn't say a word to each other, as long as she was here.

"Sure that sounds good as long as I can help with dinner."

"Deal." I smiled at her.

She left to go and take a shower and I went inside to clean up. I looked around to see what I had to make for dinner and thought I better go to the store. I threw on a pair of shorts and ran out the door.

On the way to the store all I thought of was Ivy and how good she made me feel. Then my mind wandered to what on earth was I going to cook for dinner. Racing through the store I decided that fresh grilled vegetables over pasta would be a good choice.

I couldn't drive home fast enough because I knew Ivy would be over soon. I threw everything in the fridge and went to take a shower. When I was through I came out in my bathrobe with a towel on my head to turn on the stereo, then I saw Ivy standing on the back deck. She stood there looking out at the ocean, the breeze gently blowing her hair as she ran her fingers through it. She was leaning up against the railing, her tan legs crossed and her bare toes sticking through the railing. The same breeze that was gently blowing her hair blew her thin sundress so it tightly wrapped around her thighs. I froze as I stood there and watched her. I could stand there watching her like this for hours. She then turned and saw me.

She came walking inside. "Hi, why didn't you tell me you were out of the shower?"

"I was just watching you and you look amazing." I looked away quickly when I realized what I said. "I'm sorry I shouldn't have said that." I turned around nervously.

She came closer and I started to dry my hair with the towel.

"Why?"

She was standing directly in front of me and I was staring into her eyes. I wanted to touch her face gently with my fingers and feel the warmth and softness of her skin, but I didn't, instead I continued to dry my hair. "Ivy I think that things are starting to get confusing. At least for me they are." I folded my towel and hung it over one of the kitchen chairs. Then rested my hands on the chair looking straight ahead, with Ivy standing behind me.

"I know, they are for me too."

I turned around. "Why don't you let me finish getting dressed and I'll meet you outside."

She looked down then up at me. "Alright."

I threw on a pair of jean overall shorts with a bathing suit top on underneath, then I combed out my hair. Going into the kitchen I poured us both a glass of wine, then went outside. Standing next to Ivy I handed her a glass, which she took gently from my hand as she looked at me.

"Thanks."

"You're welcome." I turned to look out at the water. "It's a beautiful sunset."

"Yes it is. Mel I think that we need to talk."

I looked at her then back out to the ocean. "I know."

She came closer to me and put her hand on mine as it rested on the railing. I looked at her hand then smiled. "Could this wait until after dinner."

She smiled shaking her head yes. We stood there quietly enjoying the sunset until our glasses were empty. I turned to her. "Why don't we go inside and I'll start dinner?"

"Now you said that I could help right?"

I laughed. "Yeah I did. Come on." I reached down and took her hand in mine. Then we walked inside.

She turned and stood in front of me. "Remember we talk after dinner right?"

"Right." Standing with her like this, feeling her soft hand in mine, smelling her sweet scent, all I wanted to do was take her in my arms and never let go. "Come on now I'm going to put you to work."

"Okay, what do you want me to do first?"

"Come on." I pulled her into the kitchen, and then took out all the vegetables I bought. "You can begin by chopping these up, but not too small because I'm going to put them on the grill."

"Okay, I can do that. As long as you pour me another glass of wine." She looked at me as she started taking the vegetables out of their bags.

"Boy you drive a hard bargain." I poured while Ivy started to cut up vegetables.

I went outside to start the grill and when I came back upstairs I stopped before I went in to watch Ivy in the kitchen. She didn't see me so I stepped through the door slowly and quietly as I watched her singing in the kitchen while she was chopping. She looked like she just fit.

Walking into the kitchen I couldn't help but smile. I felt so good, so comfortable with her. As I watched Ivy I thought of Sarah because she was the only other person in the world that made me feel this way.

She looked at me. "You okay?"

"Perfect." I helped her until the grill was hot enough to cook on. After everything was done I grabbed what I needed and went back outside.

Ivy stood at the top of the stairs and yelled down asking me if I needed any help. I told her no and that she should just relax for a while.

When I looked up again I saw that she was sitting on the railing of the lower deck. She was sipping on her wine with her feet dangling in the water. Watching her I wondered if she was my destiny, if she was my soul mate. She seems to be a little bit of everyone that I ever loved rolled into one, but she mostly reminds me of Sarah. If Windy weren't sitting back home waiting for me I probably wouldn't be so confused, if I only knew what I wanted.

Just a week or so ago I was sure that Windy was the one I wanted to spend the rest of my life with, but how could I be sure that Ivy's not really the one for me. Maybe I was meant to come here and find her. After all I don't know why I came here, I vowed that I would never come back because it was such a special place for Sarah and myself. Yet I came without a second thought. I'm beginning to believe that something steered me in this direction. Maybe it was to find my soul mate; my other half.

Ivy took a sip from her wine glass then rubbed her hand through her hair as she leaned back enjoying the sun on her face. I don't know if I could let her go, if I do my life might never be what it was meant to be. Why should I settle when I could be staring at my future right now? As I stood there staring at her she started frantically waving her arms. So I waved back, then she jumped off the railing and came running towards me. It was then that I smelled the smoke. I turned around and the vegetables were burnt to a crisp.

I quickly got them off the grill when Ivy came turning the corner. "Mel are you okay. What happened?"

"I guess I wasn't paying attention." We both looked at the vegetables on the plate and started laughing.

I looked at Ivy. "How does pizza sound?" I set the plate down and took off my oven mitt.

"Actually I was really in the mood for pizza anyway." She picked up a green pepper by the corner and dropped it back on the plate.

"Come on I'll crack open another bottle of wine and do the ordering." I dumped the vegetables in the garbage and set the plate down.

"Do you think that you can handle it or should I help?"

She started walking towards the stairs and I ran up to her grabbing her by the waist pushing her up the stairs from behind. "You can help alright."

She started laughing as she ran upstairs. I ordered the pizza then poured us both another glass of wine. "Here you go. Why don't we enjoy the night air until the pizza gets here."

We walked outside when I noticed her sister on her way over, she must have seen the smoke. The three of us sat talking on the back deck for a while until the pizza came. Ivy's sister then left to go boating.

We went inside and while I was getting the dishes and the wine I told Ivy to pick a movie to watch while we ate.

When I came into the living room carrying a bottle of wine I almost fell over when the movie came on. "Ivy, what made you choose that?" I set the wine and dishes on the table.

She looked up at me. "Why, don't you like the Wizard of Oz?"

I sat down. "It's just that it's my favorite movie. I don't know too many people who would have picked that."

She reached for the wine, and then started to pour. "Well it happens to be my favorite also."

"Now you know that you can't watch this unless you sing." I handed her a napkin.

"Oh don't worry, I sing."

We laughed, and then I dished out the pizza.

We laid in the living room eating, drinking and more than anything else we sang every song in the movie. Between the two of us there was always someone reciting or singing parts of the movie.

After we finished the pizza, Ivy laid on the couch while I sat in front of her on the floor.

Towards the end of the movie she reached down and stretched her arm around my neck. I gently rubbed her arm. When the movie was over I turned to look at her. "I want you to know that I have had a great time today."

She smiled as she lay there. "So have I."

We stared into each other's eyes then I reached up and touched her cheek with my fingers.

"Mel I don't think…"

I put my fingers over her lips. "Shh." My hand then slipped around her neck and I pulled myself to her and kissed her on the mouth. Gently at first, then I looked in those eyes and played with her hair. Moving to my knees I slipped one hand behind her back while my other arm reached around her neck. We kissed passionately, and I felt her hand on my bare back. As we kissed with such passion I realized my fate, it was with her. I just knew at that moment we were meant to be together. I thought that it was passion with Windy, but nothing compared to this. This reminds me of the passion and intensity that I had with Sarah. This is exactly where I was destined to be, right here, in her arms. I tangled my hand in her hair and pulled myself up to lay next to her on the couch.

She looked at me. "Mel I don't think that I've ever felt so strongly for one person before. I haven't known you that long but I can feel you in my blood."

I kissed her cheek then looked at her. "Ivy, when I look into my future I want you to be there by my side, just like you are now. I really believe that you are my destiny and that something drew me here so I could realize that. It's fate Ivy I really believe that. There's a lot I have to tell you though. Things aren't going to be so easy. Does that scare you?"

"No, I don't care as long as I'm with you. I can handle what ever you have to tell me, because I know that you love me. You might not know it yet, but I do. I can see it in your eyes when you look at me. When our eyes met for the first time I knew at that moment we were meant to be together. I felt the passion between us then and when we kissed, it just proved me right. I feel it every time I'm with you, and passion like that doesn't go away. Even ten years from now it will still be there because what we have doesn't die or even fade away, and I plan on being right here with you ten years from now."

I smiled at her, and hugged her tightly because I knew that every-thing she said was the absolute truth. I never wanted to move from her side let alone go back home. She ran her fingers through my hair and we laid quietly until we both fell asleep.

CHAPTER 14

I opened my eyes then laid watching Ivy sleep. We were still tangled in each other's arms. My arm under her was totally numb but I didn't care, I could lay like this with her forever. Watching her sleep I counted her breaths, they were so steady I was almost put in a trance.

As I lay watching her I started to let my mind wander, and all I could think of was what on earth I was going to tell her. I know I have to tell her all of the truth starting at the beginning with Sarah, but I was afraid. I was afraid because I was still so confused, I didn't want to lose her. Staring into her face as she slept I saw my future. I knew with every part of my being that with her is where I'm supposed to be. But I felt so guilty about Windy. I was afraid my guilt would keep me tied to Windy, making me lose her, lose this. Just then she slowly started to open her eyes. With my hand I brushed the hair from her face. "Good morning."

She looked up at me smiling. "Is it morning already?"

"It's almost 9:00."

"Really, how long have you been up?" She started to sit up.

"Only a little while, I was laying here watching you sleep." I moved, sitting up rubbing and squeezing my arm.

She rubbed her face and then ran her hand through her hair. "God I must look awful."

I laughed as I stood up shaking my arm trying to get the feeling back into it. "Hardly, want some coffee?"

"You read my mind."

I kept squeezing my arm while I started the coffee, and Ivy went into the bathroom.

When it was my turn in the bathroom I brushed my teeth then stood looking in the mirror with my hands resting on the cold porcelain. I was so confused I couldn't even think straight. I knew that Ivy made me happier than I ever thought I could be again, but I also knew that Windy was home waiting for me. I didn't know if I could hurt her like this.

Going back into the kitchen I knew I had to have a talk with her, but I just didn't know when. No time ever seems like the right time. I would much rather just be with her, and talk to and about her, then to rehash my past, not to mention bringing up Windy. Right now I didn't want to think about Windy, I just wanted to have a good time with Ivy.

"Mel that coffee smells great."

I watched as she folded blankets and put them away. "Thanks, I cut up some fresh fruit and I'm going to toast some bagels. How does that sound?"

"That sounds wonderful."

She came walking around the counter and put her arms around me, resting her chin on my shoulder as I cut the bagels in half. "Mel I have to tell you again, last night was great."

"Yeah, it was." I put my knife down and placed my hands on hers. She spoke so softly against my ear it was driving me crazy.

"What I remember most of all was the kiss that we had. First kisses, they're always the most passionate. You always remember the first."

I put the bagels in the oven then turned around to face her sliding my arms around her waist. "What do you think about seconds?"

"I don't know I haven't remembered any so far." She smiled.

I stared into her eyes and pulled her to me as I leaned against the counter. She was wrong when I was kissing her the passion is the same; as a matter of fact I think it was stronger.

With her arms around my neck she whispered in my ear. "I will definitely remember that second kiss. As a matter of fact I think that it was actually better than the first." She looked at me and I smiled at her, then I kissed her again.

"Ivy I could stand here and kiss you all day. But if I don't check my bagels in the oven we're going to be standing in a kitchen full of smoke."

She laughed. "Yeah, I'm starting to get flashbacks of yesterday's dinner."

I started tickling her sides. "You are just so funny. Now get your coffee and I'll meet you outside."

She picked up her coffee cup. "Alright, alright but don't be long."

"I'm right behind you." I opened the oven taking out the bagels then gathered everything else that we needed and went outside.

We sat quietly drinking our coffee and eating our breakfast while we enjoyed the beautiful morning. Sitting there I had no thoughts of Windy or anything back home running through my head, all I did think of was how good and totally content I felt.

Ivy turned to look at me and touched my arm lightly. "I can't even describe to you how good I feel right now."

I put my hand on top of hers. "There's no need." I laid my head back. "This is just too perfect being here with you like this."

"I know, this is the happiest I've ever been."

"I'm glad. Hey, why don't I take you to lunch and we go shopping all day."

She looked at me. "That sounds great, I could use a day out of the sun."

We sat finishing our breakfast talking and laughing until it was almost noon. I stood gathering some plates as I did. "Well you better go and get dressed before lunch passes us by and it turns into dinner."

"Alright, but let me help you clean up first."

We carried everything into the house and I straightened while Ivy ran to get ready. After I cleaned, I picked up the phone and thought about calling Windy, then realized that I didn't know what I would even say to her, so I set the phone back down and went into the bathroom.

After taking my time getting ready I threw on a pair of cut off jeans and a mid drift shirt, then went out the front door. When I looked down at my car I saw Ivy leaning up against it. Standing there I felt a smile come over my face, just seeing her made me feel good. She looked great in a little sundress with her long hair blowing in the warm summer breeze.

"Ivy you look so good."

"Thanks, so do you."

While I drove I kept going over in my head what and how I was going to tell her about Windy. I knew it wasn't right the way I kept delaying this, but I didn't want to ruin the good time we were having. I guess I'm just being selfish. One way or another I'll tell her today.

I looked at her and smiled, then she reached over and put her hand on my leg. I felt a shiver go down my spine and my heart started pounding so hard I thought it was going to jump out of my chest. The only thing I was thinking of at that moment was how badly I wanted to take her in my arms and kiss her.

Looking around I spotted a little dirt road up ahead and turned the jeep in driving about halfway down, then stopped.

"Mel where are we?"

Without saying a word I leaned towards her, taking her in my arms and kissed her. My hand slid down her side feeling her smooth leg, then back up to her waist. I moved her hair and began kissing her neck. She let her head fall back moaning softly, when she did, it drove me crazy. I began searching for her mouth again while my free hand touched and felt every part of her body. Gently I lowered the strap of her dress off her shoulder and softly kissed her bare skin. She played with the back of my hair guiding my mouth exactly where she wanted. She laid back holding my head with both of her hands, as my tongue licked and bit at her breast. Her one foot was on the dashboard and I laid almost on top of her, feeling her heart pounding in her chest and her body shivering under me.

It was then that I heard people talking. I sat up while Ivy fixed her dress. We both started laughing hysterically then managed to get back on the main road.

Ivy turned to me. "Well that was fun, I can't remember the last time I almost got busted making out in a car."

I grabbed her hand. "But like you said, it was fun."

We drove laughing all the way. Then finally pulled into a little restaurant. Sitting at our table, we were still laughing. We ordered a couple of beers and a couple of salads, and then sat talking until the waitress came with our beers. I looked up. "Thanks." She walked away and I turned to Ivy. "So are you ready to shop?"

"I'm always ready to shop, but I would much rather go back home and continue where we left off back there on the dirt road."

I smiled. "Before anything else happens between us, we are going to have to have that talk I've been trying to have with you for the past couple of days."

"You know Mel, I don't even care anymore. I know how I feel about you, and I'm pretty sure that you feel the same way about me, so what else matters?"

The waitress came back with our salads. I looked up at Ivy. "Ivy the truth is that I think I'm beginning to fall hard here, but you do need to know everything, and maybe more importantly, I feel that I need to tell you."

She poked her salad with her fork then looked up at me. "Alright, well when ever you feel like you want to talk, I'm ready to listen."

I nodded. "So how's your lunch?"

"Great, as usual."

We finished our lunch then hit every store in sight and even those out of sight. We had so many bags that we had to make several trips to the car. I turned to Ivy. "So have you had enough or shall I try to find some more stores?"

"No I think that I've had enough for now."

I laughed. "Well then how about a drink?"

"I think I need one about now."

There was a small bar down the street from where we were staying that was always pretty quiet and I thought would be perfect. We climbed into the car and started back. When we passed that dirt road I looked over at Ivy and she was laughing.

When we arrived I wasn't too surprised to find we were the only car in the parking lot. Besides the bartender we were the only ones in the bar. I ordered a couple of beers and we went to sit outside, relaxing a little bit from our shopping excursion.

We sat there looking out at the ocean, watching the dolphins swim around, that's one thing I never get tired of. It started getting a little dark and it looked like rain, so we grabbed our drinks and went inside. I ordered another round and asked the bartender for the darts.

I sat the drinks and the darts on the table. "Do you like to play?"

"I do and I'm really not bad."

"Good, because I'm horrible." I laughed.

After the first couple of throws I knew this was going to be a long game. Standing there I stared at Ivy, I watched her laugh and the way she played with her hair. It was like I wanted to learn everything that there was to learn about her. I knew I was falling hard for this woman, and I just couldn't help it. After our third beer I suggested we head back. I didn't want to drink any more and drive, so we had to give up on our dart game. "I thought you said you were pretty good at this."

She laughed. "I thought I was. I guess I was wrong."

"Come on let's get out of here."

Feeling sorry for the bartender sitting all by himself I left a generous tip and we left. I turned to Ivy. "So do you have any dinner plans?"

"No, but why don't you let me cook for you. I promise I won't burn anything." She laughed and ran ahead of me to the car.

I climbed in. "You know, you are just hilarious. But I will take you up on the offer."

"Good."

It was a short drive back and when I pulled in the drive Ivy started gathering up all of her things, then looked at me. "I'll be back with everything I need for dinner in a couple of hours."

"Really, that long, why don't you see if I have anything you need."

"No, it won't be long." She started walking away, then turned back to look at me. "I'll be back."

I watched her leave then grabbed all my packages and went upstairs. I tossed everything aside, then changed clothes. It started to clear up outside so I decided to take the windsurf out for a while to make the time go by.

Just when I was about to walk out the door the phone rang. I knew no one but my sister had the number here, so it had to be her.

She called worried because no one had heard from me in a couple of days. I decided not to tell her about Ivy because she would just give me a lecture. She would think I was wrong treating Windy like this, and maybe I am. We talked for only a couple of minutes, she just wanted to make sure everything was okay, and wanted to see if I had any idea when I was coming home. I told her I didn't know I still had some things to work out. I promised her I'd call before I left. When I hung up I got hit hard with a case of the guilt's. I knew I was wrong, but it just didn't feel all that wrong when I was with Ivy.

Dragging the board out on the water, I climbed on top and sat there letting my mind wander. Trying to think of what I was going to do. I knew I was in another one of those situations where someone was going to get hurt. Remembering last time that it was me and how I felt, I knew I didn't want anyone to go through what I did. I also knew it was inevitable, this was a no win situation, someone was going to get hurt. What I really wanted was to just think of myself and do what makes me happy, but I'm just not sure if I could do that.

Lying there with the sun beating down and the waves gently rocking the board, I started to fall in a trance. When I looked around I realized that I had drifted pretty far out. I watched a couple of boats go by, and then I pulled up my sail and headed back.

Reaching the deck I knew I had no more of an idea now as to what I was going to do, then when I first went out. Going inside I grabbed a beer and went to go lay out in the sun.

I was only out a short time when I heard Ivy's voice. "Haven't' you had enough of the sun yet?"

"Never." I jumped up and ran over to her. "Do you need some help?"

"Yeah, you can carry this in for me." She handed me a bag. I started to peek inside and she grabbed it back from me.

"I didn't say look inside."

On my way in I turned to her. "So are you going to tell me what's inside all of these bags?"

"Yes I will. Just hold on a minute." I sat on the barstool opposite her and she looked at me while she started to take things out of the bags. "I hope you like Mexican."

"Love it."

"Good, I bought everything to make vegetable fajitas. How does that sound?" She looked up at me as she continued to pull things out of a bag.

"Sounds great. I didn't know that you were such a cook."

"Well when you're alone as long as I've been, you have no choice but to learn."

I got up and walked around the counter then slipped my arms around her. "I can't imagine someone like you ever being alone."

She turned around putting her arms around me. "Well it's true."

"Somehow I don't believe you, look in a mirror, you're absolutely gorgeous, intelligent, caring, and sensitive and boy can you make me laugh. It just doesn't seem possible."

"Maybe I was just waiting for the right person." She kissed me on the cheek.

"So what can I help you with?"

She turned around reaching into the bags and pulled out a bunch of bottles. "Your job is to make the pitchers of margaritas."

"I could do that, but why don't you let me take a shower first."

"Okay, but you better hurry because cooking always makes me extremely thirsty." She started pushing me towards the bathroom.

"Alright I'll be fast." I ran into the bathroom and jumped in the shower. While the water was hitting my face all I could think of was how happy I felt. When ever she's around I just feel good. Is it so wrong for me to be happy instead of trying to make everyone else happy?

I guess that's the question I have to answer.

Climbing out of the shower I wrapped a towel around myself and went to change. After changing and combing out my hair I went back in the kitchen.

"I thought you were going to be fast. I'm dying of thirst out here" She was chopping vegetables.

I laughed. "Oh you are not."

"Well I could be." She stopped chopping and looked up at me.

I went behind her and grabbed her around the waist. With one hand I brushed her hair aside and kissed her on the neck.

"Now if you keep that up I'm going to end up cutting my fingers off."

"So stop cutting."

She put the knife down and turned around, putting her arms around my neck. I kissed her sweet lips softly, wrapping my hands in her hair. Loving the feel of it, how silky and soft it was. With both of my hands in her hair I kissed her, pulling her, as close to me as possible, I smelled her hair letting the curls fall and tickle my face. My hands had a mind of their own roaming down her back, feeling all of her. I lifted up the little dress that she had on and felt the silky panties she was wearing. I began kissing her neck as I pushed her up against the kitchen counter. Both of my hands traveled up the side of her body. I wanted to feel every inch of her. Her skin was so soft and she smelled so good, with my hand I reached inside of her panties searching and feeling every part of her. She was moaning as I was kissing and biting her lip softly then I whispered. "Ivy I don't think that I ever wanted someone as much as I want you right now."

My hands were still searching and feeling her body, she responded. "I know, me too."

We then fell to the floor. I slipped her dress over her head and we rolled around on the kitchen floor making the most intense love that I have ever experienced in my whole life.

From the kitchen floor we moved into the bedroom and continued until we were both physically exhausted. Lying there holding each other I knew that I had just experienced perfection. I knew then, that this woman had to be in my life forever. There was no longer any question in my mind.

"That was fantastic." She lowered her eyes, then looked back up at me. "Mel, this isn't just a summer fling is it?"

I lifted her head to look in my eyes. "No, it isn't. Hey are you trying to get out of making me dinner. Is that what this is all about?"

She giggled. "No. Do you have anything I can throw on since my dress is rolled up in a ball on your kitchen floor."

"Sure." I got out of bed and grabbed a couple of t-shirts and a couple pairs of shorts. I threw Ivy a set then got dressed myself.

I hugged her from behind as we both walked into the kitchen. She turned around and kissed me. "Mel I hope I don't scare you off but I think that I'm falling in love with you."

I looked away then back at her. "I know, I feel the same way."

She squeezed me tight then pulled away. "You know what's more important than dinner right now?"

I looked at her and at the same time we said. "Margaritas."

I gathered everything I needed then started searching for the blender. I looked at Ivy and she was cutting away at the vegetables on the cutting board.

I mixed then poured us both a drink and handed one to Ivy. "Here you go." I put my hand on her arm before she took a drink. "Ivy I think everything that has happened to me in my life was for a reason and that reason was to lead me right here, to meet and to be with you. I can honestly say that I haven't been this completely happy in a long time."

She kissed me lightly on the mouth. "I don't think that I have ever been this happy."

I slowly licked my lips. "Do you mind if I take a walk down to the dock? I want to make sure the windsurf is tied up tight in case it storms tonight."

"Sure, go right ahead. I'll come and get you when dinner's ready."

I brushed her hair aside and kissed her on the cheek, then picked my drink up and walked outside. As I walked down the stairs I felt like I lied to her. What I really needed to do was think about what in the hell I was going to do now.

I reached the windsurf and decided just to pull it in and put it away in the garage. After dragging it to the garage I went upstairs and poured another drink for myself then asked Ivy if she wanted another. After I poured Ivy's I went back into the garage. I secured the board then went up to sit on the back deck.

Sitting there Windy kept running through my mind. I had no idea how I was going to tell her about this, I feel as if I cheated on her. I just kept thinking that she was sitting by the phone waiting for me to call, or by the door waiting for me to pull in the driveway. But that's thinking a bit much of myself, I'm sure she is going out and who knows maybe she too met someone. God, I just can't get over the guilt.

Ivy came walking outside with the pitcher in her hand. "Dinner's almost ready, so you want another drink?"

I held my glass up. "Sure." She filled my glass then went back inside reminding me that dinner will be ready soon. I not only felt guilty about Windy, I felt like I was ignoring Ivy. I just needed to clear things up in my head, I felt so confused and I didn't know who to talk to about this

Sitting there watching the sun slowly set I just kept going over this situation in my head, over and over again. When Ivy came out to get me for dinner, I had no more answers now then when I first came out here.

Going inside I saw that Ivy set a beautiful table with flowers and linen napkins, the whole nine yards. Standing looking at the table I turned to her. "Ivy this table looks great, but you really didn't have to go through all of this trouble."

She slipped her arm around my waist. "But it's no trouble I really enjoy doing things like this. Especially when it's for someone that I care about."

I kissed her on the cheek. "Thanks."

I made another pitcher of margaritas and poured us both a glass full then sat down to dinner. "Ivy this really looks great."

"Thanks, but let's wait until after you taste it."

After taking a bite of everything I looked up at her. "This is fantastic. You're really a good cook."

"Thanks, but like I said before when you're alone you learn to take care of yourself, and for me that was learning how to cook."

I picked up my glass. "Can I ask you a question?"

She looked up at me. "Sure anything just ask."

I put my glass down. "Well I was wondering, you keep saying that you've been alone for a long time, when was your last serious relationship?"

She picked up her drink. "I was actually going to talk to you later on tonight, but now is just as good."

"If you don't want to, or you feel uncomfortable it can wait."

"No it's fine. It's really nothing, you see I was in love with and lived with a woman for eight years then she left me."

I picked up my drink and finished what was in my glass, and then I got up and poured some more. I topped off Ivy's glass and put the pitcher back on the counter. "I don't mean to get personal but why on earth would she leave you, you're probably the most perfect person I ever met." I sat back down.

She laughed and took a sip of her drink. "I hardly think I'm perfect in any way."

"But you are. I mean look at you. Quite simply you're perfect."

She laughed. "Well anyway she left me after eight years for a man."

"Really." I looked up at her. "I'm sorry, if that's any comfort and I know that it's not."

"Well it was a long time ago."

"O'yeah, how long?"

"Two years."

"Two years and you've been alone since?"

"Well I've dated but nothing ever came of any of the women I was set up with. So yeah, I guess I've been alone since then."

"You never connected with anyone?"

"Not really. Maybe I was being too picky or maybe I just wasn't ready for a relationship yet. Whatever it was I'm glad that I did wait because it was well worth it."

She reached over and grabbed for my hand. I smiled at her. "I'm glad too."

"So tell me Mel what's your story? Why did you come here? I know when I first met you; you said you were here to make a life decision. So spill girl." She laughed.

I reached for my drink and just about finished it. Getting up I turned to Ivy holding up the pitcher. "Shall I make more?"

"Why, do you think that I'll need it?" She was laughing.

"The truth, yes you will. Actually you might need something stronger."

She got up and started to clear the table. "Come on Mel it can't be all that bad."

"You have no idea."

I finished blending the drinks and grabbed our glasses and the pitcher, turning around I looked at Ivy. "Why don't we go sit outside, the sun is just about to set all the way and it's a gorgeous color."

"Give me a minute to just straighten up here."

I put the glasses and the pitcher of drinks outside, and then came back in. I grabbed Ivy's hand. "Come on I can do that later."

"All I have left to do is load them in the dishwasher and I'm done."

"Alright, here let me do it, you go and get comfortable outside. I'll be there in a minute." I reached for her hand. "Hold on, come here a minute." I kissed her lightly on the mouth. "Thank you, that was a fantastic meal. I really mean that. It's not too often that someone cooks for me, I'm usually the one that's doing the cooking."

"Well it's my pleasure." She kissed me on the cheek. "Don't be too long or you'll miss the sunset."

"Don't worry I'll be right there."

"I'll have the drinks poured and ready."

I lifted my head smiling at her. "Okay."

Watching her walk out the door I knew this was it. I couldn't get out of it this time; I'm going to have to talk to her now. I just hope everything comes out the way that I want it to. I've been trying to get things in order in my head the way I wanted to tell her, but whenever I do that things still come out wrong.

"Mel are you coming, or are you going to stay inside the rest of the night?"

I finished up and walked to the back door. "I'm right here. See I didn't miss a thing the sun's right above the water."

I sat down in the chair next to her, picking up my drink. "It's so beautiful out here isn't it?"

"It is, it's gorgeous."

We sat quietly for a minute, and then I felt Ivy looking at me. "Mel you know that you don't have to talk to me if you don't want to. I just think it might make things easier for you, that's all. I know something has been bothering you lately, and it's gotten worse since we made love. You've been pretty distant tonight."

I didn't look at her, I kept staring straight out at the water. "I know, and I know that I have to talk to you it's just that it's so hard to talk about when I have no idea what I'm going to do."

She was still looking at me. "Maybe if you talk about it things might get easier or even straighten themselves out. Who knows maybe I might even be able to help."

I looked at her. "Well if I'm going to start, I'm going to start at the very beginning."

"Everyone says that's the best place."

"It all started with Sarah she was my life, my world, and she died. She left me. I didn't know what to do, or how to act and that was obvious.

She changed me. She taught me how to love, she taught me how to live.

Through her illness and before she died I fell in love again. This time with I don't know what, a fantasy, security, it could be called many things. I fell in love with Windy. Maybe it was because she was so unattainable." I looked over at Ivy and she was nervously shuffling her feet on the deck. Then I looked out at the ocean, just talking about Sarah and being here where she loved it most made me miss her all over again.

"You must think I'm horrible. While the woman I'm in love with is dying I'm falling for someone else." I poured us both another drink and watched as Ivy stared out to ocean. "But it's not what you think."

"I'm not thinking anything, I'm just listening that's all."

"Windy's my business partner. I confided in her, I relied on her for everything, support, kindness, friendship and understanding. It grew. I couldn't help it, but I never acted on any of my feelings for her. Sarah was my number one priority. She always had been and sometimes I think she always will be. Besides I always kept my feelings to myself because I figured they were totally one sided." I could feel Ivy looking at me, but I just kept talking. "By one sided I mean that I never knew Windy was gay." I lifted my glass and kept talking. "Then long after Sarah had died and I met someone else I found out that Windy was gay and she told me it's me that she's been in love with."

I lifted my glass up to my lips and thought to myself this might have been a bad idea talking to Ivy like this. I glanced at her and she didn't move. She hasn't said a word to me since I sat down to talk to her. I really hope I didn't make a mistake. I watched as she just sat there staring straight ahead. "Ivy are you sure you want to hear this?"

"I'm sorry Mel. I'm just wondering where all of this is leading that's all." She looked at me. "The truth is I'm scared. I'm scared of what I might hear. I'm also scared that you won't want anything to do with me after you leave here."

"The truth is I don't know where this is leading after we leave here." I reached my hand out to her. "But I do know that I want to keep seeing you. I don't want this to end. Do you believe in fate?" She nodded her head yes while she looked at me. "Well I do too. I feel it was fate that brought me here. I really do feel like you are my destiny. I feel like we are meant to be together. But I can't lie, there are things I have to deal with and some of them are pretty complicated."

"I'm sorry." She squeezed my hand and looked in my eyes. "I've been acting like a jealous ass. I've been wanting you to talk to me and from now on I'm going to be supportive of you."

I took a big gulp of my drink. "Well everything boils down to Windy telling me that she's always been in love with me. She waited though until I was already in a relationship to tell me."

Ivy looked over at me. "What did you do?"

"The relationship I was in was fairly new and also a long distance one. She lived in New York. So I went to her, to talk and explore my feelings.

Then I found out." I stopped and took a big gulp of my drink. "She was married." I looked at her and she looked at me with such sympathy and caring in her eyes I couldn't help but smile, then I looked out at the water.

I got up and poured us both another drink. "It's getting kind of cool out here, do you want to go inside?"

"Okay, it is chilly." She rubbed her arms up and down.

We sat on the couch. "Are you hungry? Do you want me to make some kind of snacks or something?"

"No thanks." She sat close to me with her arm propped up on the back of the couch and her legs up at her side as she watched me. "So tell me about Sarah."

I looked at her smiling. "Sarah. She was everything to me. My whole life I could never have imagined a day without her let alone the rest of my life without her. She's still part of my life, and she always will be. Not a day goes by when I don't think about her."

We sat quietly for a couple minutes then Ivy touched my arm lightly "So this is how you ended up here?"

I stared at the drink in my hand. "Yeah, after Lily told me she married for her career, and that her career was more important than a relationship, I went home to tell Windy I had to go away and think things over. Of everything she said to me, the thing I remember the most is that she told me she didn't mind me going away because she knows I'd be coming home to her." I just stared straight ahead. After telling Ivy everything I felt better I guess, only because now she knew the truth, but I also felt guilty all over again.

"Wow, that's some story."

She was looking at me and I turned to her. "That's no story, that's my life." I got up and poured myself another drink.

Ivy came walking over to me and stood behind me. "I'm sorry, I didn't mean anything by that. All I meant was that…Actually I don't know what I meant."

I turned around. "I know."

"So what does all of this mean for us Mel?"

"Ivy." I grabbed for her hand. "I know that I'm falling in love with you. I also know that it really seems like we were meant to be together. We have so much in common. You have all of the best qualities of everyone I ever loved in my life. You remind me mostly of Sarah. I just can't get over the guilt that I feel. I feel like I'm cheating on Windy."

"What exactly do you feel for Windy?" She stared in my eyes.

I looked down, and then up at her. "I went over this and over this in my head and I don't know. I knew at one point I thought that I was in love with her. Now after I met you I think that maybe it's not love but a great friendship I feel for her. But I just don't know." I picked up my drink. "All I can think of is that she's sitting waiting for me to come home. I feel like she's waiting for something that might not happen, and it's all my fault."

"So what are you telling me Mel that you're in love with both of us?"

"Yes. I mean no." I rubbed my head. "I don't love her like I love you. It's totally different." I turned to look at her. "You Ivy could be my life, but I know that Windy will always be in my life. I know you don't understand, but I can't get over the guilt I feel."

"So Mel, where does this leave us?" She stared at the floor.

She walked into the kitchen and set her glass on the table. "I knew this was too good. I had a feeling it was just the romance of this place." She turned around and looked at me. "Mel I'm going to go so you can have some time to yourself and decide what you're going to do."

I walked over to her grabbing her hands in mine. Her eyes were searching the floor then they came up to meet mine. "Well if this is all that we are ever going to have, then it was without a doubt the best weeks of my life." She smiled and kissed my cheek softly; afterward she rubbed her face against mine. Then I watched as she walked out the door.

Standing, staring at the door I knew I should run after her, but I just couldn't move. For some reason Windy's face kept popping into my head. I sat down on the couch with my head in my hands wondering what in the hell I was going to do.

I decided to call Windy. Picking up the phone I dialed her number not knowing what I was going to say, but knowing that I had to talk to her. After the fourth ring I was about to hang up when someone answered. Who ever answered I knew it wasn't Windy. "Hi, is Windy there?"

Whoever did answer said she was out. Telling them I'd call back later I hung up and could have kicked myself for not asking who it was. I know for a fact that Windy lives alone, so I'm wondering if maybe she did get back together with Barb. What ever was going on I still had to decide what I was going to do. I walked into the kitchen and made myself another pitcher of margaritas maybe getting drunk will help me think better.

I grabbed the pitcher and a glass and walked down to the lower deck so that no one would see me out here. Actually the only one that could see me out here would be Ivy and I just didn't feel like talking. I sat there on the deck with my feet dangling in the water as I laid back staring up at the stars in the sky. Looking up at the stars I was just waiting for Sarah to come down and tell me what to do. Laying with my drink in my hand it was hard to believe that life could be this complicated. I just laid there waiting for some kind of inspirational idea to come to me, but it didn't. I kept going over everything in my head, Windy, Ivy back and forth over and over until I made myself dizzy.

Then rolling over to pour another drink I caught a glimpse of a crab in the sand beneath me. Staring at the crab brought tears to my eyes. It was the same exact crab that used to crack Sarah up. She would literally lay for hours watching them through the wooden slats of the deck.

Whenever I thought of Sarah I also thought of Ivy. I know that I would never have with Ivy what I had with Sarah, but I just can't help feeling something special for her. Sticking my finger through the boards of the deck I watched as the crab ran away into the sand. Maybe that's what I should do just pack and leave. Leaving all of my problems behind, but I know that's not possible.

Again I rolled over to face the sky. Lifting my arm to look at my watch I saw that I had only been out here for an hour. I sat up and stared out into the black ocean wondering what was out there waiting for me. Wondering if the decision that I'm going to make is going to be the right one.

I stumbled as I stood. Knowing I had enough to drink I left my glass on the deck. Making my way up the stairs my foot slipped and I laughed as I grabbed hold of the railing. Straightening up I felt a cool breeze blow past me and I turned around because I knew I felt an unforgettable breeze like that before, and I was right. "Sarah!"

Firmly holding on to the railing so I didn't lose my balance, I ran down the stairs as fast as I could. Reaching the bottom, Sarah was sitting there playing with the crabs in the sand. I went to touch her and I couldn't believe it, I actually felt her. I felt her skin and her hair. "Oh honey I missed you so much." I grabbed her hugging her as tight as I could.

"I know Mel, but I can't stay."

"Not even for a little while?" I pulled back to look at her.

"Only a short time."

I stood holding her, not letting go. Looking in her eyes I knew this was real love and I hugged her again. "Sarah I've been looking for you, hoping you would come to me. I need help. I'm so confused." I stared in her beautiful eyes.

"That's why I'm here." She touched my face softly.

"Tell me what to do, please tell me what to do. If you were still here with me none of this would be happening. I would still be happy." I grabbed her hand that was on my face and kissed it, holding it against my lips.

"What are you now?"

I pressed her hand against my cheek. "Confused." She rubbed my cheek and I let my hand slip down her waist.

"Before being confused."

"I thought I was happy." I let my head fall on her shoulder.

"Well maybe that's your answer." She stroked the back of my head.

"But I also thought I was happy at home with Windy." I felt tears falling down my face and on her shoulder.

"Were you truly happy or did you just want to believe that you were. You know you and Windy have a great friendship, are you willing to lose that to try and make it more than it should be?"

I looked at her. "I don't know Sarah. I really don't want to lose Windy but what if with her is where I'm suppose to be?"

"Do you really think that you're suppose to be with her?"

Tears were falling down my face. "Sarah I don't know, I can't talk to you about this because with you is where I really want to be."

"In good time Mel, until then you have a lot of love to give. You deserve to spend the rest of your life being happy. Happy Mel, that's what you deserve to be. Take the chance honey, be happy."

She walked out into the water and I followed her. We laughed and held hands walking through the knee-deep water until I couldn't feel her anymore. "Sarah, I can't see your face anymore." I raised my hand to where her face was, but it was no longer there.

I couldn't see her anymore all that I could do is hear her. "All I want for you Mel is to be happy."

Then I didn't even hear her anymore, she was gone. I sat down with my legs crossed and my head down in my hands.

I looked up again and still no Sarah. "God, I'm going nuts!" I smacked my hands on my head.

Reaching behind me I grabbed my drink and went upstairs. Looking next door where Ivy was staying I saw there were no lights on. I went inside flopped on the bed.

As soon as I closed my eyes I had dreams of Sarah.

CHAPTER 15

I awoke twisted in my blanket and still in my clothes from last night. Sitting up my head felt like it was going to explode. I stood and felt sick to my stomach. Walking in the kitchen I poured a big glass of water and headed straight for the shower. I leaned against the shower wall standing there until the water turned cold. Once I got out I made a pot of coffee then went to lie down again.

After getting up for the second time I went to get a cup of coffee and some aspirin. I stepped outside and as usual it was another gorgeous day. I looked down at the lower deck remembering that's where Sarah was. I also remembered everything she was trying to tell me, and from the dreams I had last night I knew exactly what I was going to do. I went back inside to get dressed, and then went next door to look for Ivy.

I stood on the back porch knocking at the door. Finally Ivy's sister came to the door.

"Hi, I'm looking for Ivy, is she here?"

"Yeah she's here, do you want to come in Mel?" She smiled at me and started to step aside.

"No, I'll just wait out here thanks." I took a step back and she stepped through the door.

"Mel what happened between the two of you last night?" She slid the door closed like she didn't want anyone over hearing our conversation. I liked the fact that she cared about her sister so much.

"Nothing, why?"

"Ivy came back last night pretty upset." She folded her arms across her chest.

"I just need to straighten some things out with her that's all." I nervously put my hands in my pockets.

"Okay, I'll go and get her." She stared at me for a moment then went inside.

I walked over and leaned on the railing watching and waiting for Ivy to come out. I saw her walking towards the door, as she slid it open she looked blankly into my eyes. "Hi Mel, I didn't think that I would hear from you today." She stepped through the door.

"I'm sorry, I know I slept in this morning but I came here to talk to you if you have a minute." I crossed my legs as I leaned against the railing.

"Sure, do you want some coffee?" She put her hand on the door handle.

"That would be great."

"I'll be right back."

She went inside and I walked down to the lower part of the deck. Sitting down I let my feet touch the water, and as I smacked my toes in the warm ocean I swore I saw Sarah's face in the little ringlets as they spread reaching out to nowhere. I stretched my hand out to touch her, and then she disappeared as she smiled at me. I smiled back and touched the water anyway.

I heard a noise behind me and when I turned, Ivy was coming down the stairs. She handed me a cup and sat down beside me. We stared out to the ocean for a few minutes, and then I reached over and put my hand on her leg. "Ivy I want you in my life."

She looked at me. "You do?"

"Yes I do. I just now have to decide how I'm going to tell Windy."

She laid her head on my shoulder. I reached over and touched her cheek as I kissed her on the mouth. Opening my eyes I looked at her. "Why don't you come over and I'll make you a nice big breakfast."

"I'd love that." She kissed me again.

We walked arms around each other over to my house.

Once inside Ivy sat on the couch while I made another pot of coffee. I walked back by Ivy and sat down putting my arm behind her and twirled her hair in my fingers.

"So Mel, tell me what happened last night." She tugged at my arm. "I mean you look a little hung over this morning." She giggled. "I know that I had quite a bit to drink last night, but not enough to look like you do this morning." She laughed.

I looked at her with my hand still in her hair. "You don't want to know what happened last night." I sat nodding my head not believing it myself.

She laughed and turned facing me. "Come on, tell me what happened. I really want to know how you came to your decision."

I looked at her hair in my fingers, then back into her eyes. "I don't know, after thinking things over for a while I decided that you make me happy, and that's what I want to be for the rest of my life."

"Happy." She smiled.

"Yeah." I smiled and pulled her hair so I could smell it. "Is there something wrong with that?"

"Not at all. It just seems like such a simple solution to such a complicated problem. So what are you going to say to Windy?"

"I don't exactly know yet. I tried to call her last night but she wasn't in."

"Are you going to call her today?"

"No, this isn't something that can be done over the phone."

"I suppose you're right about that."

We sat quietly for a minute, and then I went to get coffee for us. I handed Ivy hers and she looked up. "Mel, I'm wondering how on earth we are going to make this work?"

I sat back down. "What do you mean?"

"Well I live in Boston and you live in Ohio."

"I've actually thought about that and think I have a pretty good solution to our problem. I thought maybe I would open a gallery in Boston. What do you think?"

She smiled, then reached over and hugged me.

"I guess this means you think it's a good idea." I laughed at her.

"I think it's a great idea, but what are you going to do about your gallery now?" She pulled back with her arms still around my neck.

"Windy can still run it, and I'll come back and forth."

She just fell into me kissing me. "You're great. It's perfect."

"You do know it might not be as easy as I'm making it out to be, but I'm determined to make it work." I stood up and pulled her by her hands. "Come on let's go into the bedroom and you can tell me how great I am again."

She busted up laughing. "You are something else. I don't know what came over you last night, but what ever it was I am one happy woman."

I smiled. "I'm the lucky one." I'm lucky to have her in my life and also to have Sarah watching over me.

After endless lovemaking I laid my head on Ivy's stomach and wrapped my arms around her legs. "I'm really happy Ivy. You know I didn't realize it until last night, but I am."

"What happened last night to make you realize it?"

"You'll think I'm crazy. Hell sometimes I think I'm crazy."

"Oh come on." She stroked my hair with her hand. "How bad could it be?"

I kissed her on the stomach. "Well it was Sarah, she came to me last night." I looked up at her. "Are you sure that you want to spend the rest of your life with someone who sees her dead lover's ghost?"

She touched my face. "Absolutely. I can't think of anything that I want more than to spend the rest of my life with you. I would love to have met her, she seems like a great person. All she wants is what's best for you and I feel honored that she thinks it's me."

I laid my head back down. "So you believe that I see her?"

She still had her hand in my hair. "I believe that you see something, I don't know if it's really her, or if it's your mind making you see her. What ever it is she must have been a hell of a woman."

"She was." I laid there for a minute then raised my head and crawled up to lay next to her. "And so are you." I kissed her. "How about that breakfast now?"

"Breakfast, its afternoon."

"So is there any law against pancakes in the afternoon?"

"You're wild." She laughed throwing her head back.

"If you think that pancakes in the afternoon are wild, how are you going to spend the rest of your life with me?"

We laughed then got dressed and went into the kitchen. I started getting out all the ingredients that I needed, and then looked up at Ivy. "Do you like whole wheat banana pancakes?"

"Yes, I love them."

"Great, because I have an excellent wild berry syrup."

"Have I told you how wonderful you are to me today?" Her arms slipped around my waist.

I turned my head and kissed her. "You know Ivy I haven't said anything but I'm going to have to leave in the morning."

"I figured you would be leaving soon." She still had her arms around me from behind.

"I was hoping to leave first thing in the morning." I turned around and slipped my arms around her waist. "Even though I don't want to, I have to do this as soon as possible."

"I understand." She kissed me. "I'm not worried because I love you and I now know how much you love me."

"I do you know." I hugged her tight.

She whispered in my ear. "I know."

I pulled back. "Now come on and give me a hand with these pancakes."

We laughed and played in the kitchen until the pancakes were somewhat done. We ate what was edible, then changed into our swimsuits and laid outside. After a while of lying in the sun I went into the garage and brought out an inflatable boat and an old styrofoam cooler.

Ivy looked up at me. "What on earth are you doing now?"

I was bent down over the boat inflating it with a foot pump. "I thought it would be fun floating around for a while."

"Alright so what's the cooler for?" She picked it up looking at it.

"Come here and I'll show you." I walked down the stairs dragging the boat behind me. I rested the boat in the water, and then with a rope I tied the cooler to the boat. "See. You stock the cooler with beer, it floats, and you're off."

She stood next to me. "Boy you really did grow up here, you know all the tricks."

"Well you've got to if you're going to survive out here." I laughed.

She pushed me in the water. "You're so silly."

I dragged her by the arm. "Now come on and help me gather up all of the things we need."

We ran upstairs and Ivy grabbed the beer while I reached for towels and sunscreen. I turned to her. "I think that's it, let's go."

We raced downstairs and carefully jumped in the boat.

Ivy looked at me. "So now what do we do?"

I laughed. "Now." I handed her a beer and the sunscreen. "Now you lay back, relax and thoroughly enjoy the afternoon, without floating off too far."

"What happens if we do?"

"Well then we're screwed."

Ivy cracked up. "I don't know if I like the sound of that."

We laughed and splashed in the water until we were exhausted and more importantly out of beer.

We tied the boat off and crawled up the stairs.

"You know Mel when you leave tomorrow I don't know what I'm going to do with myself."

I laughed at her. "Get caught up on your sleep, because I'll be in Boston before you know it."

She threw her arms around me. "I can't wait."

"Come on now why don't we go jump in the shower. I've got big plans for you tonight."

"I like the sound of that."

We took a much-needed shower then lay down in each other's arms to take a nap.

❋   ❋   ❋

When I woke Ivy was gone. I looked around the house and there was no sign of her, I figured she went home to change so I poured myself a glass of water, flicked on the stereo and sat outside. It was just a few minutes before I saw Ivy walking back over. "Why did you leave?"

"I had to go home and change." She reached the top of the stairs.

"I see, you look great." She took the last stair and I was speechless as I looked at her. She really did look great. Her hair was pulled up with long strands hanging down her shoulders, and she was wearing a small tight black dress that was amazing.

"Well I thought that I would take you out to dinner tonight." She stood in front of me leaning against the railing.

"That's exactly what I had in mind for you."

"Good, so go on and get dressed. My brother in law told me of this very nice restaurant I thought we could try."

I stood up and reached for her hand. "Alright come on and help me get dressed." I went to slip my arm around her.

"Oh no you don't. If I go in there we'll never leave, so you get going. I'll wait right here, thank you very much."

She shoved me in the house. "Well at least come in and I'll get you a beer."

"Alright, but just a beer."

"You're so funny, come on." I grabbed her hand back and we went inside.

I got out a couple of beers for Ivy and myself, and then went into the bedroom to change, kissing Ivy on the way. In the bedroom while I searched for something to wear all I thought about was leaving tomorrow, and how I didn't want to.

I threw on a pair of silk cream-colored slacks and a matching vest when I heard Ivy yelling for me to hurry up. I giggled thinking of how happy she made me, just like Sarah said she would. I put on some mascara because with a tan I didn't need much else, and then walked out of the bedroom brushing my hair.

Ivy turned around. "Well, I guess you'll do in a pinch." She laughed.

I threw my arms up in the air. "Jeez you're cold."

She ran up to me trying to hug me, but I kept pushing her away laughing. "Come on Mel I'm sorry."

I grabbed her as I fell back on the couch. "Do you really want to go out tonight? I'll bet we can have more fun right here." I tried to kiss her and she pulled away.

"No you don't I'm taking you out tonight." She sat up. "Besides we have all night you're not leaving till the morning."

I sat up and put my arms around her laying my head on her chest. "You're right, what was I thinking?" I looked up at her rolling my eyes. She then pushed me off of her lap.

"Get up now and let's get going." She stood and held her hand out for me.

I grabbed it and she pulled me up. "Alright let me get my keys."

We were walking to the car when Ivy reached for my keys. "I'm even going to drive. I want you to totally enjoy yourself tonight."

"Wow, this is a treat. I'm enjoying myself already." I held my keys up in the air, and she reached for them.

While we drove Ivy turned on her 70's radio station and sang loudly, while I sat there laughing. We were having so much fun I was hoping the restaurant was further away, but we were almost there.

We sat at a great table and had a beautiful dinner. Sitting there we never ran out of anything to talk about. After a while we moved from the restaurant to the bar where a little blues band was playing. We were having a great time when Ivy leaned into me and whispered in my ear. "Come on let's go and get some air for a while."

I shook my head and we started walking outside towards the beach. The ocean air felt great and I leaned my head back and ran my fingers through my hair. "Ivy I'm having a fantastic time."

"I'm glad." She reached down and took my hand in hers. We walked quietly down the shore until we almost couldn't see the restaurant anymore.

I stopped and reached for her other hand as I turned to face her. "We better head back Ivy."

"Okay but first." She let go of my hand and reached in her purse pulling out a box. "Here I was waiting for the perfect time to give you this, and I don't think anytime could be more perfect than now, here, on the beach where we met, under this beautiful night's stars."

I looked at her and she placed a box in my hand. "Ivy what did you do? You shouldn't have bought me anything."

She shrugged her shoulders and folded her hands in front of herself. "Just open it."

I smiled as I looked at her, and then opened the box. Pulling a necklace out, a gold necklace with a small envelope at the end of a long chain. Inside the envelope was a gold plate, reading it, it said, 'Promise you'll come back to me, everything in my body and soul says you're the one.' I turned it over and on the back it read; 'I love you, always and forever. Ivy'

I looked up at her with tears in my eyes. "Ivy, it's beautiful. But you have to know that I'm coming back for you."

"I know, I just want you to know how much I care about you, how much I love you."

I stepped closer, hugging her as tight as I could and kissing her passionately. With one arm I held her tight and I wrapped my other hand in her long curly hair pulling her to me.

I whispered in her ear. "Lets go home." I looked in her eyes and it was like my whole body felt love and passion for this woman.

She smiled and held tight to my arm as we walked to the car. I stood against the car while Ivy put the necklace around my neck. I touched her cheek. "I love you."

"I know." She smiled "I always knew."

We heard people coming so she smiled at me and we got in the car. We pulled away and I rested my hand on her thigh as she drove. It was a quiet drive home, we were just happy to be together.

We got out of the car and started upstairs then I asked Ivy what she wanted most of all on our last night together. She grabbed my hand swinging it high in the air and told me she wanted to hold me until sunrise, then grabbed my arm and pulled me close. She kissed my cheek and ran into the bathroom.

I took the opportunity to grab a bunch of pillows and a couple of blankets, then ran down stairs and laid everything on the lower deck. Hurrying back upstairs I heard Ivy coming out of the bathroom and I yelled. "How about a martini?"

She came into the kitchen. "Alright, maybe one."

I mixed a pitcher, and then put it on a tray with a bowl of olives and a couple of glasses. I held my hand out to Ivy. "Come on I have a surprise for you."

She grabbed my hand and giggled. "Mel, what are you doing?"

I walked her outside and smiled. "We'll lay here all night holding each other until sunrise. That is what you wanted isn't it."

She grabbed the tray from me and put it down, then threw her arms around my neck. "You're perfect."

"Well I don't know if I'd go that far." I laughed as I kissed her.

We sat leaning on the pillows and I poured us both a drink. I handed Ivy hers, then lay back taking a sip. "It's beautiful here under the stars like this isn't it?"

"Like I said you're perfect, and this night has been perfect."

She moved close and settled into my shoulder. My arm immediately flew around her. "So tell me all about your life in Boston."

We lay there holding each other and talking until we both fell asleep.

❀   ❀   ❀

I awoke just as the sun was starting to rise. I leaned over and kissed Ivy on the forehead. "Here's your sunrise honey."

Her eyes slowly opened and she smiled while her arms tightened around my waist. "I don't know when I've been so happy."

I hugged her tight and we laid there a couple of minutes before I got up.

"Mel, where are you going?" She sat up fixing her hair.

"I had the coffee on a timer." I started to climb the stairs.

"You think of everything don't you?"

I yelled back. "I try."

Hurrying upstairs I fixed our coffee then ran back to Ivy. We quietly sat finishing our coffee then I turned to her. "I hate to do this babe but I've got to get going, I still have to pack."

She looked up at me. "I know I was just waiting as long as I could before getting up. I want to remember this moment forever."

"Don't worry we've made a lot of moments these past couple of weeks to remember."

She looked at me smiling. "We have, haven't we?"

"Yes we have."

She kissed my neck. "Come on I'll help you clean up and pack."

"Are you sure?" I held her face in my hand.

"I'm sure, come on." She stood and grabbed an arm full of pillows.

While finishing our coffee we cleaned, packed and closed the house up. I stood in the middle of the kitchen smacking my hands at my side. "Well, I think I'm all ready to go."

"Yeah." She walked to me. "I guess you are." Grabbing and hugging me she looked in my eyes. "Remember what I said." She tapped the necklace she gave me with her finger.

She slipped her hand around my neck and I kissed her. "Always. I'll never take it off until I'm with you again." I smiled and stared in her eyes. "Walk me to my car?"

She shook her head. "Come on." Then grabbed my hand smiling. We double checked all the doors and finally ended up leaning on my car kissing goodbye for a while. Then I kissed her cheek. "Ivy I really have to get going."

"I know." Her hand fell and grabbed mine. "I love you, and please be careful."

"Don't worry I will." I kissed her softly. "I love you." I kissed her again. "Don't forget that."

I hugged her one more time then crawled in the car and started the engine. Without saying anything I pulled away waving to her and watching her in my mirror as I turned out of the driveway.

The minute I could no longer see her in my mirror emptiness filled my body. It's only been minutes and I already missed her. I held the paper that she gave me with her address and phone number tightly in my hand. Then I touched the necklace she gave me and a smile immediately came over my face.

I drove for about six hours before stopping, getting only coffee and gas. The bathroom breaks and coffee stops were becoming more frequent before I finally got home.

I pulled into my drive and went inside without even unpacking the car. Going straight upstairs I fell in bed, immediately going to sleep.

❧   ❧   ❧

I woke up to banging at my door. I looked around remembering I was home and jumped out of bed rushing downstairs. Moving the blinds and looking out the window I saw it was Donna. "Hi Donna."

I leaned against the door and she came bursting inside. "Mel where the hell have you been?"

I shut the door and turned around. "What's the matter? I just got home about three hours ago."

She looked frantic and I walked closer to her.

"Nobody called you?"

I stood in front of her watching her face and I didn't like what I saw. "Called me about what? Come on Donna you're scaring me."

She turned around and ran her hand through her hair. "Mel it's Windy." She turned back to me. "She's okay now, well physically."

"Donna what the hell happened?" I grabbed her arm making her look at me.

"Windy was in the gallery late one night after she sent Tara home and a guy came in to rob her. The thing is he didn't only rob her."

I went into the kitchen and smacked my hand on the counter. "Donna why didn't someone call me?" I turned and looked at her.

"Windy said she would call. I guess she didn't want you to know." She moved towards me.

"This is unbelievable." I reached for my keys and looked up at her. "Where is she now?"

She put her hand on my forearm. I looked at it then up at her. Her eyes told me this was bad. "She's at home, but I have to warn you, her mother's there with her."

"Did they find who did this?"

"No, not yet. Don't be surprised when you see her though, he beat her up pretty bad. She was in the hospital for a few days."

I looked at her shaking my head then walked to the door. "I gotta go Donna."

She followed behind me then stopped in front of me before walking through the door. "Hey, you might want to stop by the gallery. It's a mess and Tara's there alone."

"I will thanks."

Windy's house wasn't a long drive but it seemed like it was taking forever. The whole way my head was just spinning. Every time I thought of Windy I felt guilty, and every time I thought of Ivy I couldn't help but wonder what this was going to do to us. Then I thought back to Windy working in her office waiting for me to come home, and the horror she must have faced.

Finally I pulled in her driveway. I didn't even get out of the car before I saw her front door open with her mother coming out. I had a feeling this was going to be bad as I walked up to the porch.

I got as close as the front stair when her mother yelled and pointed. "Mel you might as well turn right around and go back to where ever you were. Windy doesn't need your help now. When she did need you, you weren't there." She stood there in front of me with her arms folded against her ample chest like a pit bull guarding her pups.

"I think I should talk to her about this." I put one foot on the bottom stair with my hand on the railing looking up at her.

"She's sleeping right now, but she'll tell you the same thing."

"Well then I want to hear it from her." I raised my sunglasses and pushed them on top of my head.

"Right now she needs her rest." She stepped closer to me.

"Can't I just see her?"

"I'll tell her that you came by."

"Don't bother, I'll be back." I lowered my sunglasses back on my face and turned around, walking to my car. I heard her mother yell for me, so I turned to her.

"Mel I wouldn't bother coming back, she doesn't want to see you."

I turned back around to get in my car. I stared at her still standing there when I pulled away.

I headed straight for the gallery.

The whole time I was driving I wondered if her mother was telling the truth. I wondered if she really didn't want to see me. That couldn't be true though, her mother just never liked me. She never thought I was good enough for her daughter. Windy always said even though she loved her mother to death she was the biggest snob she ever knew. Boy, was she right.

Pulling into the gallery parking lot I saw that Tara's car was here. Finally I could find out a little bit more of what happened.

I walked inside and fell back against the door. Looking around I couldn't believe it the place was trashed.

Tara came running from the back. "Who's here?"

Finally she turned the corner and I held my hand up. "Tara, it's just me, Mel!"

She ran up to me and hugged me. "Mel, where have you been? Have you been to see Windy yet?"

I pulled back and started to walk around. "Well I went to see her, but her mother wouldn't let me in. She said she was sleeping."

She followed closely behind me. "Well good luck. Her mother's being terribly over protective. Although I can't blame her."

I turned around and looked at her. "So tell me what exactly happened here. Nobody's telling me anything." I stood, looking around. "Do you know what happened?"

She looked down then back up at me. "All I know is what I heard from Windy herself, and from what the police told me."

She started walking back by the offices and I followed behind her. I couldn't believe the things that I saw. Ripped paintings, broken sculptures, the place was a mess. Then we came to Windy's office. Her desk was over turned with all her papers thrown about; just looking at her office I could only imagine what she had gone through.

Tara looked at me. "I just started cleaning up today. The police had to finish in here first."

She started picking some papers up and I grabbed her hand turning her to face me. "Tara, what happened?"

She looked down then up at me while she pushed her hair back with her hand. "Windy told the police that she was sitting in her office when she heard a noise. She got up thinking it was me coming back for something, but the creep was already in the place. The police think that he probably didn't know there was anyone else in there after I left. They think he was going to take paintings and anything else of value in here, then leave.

Then he saw Windy, he pulled her back to her office and tied her up." She looked up at me. "Mel he beat her until she passed out. After she came to he raped her. He was here with her all night. From what Windy said he left just before I got here in the morning."

I fell down to the floor, rubbing my face with my hands, only imagining what she went through.

Tara knelt down beside me and put her arm around my shoulder. "Mel if it's any comfort I don't blame you a bit, but I have to tell you that Windy feels different."

I jerked my head up looking at her. "What do you mean blame me?" I stared at her. "How could this possibly be my fault?"

She sat next to me with her arm still around me. "She feels if you were here this wouldn't have happened. She just needed you and you weren't here. She's hurting that's all. She needs time."

I picked a book up that was lying next to me and threw it across the room. "Tara how could I have known that something like this was going to happen?"

She jerked next to me, and then grabbed my wrist. "You couldn't have."

We sat there for a minute, tears rolling down both of our faces. Then I wiped my cheeks and got up. "Well I better get in touch with the insurance company so we can get this place cleaned up as fast as possible."

I stood in the doorway and looked at Tara who was still sitting on the floor. "Tara one more thing."

"Yes?" She looked up at me.

I grabbed the doorframe with both my hands leaning inside. "How did he get in here? Why didn't someone hear the alarm and come to check it out?"

"No one could figure that out. Either he knew what he was doing or…" She put her head in her hands and started crying uncontrollably.

I knew then what she had been going through. Blaming herself probably for not setting the alarm. I went back into the office and hugged her. "Why don't you go home? I'll finish up here. I'll call you when it's time to come back. In the mean time just take some time off."

We both stood up.

"Thanks Mel."

I wiped the tears from her face. "Go on now, I'll call you. Okay?"

"Okay." She mumbled.

I put my arm around her shoulder and walked her to the door. After I watched her walk to her car I went in my office to make some phone calls.

I walked around one more time then decided I needed to go home and take a shower. Besides I wanted to get back over to Windy's house today before it got too late.

The whole ride all I thought of was how selfish I've been, and as I held the necklace Ivy gave me, all my guilt came flooding back to me. I quickly turned the radio in the car up, thinking that if it was loud enough it might push out all the guilty thoughts I was having. But it didn't work, nothing worked. I just kept remembering what Tara said. Windy thought it was my fault.

Now I was beginning to believe it myself.

Finally getting home and going inside I looked at the clock and it was already late afternoon. I grabbed a bottle of water out of the fridge and went upstairs.

I sat in the bottom of the shower trying to wash all the guilt off of me, but that didn't work either. I cried as I sat there with my head in my hands trying to think of something to say to Windy when I see her.

When I had no more tears left I crawled out of the tub.

I stood there with puffy eyes and dripping wet, looking at myself in the mirror, wondering how I could have screwed my life up so much. I held on tight to Ivy's necklace, knowing I couldn't tell Windy anything now. It will just have to wait.

I got dressed and went downstairs, and then I looked at my luggage sitting by the door and figured I'd put it away later as I flopped down on the couch.

I started combing out my hair when I heard a knock at the door and yelled for whomever it was to come in. I figured it was Donna and I was right. She came in carrying a tray of food and some beers.

She kicked the door closed behind her. "Vicky and I thought you probably didn't have any food around here so I brought you something to eat." She walked towards me.

I followed her to the kitchen. "Thanks Donna but I'm not really all that hungry. Although I will take one of those beers."

She handed me a beer and grabbed one of her own. "Did you get a chance to see Windy?"

"No, her mother wouldn't let me in. She said she was sleeping. I'm going to try again in a little while though" I put my comb down and opened my beer.

"So where have you been?" She sat down next to me.

I pulled my legs up on the couch crossing them in front of me. "At the gallery."

"So you talked to Tara then?" She set her beer down on the table then took out her cigarettes.

"She filled me in on everything that happened." I set my beer down. "Donna, do you think this was all my fault?" With my elbow resting on the back of the couch I propped my head up.

"No Mel! Absolutely not." She swiveled and turned to face me placing her hand on mine. "You couldn't have known anything like this was going to happen. Even if you were there, how could you have stopped it?"

I closed my eyes throwing my head back. "I just can't get over the guilt though Donna. It's eating me alive. I thought it was bad in North Carolina, but that doesn't even compare to this now." Then I put my hand over my eyes realizing what I had just said.

She stared at me with a puzzled look on her face. "What do you mean, guilt in North Carolina?"

I grabbed my beer and walked over to the window. "I wasn't going to tell anyone, but talking about it might help. Then again it might not."

She put her cigarette out and got up standing behind me. "Mel if you don't want to talk about it that's okay."

I turned around. "I don't know if you knew why I left…" I stared at her.

"I knew." She folded her arms and looked at the ground. "Windy told me."

I walked over and sat back down on the couch. "When I was in North Carolina I met someone."

Her head flew up. "Really?"

"Yeah, I know." I fell back on the couch throwing my head back to look at the ceiling, then my head raised to look at her. "But I really feel like she's the one I'm suppose to spend the rest of my life with. No one since Sarah has made me so happy." Just talking about Ivy makes me feel instantly better. I could feel a smile come over my face and I reached for her necklace.

"What are you going to do?" She looked at me with concern on her face, and that instantly brought me back to reality.

"Well, I came back here to tell Windy, but obviously I can't now." I looked away.

"No."

"I don't know what I'm going to do." I picked up my beer taking a drink.

"So tell me who is this person that you met while you were gone?"

I felt a smile come over my face again. "Her name is Ivy, she's a doctor who lives in Boston."

"A doctor huh, my mom always wanted me to marry a doctor." She smiled and took a drink of her beer.

I laughed. "She's really great Donna. I'm totally and completely in love with her. It's real. It reminds me of what I had with Sarah." I stared in her eyes. "Donna she's what I've been missing."

"I can see now why you feel so guilty."

"What am I going to do?" I looked in her face searching for some kind of answer.

"All I can tell you to do is follow your heart. Now whatever that is you're going to have to figure out on your own." She smacked her hand on her leg and started to get up.

"I just knew that you were going to tell me that." I picked up my empty beer bottle taking it into the kitchen, and then turned around. "Well I better get going so I can see Windy." I walked back over to Donna.

"Alright I've got to get going too, Vicky's probably wondering where I'm at by now."

I started walking her to the door. "Donna." I put my hand on her shoulder. "This is only between the two of us, right?"

"You know better than that." She hugged me. "If you need anything at all…"

"I know."

I watched while she walked home then picked up my keys, closed the door and drove off heading for Windy's house. I was going to call first but that would just give her mother the chance to tell me to stay away. I thought I might have a better chance with the element of surprise on my side. I drove trying not to think of anything at all while I held on to my necklace.

Pulling into Windy's driveway I glanced at the door and saw no signs of movement. I hurried out of the car and almost ran to the door. I rang the bell and knocked on the door, still no answer.

I rang the bell again, and then I saw a shadow of someone coming to the door. Seeing the blind move I stepped back from the door.

The door opened but I didn't see anyone, so I stepped through. I turned and saw Windy standing there. She was almost doubled over; I ran to her, grabbed her around the waist. "Windy what are you doing up? Where's your mother?"

She grabbed her ribs with one hand and my arm with the other. "She went to the store."

"Come on, I'll help you to the couch."

As I helped her to the couch with my arms tightly around her holding her up, I realized just how badly she was hurt. Her face was so bruised, her arm broken and from the way she was walking I'm sure she has some broken ribs, maybe even something worse.

We got to the couch and I set her down easily as I sat next to her. "Windy I'm so sorry. How do you feel?" I looked at her with tears forming in my eyes.

"Better." She sat back slowly, fixing her bathrobe around her legs.

I stared at my hands and played with my fingernails. "I was here earlier but you were resting."

She didn't say anything she just sat there staring out the window. I reached for her hand, but she moved it, so I pulled my hand back to my lap.

I really didn't know what to say to her and with my fingers I wiped a tear from my cheek and turned to her. "So what did the doctors say, are you going to be okay?"

Still she didn't look at me. "I'm okay. It's just my ribs, once they heal I'll be fine." She rubbed her hand up and down her side.

"That's good. Do the police have any idea who did this?" I stared at her, while she stared out the window.

"No."

I couldn't believe how uncomfortable I felt. I sat there wringing my hands and cracking my knuckles. "Windy can I get you anything?"

"No."

"Are you sure? Water, anything?" I just wanted to grab her and hold her until she felt safe again.

"No Mel, that's okay. I'm fine. The truth is I'm a little tired."

"Alright, well I'll go then." I stood, and then knelt down in front of her.

I tried to look in her eyes but she looked away from my stare. "I'll be back tomorrow to see you." I tried to find her eyes but they avoided me. "Windy look at me." I put my hand on her knee.

She turned to face me, but still wouldn't look at me. "I need time." She turned away. "I'll call you when I'm ready."

I rested my hand on top of hers. "Okay Win I'll leave you alone for a while, but only a while. If I don't hear from you, I'll be back."

"I'll call."

I stood up and looked down at her watching as she just stared out the window.

I walked out the door and I doubt she even knew, or cared. I don't know if she was in shock because of everything that happened, or if she really blames me.

Sitting in my car I stared at her house, then let my head fall on the steering wheel. Did I do this to her? Could this really be my fault? Lying there I felt like I really needed to talk to Ivy. I lifted my head and pulled away. As I drove I knew it was impossible for me to talk to Ivy, but I did know someone that I could talk to.

I stood looking down, and then fell to my knees. "Hi babe." I rubbed my fingers along her headstone. "I need you now more than I think I ever have. Honey did I do the wrong thing. Am I somehow to blame? Could this all be my fault? I need to know Sarah, you've got to help me." I sat there crying, waiting for her to talk to me. I looked up to the sky wiping my eyes. Then I looked around realizing how beautiful and peaceful it was here. Again I wiped the tears away from my eyes. "Sarah you were right about Ivy, I am truly happy, but at what cost, the cost of Windy's mental and physical being. How can I possibly repair this?"

I laid back throwing my hands over my head and looked up at the sky. "I guess I have to just wait. I have to wait for Windy to heal. No matter how long it takes, I'm not going to give up on her I would never be able to live with myself. After all she was always there for me when ever I needed her. It's only right that I'm here for her." I sat up crossing my legs. "Is that what you're trying to tell me Sarah, to wait."

I went back on my knees and brushed her stone. "I'll bet you are." I looked around thinking that maybe I would see her somewhere, but I didn't. "I'm sorry that I always come to you with my problems honey, but you're my rock. You always were. Please while I can't, take care of Windy for me. I love you so much, and no one will ever compare to you.

Sarah if I haven't told you today I love and miss you so much. With you in my life, my life was so simple." I kissed my fingers and rubbed her stone one more time before getting up. I stood looking down at her grave, then turned my head up to the sky because I knew that's where she really was. I winked then walked to my car. Actually I felt better.

Driving home I held Ivy's necklace visualizing her while I smiled. Pulling in my driveway I saw Donna and Vicky sitting in the back-yard.

Getting out of my car I went over to join them, I sat next to Vicky and she rested her hand on my forearm. "How are you doing Mel?"

I looked at her. "Actually I feel a little bit better, thanks." I patted her hand.

"How about a beer?"

"That sounds good, thanks Vic."

Vicky got up and I turned to watch her walk into the house, and then looked at Donna. "Windy said she would call me when she wants to see me."

"She just needs time, she's been through a lot."

"I know." I heard a door shut then Vicky handed me a beer and sat next to me. She turned to look at me. "Mel is Windy going to go for any counseling?"

I turned to her. "I don't know. I hope she will. I really think she needs to talk to someone." I looked at Donna. "I know she won't talk to me."

Vicky turned to me. "She won't talk to you. Why?" Then she looked at Donna who turned to me.

I turned to Vicky. "I don't know. Either she's really traumatized by what's happened or she blames me in some way."

"How could she possibly blame you?" Vicky sounded shocked and caring all at the same time.

"I don't know, but with everything that's gone on I'm starting to wonder if maybe I am to blame." I looked down.

Donna grabbed my wrist and I looked up at her. "Mel, what did I tell you? None of this is your fault. Do you hear me?"

"I hear you, but I can't help what I feel." I looked back down at my hands, which were twirling my beer bottle.

"You just don't listen to anyone else. Like Vicky said, she just needs time to get through this is all."

"I guess. Until then I'm going to concentrate on getting the gallery back in order. I think I'll remodel everything so when Windy comes back everything will be brand new."

We sat drinking beer for a couple of hours talking about everything that happened until it got pretty dark out. I stood. "Well guys it's getting pretty late and I'm exhausted. I'll see the two of you tomorrow."

Donna stood up and started clearing the table. "Alright Mel, goodnight."

I lay in bed holding the necklace Ivy gave me, hoping for her to enter my dreams as I fell asleep.

CHAPTER 16

❀

It's been a few days since I went to see Windy and I still haven't heard from her. I walked through the house with a cup of coffee in my hand and Ivy's phone number. I've tried to call her a couple times since I've been home, but there's been no answer. 'Oh what the hell.' I picked up the phone and dialed her number. This time some one picked up. "Hello Ivy?" I could feel my face light up.

"Yes."

"It's Mel, I've been trying to call you for days."

"I've had a lot of work to catch up on. God, it's good to hear your voice. I miss you so much already."

I sat down at the kitchen table and put my head in my hand, just thinking about Windy's situation made my head hurt. "I know I miss you. Things have gotten very complicated though."

"Why?" Haven't you talked to Windy yet?"

"No, I haven't. Something bad had happened."

"Are you okay?"

"I'm fine. It's Windy though, she was robbed and attacked at the gallery while I was away."

"My God, is she okay?"

"No, well yes. I don't know."

"Mel, was she…"

"Raped. Yes. She's pretty bad. The worst part is I think she blames me for not being there."

"Oh Mel that's ridiculous. Did you try to talk to her?"

"I tried, but she told me she would call when she was ready."

"So what are you suppose to do in the mean time?"

"Well right now I have my hands full with the gallery."

"It's that bad?"

"Ivy, you have to see it, to believe it. He kept her in there all night, beating and raping her. I could only imagine what she went through. I really understand her needing time, and I even sort of understand her resentment towards me. After all I wasn't there when she needed me."

"Mel, don't! You just started getting over the guilt you felt in North Carolina. This is not your fault."

"I know. So tell me, how was your last couple of days in paradise?"

"Without you, boring."

I laughed. "But relaxing right?"

"Very. I miss you though."

"I know. Me too. I'll call again soon, okay."

"Okay, I love you."

"I love you too. I always have you close to my heart." I tightened my grip on the necklace.

"Bye Mel."

"Bye hon." I hung up and lay back on the couch rubbing my eyes. Even though I talked to her what I really wanted was to hold her. I lay wondering when that was going to be.

The best thing I can do for myself right now is concentrate on work. Getting the gallery finished might bring Windy one step closer to healing.

❧   ❧   ❧

When I reached the gallery Tara was already helping direct everyone on what to do. We took it upon ourselves to change the entire place. We thought a fresh look would be good for everyone, and from what we have planned it's going to look great. Both Tara and I were there everyday early and stayed late to get this job done as soon as possible. We're both exhausted, but in the end if it helps Windy it will all be worth it.

CHAPTER 17

*I*t's been over a week now and still I've heard nothing from Windy. I kept myself busy though. If I wasn't working in the gallery, I rode my bike or talked to Ivy on the phone. She's been wanting me to come to Boston but I can't, not while I still haven't heard from Windy. If she decided to call and I was out of town again, I would never forgive myself. As for Ivy coming to visit me I just didn't think it would be appropriate. Windy didn't need to hear from anyone else about Ivy. I didn't think I could bear it if I hurt her anymore than I already have.

This weekend I'm going to an Indians game with Donna and Vicky, maybe the roar of the crowd will help me forget my troubles for a while.

Every once in a while I would drive by Windy's house wanting to go in, to see her. Just to make sure she's okay, but I'm doing exactly what she wants me to do, and that's to stay away. It's hard though because until I make sure that she's truly okay I have to put my life on hold. I only hope that Ivy can keep being as understanding as she is right now.

All the days have turned into weeks, and still no word from Windy. It's not just me, no one else had heard from her either. I've made up my mind to stop by and see her tonight though. I just can't sit around and wonder what is going on with her anymore. Besides, the gallery is almost finished now and it looks like a brand new place. All that's really left to do is replace the artwork, and that might take some traveling. If anything, it will give me an excuse to go to Windy's. Even if she doesn't want to see me personally, she had to see me, because it's business.

After leaving the office I went home to shower and change. Before I ran out the door I picked up the phone and thought about calling Ivy, then I put it back down. I decided it probably would be better if I called her after talking to Windy. I wasn't going to tell Windy about Ivy, not yet; it's still too soon. But maybe I could get some kind of idea of when I could tell her by talking to her tonight.

The drive seemed shorter than it ever has, maybe it was all the nervous excitement of seeing her. When I pulled in the driveway I saw the curtain move, that wasn't a good sign.

That meant only one thing…I was right, her mother's still here. She stood in the front door. I guess I couldn't be lucky enough to miss her twice. I got out of my jeep without even looking up, and then walked up to the house. She stepped on the porch and I pretended like I didn't see her. I kept walking.

She yelled. "Mel, Windy told me that she had a talk with you and you were suppose to stay away." She folded her arms in front of herself as she guarded the door.

"This is business, I need to see her." I stood firm at the bottom of the stairs.

"I don't know if I can allow this."

I put one hand on the railing and started to climb the stairs slowly. "Excuse me. Allow this! Now I know that you're her mother but she's a grown woman with a business to take care of. You either tell her I'm here to see her or I'll just walk right in. Don't make me do that."

She stood there a moment then turned and went inside, slamming the door behind her. I held my hand up and saw that it was shaking. I just couldn't get over how she hated me so much. I've hardly even talked to the woman. She knows nothing about me and she still hates me. I just can't figure it out. All I can think of is maybe she has some kind of strong motherly instinct that tells her I'm going to hurt her little girl. God help me that was never my intention.

I heard the door open and looked up. "Windy you look great. How do you feel?"

"A lot better. Mom said this was business." She stood leaning in the doorway with her hands folded in front of her looking down at her feet.

"The gallery is finally on it's way to being finished and I wanted to tell you I'm going out of town in search of pieces to fill the walls and empty spaces." I took one more step closer to her.

"Alright, but Mel you could have done this over the phone." She looked up but not at me.

"I wanted to see you. You haven't called me, it's been a month now." I stopped and looked at her.

"I know I was getting around to it."

"So do you want to talk now?"

"I don't know, how long are you going to be away?"

"Probably about a week."

"Alright, why don't we talk when you get back?" Her eyes went from the ground to finally look up at me. "Okay?"

I heard tears in her voice. "I understand should I call."

"When you get back."

I nodded my head. Standing there leaning on the railing with my arms folded I was so frustrated I could feel myself getting mad. I knew damn well I had no right, but I couldn't help it. I stepped forward stretching my hand out and rubbed her forearm gently, then turned and walked to my car. Halfway there I turned to look back and she was watching me. I waved, she smiled and I got in the car pulling away.

As I drove I thought about how I planned to use this trip searching for artwork to sneak off and see Ivy, although it doesn't seem like such a good idea now. I was starting to get another case of the guilt's.

I think maybe I'll just tell Ivy I can't see her, I don't know if I could handle all the guilt I would have.

I want to see her so bad, I miss her so much but I think a few more weeks won't put that much of a strain on our relationship. After all we have our whole lives ahead of us, I really just hope she's not going to be too upset.

With all of this going through my head I made it home in no time although I couldn't get out of my car because getting out might mean having to make yet another decision. I saw Donna walking towards me in my rear view mirror. I waited until she reached my window before I rolled it down. "Donna, how are you doing?"

"Good, how about you?" She leaned in my window.

"I'm okay." I still had my hand on the steering wheel.

"Well then why are you sitting here in your car?" She looked around inside.

"I'm afraid to get out." I looked at her smiling but yet half crying also.

"Mel." She laughed. "Why are you afraid to get out of your car?" She looked around outside. "Is someone following you?" She suddenly got very serious.

"No." I laughed. "Donna what are you doing right now?"

She leaned back in my window. "Right now?"

I laughed. "Yeah, right now."

"Nothing, why?"

"Do you want to go and get a drink?" I looked at her then I turned to look at my hand on the steering wheel.

"Are you okay?"

"Yeah, I just want a drink, is that okay?"

"Alright, well let me go inside for a minute, I'll be right back. I suppose you'll be waiting right here in your car?" She patted the side of the jeep.

"Hurry up will you please." I watched her run inside.

She yelled back at me. "Alright, alright."

I watched her go all the way inside then I sat tapping the steering wheel with my thumbs, trying to remember the words to 'Oklahoma.'

Then I sat there wondering what the hell I was doing. I laid my head back and rubbed my temples.

I felt the car move and a loud bang in the back of the jeep, and then Donna yelled. "Wake up!"

I bolted up in my seat. "Jeez, what are you doing?"

"Waking your butt up." She crawled inside. "So where are we going?"

"The nearest bar." I started the engine.

"Okay, I'm easy." She reached over and put her seat belt on. I watched her thinking how responsible she was and pulled away.

We drove away and Donna was talking about her job. I caught bits and pieces of what she was saying, but if she asked me a question I probably wouldn't be able to answer. My mind was somewhere else. Both Ivy and Windy were battling it out in my head as to which I felt most guilty over. Oh I knew Ivy was going to be mad if I didn't go to Boston, but I just really think it was for the best.

Trying to stop thinking of everything and everyone, I started singing 'Oklahoma' again to myself, hoping that might be enough of a distraction for me.

After my second verse we pulled in the parking lot of the bar and went inside. It was just a corner bar down the street, but it was nice. I ordered us a couple of beers and Donna was still talking about work when we sat at the bar and I looked at her laughing hysterically.

She looked at me. "What is up with you?"

I laid my head on the bar then looked up at her. "I haven't heard a word you said since we left the house."

"I don't believe you." She smacked my arm.

"I know, I'm sorry." I rubbed my arm.

"So what are you thinking of?"

"It doesn't matter, I didn't come here to talk about my problems I just needed to laugh."

Donna stood up. "Okay let's go."

I pulled her arm. "Sit down."

We drank, laughed and had a great time talking about nothing. For the first time in a long time I thought about absolutely nothing. All I thought about was who was buying the next drink.

After a couple of hours of solid drinking we were both pretty drunk so we called Vicky to come and get us.

We tried to play darts while we waited for Vicky but we were starting to get too silly, so we sat back down. When we did we were laughing so hard we didn't even see or hear Vicky come in until she was right behind us.

I turned around. "Hi Vic, want a drink?"

She stared at Donna. "No, I came here to drive the two of you home remember." She tossed her keys in her hand.

"Oh yeah, I'm sorry." I giggled falling into Donna's shoulder.

"Don't be, come on finish up and let's get out of here guys." She patted her hand on the air, like 'bottoms up.'

Donna walked over to her and put her arm around her shoulder. "Don't be mad." She tilted her head to the side and I sat back laughing at her.

"I'm not mad. I just want to get you guys out of here and home as soon as possible." She folded her arms across her chest.

I was twirling around in circles on my barstool. "Why, are we embarrassing you?"

"Yes, now come on don't make me drag the two of you out of here." She unfolded her arms and turned around heading for the door.

I stood up and finished my beer, then turned to Donna. "Come on let's go before you really get in trouble."

On the drive home all Donna and I did was giggle. I haven't laughed so much since I came home from North Carolina, and it really felt good. When we got home Vicky went inside while Donna and I sat outside at the patio table. I looked at her. "Is she pissed or what?"

"No, she went inside probably to get something to eat. Don't worry she's not mad."

I smacked my hand on the table at her. "Alright well you have to live with her. She'll probably never let you come out and play again."

"So is that what we were doing?"

"Yeah, playing."

We both busted up laughing, and then Vicky came out. "Are you two still laughing?"

We looked at each other and kept laughing. It was one of those laughs where once you start you just can't stop.

"I ordered a pizza is that okay?"

I looked up. "That's great, thanks Vicky."

Donna reached up and pulled her by the arm. "Come on babe sit next to me."

"Get outta here you're drunk."

"No actually I'm better. I think we just needed air, right Mel." She looked at me.

"Right, air, is that what you said, air?" I looked at her.

We laughed all over again and Vicky stomped back off into the house.

I looked at Donna. "Hey want a beer?"

"Sure."

I went into the house and came back out with some beers in my hand. I handed one to Donna then sat another by her. "Here this is for Vicky when she comes back out."

"Oh she'll just love that."

I sat back down and the two of us got pretty quiet. Then Donna turned to me. "So Mel tell me, what was this little outing really all about?"

"I'd tell ya, but then I'd have to kill ya!" I laid my head on my arm laughing.

"You're something else, are you incapable of being serious tonight?"

"For a change Donna, yes I think I am." I pulled my hair back with my hand.

We all ate pizza while we sat around trying to stump each other on T.V. trivia. I was the Brady Bunch reigning champ and with my crown still in tact, I left to go inside to bed. It was getting late and I could hardly keep my eyes open any longer. But I did have a great time. Although I knew I would be paying for it in the morning.

Walking into the kitchen I grabbed a bottle of water and started for bed then stopped by the phone. Standing there I wondered if I should call Ivy or not, then I decided against it thinking not only was it kind of late, but I really had no answers for her about Windy. I knew that she would be disappointed because I won't be going to see her but that was a decision I had to make, and it was a hard one. I think it will be better for everyone involved if I do this, but I really don't think Ivy's going to see it that way. Anyway I'll call her first thing in the morning.

CHAPTER 18

I sat up on the edge of the bed, and then just fell backwards. My head hurt so bad, even my hair hurt, I was so hung over. I rolled over and grabbed the phone to call Tara. I dialed the office forgetting that she wasn't there, so I called her at home.

"Tara, hi it's Mel."

"What's wrong?"

"Nothing's wrong, would you be able to go into the gallery today for a little bit? The painters will be in to do some more work, but they won't stay long."

"Mel you don't sound too good."

"Yeah, I think I've got the flu."

"Right! The brown bottle flu, what were you drinking?"

I laughed. "Beer with shots of tequila."

"Good luck. Sure I'll go in, it's no problem."

"Thanks Tara, I owe you. By the way I'll be leaving for a while to pick up some artwork, so could you hold down the fort for me?"

"Sure, just be careful, okay?"

"I will, thanks."

I hung up putting the pillow over my head. God why did I drink so much, I hugged my pillow and fell back to sleep.

I woke up to the phone ringing off the hook. I reached over and grabbed it, and then I laid my head back down. "Hello."

"Mel, is that you?"

"Ivy! I was going to call you this morning."

"Well morning's over. What's going on?"

I heard the sound of concern in her voice as I sat up. "What time is it?"

"2:00."

"I went out with Donna last night and we drank a little bit too much."

"Well you needed to get out, you just should have paced yourself." She was giggling.

"It's a little late for advice now."

She laughed. "Sorry, do you want me to let you go?"

"No, not at all. I wanted to tell you I talked to Windy yesterday."

"So how did it go?"

"I don't know, okay I guess. No not really."

"Mel, what happened?"

"She still wasn't very receptive of me. I told her I was going on a business trip. She said when I came back she wanted to talk to me."

"Why when you come back? Why not now?"

"I don't know, all she said was she would be ready to talk when I come back."

"Mel, what are you saying?"

"Well." I laid back down. "Ivy, I was thinking of making this just a business trip."

"So you're not coming here?"

I heard disappointment in her voice. "No." My eyes closed because I knew that I was hurting her.

"Because of Windy?"

"No, because of me. I can't be with you then come back here and pretend nothing's going on when I talk to her."

"I see."

"Are you mad?" I put my hand over my closed eyes.

"I don't know Mel. Disappointed yes. Mad not really."

"Thanks hon. you really wouldn't want me to be the kind of person who could do that, would you?"

"No, of course not, but if you came I wouldn't tell you to leave."

"Soon, I just feel like she's been hurt enough."

"I know I really have to get going though I've got to get to work."

"Alright, I love you and thanks babe for understanding."

"I love you, talk to you soon."

We hung up and I crawled into the bathroom to take a shower.

Going downstairs I picked up the phone and started making calls for airline tickets and hotel reservations to New York. Then I packed for my flight in the morning. All I had to do now was go up to the bar and get my car. Instead of calling Donna I decided that the walk would do me good.

On the way to the airport and on the flight to New York all I thought of was the last time I came here. I thought about looking Lily up, and then thought that was probably the worst idea I ever had.

I had every stop mapped out so maybe I wouldn't need a whole week, because the quicker I got back, the quicker I can find out what's going on with Windy.

I checked into the hotel and headed straight for my first slotted stop. After that I thought I would do a little shopping and buy something nice for Ivy. I looked around for hours then settled on a gorgeous diamond tennis bracelet. Looking at it I knew it would look prefect on her delicate wrist. I couldn't wait to get back to my hotel and call her. I rushed out of the taxi and into the hotel, and then I heard someone call my name.

I snapped my head around and felt a smile immediately come over my face. "Ivy, what on earth." She was standing in the middle of the lobby looking great as usual. I headed straight for her, as I did I could only think of all the queer movies where people meet and run to each other in slow motion and I started laughing.

She looked at me with a smile on her face. "What are you laughing about?"

"Nothing, come here." I hugged her so tight I never wanted to let go, but I did. "How did you know where I was?"

"It took a lot of tracking down, but I did it. Come on I'll tell you about it over a drink." She grabbed my arm.

As we walked I looked at her. "God it's great to see you."

"I know, you too."

We walked into the hotel bar and sat down at a secluded booth in the back. The waitress came over and I ordered a couple of martinis. We just couldn't stop staring at each other.

I was the first one to break the silence. "I missed you so much."

"Me too." She smiled at me and I could feel my heart beating faster.

"I was just headed up to my room to call you." Without taking my eyes off of her I reached in my bag. "I bought you something." I slid it over to her on the table and she put her hand on it smiling at me, the waitress came over with our drinks and set them down on the table.

I smiled, still staring into her beautiful green eyes. "Go ahead, open it."

She looked up at me then down, as she slowly opened the long black box. I watched her eyes smile as she carefully pulled it out. "Mel this is gorgeous. You shouldn't have done this."

"Yes I should have." I reached over the table. "Here let me help you." I shut the clasp then gently and slowly rubbed her hand as I pulled away. "It looks beautiful on you. I knew it would."

She raised her hand to watch the diamonds dance in the light. "This is the best thing anyone has ever given me."

I smiled then took a sip of my drink as I just watched her. "I'm glad you like it."

"I love it." She looked up at me. "And you."

She watched the diamonds dance when she raised her glass.

"So you never did tell me how you were able to track me down."

"Well let's see if I can even remember my trail." She set her glass down. "First I called the gallery and a woman named Tara answered, but she didn't know your plans. She asked who I was and I told her that you had called me because you were coming to my gallery to buy some artwork."

"Get outta here." I laughed at her as I rubbed the rim of my glass with my finger.

She laughed. "No kidding."

"So what did she say?"

"She told me to call Donna she probably would know your plans. So I got Donna's number from her, then called."

"You're something else." I picked up my drink sipping it as I stared at her. "Have I told you how glad I am that you came here?"

"You just did." She touched my hand lightly. "How about I buy you dinner."

"I'd love that, but why don't we eat in the room instead."

She grinned. "You read my mind."

I had her luggage put in my room, and then we followed. The minute we got in the room I threw my arms around her pulling her to me. "I've been waiting for this moment since I saw you standing in the lobby."

We started kissing and fell down on the bed. She rolled over and brushed the hair out of my eyes. "Are you sure that you don't want me to get my own room. I mean that is what I had in mind anyway."

"No, why would you do that?" I held her face in my hands kissing her lightly on the mouth.

"Well I was doing it for you. I didn't want you to feel guilty about Windy. I know it would be hard for you to be with me and then go home to her and pretend that nothing happened. I just didn't want you to go through that. I knew it was hard for you when we were in North Carolina. Like you said before, she's been hurt enough."

"You're amazing." I kissed her. "Even though I love you for thinking of me, and of Windy I really want you to stay. Having you here in my arms I realize how very badly I missed you."

She kissed me. "You're sure?"

"Positive." With my hands I held her hair back kissing her neck.

"Okay." She rolled off me and sat up. "Well then I'm going to go and take a shower. I went straight to the plane from work." She stood up.

"Alright, then I'll take it upon myself to order us some dinner."

"That sounds good."

I got up and hugged her. "Do you want anything special?"

"Anything you order is fine."

"Okay, go ahead and get in the shower." I kissed her lightly on the mouth then she grabbed her bag and went in the bathroom. I moved across the room and watched as she undressed. I saw her step into the shower and I started taking my clothes off as I followed her.

I slid the door open and she turned around smiling.

I slipped my arms around her waist. "I thought we would eat later." I started kissing the back of her neck and she reached around for the back of my head.

"Are you sure that you want this?" She laid her head back on my shoulder.

"I'm sure."

※   ※   ※

After the shower we ended up in bed. While we lay tangled in the sheets, I played with her feet that were on my pillow next to my head. With one finger I drew a line down the middle of her foot. "So are you hungry yet?"

"Starved. Did you ever get around to ordering room service?" She giggled and rolled over on her side.

"How could I have thought of food when I saw you standing naked in the bathroom."

She rolled back on her stomach and started massaging my calves. "So what you're telling me is that there's no food on the way and we have to lay here starving to death."

"Yep!"

She rolled over on her back laughing hysterically. "Come on and get dressed I'll take you out to dinner." She smacked my thigh lightly.

I knelt up and lay on top of her. "Where are you taking me?" I kissed her.

"I don't know, we'll find somewhere to go. Come on." She tickled my waist and rolled me off of her. "I'm starving."

"Okay, okay!"

We got dressed and headed out of the hotel finding a little restaurant and bar down the street, it looked nice so we went inside.

We ordered a vegetable pizza and a pitcher of beer then just sat there catching up. Ivy told me absolutely everything that has happened to her since the last time I saw her.

After we ate we sat there dinking beer, talking and of course laughing. I grabbed the pitcher and carried it up to the bar to get it refilled when I heard someone call my name. Turning around I just had a feeling I knew who it was, after all I didn't know anyone in New York except for…I smiled. "Lily! How've you been?"

"Good, by the way, you look great." She stared at me smiling.

"Thanks, so do you." I set the pitcher down on the bar.

She moved closer to me. "So what brings you to New York, and why haven't you looked me up?"

I laughed. "I'm here on business."

"So, why haven't you looked me up?" She set her drink down next to me and leaned against the bar putting her foot on the brass foot bar.

I looked at her leg smiling. "I just got in today." Staring at her I remembered all the fun we used to have. "You look fantastic as usual." I watched as the bartender filled my pitcher.

"Thanks, I really wish we could talk, I hate leaving things the way we did."

I stared. "That's in the past, don't give it a second thought."

She smiled. "Why don't you let me buy you a drink? Then maybe we can talk and who knows…" She moved even closer to me.

I paid the bartender then looked up. "Lily I'm with someone now."

She lowered her leg and picked up her drink. "Oh."

"Are you still married?"

She avoided my eyes, and then in the background I saw Ivy walking over. I smiled at her as she reached us at the bar.

She slipped her hand in mine. "Mel what's taking you so long?"

"Hi, I was just talking to an old friend."

She turned to look at Lily.

Lily was laughing. "Old! How dare you."

"Ivy, this is Lily."

Ivy looked at her smiling. "Nice to meet you. Excuse me for asking but do I know you from somewhere, you look really familiar to me."

Lily smiled. "I don't think we've met." Then she turned to me. "Well I'll leave the two of you alone." She smiled at Ivy then turned to me. "It was really nice to see you again." She stepped close as she hugged me, then whispered in my ear. "I really miss you."

I just smiled at her. "Bye Lily, it's been nice seeing you again."

She winked at me, then said goodbye to Ivy. As she walked away I turned and grabbed the pitcher of beer from the bar and looked at Ivy. "Come on let's go back and sit down."

Sitting at the table I poured our beers and looked up at Ivy. She was just sitting there grinning at me. "What?" I giggled.

"What? What?"

"What are you smiling about?"

"You."

"Why?" I laughed nervously.

"Bumping into an old girlfriend and you weren't even going to tell me." She leaned back in her chair folding her arms in front of her.

"I told you about her when we were in North Carolina."

"Yeah, but it took me going up to the bar to pull you away."

"Well I haven't seen her in a while."

"Come on, who do you think you're fooling?"

I laughed. "Oh stop it!"

"So what did she say to you when she hugged you?" She picked up her beer.

"Jeez, you don't miss a trick do you?"

"Nope."

"She just told me that she missed me."

"I didn't see you say anything."

I was giggling. "That's because I didn't."

"So you don't miss her?"

"No, I have you." We both took a drink of our beers.

She leaned in close and measured with her fingers. "Come on just a little."

"Ivy!"

"I want you to be totally honest with me." She sat back in her chair and picked up her glass.

"You sure?" She nodded her head as she drank. I looked back at Ivy. "We had some good times, I wouldn't be normal if I didn't. But that's all over now. I've got something much better with you." I smiled and stared in her eyes.

"I knew that you missed her, I could see it in your eyes. I'm glad you were so honest with me."

"What's that suppose to mean, that you could see it in my eyes." I smiled at her nervously

"Just that I could tell you're still attracted to her. I'm not worried though." She took another drink smiling. "I know that you love me."

I laughed out loud. "You're something else."

We sat drinking for a while then walked back to the hotel.

＊   ＊   ＊

I forgot how good it felt to rollover in the morning and have Ivy in bed next to me. I kissed her softly in the neck. "Morning."

"Mel what time is it?"

"Early. I'm going to shower; I have an appointment in an hour. Go ahead and go back to sleep."

"I can't now." She rolled over and hugged me. "Can I tag along?"

"Sure if you want. It might be boring for you though."

"If I'm with you it won't be."

"Alright then you better get up."

I was dragging Ivy all over New York, from one gallery to the next, from one auction to another and after calling Tara to check in, I turned to Ivy. "Come on I'll buy you lunch."

"I was wondering if you were going to slow down for a minute."

I laughed at her. "Just wait until this afternoon, I have even more stops to make."

She turned to me as we walked. "Maybe I'll take this afternoon to do some shopping. That is if you don't mind."

I laughed at her. "I told you it might be boring for you."

"It wasn't that bad, just exhausting."

I grabbed her arm. "Come on let's eat."

We sat and had a nice lunch. Talking for a little bit until I had to run.

Ivy went her way to do some shopping and I went mine. I told her I would meet her around 6:00 o'clock at the hotel then touched her lightly on the forearm telling her to be careful.

I finished everything I needed to and remembered Ivy was waiting for me, so I ran to her. Seeing my room number and reaching for the door handle I felt a smile take over my face, because I knew she was waiting for me on the other side. I walked in and heard the shower

running. I quietly set my briefcase down and walked into the bathroom.

"Ivy, is that you in there?"

She slid the door open. "Now I better be the only one that's in
your shower...Ever!" She laughed and held her hand out. "Join me?"

"Of course." I went into the shower with my clothes on.

She screamed. "You are too funny."

I soaped up a loafa sponge and turned her around so I could wash
her back. My hands wandered all over her body and I started kissing
her shoulder, slowly moving down her back until I knelt in the tub
turning her slowly at the hips.

I tasted her body as the water steadily beat down on my face. She
leaned back against the shower wall moaning softly as she tangled
her hands in my wet hair.

After I felt her body rush I stood and licked the water off her neck.

I rested my hands above her shoulders on the shower wall. "I
think I better get out of these wet clothes."

She reached for the buttons on my shirt. "Here let me help you."

After she undressed me she poured some shampoo in her hand
and washed my hair. With the shampoo dripping down my back she
massaged my shoulders. Her hands slowly fell down to my hips then
around my stomach. She rubbed the shampoo all over my body, her
hands sliding everywhere with the fragrance of the shampoo and the
steam of the shower invading our senses.

All I wanted was the feeling of her mouth all over my body.

She started with the spot right between my shoulder blades.

❧   ❧   ❧

Ivy sat behind me in bed combing my hair. "So what do you want
to do tonight?"

She got out of bed and grabbed the newspaper. I fell back on the
pillows and watched her. She is amazing; whenever she's around I
can't seem to focus on anything but her.

She turned around and looked at me. "What?"

"Nothing." I smiled. "It's just that when ever you're around I'm so happy."

She smiled. "I love you."

I stood up and walked over to her, taking the comb from her hand. "Why don't you go and get ready, we'll see a movie then grab some dinner. I have some phone calls to make."

"Alright, but don't be long." She kissed me gently on the mouth.

I sat down with the phone in my hand and watched her. Being with her made me feel so content. It's like she makes me whole. She makes me be only who I dreamt of being.

I called Tara getting all my messages, we talked for a while, and then I asked her if she heard from Windy, but she didn't. I told her I might be longer because after I leave New York I was on my way to Boston. There were a couple of artists there that I wanted to see.

I hung up with her then went to talk to Ivy. She stood putting on her make-up.

I leaned in the bathroom doorway with my arms and legs crossed and my head leaning against the wood watching her in the mirror.

"So are you all done with your business?"

"Yeah I'm done. By the way, when do you have to leave?"

She stopped what she was doing and looked up at me in the mirror. "Why, are you trying to get rid of me?"

"I think you know better than that." I smiled.

"I was going to talk to you about that. I'm probably going to have to leave tomorrow. I've got to get back to the hospital."

"Alright."

She spun around and looked at me. "What, that's it, alright."

"Yeah." I laughed. "I'm going with you, if that's okay."

I saw her eyes dance and a smile come over her face. "Really!"

I laughed. "I have some people I have to see in Boston."

She stood throwing her arms around me. "Great. This is turning out to be perfect."

"I know." I hugged her back. "Now hurry up in here so I could get ready."

"I'll just be another minute."

I pulled the towel off her as she turned to go back to the mirror. "Hey!"

I laughed and threw the towel at her, then went to go and find something to wear.

The night was perfect as was any night with her. We went back to the hotel room and fell into bed tired, but happy.

The next morning we laid around in bed eating breakfast and reading the paper until I had to leave. I got dressed as Ivy lay in bed watching the news.

I kissed her on the head. "I've got to get going, be good."

I reached for my briefcase and she jumped out of bed. She hugged me and dropped her robe. "Hurry back."

I slipped my hand around her waist. "Don't worry I will."

I kissed her then walked out the door stopping and turning around half way through. Taking one last look at her standing there naked, I threw my head back. "Phew, boy will I hurry." I closed the door behind me.

After several hours of buying, I called Ivy to check in. She was in the process of purchasing the airline tickets for us. I told her I'd be back in a couple of hours, and then hung up. I finished all the business that I could take care of in New York, and headed back to Ivy.

I burst through the door and saw her standing in the middle of the room. Her beauty took my breath away. I grabbed her around the waist and we both fell on the bed. "So when do we leave?"

"In a few hours. You have time to shower, and I'll order us some take out."

"Sounds great." I kissed her.

She crawled off of me. "Okay now go on so you have time to pack."

"You're just a slave driver." She stood above me pulling at my arms.

I eventually got up and somehow managed to drag myself into the shower. Standing there with my hands resting on the wall I let the water hit me in the face. I was thinking about Windy and how she was doing. I wondered if I should call her, then I remembered she said to call when I got back.

I stepped out of the shower and wrapped a towel around myself, then went to see what Ivy was up to. She had clothes already laid out on the bed for me and started to pack my bags. "Are you in a hurry or something?" I laughed at her.

"Yeah I am, what's wrong with that. Besides I can't wait to get you home." She hugged me. "Now you get dressed, our food will be here soon."

"Okay." I grabbed my clothes and went into the bathroom. When I came out we ate, then went to the airport.

We had a drink at the airport; it was then that I realized exactly how nervous I was. Not of being with Ivy, but being at her home, with her friends and family. It might be just a bit overwhelming. But as long as she's with me I'll be fine. I looked at her sitting across from me and felt happy and proud to have her there.

The plane ride was short but it felt like forever. I absolutely hate to fly. Once we landed in Boston we went straight to Ivy's apartment. She lives in the city in a huge loft.

I walked through her place looking around; she had big vaulted ceilings with hardwood floors. Her furniture was big and comfortable looking. Bookcases lined her walls filled with books, and her kitchen was huge and immaculate with everything lined in steel and glass. I stepped out onto the balcony and the view was spectacular.

Turning around with my hands leaning on the railing I smiled. "Ivy this place is great."

"Thanks, I like it." She came walking out on the balcony and hugged me. "Do you think you could live here?"

"I can live anywhere as long as you're there." I kissed her and she took my hands in hers. "Come on, I'll make us something to eat. You can pour the wine."

I followed her into the kitchen then picked a nice red wine while Ivy started making some eggplant. I poured us a couple of glasses, and then helped her with a salad. The whole night was pleasant and relaxing. After dinner we sat out on the balcony, staring out at the city.

We went to bed early.

CHAPTER 19

Waking up I felt surprisingly comfortable in Ivy's home. She had her arm stretched across me and I picked up her hand kissing it. "You better get up, your alarm's going off."

"Already." She rolled over pushing her hair off her face.

"Yeah, already. Come on I'll make some coffee." I started to get up then fell back down. "Except that I have no idea where anything is." We both laughed and she pulled me up.

We got up and eventually Ivy was off to work. I walked around her apartment and felt like I was in a different world. This was her world; I just hope that I'm able to fit into it. I called a cab and as I sat drinking my coffee waiting for it to show up, I thought about how drastically my life had changed.

I got up and walked out onto the balcony, looking out at the city of Boston. As I stood there I thought of Sarah, I looked up at the sky. "Is this what you had in mind for me?" I looked down and saw a cab pulling up. Grabbing my briefcase I ran downstairs.

I actually made all of my appointments, and then was on the phone the rest of the day. I got back to Ivy's place around 7:00 and she was already there. I walked in setting my briefcase on the table, and then went up to her hugging her.

"I didn't think you were coming back."

"You didn't huh." I put my arm around her waist and kissed her, and then we walked in the kitchen. "Do you mind if I use the phone?"

She turned to me. "Mel, feel free to use and do whatever you want." She kissed me and handed me the phone. "Here, if you need some privacy you can use the bedroom."

I kissed her. "There's no need for that." I sat down and opened my briefcase then started making calls.

Ivy came over and set down a martini next to me. "I went out and got olives today just for you."

I smiled up at her. "You didn't have to do that, but thank you."

I was on the phone until after 10:00 and Ivy was great. She ordered a pizza and most of the evening she sat on the balcony reading. I did manage to get everything done that I needed to get done.

The shipments should be rolling in any day now, and the gallery will be officially finished. I called Tara at home to tell her. Now all I have to do is go back home and perfectly place each piece in the gallery, then plan a grand reopening. Tara was excited about the reopening. I asked her again about Windy but she still didn't hear from her. When I was talking to her I told her I would try to be back in a day or two. I was actually pretty anxious to see how Windy was doing. Even though I was having a great time with Ivy. I just feel like I needed closure with that part of my life before I could really move on and be happy. I finally hung up with Tara then went outside to see Ivy.

I knelt down beside her, grabbing her hand. "I'm sorry that I've been busy all day and actually all night." I looked at my watch.

"That's okay, I understand. Here sit down next to me." She pushed a chair over to me.

I sat down and quietly stared out at the city. "Ivy I'm going to have to leave soon."

"I thought you would be."

"I'm sorry."

"Don't be. I know that you have things to take care of and I understand." She looked at me smiling.

I put my hand on hers. "Have I told you today that you're wonderful."

She smiled. "Let's go to bed."

I followed her back inside. Watching her walk I knew that I would follow her just about anywhere.

❦   ❦   ❦

I woke up with Ivy and made her coffee while she dressed for work. She handed me the cream. "So what are you going to do today?"

I picked up my mug. "I have no idea. I guess I'll make a few more phone calls and then maybe go for a walk."

"Why don't you meet me at the hospital for lunch today."

"That sounds good. What time?"

"About 1:00." She set her coffee cup down then walked into the bedroom. I followed her with my coffee in hand and watched every move that she made. I knew I would be going home and I wanted to have strong memories of everything she did in a day. She ran her fingers through her hair, checked her make-up then reached in her jewelry box and pulled out the bracelet I bought her.

I walked over to her. "Here let me help you with that." I set my cup down and fastened her clasp on the bracelet.

She kissed me. "Thanks."

"You're welcome." I followed her to the front door. "Have a good day honey." I kissed her.

She giggled. "Remember, 1:00 okay. I'll be waiting for you."

I smiled. "Okay." She kissed me then I watched as she walked to the elevator. When she left I sat on the couch throwing my head back. For some reason and all of a sudden I was in a terrifying state of confusion. I guess knowing that soon this will be my life is making my head spin, a new city, a new job, a new girlfriend everything is happening so fast.

I got up and poured another cup of coffee. This time I walked and sat out on the balcony. Sitting there looking around I knew I had to get back home. I think I just need to be in familiar surroundings for a while. I grabbed the phone and booked the first flight home in the morning, and then I got dressed and thought I'd do a little shopping before meeting Ivy for lunch.

I basically just walked around taking everything in. For some reason all I thought about was Sarah. Sarah always seems to pop into my head whenever I'm having some sort of crisis.

I walked thinking of her and how easy things used to be and how different they are now. Then I started thinking of Ivy and even though things are different now, I'm happy, really happy.

I walked a little further then caught a cab to meet Ivy for lunch. On the drive over I knew I had to tell Ivy I was leaving in the morning. I also knew she would be very disappointed, but I really needed to end this part of my life back home so I could go on and be happy with her.

I reached the hospital a little before 1:00, but Ivy was already standing outside waiting for me. Seeing her and walking up to her all my confusion seemed to slip away. Every time I see her I smile to myself, and just plain feel good.

"Hi, you didn't have to wait out here." I walked up to her and hugged her.

"That's okay. I didn't want you to get lost. Come on inside while I leave word where I'm going and when I'll be back."

We went inside and Ivy took me up to a desk where she huddled in a group talking. I immediately felt all eyes on me as I stood there. She then came walking back over to me grinning as she took off her lab coat.

"Ivy does everyone in this place know you're gay?" I walked beside her as I glanced back at everyone standing in a little group, smiling at us.

"Just about." She kept walking as she smiled.

"And what, they're checking me out."

"Yes." She laughed. "They were."

She put her coat in her office, and I turned my head slightly to see if everyone was still watching, and they were. Ivy came back out into the hallway.

I turned to face her. "What did you tell these people about me?"

"Not much." She grabbed my arm. "I just told them how wonderful you are, and how in love I am."

I laughed at her. "You didn't."

"I did. Now come on, I have only an hour."

We walked to a restaurant down the street and were seated right away. After we ordered I looked at Ivy. "So how's your day?"

"Mel, what's wrong?" She stared at me.

"What? What makes you think something's wrong?"

"I can tell."

"Really?"

"Yeah, so tell me. What's wrong?"

I looked down at the table smiling, then back up at her. "And I wonder why I love you." I smiled then got very serious. "I wanted to tell you I was leaving to go home in the morning."

"I figured that's what you wanted to tell me. That's okay. It's all a bit overwhelming isn't it?"

I fell back in the booth. "So it's not only me."

"No, I'm afraid too. But I do know that afraid as I am, I love you more."

I rested my hand on top of hers. "I might be gone a while."

"I'll be here."

"You sure?"

She smiled at me. "Don't worry. I'll be right here."

The waitress then came back with our food and we talked a little bit before we had to leave. The rest of the lunch hour we never brought the fact that I was leaving up again.

As we walked back to the hospital I asked Ivy if she wanted me to make her anything special for dinner tonight.

"I thought that we would go out tonight when I get home from work." She turned to me. "Is that okay?"

"Yeah, that sounds great."

I walked inside with her and she introduced me around a little bit before I left. When I got outside I caught a cab back to Ivy's place.

I went inside and decided upon a long hot bath. I took the phone with me thinking that maybe I would call Windy and tell her I'd be back tomorrow.

I slipped in the tub and dialed Windy's number. The phone rang then finally someone answered.

"Hello?"

"Hi, is Windy there?" I knew it was her mother.

"Who's calling please?"

"It's Mel, Windy told me to call her, is she in?"

I heard a sigh, then nothing. The next thing I heard was Windy's voice.

"Hi Mel, are you back already?"

"I will be tomorrow, that's why I'm calling."

"Okay when will you be back?"

"Around 10:00 in the morning."

"Good why don't you stop over around 12:00, is that okay?"

"Sounds great."

"Okay, I'll look forward to seeing you then."

"Okay, bye Win."

I hung up thinking that was way too easy. But I decided not to think about it anymore and just relax. I lay back in the tub reading one of Ivy's trash tabloids. Even though you know they're all lies you have to admit they are fun to read.

Just when I got to some story of some guy who had millions of tumors all over his body the phone rang. "Hello."

"Hi Mel, it's me."

"Hi, do you miss me already?"

"Sure do, I'll be home in a couple of hours, are you keeping yourself busy?"

"Right now I'm laying in the tub reading about tumor man."

"What?"

"Never mind. So what do you have planned for tonight?"

"It's a surprise."

"Oh, by the way how did I do?"

"How did you do?"

"Yeah, when everyone was checking me out, how did I do?"

She laughed. "You actually scored very high. I think the phrase was, 'she's a keeper.'"

I started laughing. "A keeper huh, well I guess that's good."

"Listen Mel I gotta go. I'll be home soon."

"Alright bye."

I hung up the phone and felt good. I think it was when Ivy said she'd be home soon. It feels good to have someone coming home to me.

After my bath I took my time getting ready. I packed everything then called a florist to have someone bring over flowers. I wanted the place filled with flowers when Ivy came home.

By the time she did come home I had a pitcher of martinis ready for her and flowers throughout the whole apartment. I heard her at the door and started to pour the drinks, when she came inside the look on her face was incredible.

First astonishment, then it turned to joy, then I don't know what happened but she started to cry. She dropped the bag that she was carrying and I walked over to her with a drink in my hand. "Do you like them?"

Her eyes just kept looking around the apartment. "I love them."

I handed her a drink, then kissed her lightly on the mouth. "Come on, sit with me." I opened up the balcony door and there were even flowers out there.

"Mel this is unbelievable. No one has ever done anything like this for me before. I wish you never had to leave."

She came up to me and hugged me, then went over to all the flowers and started smelling them. She turned and just stared at me. "I'm so happy right now. I feel like I'm in heaven and it's full of flowers." She ran up to me and hugged me. "Have I told you lately how much I love you?"

"You don't need to. Now you better go and get ready." I grabbed the glass out of her hand. "Go on, I have a bath ready for you. I'll bring your drink into you."

I stopped her just before going in. "Take your clothes off here."

"What?"

"Go ahead. I have a surprise for you in there."

She looked at me questionably, and then started to undress. She stood before me naked and I couldn't take my eyes off of her.

"Mel."

"Okay come on." I stretched my hand out. She grabbed it. "Now close your eyes."

"How did I know that was next?"

She closed her eyes and I looked at her to make sure they were closed then guided her into the bathroom.

"Mel what's that smell?"

"Just come on, I'll help you in the tub."

I helped her gently sit down and heard her moan softly, a moan of comfort.

"Open your eyes."

All I heard was Ivy taking the deepest breath of her life. "Oh Mel!"

I covered the bathroom in red roses and candles, and in the tub I put fragrant bath oil. She lowered herself in the water so it washed over her shoulders, and then rubbed her arms up and down.

I sat on the edge of the tub rubbing her shoulders. "Do you like it?"

"How could you even ask?" She lowered herself in the water again.

I walked out of the bathroom, only to return with Ivy's drink in my hand. "Here you go." I kissed her. "Enjoy."

"God I love you."

I smiled and walked out, then sat on the balcony feeling good about making her so happy. I relaxed for a while then thought about going to check on her, but thought I'd just let her be alone and enjoy it.

I got up to pour myself another drink when I heard a noise from the bedroom. "Are you all done honey?"

She yelled. "I'll be there in a minute."

I went back outside and sat down. Some time went by, then I saw her coming out of the bedroom. She looked amazing; she had on a little, tight, blue dress.

I took a deep breath. "Ivy, you're beautiful."

She lowered her eyes, then looked up at me smiling. I walked over and grabbed her hands lightly kissing her. I caught a glimpse of us in the mirror and we looked great together. She had on that little dress and I had on a white silk suit. The jacket was very low cut with nothing underneath and we just looked like we belonged together.

Ivy looked in the mirror. "We look great, don't we?"

"We sure do."

She looked back at me. "I really love what you did for me. This was so special."

"I'm glad you liked it."

She grabbed my arm. "I have a great evening planned for us."

We walked out of her apartment and stepped into her car. The restaurant was just fabulous. Afterwards we went to a great club. What she neglected to tell me was that all of her friends from work were there, it didn't matter though, and all that mattered was that she was there with me. We danced, we laughed and Ivy took her time introducing me to all of her friends.

We finally moved to a booth and managed to grab a few minutes alone. I rested my hand on top of hers. "I'm having a great time, your friends are fun."

She looked around. "Yeah, they are. They were dying for us to go out with them after they saw you at the hospital."

I smiled. "Oh yeah."

"I tried to get them all to go to a gay bar, but I had to draw the line somewhere."

We laughed as we leaned into each other. I then took the opportunity to lay my hand on her thigh.

"Mel!" She looked at me shocked.

I laughed. "Come on, you can't see, and who cares. It's not like no one here doesn't know about us."

"You're bad."

She then reached under the table. I expected her to remove my hand but she moved it up her thigh. I whispered in her ear. "You're the one who's bad."

Her friends came to the table and broke up our stolen moment. I watched as they dragged her to the dance floor. We partied until the place closed, and then I drove Ivy home.

I helped her upstairs, undressed her and put her to bed before she fell asleep. As I stood above her I laughed at what a good time she had.

I jumped in the shower then crawled in bed next to her. I lay there holding her, listening to her body, until I fell asleep.

CHAPTER 20

❀

I shook my head laughing as Ivy lay there sleeping. I didn't want to wake her because I knew when she finally did wake up, she'd be feeling rough. I don't think I've ever seen her drink so much.

I showered, dressed and drank about a pot of coffee before going to wake her up. I went in the bedroom and she was still fast asleep. I slowly sat on the edge of the bed next to her and put my hand gently on her shoulder. "Ivy." Still nothing. Again I shook her a little. "Ivy, are you going to get up? I'll be leaving soon."

She moaned softly, and then she rubbed her head with her hand as she rolled over. "Mel, what time is it?"

"Almost time for me to leave."

"Oh my God my head is killing me."

"Well it should be I never seen you drink so much."

She tried to sit up, then laid back down. "Jeez Mel, I'm sorry your last night here and I end up getting drunk and passing out."

"That's okay I had a blast watching you have so much fun."

I covered her with a blanket. "Why don't you lay back down? I'll call a cab to the airport."

She sat back up slowly. "No you don't, I'm going to drive you even if I'm sick the whole way there."

"Well that should be a fun drive."

She laughed. "Stop it, all I need is a shower and I'll be fine."

"Alright." I helped her up. "Do you want me to bring you some coffee?"

"No, but I'd love some ice water."

I laughed. "I should have known."

She managed to get herself in the shower and I came in with her water, handing it to her.

She reached for it. "Thanks." She drank the whole glass down and handed it back to me.

"Okay." I laughed. "Would you like another?"

"Please." She put her head directly under the water with her hands on the wall. I left laughing at her, and then came back with another glass. I also handed her some aspirin. "Here you go."

"Thanks."

"Take your time I'll be in the kitchen." I left then called Donna. Neither her nor Vicky were home. I started reading the paper when Ivy came walking out of the bathroom. I tipped the paper and looked up. "Do you feel any better?"

"Yeah, I do." She sat down.

"I've got about a half hour before I have to leave, okay."

"Okay." She rubbed her head with the towel. "I'll be ready." She looked at me. "Mel I'm really sorry."

I put my arm around her. "Don't give it a second thought." I laughed and kissed her. "Umm, tequila."

She smacked my arm. "I'm ready for coffee now."

"I'll get it for you." I got up and poured her coffee and let her relax for a while, while I put my bags in her car.

I came back up and she was already to go with her keys in her hand. "After much effort, I'm finally ready."

I walked up to her and hugged her, then kissed her. I saw a tear in her eye when I pulled away. "Ivy, don't start."

"I can't help it. I don't want you to go."

"I know, but I have to. It won't be long before I'm back to stay." I hugged her again so tight I thought I was going to squeeze every last breath out of her. "I better be going."

The drive to the airport was a scary kind of quiet.

Then while I waited to board my plane we still said nothing to each other. Ivy just held tight to my arm. I hugged her one last time with tears running down my face and looked into her eyes. "I promise you, I'll be back."

She just looked at me. "I love you."

"I love you too." Then I turned, and without looking back I walked on the plane.

I sat there wondering what was waiting for me when I landed. I laid my head back and closed my eyes. The next thing I knew, we were landing.

I opened my door and walked inside dropping my bags on the floor. It felt so good to be home. I went into the fridge and got out a bottle of water, then sat down on the couch and kicked my feet up on the coffee table.

I looked at my watch and figured I would leave for Windy's after I finished my water. The fact is I was scared. Scared of what I might hear.

On my drive to Windy's I felt incredibly nervous. I thought about what she was going to say to me, if she was going to tell me that she hated me or not. I don't know if I could handle it if she told me that she hated me. I pulled into her driveway and sat there a minute. I looked around and didn't see her mother anywhere; at least that was a good sign.

I slowly got out of the car and debated taking my sunglasses off, but decided to leave them on. I thought they might hide my lying eyes. I got halfway to the porch when Windy came out. I smiled as she met me in the driveway.

She grabbed my hand. "Let's go and sit out back, it's such a beautiful day."

"Okay." I looked at her not believing the change from the last time I saw her.

"So how was your trip?"

"I think you'll be happy with all my choices."

"I'm sure I will be."

We sat down at her patio table. "So Win, how do you feel?" I looked at her.

"I'm feeling good, thanks."

"Well you look good." I turned to face her and I don't know why, but I felt incredibly nervous.

She smiled. "Can I get you anything?"

"No, I'm fine."

"I'm really looking forward to coming back to work."

"Great you can help me plan the reopening."

"That sounds like fun."

"Good, it'll be fun working together again." I smiled at her, and then we both got pretty quiet.

We sat looking around, and then Windy started. "Mel, I don't blame you."

I looked up. "No?"

"No Mel I don't. It did take a while for me to realize that though, and I'm sorry for that." She leaned forward in her chair and rested her elbows on her knees. "Actually I didn't really blame you. I was just mad because you weren't there when I needed you most. But I realize now that it was wrong of me to be mad at all."

I moved closer to her and rested my hand on her arm. "Win I don't blame you for being mad at me, and there's no need for you to apologize to me. I can't say that I wouldn't have been mad either."

"I was just so hurt." She put her hand over her eyes. "I wanted you, I needed to have you hold me. I needed to hold you. What I needed was to feel safe again, and for me feeling safe is having you near me."

With her hand over her eyes she wiped the tears away and turned to me. "Mel, I was wondering if you would come to counseling with me. I think it will help and so does my therapist."

"Sure if it will help then of course I'll go."

She put her hand on top of mine. "Thanks."

I held her hand. "There's no need to thank me. You know I'd do anything for you."

"I knew you'd be great about this." She smiled at me.

"I missed your smile."

She stood. "Come on I'll walk you to your car."

Her hand slipped in mine and we walked to my car. I hugged her goodbye then closed my car door.

Her head lowered by my window. "I'll call you later, okay?"

"I'm going to the gallery, then I'll be home the rest of the night."

"Okay, bye Mel."

"Take care." I pulled away smiling.

As I drove to the gallery I knew I had to tell her about Ivy. I also knew I had to tell her soon. I didn't want her thinking there would be anything more between us than a great friendship. After everything she's been through I didn't know if she would be able to handle it.

I reached the gallery and went straight to my office. Picking up the phone I dialed Windy's number.

"Hello."

"Windy it's Mel, I know I just left but I really need to talk to you about something." I brushed my hair back as I closed my eyes because I really didn't want to do this.

"What is it Mel?"

"I can't do this over the phone."

"Alright why don't I come over to your house around 7:00."

"That would be great."

"Okay, I'll see you then."

I hung up and knew that I was doing the right thing, but boy did I feel lousy. My hands were sweating and my face was so hot I got up and walked around the gallery, when Tara came walking in.

"Mel I'm glad to see you're back."

"Thanks. The place looks great."

She looked around. "Yeah it does. So, have you talked to Windy?"

"Yeah, she might be back to work pretty soon."

"Mel, that's great."

"Yeah, I think it'll be good for her." I walked closer to her.

"I hope so."

"Come on and show me everything that's come in so far." I grabbed her arm.

"Alright."

We walked in the stock room and I instantly remembered the last time I was in here. It was when I was first leaving for North Carolina and I said goodbye to Windy. Tara was talking away and I barely heard a word she said.

"Mel!"

"Yeah." I looked at her as I spun around.

"Have you heard anything I said?"

"No I'm sorry. What did you say?' My hand ran through my hair.

Tara and I worked in the gallery until around 5:00 then we both left. I rushed home to shower and change.

After my shower I finally had some time to unpack. With everything that I put away there seemed to be a memory attached to it. Halfway through I had to quit because I was starting to miss Ivy terribly. I went downstairs and cut up some cheese and fruit for when Windy came, then made a pitcher of martinis.

Pouring myself a drink I looked at the phone and thought about calling Ivy, then decided to wait until Windy left. I walked outside and sat down at the patio table waiting for Windy to show up.

I was outside enjoying the fresh air when Donna came walking out. I watched her until she was right in front of me. "I tried calling you the other day, but there was no answer."

"I was probably at work. I've been putting in a lot of hours lately." She sat down next to me.

"Is that a good thing, or a bad thing?"

"Bad, definitely bad."

I laughed. "You want a drink I have more in the house?"

"No thanks, I'm fine. When did you get back?" She folded her hands in front of her and turned to me.

"This morning." I stared at her hands.

"Did you see Windy?"

"Yeah, but I still have to talk to her, she's on her way over now."

"So what did she say when you did see her?" She looked at me.

"She said that she's not mad anymore, and that she wants me to go to counseling with her."

"Did you tell her about what's her name, Eileen?"

"No I didn't, and her name is Ivy." I laughed. "I'm going to tell her when she comes over. I thought it would only be right for her to know, especially if she wants me to go to counseling with her. I don't want her getting the wrong idea about us."

"Well you're doing the right thing, but I wouldn't want to be in your shoes right now. How do you think she's going to take it?"

"I don't know." I looked up. "Well, I guess I'll find out, here she is."

Donna got up. "I'm going inside, if you need me or Vicky we'll be home all night, okay?"

I stood up. "Okay, thanks Donna."

I watched as Windy pulled in the drive. Donna walked up to her car and started talking to her as she stepped out. Then I watched Donna go inside looking back at me as she stepped through the doorway.

Windy walked towards me. "Hi Mel, you got one of those for me?" She pointed to my drink.

"Sure come on in." I walked inside and Windy followed behind me.

"Mel the place looks great." She turned looking around. "You really have done a lot with it since that first day I helped you move in here." She looked at me. "Remember?"

I stared at her smiling. "How could I forget, you helped me through a lot that day. I'll never forget it." We walked into the kitchen and I poured her a drink, and then freshened mine up.

"Here you go." I handed her, her drink and walked into the living room. "Windy please, come and sit by me."

She sat next to me on the couch. "Mel this feels good."

I looked at her. "We have to talk."

"Mel, I think I know what you're going to say." She turned to look at me and I saw sadness in her eyes.

"You do?"

"Yeah, you don't feel for me the way that I feel for you. Do you?"

I lowered my head, and then looked at her. "No." I started to wring my hands, and then I started to twirl my hair. "Windy there's more."

"Is there someone else?"

I looked in her eyes. "Yes, Win there is."

"Mel it might be for the best. You see I'm not ready for a relationship right now anyway." She looked away.

"You're not mad?"

"No, I need you to be my best friend right now, and that's it."

I moved closer to her and hugged her. "Windy you don't know how glad I am that I'm not hurting you." I stared in her eyes. "I would never intentionally hurt you." Although I knew I did. I could tell she was hurting.

"I know." She looked down, then up in my eyes. "Do you love her?"

"I do." I looked at her. "There's no one thing that I love about her though, it's her. It's everything. It's her whole package." I couldn't believe that I was telling her all of this, but I thought of Ivy and couldn't help myself, it just all came pouring out.

"Mel if you found true love, then I'm happy for you. I can't say that I'm not disappointed because I am, but if it's her that you want, then I'm happy for you, and she's a lucky woman to have you."

I put my hand on hers. "You're great." She smiled at me and I stared at her. "But Win, how did you know?"

"Well the first thing that gave it away was the fact that when you came back to see me from North Carolina you never said once that you loved me."

I looked down. "I'm sorry."

"Don't be." She lifted my face with her hand.

"But Windy I do love you. It's just different."

She smiled. "Mel it's okay, really. I just want you to help me through this, that's all. I still need you." She grabbed my hand and leaned into me.

My head fell to her shoulder. "I'll always be here for you."

"I know." She squeezed my hand. "Now come on, let's have a good time."

"Sure." I looked at her. "What do you say I take you out for a drink and a game of pool." I pulled her by her hand.

"I'd like that." She lunged forward.

We both stood, then I hugged her. "Windy, I'm so glad everything is going to be okay." I pulled away. "It is isn't it?"

"Of course." She smiled. "Let's go."

We walked out, and climbed in Windy's car. Before pulling away she turned to me. "Do you want to ask Donna and Vicky to come along?"

"Sure, if you want."

"Yeah come on, it'll be fun."

She beeped the horn and Vicky came out. Windy rolled down her window. "Mel and I are going to shoot some pool, would you and Donna like to join us?"

Vicky looked at me through the window.

I leaned forward. "Come on it'll be fun."

"Okay, let me go and ask Donna though."

We both watched as she jumped on the porch and went inside.

Windy turned to me while we sat waiting for them to come out. "So, what's her name?"

I looked around, then back in her eyes with a crooked smile on my face. "Ivy."

She turned away and I nervously looked out my window. Then she started laughing uncontrollably.

I turned to look at her. "What's so funny?"

"Ivy, what kind of name is that?"

I smacked her arm laughing. "I guess about the same kind of name as Windy."

"Touché"

I put my hand on hers. "I love you Win."

She turned and winked at me, smiling. "I know."

We all had a great time shooting pool, drinking but mostly we laughed. I think that's what Windy needed the most. Was to laugh.

The night was over and I turned to Windy while we sat in the driveway. "Win, I'm really sorry about everything and I mean that. I just can't seem to say it enough."

"I know you are."

I touched her face and let my hand rest there. "Goodnight Win."

I got out of the car and went to unlock my door, then turned to her and waved as I walked inside. I thought it was terribly sweet of her to sit there waiting in her car for me to get inside first.

Moving the blind I watched her pull away, then I went upstairs and fell on the bed. Lying there I knew I should call Ivy, but I was just exhausted, then I passed out.

CHAPTER 21

Surprisingly enough when I woke I felt pretty good. I went downstairs and called Ivy while I waited for my coffee to finish.

Finally after the sixth ring. "Hello."

"Hi hon."

"Mel, I was waiting for you to call yesterday."

I walked in the kitchen. "I'm sorry I meant to call, but there was a lot going on here."

"Did you talk to Windy?"

"I did, and everything went great."

"Really?"

"Yeah, I told her about you."

"You did?"

"First I went to her house and she wanted to tell me that she didn't blame me, nor was she mad at me anymore."

"That's great!"

I poured my coffee. "Yeah it was, then she asked me to go to counseling with her."

"She did?"

"She did and I told her I would, then I left to go to the gallery. The more I thought about it the more I knew I had to tell her about you. So I called her, and she came over last night."

"If I didn't know you so well, I might be jealous."

I laughed. "Anyway! She already knew."

"She knew?"

I sat down at the kitchen table. "She knew, and she wasn't mad. I could tell she was hurt but she wasn't mad. She wants a friend to help her get through this."

"Mel that's great, you've got to feel better."

"I do. Pretty soon I'll be all yours."

"I can't wait."

"Me either."

"Oh Mel, I gotta go my pager's going off, I have to call the hospital."

"Okay, I love you!"

I hung up the phone and not five minutes went by before it started ringing again. I looked to see who it was and then picked up. "Hi Windy."

"You know I hate those caller I.D.'s."

"Why?"

"Well you could act a little surprised. I was wondering if you would be willing to go to one of my counseling sessions today around 2:00?"

"Of course I will."

"Thanks Mel."

"Windy there's no need to thank me."

"Why don't you come by about quarter to?"

"I'll be there."

I hung up with her then left for the gallery. I spent the whole morning working with Tara. No matter what I did all I thought about was going to counseling with Windy. I was honestly terrified. The whole morning I felt nervous and scared. I had no idea why, all I did know was I was dreading this appointment.

Finally it was time. I drove over to Windy's house and by the time I got there I was almost in a state of panic. Windy was already waiting for me and when she saw my car she came walking down the porch stairs and across the grass. When she reached the car and sat down next to me I looked over at her.

"Windy I don't mind telling you I'm a little nervous about this whole thing."

"Oh Mel don't be, it's really not all that bad."

We still sat in her driveway. "Well maybe if I knew before hand what was going to happen it might make me feel a little more at ease."

She put her hand on my arm. "You don't have to say anything. I just want you there to support me."

"So this isn't a one on one session?"

"No, there's a group of about seven. Mel, have you been making yourself crazy all day over this?" She rubbed my arm.

"A little." I looked at her.

"You should have talked to me about this sooner."

"I probably should have. Well let's go before we're late, then every-one will stare at us when we walk in."

"Would you calm down?"

I laughed. "I am calm, this is calm."

We pulled away and for most of the ride we talked about work. When we stopped talking about work, we just didn't talk. I sat there wondering if we still had anything in common, or if we ever did to begin with.

CHAPTER 22

The counseling sessions with Windy turned out to be good for both of us. She talked through her fears of going back to the gallery and of being alone, and I talked through all of my guilt. I've gone to every session Windy's had for the last two weeks, and I really believe we both have benefited from it. She finally learned of all the guilt I carried around with me everyday, guilt from North Carolina as well as the guilt I felt by not being there when all of this happened.

The gallery is finally a go and we've made some plans for the reopening but not many, I want Windy to be there and feel secure about being there.

In the last two weeks I've gotten a lot of work done, but mostly I've taken care of Windy. When I wasn't with her I occupied my time by either riding my bike or playing basketball with Donna. Donna is all of a sudden on a fitness kick. She claims she needs to lose weight, although I don't see it. But whatever, the workouts if nothing else clears her head and mind from everything.

Sitting in my office I stared at the phone wondering if I should call Ivy now, or wait until I get home. We talk to each other everyday, it's hard, but we're really making it work. I put my hand on the receiver, and then heard a knock at the door.

"Mel." Tara popped her head in the door. "Windy's here."

I snapped my head up. "Really. I didn't think she was coming until later, and then I thought she'd call first."

"Well she's here now." She smiled at me.

I let go of the phone. "Okay." I jumped out of my chair and hurried out of the office.

I saw her just standing by the front door and walked to her. "Win I thought you would call first."

"I wanted to surprise you and to test myself to see if I was really ready to come back."

I watched her eyes were all over the place, then I walked up to her and grabbed her arm. "So what do you think?"

She looked around and her mouth was wide open. "This doesn't even look like the same place."

We walked around. "It's great isn't it?"

"It's fantastic!"

"Do you want to see your office?"

She turned to me. I didn't know if I should have asked or not. Maybe the memories were still a little too strong.

Then she smiled. "Mel I'm stronger than you think."

I watched her.

"I seen that look on your face. Like I'm still too fragile."

"Win I didn't mean…"

"Don't worry, come on." She tugged on my arm. "Show me."

We walked around then back to her office. I stood there a minute, and then opened the door. She slowly walked in as I stood aside holding the door. I didn't say anything I just stayed one step behind her as she walked around taking everything in. She then turned and looked at me, and I saw everything I ever loved in her. She was her old self again, she looked happy. I could see it in her eyes they danced with happiness.

"Mel I don't know what to say."

"You don't have to say anything." I smiled at her then walked up to her with my arms stretched out to hug her. I hugged her feeling proud in the fact that I made her so happy.

She pulled away from me. "Mel what ever happens between us I will always love you. I feel ashamed in the fact that I could even have been mad at you for what happened."

"Win, forget it." I hugged her. "I'll always be here for you I promise you that."

"And me for you."

I laughed at her. "Come on, why don't we start making some serious reopening plans here, that is if you feel up to it?"

"That's why I'm here. Let's go." She grabbed my arm and we were off. We spent the whole day and a lot of the evening working, and it felt great.

It felt like old times.

We planned to have the reopening in a few weeks, but what I was most excited about was that Ivy was coming in for the weekend. We planned this for weeks and I was going to make sure this was the best weekend of her life.

I spent days preparing for this, buying Ivy's favorite cotton sheets, stocking the refrigerator and planning every minute that she'll be here. While I was shopping for the sheets I stopped in a jewelry store searching for the perfect gift, and I found it. A fabulous diamond necklace that I know she'll love.

I stood at the airport anxiously awaiting her plane. When I finally saw her walking toward me I felt like a teenager. My heart was pounding so fast I thought it was going to leap out of my chest. When I reached her I hugged her so tight I actually felt our bodies become one. We were in each other's soul. I knew I loved her more than I ever thought possible, and God…how I missed her.

"Come on I want to get you home."

"I can't wait. I missed you so much."

I smiled at her as I helped her grab her bags.

We were home in no time, pulling in the drive I looked at her. "Well this is it. Home sweet home."

"Mel, it looks like a barn." She was laughing.

"It is."

"Cool."

"Come on leave your bags I'll get them later."

"I was planning on it."

We both got out of the car and as she walked in she turned around checking the place out. "Mel this place is great. I love it. I feel like I'm in the mountains or something."

"Can I get you anything?"

"A beer would be great."

I walked into the kitchen. "Are you hungry?"

"Yeah, actually I am."

"Alright." I walked into the living room and handed her a beer. "Let's catch our breath then I'll take you out to dinner." I put my arm around her. "How does that sound?"

"Good." She put her arm around my neck and kissed me.

I whispered in her ear. "You feel so good."

I slowly kissed her eye, and then her cheek, and then I kissed her passionately on the mouth and reached down taking her beer out of her hand, setting it on the table. With one hand sliding under her shirt on her bare back, my other was on her neck under her hair pulling her to me. Finally after weeks I felt whole again. I held her body, feeling her soft skin and listening to her soft moans of happiness and desire. With my hand I moved her hair biting and kissing her neck, while my other hand slipped in the waistband of her pants.

Ivy threw her head back. "Oh Mel I missed you so much."

I softly kissed her neck while both of my hands worked on the buttons of her shirt. Then both of our heads snapped up when we heard a knock at the door.

She looked at me. "Are you expecting anyone?"

"No I'm not." I fixed Ivy's shirt then walked to the door, checking through the blind before I opened the door. I turned back to Ivy. "It's Donna. I don't think I told her you were coming in today."

She laughed. "That's okay. I would like to meet her."

Smiling I opened the door. "Hi Donna."

She walked in then spun around to face me. "Mel I'm sorry. I didn't know you had company."

Ivy walked up to her with her hand stretched out. "Well if you ever see her with any other company then me, you be sure to let me know."

Donna took her hand in hers as she laughed. "You must be Ivy. It's nice to finally meet you."

"Same here, with you that is." She laughed.

"So Donna what's going on?" I looked at her and closed the door.

"I came over to see if you wanted to do something tonight?"

I looked at Ivy, she smiled and nodded her head yes. "We were going to get something to eat, you guys want to join us? Then we can go out after."

"I'll check with Vicky, but it sounds good to me." She stared at me grinning as she walked out the door.

I turned to Ivy. "I'm sorry, I really wanted this whole weekend to be just the two of us."

"Don't worry we have plenty of time, besides I'm looking forward to meeting your friends."

"You're sure?"

She walked up to me taking me in her arms. "Yes, I'm sure."

I kissed her lightly. "Why don't you go and take a shower and change. I know how Donna is she'll be here shortly with Vicky ready to go."

"Okay." She let me go. "Just direct me to the bathroom."

"Oh I'm sorry, come on." I grabbed for her hand. "I'll show you."

Knowing that Ivy was upstairs in my shower felt great. I fiddled with the stereo to find her 70's music; I wanted everything to be perfect for her. I grabbed a couple more beers out of the fridge then went upstairs. Ivy was out of the shower and drying herself off, when I wrapped the towel around her.

I walked in and handed her a beer. "Here you go." I took her hand in mine. "Come with me I have something for you."

"Mel there's never a dull moment with you."

I laughed. "It just feels so good to spoil you."

She stood in the middle of the bedroom. "Now close your eyes." She did and I took out the necklace I bought her and put it around her neck. Right away her hand reached up to feel it.

"Mel, what did you do?"

"Hold on, one more thing." I grabbed the towel from around her and let it fall to the floor then turned her to face the mirror. "Okay now open your eyes."

She stood there naked except for her diamond necklace.

I reached around her waist with my hands and rested my chin on her shoulder. "So do you like it?"

"It's unbelievable, but Mel you really don't have to keep buying me things."

"I know I want to."

She spun around and kissed me as she threw her arms around my neck. "I love that you spoil me. Is that horrible?" She stared in my eyes and I felt myself melting from her stare.

"Not at all." I fell back on the bed as I held onto her. She laughed and screamed at the same time. Feeling her naked body on top of me I wish we were just staying home tonight.

"You better get up and get dressed or we're not going anywhere tonight." She rolled off me with her arms still around me.

"You know Mel I can picture us 30 years from now still so happy, and so much in love."

"So can I."

I had to leave and go downstairs while Ivy got ready or we really wouldn't be going anywhere.

Just as I thought, Donna and Vicky were already knocking at the door. I opened it laughing while Donna stepped in.

"What are you laughing at?"

"Nothing, come on in Vic." They both walked in and followed me in the kitchen. "Anyone for a beer?"

"Yeah I'll take one." Donna turned around. "What about you Vic?"

"No I'm fine for now."

I looked at them in the kitchen. "Ivy will be down soon she's changing."

Vicky came walking up to me. "I can't wait to meet her Mel, she sounds great."

"Yeah she is." I looked upstairs to see if I could catch a glimpse of her. "Well come on let's go and sit down."

We all walked into the living room and when Ivy came walking downstairs all eyes turned to her. She had on beige slacks with a white silk blouse, plus she was wearing the necklace along with the bracelet I gave her.

I went up to her and reached for her hand, pulling her to me, whispering in her ear. "You look great." She smiled at me then we walked to meet Vicky.

Vicky walked up to her with her hand out. "You must be Ivy."

"And since I already met Donna, you must be Vicky. It's nice to finally meet you."

"Same here."

We sat around talking for a while letting everyone get acquainted. I kept a watchful eye on Ivy and it seemed like she was really having a great time. Both Donna and Vicky seemed to like her a lot, then I thought who wouldn't, she's perfect, or maybe I'm just a little biased. I stood up. "Is everyone ready to go?"

We all started walking towards the door when Ivy came up to me slipping her arms around my waist. "Your friends seem great."

I watched them as they walked to the car. "Yeah, they are. They have always been there for me and sometimes I'm ashamed to say, I need someone else to remind me exactly how great they are."

She smiled. "You're really blessed Mel."

I kissed her. "Sometimes I think so."

All of us piled in Donna's car. Sitting in the back seat I rested my hand on Ivy's thigh and kissed her cheek. "I'm glad you're here."

She put her hand in mine. "Me too."

That night we had a wonderful time. I basically sat back and took everything in, watching Ivy make everyone love her as much as I did. We had some drinks after dinner then headed for home. It was a very relaxing evening.

On the drive home I leaned over and kissed Ivy on the ear as I whispered. "I can't wait to get you in bed."

She turned to face me. When she kissed me I felt my heart pounding as I stared into her eyes, letting her see how much I love her.

CHAPTER 23

❀

Standing in the kitchen sipping our coffee I went up to Ivy and hugged her from behind. "Last night you were amazing."

She giggled. "Yeah I was, wasn't I?"

I hugged her tighter. "You're something."

The phone then started ringing. I looked to see who it was, and it was Windy. I looked at Ivy, wondering if I should answer or not, then I knew I had to. What if something was wrong?

"Hello."

"Hi Mel."

She sounded like something was wrong. "Windy are you okay?"

Ivy came walking over with a look of concern on her face.

"Mel, could you come over?"

"Is everything okay?"

"Please Mel, come over and hurry."

She hung up. I looked at Ivy. "I gotta go, is that okay?"

"Sure hon, is everything okay though?" She followed me to the front door.

"I don't know." I grabbed my keys. "I'll be back as soon as I can."

I ran and jumped in my car. While I drove all kinds of horrible things went through my head. I couldn't get there fast enough. It seemed like I hit every single red light there was. Finally I pulled in her driveway and Windy was sitting on the front porch.

I ran to her and knelt in front of her, putting my hands on top of her knees. "Win what's wrong? Are you okay?"

She looked at me with tears and fear in her eyes. I took my sunglasses off. "Win, talk to me. What's going on?"

"Mel." She lowered her eyes, then looked back at me. "I'm pregnant."

"What!"

"Pregnant Mel, I'm pregnant!" She wiped her face with a tissue.

"When you were in the hospital didn't they do tests not only pregnancy, but HIV and STD's?"

"They said it might have been too early for a pregnancy test though. All I know is that my period is never late, and I've already been showing signs of morning sickness."

"Did you see a doctor?"

"First I took one of those at home pregnancy tests and when it came out positive I made an appointment with my doctor, and sure enough, I'm pregnant."

"Oh Win." I sat next to her on the stairs and put my arm around her.

"Mel, what am I going to do?" She laid her head on my shoulder.

"I don't know, but what ever you decide I'm here for you." Tears came rolling down her cheeks and she covered her face with her hands.

"Mel could you stay with me for a while?"

"Sure Win, what ever you want, you got." I helped her stand up. "Come on let's go inside. By the way where is your mother?"

"She's out. She doesn't know yet. Please just stay with me until she comes back." She turned to look at me, and all I saw was fear in her eyes.

"Alright sure. Are you going to tell her?"

"No I don't think so. She's leaving in a few days. I'm not going to say anything until I know what I'm going to do first."

"That's a good idea."

We went inside and sat on the couch, then she laid down with her head in my lap.

"Mel, could I really love this child knowing how it came to be?"

"I don't know, you're going to have to figure that one out by yourself, no one can tell you how to feel. Although I think that you should start by thinking of this baby as an innocent part of you." I carefully stroked her hair then gently wiped the tears from her cheeks.

"I guess." She hugged my knees.

"If you think about it this child is as much a victim as you are."

"That's true, but every time I see it would I think about what happened to me and how it was conceived?"

"I think that's what you have to decide by yourself."

I stroked her hair until she fell asleep, then sat there with her until her mother got back.

Driving home I thought about how much she's been through and I didn't know if she could handle this or not. Putting myself in her situation I had no idea what I would do. I looked at my clock in the car and realized I was gone for about three hours. Ivy was probably going out of her mind with worry. I pulled in the driveway and sat there for a minute. Looking at Donna's house I wondered if I should talk to Vicky about this, after all she knows a lot about this because she deals with it everyday. Most of the abused children she counsels are girls who are pregnant from either incest or rape. I just didn't know if I should say anything or not. Getting out of my car I stood there trying to decide what to do, then Ivy came walking outside.

"Mel is everything okay?"

I walked up to her and hugged her. "No hon it's not."

We sat down outside. "Can you tell me about it?"

I looked at her and smiled. "I'm so lucky to have you."

She put her hand in mine. "Mel?"

"It's Windy, she's pregnant from the rape."

"My God!" She moved closer to me. "Is she okay?"

"No, she's confused, scared, worried and she has no idea what she's going to do." I looked down at our hands.

"Mel if you need to go back to her go right ahead, I understand."

I kissed her. "I love you." I smiled and brushed her hair out of her eyes. "Right now she's resting."

She put her arm around my shoulder. "Let's go inside."

We both got up walked inside and went straight upstairs to lie in bed and just hold each other. Lifting my head up from where I had it nestled in her neck I looked into her eyes. "Ivy, if it were you what would you do, and would you blame me for ruining your life?"

"First of all she doesn't blame you anymore, does she?" She looked at me.

"She says no."

"I'm sure she wouldn't say it, if she didn't mean it."

"I guess. It's just hard not to blame myself."

She played with my hair while my head rested on her chest, and my arms wrapped tightly around her waist.

"As far as what I would do. I don't know, I hope to God I'll never have to make that kind of decision."

"Yeah, I know."

We laid there for I don't know how long. Both of us fell asleep for a while then the phone woke us up. I jumped out of bed and answered. "Hello."

"Mel its Windy."

"How are you doing?"

"Okay, but my mother's driving me crazy."

"Well that's no surprise." I laughed.

"I was wondering if I could come over."

"Win." I didn't say anything. "Win, I've got company from out of town."

"Oh, your new girlfriend?"

She sounded disappointed. "Yeah." I looked at Ivy. "You can still come over. I really would like you to. That is if you wouldn't feel to uncomfortable."

"I don't know Mel, I don't want to intrude."

"You won't be." I stood up. "I'll even make us all dinner. What do you say?"

"Well I guess if she doesn't mind."

"Win you'll like her, she's great. You're my best friend in the whole world and I want the two of you to meet."

"I don't know Mel. This might be uncomfortable. You know I still care about you."

I didn't say anything. "Win, I love you, I want you here but only if you can feel comfortable being here."

"Is she there?"

I looked at Ivy. "Yes."

"Right there?"

"Yes."

"And she heard you tell me you loved me?"

"Yes."

"She's not mad?"

"Not at all."

"She must be great."

I winked at Ivy. "She is."

"Okay, I'll be there in a while."

"Great."

I hung up and stared at Ivy. "You don't mind do you?"

She hugged me "Not at all. I've actually been dying to meet her."

"You sure?"

"I'm sure." She kissed me. "Now why don't you go and take a hot shower. I'm the one who's going to cook dinner tonight."

I stroked her long curly hair. "I love you."

She smacked me on the butt. "Go while I figure out what I'm going to make."

I stood in the shower feeling guilty all over again about Windy. No matter what she says I can't get it out of my head that I'm some how responsible. I let the water rinse the shampoo out of my hair and down my body when I heard Ivy coming through the door. I didn't know what she was doing; all I saw was a black silhouette on the other side of the shower door.

She opened the door and stepped in. "I thought you could use some help."

I grabbed her, kissing her hard, then licked the water as it ran down her neck. Pulling her hair so her head leaned back, I kissed her on the mouth again. This time my hands grabbed at her body while I had her pressed against the shower wall. My mouth worked feverously on her neck and breasts as she pulled at my hair and moaned with delight. My fingers entered her body, making her pull my hair even harder, because she knew that the harder she pulled, the more frantic I got.

I raised my mouth to hers while my hand still worked her body. She had one foot up on the side of the tub and I lowered myself to kneel in front of her. The water turned ice cold and I pushed her hands to play with her breasts as I licked and tasted every part of her. I watched her hands pinching and pulling her nipples, and then they suddenly fell to grasp my head. She pushed my face into her until I could barely breath, and she screamed louder then I ever heard her before. Her whole body shuddered and she pulled me back up to her mouth.

I stood before her and turned the water off.

"Mel, I came up here to surprise you, but wow, what got into you?"

"I guess I just didn't want what happened to Windy, to happen to you. That is, I don't want to hurt you. No matter what, I want to give you all the love that you deserve. I never want you to doubt how I feel about you." I fell into her.

"I don't, I never will." She hugged me tight.

She pulled me to my bed, and then pushed me down. While she made love to my body I laid there thinking how much I love this woman.

We both dressed then went downstairs. Ivy started cooking while I paced and waited for Windy.

Ivy yelled from the kitchen. "Don't worry she'll be here soon and everything will be fine. Trust me."

I looked at her smiling. "You know that I trust you, I just hope that everything turns out alright."

"It will. Does she like Mexican?" She looked up at me smiling.

"The hotter the better."

She smiled. "See we're going to get along great."

I smiled at her. "You know you really are being great about this."

She smirked. "I know, now come on and help me chop vegetables."

She grabbed me by the waist and pulled me in the kitchen. We laughed for a few minutes, and then I heard a knock at the door. I turned to Ivy and reached my hand back. "Well, come on."

She took my hand and when we reached the door she let go.

I opened the door and immediately hugged Windy, then stepped aside as she came in.

Ivy looked at her and smiled. "Hi, I'm Ivy." She reached her hand for Windy's.

"Ivy, nice to meet you. As you probably know already I'm Windy."

I grabbed Windy's shoulder and smiled. We all walked in and sat down. I got everyone drinks and it wasn't long before we were all laughing out loud. I excused myself and Windy told Ivy what she called, stupid Mel stories. I stood in the kitchen and watched them, if you didn't know better you would think they were best friends the way they laughed and joked and pushed each other around, you actually would think that they knew each other for years.

I walked into the living room. "Hey can anyone join in?"

Ivy stood up laughing. "Sure." She moved over and then pulled me to the couch. "We were just talking about you."

"I'm sure you were. Windy what have you been telling her?"

"Oh nothing that bad."

They both laughed and I just looked at the two of them thinking this is too weird. Ivy then got up to get dinner.

I looked at Windy. "So?"

"Mel she's great. I can see why you love her." She looked at Ivy in the kitchen.

"Yeah she is, but I was referring to whether you have thought about your problem or not?"

She looked away. "No, I haven't. I'm here because I don't want to, not yet, not today."

"I understand. So you like her huh?"

"Yeah I do, she's great."

Windy and I talked about work until Ivy called us for dinner. We all ate slowly while we talked until the late hours of the night. Windy looked at her watch then stood up to say she was going home. I stood to walk her to the door.

Ivy got up and hugged her. "Windy it was really nice to meet you. I hope we can become great friends."

"We will." She looked at me. "We have a lot in common."

Windy then grabbed my arm and Ivy started to clear the table. I walked Windy to her car and stood leaning against her door. "Win I had a good time tonight."

"Me too. Mel she is great and she really loves you."

"I'm glad that you like her. Your opinion means a lot to me."

"Well then I can't stand her and you should get rid of her." She laughed.

I hugged her. "I love you Win."

"I know."

I watched as she pulled away. Going inside I stood behind Ivy tightly wrapping my arms around her waist. "This was a great evening."

"It was." She touched my hands. "She's nice Mel, I mean really nice. Now I understand your guilt."

I kissed the back of her head. "Let's go to bed."

CHAPTER 24

❀

I vy and I sat in the kitchen talking over stacks of cinnamon apple pancakes. We talked mostly about Windy. Ivy agreed when I wanted to spend as much time with her as I could until she makes some sort of decision, then I just stared at her, wondering how I got so lucky.

Together we did the breakfast dishes then lay on the living room floor. I held her tight knowing she had to leave soon, but not wanting her to.

I turned to her. "Our reopening of the gallery is pretty soon, can I count on you to be my date?"

"Try to stop me." She hugged me and kissed my ear. "God I wish I never had to leave you. I could see myself being here with you for a long time." She looked around.

"I could see you here too."

We lay there holding each other until it was time for her to leave. She was already packed so I just carried her bags to the car then came back inside.

Ivy pinned me against the door. "How long do we have?"

"Ivy I don't know, you don't want to be late."

"Maybe I do." She threw her body against mine, kissing me, as her hands ran through my hair. Her one hand was behind my neck under my hair pulling me to her while she kissed and bit my neck. I threw my head back closing my eyes as my hands tangled in her hair.

I hugged her head. "Ivy, there's no time for this."

She kissed me then slipped her hand down my shorts. With my head back and my eyes closed I finally thought about nothing except how great I felt. She kissed my mouth and I whispered to her. "I'm addicted to you, I don't know what I'd do without you."

"You're never going to have to worry about that while I'm still alive."

I pushed her back lightly. "Why would you say that?"

"What?"

"Never mind, we better get going so you're not late." I grabbed both of her hands. "Come on let's go."

"Mel what's wrong?" She was staring in my eyes.

"Nothing I'm sorry." I looked down at the floor.

"Oh Mel, I'm sorry I just realized what I said. I'm not going anywhere though, you have to realize that." She lifted my face up to look at her.

"You don't know that." I felt tears in my eyes.

"No I don't, but I can't control what's going to happen, we can't live in constant fear. I'm not Sarah, I'm not sick."

"I know, I'm sorry." I swallowed hard. "I guess I'm just scared, things are just so good it feels like it can't possibly be this good all the time."

"Mel it can, and I'm going to prove that to you."

I hugged her. "We really should be going."

"Okay." She smiled and kissed me.

After seeing Ivy off I went to see Windy. Before I had a chance to knock, she came out. "Come on Win." I grabbed her arm. "Let's go for a walk."

She smiled at me. "Alright."

"So did you tell your mother yet?"

She looked at the ground. "No I haven't, but I think I have made a decision."

I looked at her. "You have?"

"Yeah." She stopped and turned to me. "I've been up all night thinking about this. Mel, it's just a baby. I don't blame it for what happened. This baby didn't choose to come into this world but now that it's going to, he or she deserves everything I can do for it."

"That's true."

"I think what's best for me is to have this baby. I've really thought long and hard about this."

"Win that's great." I felt a huge smile come over my face.

"Will you help me?" She grabbed my hand.

I turned to face her. "You know that I will."

"I mean everything Mel, doctors appointments and all. You better think about it before you answer."

I put my hand on her face. "Win, I don't need to think about it, of course I'll be there for you, through everything."

"What about Ivy? Won't it bother her just a little bit?"

"You know how great she is, she would love the idea."

"Mel I don't know how to thank you. I don't know what I'd do without you."

"You'll never have to find out."

"So where is Ivy anyway?"

"I just dropped her off at the airport."

"I like her, she's really nice. Is she coming in for the gallery opening?"

"She wouldn't miss it, but do you still want to open on time?"

"Why not?"

"I don't know how hard this pregnancy is going to be for you."

She laughed. "Mel I'm just pregnant. I'm looking at this as a blessing. Believe me I know that the circumstances aren't the best but this child is already a part of me. It's strange but I can already feel it alive inside me."

I hugged her. "I'm so happy for you. Actually I envy you. Win you're going to be a mother." I smiled at her. "Congratulations."

"Thanks." She smiled. "A mother…Wow!"

"So?" I grabbed her hand. "When is our first doctor's appointment?"

I was swinging her hand as we walked, then she grabbed my arm. "In a couple of weeks."

"Great, I'll be there. I'm really looking forward to this."

"You are so good to me."

We walked for a while making some more plans for the gallery reopening. We also talked baby talk. I haven't seen her this excited about anything in a long time. She literally beamed when she talked about the baby. I really think this is going to be good for her.

In the coming weeks we worked constantly in the gallery preparing for the reopening. In that time we also went for Windy's first ultrasound, it was also the first time we got to listen to the baby's heartbeat.

I held Windy's hand as we stood in the doctor's office. "I'm so proud of you."

"Mel did you hear that. That's my baby." She looked up at me. "I'm so glad that you're the one who's here with me."

"Me too Win." I looked at her and never felt more proud of her. This is probably the hardest thing she's ever going to have to go through, and she's doing great. I plan on being by her side the whole time, and after the baby's born I will be there whenever she needs me. I'll be there for her and I will always take care of her baby as if it's my own.

On the way home from the doctor's office Windy surprised me with a picture of the baby. I told her as soon as I got home I was going to send it to Ivy. She looked at me and grabbed my hand.

"Ivy is really being great about this, even though I hate to say this, I really like her a lot."

"What do you mean, you hate to say it?"

"Come on Mel you know that I've been secretly hoping…"

"Win." I looked at her.

"I know. I love Ivy too." She looked at me. "Bitch!"

"Windy!"

She started laughing. "Why don't you take me out tonight for a big dinner?" She patted her stomach. "You know the old saying…"

At the same time we said. "Eating for two."

We laughed. "Okay. I'll pick you up in a couple of hours."

"Why don't I just stop by and pick you up."

"Alright but why?"

"I'm going out shopping this afternoon."

I laughed at her. "I can see now this baby's going to be spoiled to death."

She smiled. "Why shouldn't it be?"

"Why indeed."

I went home to get a quick workout in before going out with Windy, but first I wanted to call Ivy.

"Ivy." I sprawled out on the couch.

"Hi babe. I was hoping to hear from you."

"Oh yeah…why?" I twirled my hair and stared at the ceiling.

"Is the fact that I miss you enough."

"Yeah, but it sounds like more."

"It might be."

"So." I crossed my stretched out legs and grinned.

"Well…"

"Come on."

"I can't, not yet maybe when I come in for the reopening."

"Okay, well you really have to hear this." I sat up.

"What?"

"I just got back from the doctor with Windy and we both heard the baby's heartbeat. I also have a surprise coming in the mail to you."

"A picture?"

"How did you know?"

"Mel, I'm a doctor."

"That's right. Hey Ivy, Windy asked me today if this bothers you or not, does it?" I sat back and threw my legs up on the coffee table.

"Mel." She sighed on the other end of the phone. "You know I'm okay with this. As a matter of fact I'm better than okay with this. I love the fact that you're helping her so much. I know, and am very secure in the fact that you love me."

"You are so great. Why don't you come early for the reopening?"

"No, that wouldn't be good, but I can definitely stay later."

"Great. I love you. I'm going to go for a bike ride."

"Alright, be careful."

"I will."

I hung up with her and went for a great ride. I really felt good when I got home. After a shower I waited for Windy while I opened a bottle of water. I heard a light knock at the door and sure enough it was Windy standing there with a million bags in her hands. I opened the door and helped her carry everything inside.

"Hold on I'll be right back." She went back outside then came back carrying armloads of Chinese food.

I laughed. "I thought I was taking you out to dinner."

"Well I was craving Chinese. That's okay isn't it?" She set everything on the table.

"Sure, Chinese is great."

We sat around the rest of the evening eating and talking. She showed me everything she bought for the baby. She really was excited about this and I was never happier for her.

"Mel there's another reason that I wanted to come over here tonight."

I looked at her. "There is?"

"Yeah, I didn't forget you know."

Staring at her I smiled and felt tears starting to form in my eyes. "If it's okay I won't be at work tomorrow."

"That's fine I understand. Does Ivy know?"

"No, actually Win I think you're the only one besides me that remembers."

She moved to sit next to me on the couch putting her arm around my shoulder. "You know I'm here if you need me."

"I know, but I just really want to be alone."

"Okay, well I better be going. I'm pregnant and I need my rest."

I laughed at her, then hugged her goodbye and walked her to her car. I watched her pull away then headed upstairs to bed.

CHAPTER 25

*D*riving in my jeep I let my head fall back because the bright sun felt good on my face. I drove to the nearest florist and picked out two-dozen of the most beautiful yellow roses they had. Back in the car I drove thinking about all the things that have happened to me in the last year. I had to laugh out loud at some of the times I had with Lily. God, she always made me laugh. We barely had one serious moment between us. I'll never deny the fact that I had a great time with her. I knew when we first met it probably wouldn't last, but we always had a laugh when we were together. She was fun even when she was tying to be serious. Life with her would most definitely have been a roller coaster ride. I'm still not mad at her for what happened. I just really hope she finds what she wants out of life, she deserves it, she really does. As I rode I smiled thinking of her and feeling good inside.

From Lily I thought of Windy and how much that poor woman had gone through. But maybe it was all suppose to end up this way, Windy a mother, she would be great.

Getting out of my car the walk felt good. The sun was even warmer than when I first left. I laid the flowers down as I rubbed the letters on Sarah's stone.

"Hi babe, you know I wouldn't forget, how could I. I love you so much." I sat down on the cold ground. "You probably know already.

Windy's pregnant, Sarah she's going to be a mother. I'm helping her through all of this." I smiled at the sky because I missed her so much, but I also felt so happy. "Honey yesterday we heard the baby's heartbeat, it was amazing. It was the most beautiful thing I ever heard. Then we saw the baby. Sarah it was just amazing. I've never seen such a thing. It makes me think of when we used to talk about adopting." I looked at the ground. "I really wish we would have, I could be raising our child right now." I rubbed her stone then I felt the coldest breeze on the back of my neck. I turned around smiling because I knew. "Sarah!"

"Hi honey." She stretched her arms out and came walking towards me.

I ran to her and when I reached her I was almost afraid I wasn't going to be able to feel her. But I did, I could feel her, I could even smell her. It felt like we were never apart. As I hugged her I brushed her hair aside and stared in her eyes. God I would always melt in those eyes. I leaned in and kissed her and it was everything that I remembered.

I brushed her hair over her shoulder and kissed her ear. "God Sarah, I missed that, I miss you."

"I know I miss you the same."

We kept hugging each other. "Sarah I'm afraid to let you go. I don't want you to leave."

"Mel I'm glad you came today. Today's been one year."

"I know honey." I picked up the roses and handed them to her.

"Mel, they're gorgeous." She lifted them up to her face and smelled them. "They smell so good."

"Mel today is our last day."

"What does that mean?"

"After today I'll never see you again."

"What?"

"After today you'll never see me again. Although you know that I'll always be here for you."

"But why?" I stared in her eyes.

"My year's up."

"So how long do we have?"

"Until midnight."

"Can you leave here?"

"I can, the only trick was that you had to come to me first."

I grabbed her hand. "Let's go." We walked to the car and she crawled in. I knew exactly where I was going to take her first. I held her hand as I drove.

"Mel, are you taking me home?"

"Well I'm taking you past our old house, you know that I don't live there anymore."

We drove by our old house and sat in the car across the street while we watched a bunch of kids playing in the back and the front yard. I held tight to her hand. "See honey I told you I would pick the perfect family to live in our house."

"I knew that you would. I never had any doubt." She turned to look at me.

I lightly rubbed her face with my fingers. "Now I'll show you my new home."

"Could we go somewhere else first?" The way she looked at me I knew I could deny her nothing.

"Sure what ever you want."

"Okay drive straight for a while."

We drove for a while talking about everything and anything. I just wanted to hear her voice.

She pointed. "There Mel, pull over here I want to go there."

"Sarah, this is just an empty lot. Why did you want to come here?" I turned to look at her.

"Mel, look at the view. Can't you look at this view forever, with the lake right here this place is really perfect."

I put my arm around her from behind. "It is beautiful here."

"Mel I could stare at this sky for hours."

"Yeah. So could I." We both sat down on the grass and Sarah lay back in my arms. I held her as tight as I could for a few hours of total bliss, then I stood and held my hand out to her. "Come on, let me get you home." She put her hand in mine and stood in front of me. She was so close I could feel her breath on my face. I stroked her face with my hand and stared into her soul through her amazing eyes. I slipped my arm around her delicate waist and we walked back to the car.

We pulled in the driveway and Sarah turned to me smiling.

I squeezed her hand. "Come on I can't wait to get you inside in front of the fire." We were in front of the door when I heard Donna coming.

I looked at Sarah. "Can anyone see you?"

She smiled. "Only you babe."

I looked over at Donna. "Donna, hi."

"Mel, are you okay?"

"I'm great, why?"

She stared at me strangely. "It's just that Windy called me to come over and check on you. She reminded me what today was. Mel I'm sorry that I forgot."

I put my hand on her shoulder. "Donna that's okay, really. There's no need to worry about me. Okay."

"If you say so."

"So. Now I'm going inside. I'll see you tomorrow."

"Okay." She stood there and watched as I went inside.

When Sarah and I stepped inside we both started laughing and she fell into my arms. I hugged her tight. "I can't believe this honey, it's like you never left me."

She giggled as she hugged me. "I never have."

"Do you want a beer?"

"A beer, I'd love one."

I went into the fridge and pulled out a couple of beers. Sarah walked over by the stereo and turned it on. It was still on the 70's station from when Ivy was here.

She looked at me smiling. "I love this music."

"I know." I stood there smiling and laughing at her as she sang and danced around the living room. She grabbed my hand and pulled me to dance with her. I wondered what Donna would think if she came walking over to see what I was doing with the music so loud. I told Sarah and we laughed out loud while we danced and held each other. The phone started ringing and I grabbed a hold of the cord unplugging it. Then went back to Sarah.

She had her arms thrown around my neck. "How about another beer?"

"Tonight, anything your little heart desires." She smiled and kissed me.

"I'll be right back." I turned around and walked into the kitchen. As I stood there I watched her still dancing and singing loudly. All I could remember right now was all the fun we had together. It was like no one else existed but us. I wish my life would stay like this forever. I smiled to myself, I love her so much.

"Mel, what's keeping you?"

"I'm coming." I walked back to her handing her a beer. "Aren't you tired yet?"

"Not at all."

I watched her laughing, then after a while she fell next to me on the couch. "Okay I'm tired now."

"Well you should be."

"Sarah." She turned around. "I'm going to go and take a shower you'll be here when I get back won't you?"

"Yes, I'm all yours until midnight."

Her eyes smiled at me and I ran to take the fastest shower ever. I threw on some sweat pants and a t-shirt, then ran downstairs. I looked around for Sarah and got frantic when I couldn't see her.

"Mel, are you done already?" She came walking from the kitchen.

"I couldn't see you, I was afraid you were gone."

"I was just making your favorite."

She held up a martini glass. "Here try this." She walked up to me handing me the glass.

I took a sip. "You always did make a better martini than I could."

She smiled and picked up her own glass then we walked into the living room. Sarah sat on the couch while I built a fire.

"Mel this place really is nice."

"Yeah, I really like it." I looked around.

"Maybe you should think about getting your own home though."

"I've been thinking of that a lot. I would love to build my own house."

"Why don't you?"

"I don't know where I'm going to be living."

"You'll know soon enough."

"Are you trying to tell me something Sarah?" I grinned at her.

I threw some pillows on the floor and lay down next to her, in front of the fire. I held her so tight knowing this would be the last time. We said nothing and my head rested on her stomach, with my arm around her hip. She stroked my hair with one hand; while she sipped her drink with the other I couldn't stop smiling I was in total bliss.

I stood then looked down at her. "I'll be right back." I ran upstairs.

I returned grinning in front of her. "I have a surprise, your favorite thing."

She smiled up at me. "Mel!" She stood. "Monopoly?"

I pulled it from behind my back. "What else."

She went in the kitchen and came back with the pitcher of martinis, then jumped on my back. "Remember I'm the shoe."

I laid a blanket on the floor and went to get plenty of logs for the fire. When I went outside Vicky was walking to her car.

"Hey Mel." She came walking up to me. "Donna told me she talked with you earlier."

"Yeah, she did." I just kept picking up logs.

"Are you okay?"

"Vicky I'm fine. The truth is I'm great." I looked up at her.

"Are you sure?"

"Yeah Vic, thanks for caring but I'm okay, really." I couldn't stop smiling.

I finished picking up my wood then turned to go inside. I waved to Vicky and walked through the door.

I opened the door and once I was inside I fell up against it.

Sarah turned to me. "Mel what's wrong?"

"It's Vicky she thinks I'm losing my mind."

She laughed. "Why didn't you tell her I was in here waiting for you?"

"Oh right, that would go over big."

We laughed and I put the wood next to the fireplace, and then turned to Sarah. "Are you ready?"

"Ready."

We played Monopoly, we laughed, and we drank. While we played I laid there watching her and nothing about her changed. Her smile, her laugh, everything that I ever loved about her was still there.

She sat with the glow of the fire on her face and shadows dancing in the background, she looked as beautiful as ever. I sat up and ran my fingers down her face, while I stared in her eyes. I felt tears forming, and then felt them running down my cheeks. Sarah reached with her fingertips and touched my tears, then leaned forward and kissed them away.

I closed my eyes and put my hand gently around her neck kissing her like I've been dreaming of for the past year.

I looked in her eyes, then brushed the Monopoly game aside with one arm while I gently laid her down. "Sarah I'll never love anyone the way that I love you."

"I know."

I kissed her then laid on top of her burning her beautiful face into my memory. The glow of the fire struck her so perfectly; I never wanted to forget the way she looked at this moment.

She reached up with her hand and touched my cheek gently. "Mel." She ran her fingers over my lips. "Make love to me."

I closed my eyes and lowered my head to kiss her. My hand traveled down the side of her body, stopping at her thigh and pulling her leg up, putting it around my back. With one arm around the small of her back and the other around her neck I held her tight. She held me just as tight with her arms and legs.

After hours of lovemaking I felt like I could sleep forever. I could barely keep my eyes open. My head was on Sarah's stomach while she played with my hair. "Sarah I'm so tired, I can hardly keep my eyes open."

"Go to sleep honey." She stroked my head.

"No I don't want to."

"Don't fight it Mel, go to sleep baby. Dream of what a perfect love we had. Dream of your future Mel, dream of your happy home." Her hand slid through my hair. The sensation was so soothing I could feel myself drifting off. "Don't forget Windy. She's going to need you, don't disappoint her."

I fell into the deepest sleep I've ever been in.

❧   ❧   ❧

I woke up freezing on the living room floor. It was just before sunrise and I made some coffee then walked back into the living room looking around. I rubbed my head, 'Jeez I must have drank a lot last night.' I looked around and picked up the empty martini pitcher and glass. Going back in the kitchen I poured a cup of coffee then went outside. I sat at the patio table with my feet kicked up on a chair watching the sunrise.

As I sat there I couldn't remember anything from last night. The last thing I remember is going to the cemetery.

I watched the sunrise and thought I'd go for an early morning bike ride. I went inside and poured another cup of coffee when I saw something next to the coffee maker. I reached for it knowing what it was right away it was the shoe from the Monopoly game. I looked at it as I turned it in my fingers. How on earth did this get down here? I held it in my hand and thought about how every time Sarah and I played Monopoly she always had to be the shoe. I laughed at the memory then I put it in my pocket, and poured another cup of coffee.

I carried my coffee upstairs and sat at the edge of my bed. I took the shoe out of my pocket and stared at it, when all of a sudden I had a sharp image of Sarah with a glow surrounding her. It seemed so vivid, I smiled shaking my head then put the shoe in my jewelry box and changed.

The whole time I rode my bike I had thoughts of Sarah for some reason I couldn't get her out of my mind. I kept picturing her face, but it was so dark, I could barely see her. I kept trying to focus on her while I rode. With all these memories of her I was turning the corner for home before I knew it.

As soon as I stepped through the door I called Tara at the gallery and told her I wouldn't be in.

I hung up with her and went to take a shower. I stood and let the hot water run down my face and work its wonders on my tired body.

Wrapping a towel around myself I walked in the bedroom.

Standing in front of the mirror I dropped the towel to change and I saw what appeared to be a sucker bite on my collarbone. I knew it couldn't be, Ivy hasn't been here for weeks. I shrugged it off and threw some sweats on going downstairs.

When I reached the bottom I looked up the stairs remembering the shoe, then went into the kitchen. I made some more coffee and sat with my photo albums. I reached for a video tape of me and

Sarah on vacation but before I played the tape I ran upstairs, and in the back of my closet I took out Sarah's pillow, which I had tucked away back there.

I ran downstairs and sat on the couch clutching Sarah's pillow while I watched the videos. I watched and flipped through the photo albums with tears rolling down my face. After a while the photo albums dropped from my hands and I clutched her pillow laying my head down as I cried myself to sleep.

I awoke still holding Sarah's pillow stained with my tears. I got up getting a bottle of water from the fridge then went back to the couch. Lying there I watched video after video with tears running down my face. I couldn't understand why all my memories and feelings for her were back, and so strong. It must be the one-year anniversary of her death.

I got up again to get a beer out of the fridge and when I opened the door a single yellow rose laid next to the grapefruit juice. I sat on the floor of the kitchen totally freaking out. I screamed for her to show herself. I squeezed the rose so hard the thorns pierced my skin and blood trickled on the floor while I screamed for her. I turned when I heard a pounding at the door.

"Mel, open up! I know you're in there, open up Mel!"

I heard Donna at the front door, but paid no attention. I ran upstairs getting the Monopoly shoe from the jewelry box. I held that in one hand and the rose in the other as I cried for Sarah.

I felt arms around me before I realized it and Donna was holding me. "Mel, are you okay? There's blood on the kitchen floor."

I looked at her, and then looked to see Vicky running up my stairs she looked at Donna, and I looked at the both of them. I whispered. "What are you guys doing here?"

Donna looked at me, then up at Vicky, then back at me. "Mel I heard you screaming. I tried to get the door open but it was locked. By the time I found the key, I found you up here, on the floor." She looked at Vicky then back at me. "Then Mel, you were screaming for Sarah to show herself to you."

I looked at her, and then dropped my head in my hands. "Am I going crazy?"

Vicky knelt in front of me. "Mel, I think you've been through a lot lately."

"I don't know."

Donna laid me down on the bed. "Why don't you rest for a while?"

"Sarah's pillow. Donna, where's Sarah's pillow?" I tried to sit up but Donna held me down.

"Don't worry, Vicky will find it." She turned to Vicky. "Won't you Vic."

"Sure Mel, I'll go and get that right now."

Vicky left and I laid my head down. "Donna how can you explain this."

"Mel, what happened?"

"I don't know, yesterday the last thing I remember is going to the cemetery. After that it's a total blank. I tried to tell myself I drank too much, but I never drink like that, and especially alone. When I got up I found this shoe next to my coffee maker. Then there's the rose, I went in the refrigerator and there it was. Not to mention this." I pulled my shirt aside and showed her the sucker bite on my neck.

"Mel I don't know what to say or think."

Vicky came in with Sarah's pillow in her hand. She handed it to me and I laid my head down, talking to Donna was the last thing that I remember.

❧   ❧   ❧

Opening my eyes I felt someone else in the room with me. I bolted up. "Who's there?"

"Mel calm down, it's just me, Windy."

She crawled in bed next to me and put her arm around me.

I giggled nervously. "I guess Donna told you that I'm losing my mind."

"No! I'm here because for a change you need me."

"I've always needed you Win." My hands flew to my head. "Do you know what's happening to me?"

"Mel, I really think you believe Sarah's trying to tell you something." She sat staring at me.

"Really? You really believe that."

"I do."

"So, I'm not crazy?"

"No."

I smacked my head with my hands. "I don't know Win…I don't know." I threw my arms around her. "I'm so glad you're here."

"I'll be here whenever you need me, you can count on that."

"I know I can."

With her arms around me she looked in my eyes. "Mel you really have to try and remember what happened last night. That's the key."

"I know." I rested my head on her chest and she stroked my hair until I fell asleep again.

❧   ❧   ❧

Waking up again I looked at the clock and it was the middle of the night. I looked to my side and Windy was lying in bed next to me. I put my head on her stomach. "Little one you are probably the luckiest baby in the world, your mother is one wonderful human being I happen to love her to death." I got out of bed, after I kissed her stomach.

I went downstairs to get some water. Sitting on the couch I kicked my knees up at my side and stared at the fireplace, I swore I saw visions of Sarah's face. I squinted my eyes and stared, I wasn't seeing things it was Sarah.

"Sarah!" I moved to the edge of the couch. "Sarah what's happening to me?"

"Mel it's not you. It's me I didn't know the rules."

"Sarah, what rules?" I could no longer see her; I sat there until my eyes could no longer stay open then I climbed in bed next to Windy. I lay there wrapping my arms around her falling asleep as I had my head nestled in her neck.

Waking up I still had Windy wrapped in my arms I felt her moving but I just kept holding her. Then I heard my top stair creek and my head bolted up only to see Ivy standing looking at me. I turned to Windy lying next to me then looked back at Ivy as she ran back downstairs. Donna ran up to stare at me, then chased after Ivy. I woke Windy up, and told her what was going on, she then ran downstairs.

I laid in bed feeling like my whole world was falling apart around me. I had absolutely no energy left; besides no matter who was here I couldn't get Sarah out of my mind. I sat on the edge of my bed scared that Ivy was here, but I knew I did no wrong and after a while she'll realize it too, until then I needed to distinguish what was reality and what wasn't.

I headed into the bathroom and ran a shower; I stepped in and sat on the bottom curled up in a ball. As the water pelted the top of my head I stared at nothing and when the water turned cold I began to see Sarah's face. The colder the water, the more clear she became. I reached up and turned the hot water totally off. I sat there focusing my stare straight ahead trying to see her again. After a while she became clear to me.

"Sarah I've been going crazy. What did you mean when you said that you didn't know the rules?"

"Mel do you remember anything that happened?"

"No Sarah, I don't."

"Mel I told you things that I shouldn't have, but more importantly we shouldn't have done what we did."

"Sarah, what did we do?"

"It was fine for us to talk, it was even fine for us to touch, but Mel we should never have slept together."

"Sarah why all the things laying around the house?"

"I wanted you to remember the most important things. I want you to be happy and to watch over Windy she's going to need you."

"Sarah why can't I remember anything? Why can't I remember making love to you?"

"Honey you're not suppose to. I'm not suppose to even be talking to you now. But I really screwed things up, and I needed to make them right. I hate seeing you like this."

"So I'm not going crazy?"

"Honey you are probably the most sane person I know."

"Sarah will I remember any of this?"

"In time you may, but right now it's best that you don't."

"Sarah!" My hand reached out. "Sarah!"

I felt someone holding me and I looked around to see Ivy's eyes staring at me. She was shaking me. "Mel! Mel, are you okay?"

I stared. "Ivy." I hugged her. "I need you so bad right now, please hold me."

"You're freezing, you have to get out of this shower."

She wrapped a towel around me and lifted me out, then squeezed me tight. "Mel I'm right here, I'm sorry I should have known better. I love you." She rubbed my arms and body. "Mel I love you."

I stared in her eyes and I heard a voice in the back of my head telling me to be happy. "Ivy I love you, I'm sorry I don't know what's happening to me."

"I'm here babe, I'll always be here." She held me as she walked me into the bedroom where she pulled out some warm clothes to put on me, and then laid me in bed. She curled up next to me and rubbed my arms up and down. "Mel, are you warm yet? That shower was ice cold."

"Yeah, I think I am." I touched her face. "I'm glad you're here but I really don't want you seeing me like this."

"Don't worry, just lay back."

"Ivy where's Windy, does she need me?"

"Windy left for the gallery and she's fine. I checked her out myself."

"You're sure?"

"I'm sure."

I laid my head on her chest. "Ivy I have to tell you what happened."

She stroked my head. "When you're ready babe, tell me when you're ready."

I just lay in Ivy's arms and she held me tight. Again I fell asleep, being the most comfortable that I've been in days.

CHAPTER 26

Opening my eyes I felt amazingly better, I think it was because Ivy was here with me. What is it people say about true love overcoming all? I smiled and reached over for Ivy but she was gone. I swung my arm around frantically feeling the bed, searching for her. Then I heard a noise downstairs, I walked down and saw her in the kitchen.

She turned around. "Mel you're up, I was just making coffee."

"Great."

She looked up at me. "So you want some?"

"Yeah, that would be great." I sat down on the couch and stared at the fireplace.

"Mel you okay? How do you feel?"

"Sane. I feel sane today. Okay!" I screamed.

I rubbed my head with my hands. Then I stood up and walked over to her in the kitchen. "I'm so sorry." I put my arms around her. "Ivy I just don't know what's happening to me."

"Don't worry babe, you're not going crazy. Like Windy said, Sarah is trying to tell you something, either you have to try and figure it out or just relax and let everything come back to you naturally."

"Ivy." I looked at her. "I think Sarah was with me the other day. Remember I told you she came to me before."

Ivy shook her head yes.

"Well I think she came to me again, for' some reason I don't remember." I let go of her and sat down at the kitchen table.

"Mel, I really think you're thinking about this too much. Do you need someone to talk to?" She sat down across from me.

"What like a psychiatrist or something?"

"'Well yeah, it might help."

"No, I'm going back to work, I just need to keep myself busy."

"Maybe that's what the problem is. You might be taking on too much, with Windy and the baby, work and trying to figure out a way to be with me. It all might have caught up to you."

"Maybe." I looked down at my coffee cup.

"Why don't you just take some time and settle down for a while. I already talked to Windy and everything at the gallery is fine. She's just waiting for opening day."

"What about her doctors appointments?"

"I've already discussed that with her and I'm going with her on her next appointment."

I looked up at her. "Really?"

"Yeah. Mel, I'm here to help." She reached across the table putting her hand on mine.

"By the way how were you able to get out of work?"

"I just took some time off, right now your health is more important to me."

I squeezed her hand. "I wish you were here all the time."

"Well sometimes wishes come true."

I smiled at her. "What?"

"I put in to be transferred here. With all that you're going through I thought that you needed me around."

"I do, but you don't have to disrupt your whole life for me."

"You were going to do it for me. We love each other right?"

"Yeah, but that's a big step."

"It's no bigger than the step that you were willing to take for me."

I stood up and hugged her. "You're so wonderful."

She laughed. "Now take your coffee and go sit down, while I make you some breakfast."

"That sounds good."

I walked into the living room and sat down as I watched Ivy in the kitchen. Then I realized this is what I needed, I needed her to be with me, always. Sitting there all I thought about was how ridiculous I had been acting for the last couple of days. I love her so much it scares me.

Ivy and I sat down to a great breakfast and a much needed talk. We discussed in depth her moving here and decided that it would definitely be for the best. She would be transferring right away because the clinic downtown needed a pediatrician of her stature, so our plans were already in motion. We talked for a little while then I went for a bike ride while she went to check out the hospital.

Ivy was reluctant to let me go, but I insisted that I'd be okay. I gave her the keys to my jeep, kissed her goodbye and took off on my bike. As I rode I turned down Windy's street, I just had to see her to let her know I was okay.

Knocking on the door I didn't think she was home then I saw the door beginning to open. "Mel, what are you doing here?"

"I'm just out for a ride."

"Should you be?"

"Win I'm fine, I wanted to stop by and say thanks."

She swung the door open and stepped aside. "Come on in."

I walked in. "I really can't stay I want to finish my ride, but I did want to say thanks."

"Mel, there's no need. So how are you feeling?"

"A lot better thanks, although totally embarrassed."

"Don't be." She put her arm around my shoulder. "I really should have seen this coming. You have just been too stressed out lately."

"Well I hope that's all it was."

"I'm sure it is."

"Okay, well I'm going to get going then."

She stepped on the porch with me. "Oh, by the way absolutely everything's done for the gallery opening, all you have to do is show up. Actually that's all any of us have to do; both Tara and I are off until then too. So just relax."

"Thanks Win. What about…"

She put her hand over my mouth. "Ivy will be there for me, just until you're back on your feet, okay?"

I nodded my head then she took her hand off my mouth. "You're sure?"

"I'm sure. Its probably only going to be one appointment."

"Alright." I hugged her then headed on my way.

After visiting Windy I rode for a while until I ended up sitting rubbing my fingers along Sarah's stone.

While I sat there I looked up at the sky. "Sarah what the hell happened the last time I was here, because after that my life has been one big jumbled mess. I can't seem to remember things, and then there are certain things that pop into my head for no reason. Everyone says it might be stress and maybe they're right, after all I have been pretty busy. But I don't mind saying it has been scaring the hell out of me." I leaned back resting on my elbows. I lay there looking around wondering if anything would bring back any kind of memory. Nothing did.

I sat up with my legs crossed and my elbows on my knees, as my hands held my head. I stared down at Sarah's stone. "Well I better be going I know this was a short visit, but I don't want anyone worrying about me. I'll be back soon." I kissed my fingers and rubbed her stone.

Climbing on my bike I rode off and it seemed like all of a sudden all I thought about was getting home to Ivy. Ivy and home sounded so good.

I turned in the drive and my jeep was still gone so I had time. Running in the house I quickly jumped in the shower, then went downstairs to fix Ivy a great dinner. Looking around I realized I hadn't gone shopping in a while so there was a quick change of plans.

I went back upstairs to change so I could take her out to dinner instead.

By the time I finished I heard Ivy downstairs.

"Mel, you home?"

"Yeah, I'll be right down." I put the finishing touches on then went downstairs. Walking into the kitchen Ivy looked at me.

"Wow, you look great what's the occasion?"

"I thought I would take you out to dinner tonight. I've been in the house for days and just need to get out of here for a while and be alone with you."

Looking in her face, I saw a look of concern.

"Honey, don't worry I'm fine. I don't need anymore rest, okay."

I went up behind her and put my arms around her. "So how did everything go for you today?"

"Great, I think I'm going to like it here."

"Yeah." I spun around so that she faced me. "I think I'm going to like having you here."

CHAPTER 27

The time before the opening was long and boring. Ivy was traveling back and forth to Boston, trying to get everything in order and I had nothing to do.

I did take the spare time to play catch up with my family, but that was about it. Other than that with all the exercise I was getting, I must say I never felt better. I actually felt like I was regaining my sanity.

Windy was starting to show and I was going to pick her up so she could buy something for our big event tonight. Finally the reopening of our gallery was here. Ivy's plane was coming in late this afternoon so I had all morning to help Windy shop.

Pulling in her driveway I got out of my jeep and stared at her as she stood on her front porch. "Win, you look great today. I really mean that, it's something about you."

She laughed at me. "No I don't. Look at me Mel I'm getting fat."

She sounded like she had tears in her throat. "You're not fat." I smiled and waked up to her rubbing her stomach. "You're pregnant."

I bent over and spoke to her stomach. "Don't worry little one, your mom is going through her fat stage now. It won't last."

She pulled me up by the hair. "Win, ouch. That hurts." I smacked her hand while I laughed loudly.

"Well stop making fun of me."

"I'm not, I'm just teasing you, and there is a difference."

"Not much."

"Oh, come on, get your big butt in the car."

"I'm not going with you if you're going to keep this up."

"I won't, come on."

We walked to the car and when she got in I walked to her side of the car.

"Mel what are you doing?"

"Just checking the air pressure in the tires."

"You know!" She looked around disgusted. "I think I liked you better when you were temporarily insane."

"Oh Win, that was uncalled for." I laughed and walked around the car, and when I sat down I looked over at her giggling. "That was really uncalled for."

"Well then you just keep it up."

"Ouch…you're pregnant and you're feisty."

"Mel!"

I looked at her.

"Let's go."

"For you anything." We both laughed and I pulled away watching her as she shook her head at me. We had a great time, Windy couldn't find one thing that she liked, and believe me, we looked everywhere.

"Win, what next?" We stood by the car talking.

"I have no idea."

"How about you let me buy you lunch, I have an idea."

"What?"

"I can't tell you just yet. Let me make one phone call then we'll go to lunch, okay?"

"Alright, I'll just wait here." She leaned on the car.

I walked over to the pay phone and called my sister. If anyone had a load of maternity dresses she did. She had everything from formal wear to bathing suits. Kimmie said she would unpack everything that would be suitable for Windy.

I started walking over to her smiling. She stared at me as if I had some ulterior motive. "Mel what have you done?"

I grabbed her arm clutching it as we walked. "Well I think you'll be pleased." I looked at her.

"Come on don't keep me in suspenders, tell me."

I looked at her. "You're getting pretty goofy on me. I called Kimmie."

"Your sister?"

I nodded my head.

"Mel, that's perfect we are just about the same size and she had great taste."

"I told you that you would be pleased. Now let's eat."

We went to a little restaurant on the water and I sat across from her staring. "Win you really look great. Pregnancy really agrees with you."

She smiled. "Thanks, even through all the morning sickness, and cravings, and weight gain I just think about this baby growing inside me and feel warm all over."

"That's so great. Have you thought about names yet?"

I saw a twinkle come to her eyes. "A little. I wanted to talk you about it."

"Me?"

"I thought you could help and give me some input, besides I want to make something official."

"What?"

"I want you to be my baby's Godmother. You know in the event…"

"Don't even Win!"

"I'm sorry I shouldn't have phrased it that way, but you will, right?"

"Of course I will. I love this baby."

She smiled. "I know you do, it shows every time you look at me."

We finished our lunch then drove to my sister's. Kimmie and I sat on the couch while Windy put on a fashion show for us. Everything she tried on looked great, she picked out the most perfect one, then we kissed Kimmie goodbye and thanked her.

After I dropped Windy off I hurried home to get myself ready. I looked at the clock and Ivy should already be home, her plane landed an hour ago.

As I pulled in the driveway I saw her rental car. I rushed inside. "Ivy!" I walked around, and then I heard the shower on.

I poured a glass of water and went upstairs. Ivy was finishing her shower while I picked up the dress I bought just for this occasion and took another look at it in the mirror, when Ivy's shower stopped I went into the bathroom. "So when did you get home hon?"

"I just got in a few minutes ago. How was your shopping extravaganza?"

She stepped out of the tub and I wrapped her in a towel. "It was fun but tiring, very tiring."

I stepped back and watched as she toweled off her hair.

Leaning up against the doorframe I couldn't take my eyes off of her. She really was beautiful I loved everything about her.

Her shoulder blades almost put me in a trance as they moved up and down, and in and out. I trailed her spine all the way down to the spot right above her perfectly shaped ass. I stared at her long and slender legs and suddenly realized I wasn't paying attention to a single word she was saying. I shook my head smiling and looked back in the mirror at her gorgeous face.

"Mel you weren't listening to a word I was saying. Were you?"

I stepped forward and slipped my hands around her waist. "How could I?" I kissed her shoulder. "Now what did you say?"

"Oh it doesn't matter." She put her hand on the back of my head. "Mel, you don't want to be late do you?"

I dropped my forehead on her shoulder. "Okay, but we pick it up right here when we get home."

"Deal." She turned around and kissed me. "Now you better get in the shower."

I took an extra long shower so Ivy had time to get herself ready. If I went out there and she was still naked we really would be late. When I stepped into the bedroom Ivy was already downstairs. I sat in front of the mirror putting on my make-up when I heard Ivy coming back upstairs. I saw her coming towards me in the mirror with a martini glass in her hand. "Is that for me?"

"Sure is." She handed it to me. "I don't know how it tastes. I haven't perfected the martini yet."

"I'm sure it's fine." I sipped it and opened my eyes as wide as possible. "Oh it's good."

She smacked me on the back. "Stop it."

"No really, it's fine."

She walked over and sat on the bed. "So are you excited?"

"Nervous is more like it."

We were sipping our drinks, when the phone rang. I saw it was Windy and I looked at Ivy. "She's probably having a panic attack."

I picked up the phone. "So, are you nervous?"

"Mel I just don't want anyone talking about what happened and I know they will."

"Don't worry Win. If they're going to talk let them. You're bigger than that."

"What about my being pregnant? They're going to know."

"I think you're worrying too much. Just relax and enjoy the evening, screw what everyone else says, okay?"

"Okay. So when are you and Ivy coming by?"

"Is 6:00 okay? That gives us time to make sure everything's perfect when people show."

"I'll be ready."

"I'll see you then."

"Okay."

I hung up then looked at Ivy. "She's really scared."

She came and sat next to me with her arm around me. "Can you blame her I mean think about it?"

"I know. I just didn't want to let on I was scared for her."

"Don't worry everything will be fine. We'll all get through this and then it will be over. You'll see."

"I hope so."

"Come on let's finish getting ready."

When we were all done we stood in the mirror, Ivy behind me with her hands on my shoulders. "God I love you."

I crossed my shoulder and put my hand on hers. "I love you more."

She looked at me in the mirror. "Stay right here."

I watched as she ran downstairs. She looked fantastic wearing a white, lightly pinned striped suit. I stared in the mirror and again we looked great together, her in white and me in black. I fooled a little bit with my hair when Ivy started back up the stairs.

"Ivy, I don't think I told you how great you look tonight."

She walked up behind me and kissed me on the neck, and then from behind her back she pulled a pearl necklace and placed it around my neck.

I touched it lightly with my fingertips. "Oh Ivy, it's beautiful."

"It looks great on you."

I turned around and with my arms around her neck I pulled her to me and kissed her. "I am so glad you're here with me."

"Me too."

We kissed again. Then I pulled her hair back with my hands. "Come on I'll make you a perfect martini."

"Are you saying that mine's not perfect?"

"Your what?"

"My martini."

"I didn't say that at all." I giggled as I kissed her neck.

We stood in the kitchen sipping our drinks when there was a knock at the door. I looked at Ivy. "That must be Donna and Vicky." I walked to the door and let them in. Donna came walking in first followed by Vicky. "Well the two of you look great. We were just having drinks, anyone for a martini?" I closed the door.

Donna turned around. "Sure I'll have one."

I looked at Vicky. "I'll just take a beer thanks."

We all walked into the kitchen and Ivy giggled. "Boy we make a mighty fine looking group."

Donna sat down. "We sure do."

After our drinks and small talk we walked outside. I turned to Donna.

"Alright, follow us we're going to stop by and pick up Windy."

She looked at me. "Okay."

We got in our cars and pulled away. I rested my hand on Ivy's thigh. "You better stay close to me. I want everyone to know you're with me."

"Oh you don't have to worry about that." She put her hand on mine.

Once we all got to the gallery Windy and I proudly showed everyone around. Ivy clung tightly to my arm. "Mel, I'm impressed. This place is really fantastic."

"Thanks." I looked at Windy. "Win you and Tara did a great job."

"You did most of the work, we just put the finishing touches on. You should be proud Mel." She smiled at me.

"We all should be proud. By the way where is Tara?"

Windy walked to the front of the gallery. "I don't know, I called her and she was on her way."

"Well I'm going to go and check on the caterers, I'll be right back." I patted Ivy's hand, then walked and checked on the bar and the hors d'oeuvre's. I stood there looking around smiling with pride. I saw Ivy walking towards me.

She stretched her hand out and grabbed mine. "I'm so proud of you honey."

I smiled. "Thanks. Hey did Tara show up yet? I want to introduce you."

"I don't know someone came in when I started over here to see you."

I looked over Ivy's shoulder. "Yeah that's her." I tugged her hand. "Come on."

I introduced Tara to Ivy, then we all stood around talking until people started coming. Once they did though it seemed as if they all came at one time. I kept one eye on Windy and the other on Ivy. Windy worked the room like a pro. Once she started all of her fears disappeared. Ivy on the other hand mingled with everyone, but mostly she hung around Donna and Vicky. I started making my way over to Ivy but was stopped several times trying to get to her. The harder I tried, the more I was stopped. Then someone grabbed my arm and I turned around.

"Lily!" I couldn't believe that she was here.

"Mel you look like you're in absolute shock."

"Well." I hugged her. "I am, so how have you been?"

"Great, and yourself?"

"Good, real good."

She grabbed my arm and pulled me to the bar as I looked at Ivy. "Come on Mel, I'll get you a drink. If I remember you're pretty fond of martinis."

I smiled at her. "A martini sounds great."

After we got our drinks Lily turned to me. "Mel the place looks great. It really does."

"Thanks."

"I heard what happened and I'm really sorry." She placed her hand softly in front of me on the bar.

"Well, we're trying to get past that now."

"So how is Windy? She looks great."

"She is great."

"That's good." She looked around. "So are you still seeing some-one?"

I smiled. "Yeah, I am."

"That's too bad. You really look great. I keep thinking about all the fun we used to have together." She stared at me smiling.

I laughed. "We did have fun."

My hand rested on the bar and she touched it lightly. "Mel it could be like that again." She smiled. "Remember the passion we had. I can still feel it. No one has made me feel they way you did. I still want you. I think about you all the time." She took a sip of her drink.

I stared at her, knowing she was being totally sincere. She touched my hand again. "Mel, am I making a total fool out of myself?"

I put my hand on hers. "No Lily you're not, but things are different now."

"They're not that different. I would leave him Mel. I would do that for you. I want you that bad. I miss the passion we had…Mel I miss you."

"Lily." I shook my head. "You're making this so hard."

"That's what I intended." She smiled.

"You would leave him?"

"Yeah, Mel you have to know he never meant anything to me. I was just afraid. Knowing what we had and how happy I was, well, I'm no longer afraid. I don't care anymore what people think."

I couldn't believe I was standing here listening to her tell me all of this. Standing here I realized how much she meant to me. "Lily I wish you would have said this to me when I went to New York that day. If you had I never would have left, and things might be different today."

"You wouldn't have?"

"No, I wouldn't have."

"See you still care, I know you do."

Then I felt a hand on my back. Turning around I saw it was Ivy; a smile came over my face. She reached her hand out. "You're Lily right?"

"Yes." Lily took her hand.

"It's nice to see you again."

Lily looked at me. I smiled at her then looked at Ivy. Lily finished her drink and set her glass on the bar. "It was nice seeing you again Ivy." Then she turned to me. "Mel, think about what I said. You know where I am."

I smiled at her, and then she walked away.

"Mel what did she mean by that?"

"It's not important."

"Are you sure?"

"I'm sure, let's go find my sister and Windy." I pulled her by the arm.

"Okay."

We made our way through the crowd and when we reached Kimmie I saw Lily watching us. Ivy tugged at my arm. "Are you sure you don't want to tell me anything?"

"I'm sure."

We talked for a while with Kimmie, then I stepped back. "Well guys you're going to have to excuse me, I have to sell some of this art." I looked at Ivy. "I'll be back soon."

"Don't be long."

I smiled and walked away. Finally I reached Windy. "So how are things going?"

"Mel, things are great."

"Good."

She looked around the room. "Hey, I saw Lily walking around, have you talked to her yet?"

"Yeah, I did."

"So."

"Well she basically told me that she wants to start over. She said she would leave him."

"Really." She looked at me shocked.

"Yeah, you know Win how much I love Ivy, but I gotta tell you when Lily told me how bad she missed me, I don't know, I remembered all we had together and I guess I miss that too."

"You've got to think about what you have now." We both looked at Ivy. "She's pretty great."

"I know she is. I better get back to her I've already been gone too long." I looked at Windy. "You know Win." I hugged her. "I really love you. You always know just what I need."

"Go ahead and go to her. There's nothing more that we can do tonight the evening's starting to wind down."

"Are you sure that you're okay?" I held her hands.

"I'm fine."

"The baby?"

"Mel. Please." She pushed me from behind. "Quit worrying, I'm fine and so is the baby, now go and enjoy the rest of the evening. There's something I have to do then I'll join you."

"Okay but why don't you sit down and relax a little. You shouldn't be on your feet for so long. Okay."

"Mel..."

"Promise me."

"Okay, I promise, I'll rest, alright."

I smiled. "That's all I ask."

"Now go."

I started my way back to Ivy. It was a lot easier this time because the crowd thinned out. I finally reached her. "Hi, so where's Kimmie?"

Donna looked up from her drink. "Oh she said to tell you bye and to call her tomorrow."

"Thanks. So has everyone had a good time tonight?"

Vicky walked up to me. "Mel I think everyone has had a great time. Jeez just look around the room, people don't want to leave."

"Yeah." I looked around. "This is good."

Ivy turned to me and held up her glass. "One more for the road?"

I reached for her glass. "Sure."

She grabbed mine. "No, I got it." She took my glass and I watched her walk away. I looked back at Donna. "This has been a perfect night."

"Well it's not over yet. I thought we would all go out for a while."

"Sounds good to me, but I'll have to ask Ivy when she comes back."

Vicky grabbed Donna. "I don't think so, it was originally her idea."

"Is that right." I laughed.

I turned around just in time to watch Ivy walking back to me, and thought about how lucky I was. I have great friends, a career I totally love, and a woman who I couldn't live without. She finally reached me and handed me my drink. I knew after finishing this drink I wouldn't be able to drive, so without Windy knowing it we all designated her the driver. Now we just have to convince her to come along.

I convinced Windy to leave everything for tomorrow and she agreed; she just wanted to get off her feet. I didn't think it was a good idea for her to come with us and deep down I really didn't think she wanted to. She was pretty tired. Vicky as usual was then appointed the designated driver while my car stayed at the gallery.

When we dropped Windy off I walked her to the door, just to make sure she got inside safely. She's still nervous; I could tell by the way she left every light in the house on when she left earlier. She unlocked the door and I went inside with her for a minute. "Win, you sure you're okay?" I stood in front of her.

"Yeah, just tired. Go ahead, I'm fine."

"Alright, I'll call you tomorrow."

"You guys be careful."

"Always." I hugged her. "Good night Win."

On the way to the car I heard Vicky blasting Ivy's 70's music while everyone in the car sang the Bee Gee's, Staying Alive. I don't think that one person was singing on key.

We reached the bar and not soon enough, my ears were ringing. I swear everyone in the car was tone deaf, one sang worse than the other.

As soon as we walked in I slipped my hand on the small of Ivy's back and we all sat down at a table. Donna went up to the bar and ordered drinks, then came to the table and kissed Vicky's head before sitting down. "Mel I've got to tell you, this opening was even better then the last show we went to. Right Vic."

"It was. By the way Mel how is Windy feeling? She looked pretty tired."

"She was really tired, her feet were killing her. I told her to rest I'd take care of everything at the gallery tomorrow."

Ivy put her arm around my shoulder. "Mel you know she's only pregnant."

"I know." I took a sip of my drink. "I just can't help but feel like she should be pampered. Hey did I tell you she's making me the Godmother of her baby." I looked around the table proudly.

Ivy looked at me. "Really!"

Vicky grabbed my hand as it sat on the table. "Mel, that's great."

Ivy then kissed my cheek. "It is hon."

I sat back in my chair holding Ivy's hand, just watching and listening to everyone. Sitting there looking around I knew this was going to be one of those moments. You know, one of those memories that will be with you forever.

I watched Ivy laughing with everyone, and how she had them captivated. With my elbows on the table and my hand propping my head up I stared in her eyes. I wanted to see all the way into her soul.

I wanted to see what she was thinking and feel what she felt. I loved her so deeply I wonder if she had any idea.

I smiled while she told Donna and Vicky one of those stories that people always repeat over and over, especially when they're drinking. The thing of it is, I wasn't even tired of hearing it. As long as she was the one telling it, I could listen to it over and over again. Which only means one of two things. One...I really love this woman, or two...I really love this woman.

Walking through the parking lot on our way to the car I had both of my hands clutching Ivy's arm and my head on her shoulder. Then I whispered in her ear. "I can't wait to get you home alone."

"You can't huh?"

"No."

She turned her head to me while we walked and kissed me lightly on the mouth.

CHAPTER 28

❀

With every month that passed the gallery did better and better, and Windy got bigger and bigger. It was nearing the holidays now and Windy was going to be leaving soon. She's going home to visit her parents. I'm going to miss her, not to mention worrying about her. It'll be nice to turn all of my attention to Ivy though, she has been wonderfully understanding through all of this. I can't say that I would be the same.

After dropping Windy off at the airport I turned to Ivy and put my hand on hers. "Hungry?"

"Sure, I could eat." She looked at me as we walked to the car.

We drove for a while and then eventually ended up on a beautifully quiet street. We were admiring all the gorgeous homes, and then I just stopped the car and got out.

I heard Ivy's voice yelling from inside the car. "Mel, what on earth are you doing?" Then she got out of the car and walked to me.

"I don't know for some reason I remember this place. But I don't know from where."

We walked around looking at the unbelievable view. It was a great piece of land and I turned to Ivy. "Why don't we buy it?"

"Buy it?" She looked at me with total shock on her face.

"Yeah, there's a For Sale sign right over there." I pointed across my chest.

"And do what with it?"

"Build a house."

"What?"

"Can't you see it? Ivy it would be perfect. Imagine it. The house could be right here, we could put a built in pool over there. Can't you see it?" I looked at her. "What do you say?"

"Mel I don't know what to say. This would be a huge step for us."

I took her hands and held them in mine. "I know, but I think that we're ready." I looked up in her eyes. "Don't you?"

"Yeah...I don't know. Why don't we talk about this for a while first."

I looked down at the ground trying to hide my disappointment. Then I let her hands go and turned imagining how so perfect it would be.

I then felt Ivy tugging at my arm. "Come on let's go, I'm freezing."

"Okay."

I turned around and started walking back to the car. I stood looking around knowing that I've been here before, or at least I thought so. We got in the car and headed home, forgetting all about the restaurant.

Windy called when she finally got to her parent's house so I knew she was okay. I wished her and her parents a Merry Christmas and told her to call before she left. She promised she would.

I then had the important task of finding the most perfect Christmas present for Ivy. I shopped for hours and still nothing struck me. Then as I walked to my car looking up at the sky, it hit me. I knew exactly what I was going to get her.

With that out of the way I went home to bake cookies with Ivy. We were going over to my sister's house for Christmas Eve dinner, and decided to bake cookies to bring along.

We wanted to do the whole family thing Christmas Eve so that we could be alone on Christmas. Ivy's parents go to Hawaii every year for Christmas, they've done that I guess ever since she was a little girl. She told her sister she would come back to Boston next year for Christmas and I was glad. Even though it was selfish of me; I wanted her all to myself.

I woke up early Christmas morning and started a big breakfast for Ivy. I made waffles with bananas and raspberries sprinkled over them, and then I put everything on a tray and carried it up to her.

Setting it down I crawled into bed next to her, kissing her on the forehead. "Get up sleepy head."

She opened her eyes slowly, and then rolled over putting her arm around me. "What is that heavenly smell?" She opened her eyes slowly.

"I made breakfast."

She brushed the hair out of her eyes and lifted her head. "Really?"

"Really, we have waffles with fresh fruit and coffee."

She sat up slowly. "Mel this is wonderful. Breakfast in bed. What did I do to deserve this?"

"You didn't do anything, you just being you is enough." I kissed her. "Now come on let's eat before everything gets cold."

We lay eating in bed until everything was gone. Then crossing over Ivy I set my coffee cup on the table next to her, as I did, I kissed her. "Now don't move."

I went downstairs and set my Christmas present up for her. I wanted everything to be just perfect, after all it was our first Christmas together. I had all the lights out except for the lights we had on the tree, and around the house. Then I ran back upstairs.

"Come on I have your present ready for you. We have to hurry though before the sun comes all the way up." I jumped on the bed kneeling over her pulling her up by her hands.

We reached the bottom of the stairs and Ivy turned to me. "Mel, what on earth is this?"

"Haven't you ever seen a telescope before?" My arms flew around her.

"I have." She turned to me. "But…"

"Here maybe this will help." I handed her an envelope.

"Mel, what is this?"

"Look through the telescope."

She smiled at me then walked to it. "What am I suppose to be looking at?"

"It's a star."

"A star?"

"Yeah, that's your present." I rested my hand on her back.

She stopped looking and turned to me. "What?"

"I bought you a star. That's what the certificate is for. That star you see there is yours, well it's named after you anyway."

She looked back into the telescope, then back at me. "Really?"

"Yeah, I named it Ivy." I sat down on the couch. "So?"

"Mel this is really one of the best gifts I think I ever got. You bought me a star." She laughed and sat down next to me putting her arms around me. "A star. You actually bought me a star, I just can't get over it."

"I look at you and see your radiant beauty." I twirled my fingers in her hair. "Now everyone in the whole world can do the same. Everyone can love you like I do."

With her arms wrapped tightly around my neck she started kissing me. "I love you so much, do you know that?"

"So you like it? I mean it's not your usual type of gift."

"I love it, and I love the fact that it's so unusual."

She jumped off the couch. "Now stay there I have something for you."

She picked her briefcase up off the floor and started digging though it. Then she pulled out an envelope and came walking over to me. She kissed me. "Here you go honey, Merry Christmas."

I looked at her then opened the envelope. I couldn't believe my eyes. Immediately I stared at her then back down at the paper. "Ivy I don't believe you did this."

"I did." She giggled.

I looked at the paper again; it was the deed to the land that was for sale. "Does this mean I can build our dream house?"

She nodded her head. "That's what it means."

"Are you sure about this?"

"Absolutely." She sat smiling next to me.

"It's just that you had concerns about it before."

"They weren't concerns. I knew when we pulled over to that land we were meant to have it."

I hugged her. "This is going to be a perfect house."

"As long as we're together any home is a perfect home."

"But this one will be special…it will be ours."

I hugged her. "Ivy this has been a terrific Christmas."

We lounged around for a while, and then I got up to start cooking a traditional holiday meal.

CHAPTER 29

*F*or the first time in my life I've been carrying around a beeper, and I hate beepers, but I need one now. Windy gave it to me so she can get hold of me when she's ready. The baby's due any day now and I have been nervous and jumpy everyday for the past week. I'm her coach in the delivery room and each day that goes by I get even more scared, but also more excited. I go to work wondering if today is going to be the day or not. I try to sleep through the night, but no matter how hard I try I can't. I keep picturing myself in the delivery room with Windy and right when she needs me, I pass out.

With all of my nervous energy when I'm not at work, I'm checking on our new house. Ivy and I started building right away. I worked day and night with an architect to help design our perfect home.

It was now almost through and I wouldn't let Ivy come look at it until it was finished. I wanted to surprise her, I even hired a decorator. I roamed around for a little while longer then headed back to the car. Once inside I called Ivy to let her know I was on my way home.

While I drove I reflected back on the past year and realized that I have been blessed. I hope to have the house finished and be able to bring Ivy here for our one year anniversary.

Right now everything in my life is perfect. The gallery is doing better than I ever thought it could be. Windy on the other hand is one of those women who loves to be pregnant, and it suits her. Just as

I was thinking about her, the beeper went off. I reached in my pocket, pulled it out and saw 9-1-1 that was Windy's code.

I tossed it in the back seat and called Ivy. "Ivy, it's time."

"You mean…"

"Yeah, she just beeped me. I'm going to her house right now."

"Okay I'll be at the hospital."

"I'll see you there."

"Mel!"

"Yeah?"

"Drive carefully. Don't be in so big of a hurry, I'm sure she has a lot of time before her delivery, okay?"

"Promise, I love you."

"Me too."

I hung up and rushed to Windy's. Once Ivy transferred to the clinic, Windy changed to have her become her doctor, that way Ivy and I will both be in the delivery room giving her support. Not to mention Ivy is a fantastic doctor.

Finally I reached Windy's and ran inside, she was calmly sitting at the kitchen table. I grabbed her bag and put my arm around her helping her up. "Come on mother, it's time for this little one to enter the world."

"Where's Ivy?"

"She's already on her way to the hospital. Let's get going."

We walked out to the car and were on our way. I held her hand the whole way and talked her through her contractions.

Ivy was waiting for us when I pulled into the parking lot.

Windy was checked in and in her room when I called her mother to tell her she was about to deliver.

Finally after hours, she was ready. She was taken to the delivery room and Ivy came to help me get dressed, then we both went inside. I looked at Ivy while Windy lay there screaming in pain, she was so scared, and she never looked more beautiful. I ran to her and grabbed her hand tightly in mine.

With my hand I turned her head to look at me. "Win! Win!" She kept looking away. "Windy!" She finally looked at me. "Win, hold me in your stare, let me help you through your pain."

As she looked at me I thought I saw a slight smile come over her face. I looked at Ivy and heard her yelling instructions to Windy.

I looked back at Windy. "Win, you're doing great. I'm so proud of you. You never looked more beautiful."

I held her tight and coached her through the roughest parts. Praising her the whole way. After hours in the delivery room I heard Ivy yell. "You're doing great Windy, just one more push."

Windy screamed in pain as I watched her face turn from pain to joy at the sound of her baby crying, I cut the umbilical cord and looked at Ivy.

Ivy held up her baby. "Windy you have a beautiful baby girl!"

I walked over taking the baby from Ivy, and then laid her on Windy's chest. "Win she's gorgeous."

She held her smiling. "Mel look, she's perfect."

I turned to Ivy as she walked to me putting her hands on my shoulders. I reached down and grabbed Windy's hand, the three of us never seen or felt so much love.

"Windy have you decided on a name?" Ivy asked over my shoulder.

She looked at her baby, then back up at me. "I have." She smiled and rubbed her baby's head. "Koko Melissa Berrington."

I felt Ivy's hands gripping my shoulders tightly as tears started rolling down my face. I sat down on the edge of Windy's bed and wiped the sweat off of her forehead. Then I kissed little Koko on the head.

I looked at Windy smiling. "I love you, do you know that?"

"I know." She grabbed my hand. "Thanks Mel for everything, you too Ivy. Thanks."

I smiled at Ivy then turned back to Windy. Ivy moved closer. "Windy why Koko?"

Windy looked at me smiling. "From Koko Taylor, one of the great Blues singers."

Ivy looked at me. "And you knew this?"

I smiled shaking my head. "Actually it was my suggestion."

She turned back to Windy smiling. "Okay, whatever." She put her hand on Windy's shoulder. "Get some rest, okay."

After Windy was fast asleep I went to look once again at her baby. She was so perfect; I just knew this little one was going to change all of our lives. I felt a hand on my back and I turned around to look into Ivy's eyes.

We stood there quietly watching Windy's baby.

CHAPTER 30

Our house was finally finished and just in time. I made Ivy promise me to be home on time today. I left the gallery early so I could prepare everything for her surprise.

Going from our new home to our present home I saw that she still wasn't home. I ran in to shower and when I was toweling off I heard Ivy coming through the front door.

I hurried down to meet her and ran to her arms. "You had better hurry and change. I have a big surprise for you today."

"You do?"

"I do. Now hurry." I pushed her towards the stairs and watched as she climbed them.

While she was in the shower I called Windy to check on her and Koko. "Hi Win."

"Mel, hi. I thought you were taking Ivy to your new house."

"I am. I just wanted to give you a call to see how things are going."

"They're perfect."

"Is your mother still there with you?"

"No, she left this morning."

"So it's just you and Koko now."

"Yeah, and I'm loving it. Mel, I never thought that I could love like this before. So completely, and so totally."

"Win I have never been happier for you. Now you remember tomorrow you and Koko are coming over, right?"

"Don't worry, I can't wait."

"Okay, you kiss that sweet child for me."

"I will."

When I hung up Ivy was on her way downstairs. She looked at me throwing her arms in the air. "So now what?"

"Now you come with me."

"Where are we going?"

"You'll see." We started walking to the car. "First let me ask you, do you know what today is?"

"Should I?"

"I don't know I'd hope you would."

She stood there thinking.

"Ivy I don't believe you. It has been one year today. It's our anniversary."

"Really, a whole year."

"You make it sound like it's been torture."

She threw her arms around my neck. "It's been heaven, and yes I remember what today is." She reached in her pocket and pulled out a small box, then opened it.

She took out a beautiful silver ring surrounded in diamonds. "I thought this would look beautiful on your long slender finger." She picked up my hand and pushed it on my finger.

I looked at it holding my hand up to the light watching the diamonds sparkle as I turned my hand around in the sun. "Ivy, this is gorgeous." I looked at her smiling.

"It looks great on you." She smiled and rubbed my arms with her hands.

I hugged her. "Come on, it's time for my surprise and it's killing me, this waiting."

"Am I dressed okay?"

"You look great." I kissed her.

We got in the car and I handed Ivy a handkerchief to put over her eyes.

"Mel!"

"Please, do it for me."

"Oh, alright."

I turned the music up loud and I saw Donna waving to me as I pulled away. I drove fast because I was so excited to show her our new home.

As I drove I looked at how beautiful the ring that Ivy gave me looked while my hand rested on the steering wheel. The drive went fast with little conversation. Finally I pulled into our new driveway.

"Can I take this off now?" She reached up and touched the handkerchief with her fingers.

"Not yet, I'll let you know when."

I got out of the car and went around to open her door. I helped her out and I looked around, loving how private and secluded it was. I walked her into the middle of the front yard and gently took off her blindfold.

She slowly opened her eyes, squinting from the light. Finally she focused in on what was in front of her. I saw her mouth open wide, then she spun around to look at me. "Mel, is this our new home?"

"It sure is. What do you think? Do you like it?"

"It's gorgeous. Absolutely unbelievable I never dreamed that I would live in such a house."

I smiled and watched her eyes. "Come on, I'll show you the inside." We started walking to the front door. "Ivy, before I open the door I did something, I hope you don't mind. I worked with a decorator. I just wanted to surprise you. I wanted everything to be perfect."

"Mel, what ever you did I'm sure it's perfect."

I squeezed her hand and we walked to the front door. I stopped and stared; I've dreamt of this house my whole life, a log cabin style house with a solid glass back facing the water. Now I just hope that

Ivy likes it. Before I opened the door I turned to her. "This is our new home." I opened the door and we walked in.

I stopped and proudly looked around. I felt Ivy's hand tighten in mine. "Oh Mel..." she was at a loss for words and I know what she was feeling because I felt the same way every time I stepped through the door. We both stood staring in the foyer amongst all the ceramic and marble, and in the center of the house was a tree, a ficus tree reaching and touching the skylights on the second floor.

I turned to her. "Do you like it?"

"Like it." Her arms flew around my neck. "It's amazing."

She just stood, looking around. The staircase was extra wide going upstairs, and the second floor was open and circular with three rooms at each end of the house. I held tight to her hand as I toured her through the house starting in the kitchen.

I showed her every room, the rec room with pinball machines and a pool table, her very own office then ended up in front of two big doors. Ivy turned to me smiling, watching her has been everything I ever thought it would be.

I opened the doors and we both stepped inside. This was my favorite room, the bedroom. The back wall was glass and had a balcony overlooking the back yard. The whole room was filled with comfort, over stuffed chairs and the ultimate four-post king size bed.

She said nothing just staring and I put my hand on her waist turning her around to walk into the bathroom.

"Oh my God!"

The bathroom was huge with stained glass windows, a sunken bathtub and big glass circular shower. "So what do you think? I know the tour was kind of rushed but I just couldn't wait to show you everything." My arms slipped around her waist.

"Mel, I don't know what to say, I'm floored. I love everything about it."

We stepped out onto the balcony. "This yard is something else. I love the pool and I can't get over the basketball court. This is a dream house, I can't believe that we're actually going to live here."

I softly kissed her neck. "Happy anniversary."

"You are amazing. This home is amazing." She threw her hands in the air and turned to face me.

"I'm glad that you like it."

"I love it. I'm going to feel like I'm living in a palace. This is the kind of place that movie stars live in." Her arms landed around my neck.

"You deserve to have beautiful things around you all the time. As long as we're together I'm going to do my best to make that happen."

She kissed me and pushed me to the bed. "I love you." Then she started to laugh. "This bed is so huge."

"Plenty of room to roll around."

She laughed. "You're so funny." She moved to sit on top of me.

After a tiring session of lovemaking Ivy rested her head on my stomach. I twirled her long curly hair in my fingers. "Are you hungry?"

"Famished."

"Good." I rolled over on my side and let my arm fall across her chest. "I have a big dinner planned."

Finally we dressed, and then I looked at Ivy. "Oh by the way, tomorrow I invited everyone over for a barbecue, I hope you don't mind. Do you?"

"Of course not. I can't wait for everyone to see our new home." She ran up to me, pushing me back on the bed. "God I love you."

I pulled the necklace that she bought me in North Carolina from around my neck. "I told you I would wear this until we were together again. Now we'll always be together."

She kissed me. "I have never been so happy."

"I'm glad because you've made me happier than I ever thought I could be again." I hugged her, and then whispered in her ear. "With your love in my life, I feel happy and whole again."

She squeezed me tight. "I can't imagine my life without you."

"You'll never have to."

We went downstairs in the kitchen and cooked dinner together.

"Mel you even stocked the fridge." She was laughing.

"Of course." I reached in and pulled out a couple of beers. "I never do things half way."

"I know that!" She giggled.

I watched Ivy in the kitchen, and I really felt at home. I smiled just thinking about how happy we were going to be here. I suddenly felt so content…Happy.

After dinner we walked around outside.

Ivy moved close to me as we walked. "Mel I just love it out here. It's so secluded, do we even have neighbors?"

"I think so, probably somewhere." We laughed and I grabbed for her hand. "Let's go for a swim."

"Now that's a great idea."

We ran inside and changed into some suits that I brought with me. Then went back out to the pool.

While Ivy jumped in I went into the pool house and pulled out a couple of rafts and turned the music on.

Throwing the rafts in the pool Ivy looked at me. "You just thought of everything. I can't believe it."

I shrugged my shoulders. "I try."

I dove in coming up out of the water right in front of her. She threw her arms around my neck and my arms went around her waist. "Ivy I am totally and completely in love with you." My eyes never lost hers.

She kissed me and we fell back against the pool wall. My hands traveled up her spine, slowly feeling every bump along the way. Then they made their way back down, while Ivy drove me wild by biting and kissing my neck. My breathing got deeper and deeper as the passion took over me. I pressed her against the wall as my hand found it's way inside her swimsuit. I kissed her neck and bit her shoulder as she wrapped her hands in my hair and threw her head back.

She then lifted my head to look in her eyes. "Mel should we be doing this out here?" She giggled softly.

"Sure, why not we basically don't have any neighbors." I laughed and bit her neck softly.

She took my face in her hands and started kissing me. "Why not?"

CHAPTER 31

❈

The next morning I opened my eyes and smiled when I felt Ivy's arms wrapped tightly around me. I put my hand in hers and rolled over to face her. "Good morning."

"Great morning. I don't believe I've ever slept so peacefully."

Her smile was all I needed and I squeezed her tightly. "Come on I'll make us some coffee."

We sat drinking our coffee and I looked at her. "So you want to go and pick up the rest of our things. It shouldn't take long. I told Donna she could keep any of the furniture she wanted. She could probably rent the place out furnished now."

"Okay sure."

We spent the morning packing up our clothes and personal belongings. Ivy sure did accumulate a lot of things in the short amount of time she was here.

After a couple hours of packing I heard Donna yelling downstairs.

"We're up here Donna." I yelled down to her.

She came upstairs. "So it looks like you guys got a lot done."

"Yeah, we'll be by tomorrow to make sure we didn't forget anything. But I'm pretty sure we have everything."

Donna moved next to Ivy. "So tell me what's this secret house look like."

Ivy stopped packing and looked up. "Donna you have to see it, to believe it. It really is fabulous."

"Really?"

"Really, it's great."

"Well, I'll let you guys finish up here and I'll see this fabulous house later on then."

I lifted my head. "Alright, remember, 3:00."

"Can't wait."

"Donna."

She turned. "Yeah?"

I walked up to her and hugged her. "I'm really going to miss you guys, you know that, right?"

"I know we're going to miss you too. No matter who moves in, it just won't be the same."

I felt tears starting in my eyes. "Okay, go now before I start to cry."

"I know." She wiped her face then turned to walk down the stairs.

I watched her then followed her down. Ivy went out to the car and I stood in the middle of the house looking around. I knew that I wouldn't stay here forever, but the time that I've been here has been fun. It's been home.

I heard Ivy coming back inside. "Mel you okay?"

"Yeah." I turned to her. "Yeah, I'm fine. Let's go home." I put my arm around her waist. "That sounds so good doesn't it?"

"It sure does."

"Think about it Ivy, we're entering into a whole new part of our lives."

She put her arms around my waist. "It's exciting isn't it?"

"Yeah, it is." I opened her car door. "I'll be home in a little bit, I have somewhere I have to go. "Okay?"

"Sure, take your time." She started her car. "Tell her I said hello." Then she pulled away.

I smiled watching her turn out of the drive; it's scary because sometimes she knows me better than I know myself. How did I ever get so lucky? I shook my head and walked to my car.

Standing there looking at Sarah's stone I bent down to my knees. "Hi honey. I know that it's been a while, but I've been unbelievably busy. Windy had her baby and she named her Koko Melissa Berrington. Sarah, I was there when she was born, I have never seen such a thing. It truly was a miracle honey."

I sat down on the ground with my knees bent and my arms around them. "I finally built my dream house. You should see it Sarah it's the home that we always talked about having. I just wish that I were able to give you something so nice. I feel guilty hon." I blinked back tears. "I feel like I shouldn't be this happy without you." I wiped my face. "I am happy though. I have a picture of you in my office and I look at it everyday, remembering what we had together. It's because of you that I am who I am today Sarah, and I want to thank you for that. It was because of the great love we shared, that I was able to recognize it again when I saw it in Ivy." I stretched my legs out in front of me then crossed them. "She says hello by the way. You would really like her Sarah I know that you would. If I didn't know better I would say that you hand picked her for me." I brushed my hands together then moved back to my knees. "Well Sarah I better be on my way, I'll be back soon." I kissed my fingers and rubbed her stone.

When I finally got home Ivy came outside to help me unload the car. "I didn't think you were going to make it back in time."

I looked at my watch. "I even have time to spare."

I didn't bother to unload; instead I followed Ivy into the kitchen. "Need help?"

"Sure, here you can chop up vegetables for the pasta salad." I picked out a knife. "I could do that." I laughed, and then got very serious while I stared at the green pepper I was cutting. "Ivy, could I ask you something?"

"Sure anything babe, is there something wrong?"

"No...no, I was just wondering if my going to the cemetery bothers you at all?"

"No, not at all." She stared at me.

"Are you sure? Come on Ivy I want the truth. The real truth does it bother you?"

"The truth?" She stared dead in my eyes.

I nodded my head. "The truth."

"Well truthfully at first it did bother me, but after a while...no, it doesn't bother me. I've accepted the fact that you had someone before me that you loved a great deal. I can't say that sometimes I don't get jealous." She moved closer to me. "If you loved her so much, then she must have been a great woman. Someone that special should never be forgotten."

I hugged her. "Thank you."

"For what?" She looked at me with her arms around my neck.

"For telling me the truth, and for understanding." I kissed her lightly and softly on each of her lips then on her cheek.

We finished up in the kitchen then sat outside. Ivy turned to me. "This feels like it's going to be a great day."

I smiled and lightly kissed her lips tenderly. "With you everyday is a great day." My eyes slowly opened and I smiled with my heart while I cupped her cheek in my hand.

We then heard a horn beeping out front. We both jumped up and ran to see who our first guest was. We went out the gate and saw that it was Windy and Koko. I ran to her and helped her with her bags. "Did you have a hard time finding the place?"

"No not at all, they were great directions. Hey guys this place is gorgeous." She stood there staring at the house.

"Thanks." I threw a diaper bag over my shoulder.

Ivy grabbed Windy's arm, as Windy held onto Koko. "Windy just wait until you see this place, it's unbelievable."

They both ran off and left me to get the bags. "That's okay I got everything." They turned around and looked at me as they continued to walk. I made it to the house carrying everything and watched while Ivy gave the grand tour.

I grabbed a beer and went outside. Walking over to the pool house I turned the stereo on then decided to go back inside and see what they were up to. I heard them walking around upstairs, then watched as they came walking down the stairway.

Windy walked up to me. "Mel I don't believe this house. You did all this by yourself?"

"Well I did have help." I laughed "So I guess you like it?"

"Absolutely."

I put my arm around her shoulder. "Come on, let me get you a beer."

"Now that sounds good."

Everybody walked in the kitchen and Ivy grabbed the baby as Windy reached for her beer and sat down. Windy and I watched while Ivy walked around carrying Koko.

Windy turned to me. "She's really great with her."

"Yeah, she is." I watched and smiled.

Ivy looked out the front door. "Donna and Vicky are here."

I watched as she went outside then I turned to Windy. "I think she was a tour guide in her past life."

Windy laughed and smacked my arm. "Oh, leave her alone she's happy, and who wouldn't be. Mel, the two of you have a great life here."

I stopped and looked at her. "Yeah, I guess we do. By the way so do you." I reached for her hand. "I can see every time I look in your eyes how much joy that little one has brought into your life. Now all you need is someone to share that with. I worry about you being all alone."

I held her hand while we walked to the front door.

"There's no need to worry. I have all that I can handle right now." She stared at her baby in Ivy's arms."

I laughed. "Yeah I guess you do have your hands full."

Then Donna yelled. "Mel I can't wait to see the inside."

Vicky grabbed her arm. "Me either."

They climbed the stairs and Ivy handed the baby over to me, then grabbed Donna and Vicky's hand. "Come on I'll give you the official tour."

I shook my head and laughed at her, then turned around looking at Windy. "There she goes again."

She smacked my arm. "Come on I'll set up her porta—crib, she should sleep for a little while."

After we finally got Koko settled we quietly sneaked off to the backyard where Donna and Vicky came up to us with a glass of champagne.

I looked at them. "What's this for?"

Vicky handed one to Windy. "Just wait you'll see." She grinned.

Ivy came over and stood by me. "Don't look at me, I have no idea."

Donna walked over and held her glass raised in one hand, her other was around Vicky's waist. "First I'd like to make a toast to Windy and her beautiful baby girl and hope that she brings her nothing but joy in the coming years."

We all drank.

"Hold on I'm not done." Everyone giggled. "Second I'd like to toast Mel and Ivy on their new life together in this magnificent home."

We all drank again and I smiled at Ivy.

"And third." The two of them looked at each other then back at us. Vicky moved closer to Donna. "I'd like to toast Donna and myself. Because we are adopting a beautiful baby boy." Vicky grabbed a hold of Donna's arm smiling.

I looked at Ivy then back at Donna. "Donna, Vicky that's great but..."

Donna was staring in Vicky's eyes. "Well there's a young girl where Vicky counsels and she had a baby she wanted to give up all rights to saying she couldn't even care for herself, let alone a baby. So we discussed it, and we're in a secure relationship, with a home, good jobs and some savings. So naturally we thought this is the next logical step in our relationship."

I walked up to them and hugged them both. "Guys this is so great."

As I stood there looking around at everyone I realized how much each one of us has been through, and exactly how much we all deserved this moment of joy and happiness.

The rest of the day we ate, drank and laughed.

Everyone took turns playing with Koko and I just couldn't get over the way Donna and Vicky glowed every time they told us about their new addition. It definitely was a day to remember.

Ivy and I both sat on the edge of the pool with our feet hanging in the water and I put my hand on top of hers. "This is what life's all about."

She started laughing hysterically, and I looked at her smiling.

"What?"

"Just the way you said that. I felt like I was in a beer commercial."

I pushed her in the water then jumped in after her.

CHAPTER 32

While I was holding on the phone, I heard a knock at my office door, and watched it open slowly.

"Mel?"

"Come on in Win." I pushed the phone to my neck.

"Oh, I didn't know you were on the phone, I'll come back." She started to leave.

"No." I hung up. "That's okay I'll try again later. Boy she's getting so big, bring her here." I held out my hands for Koko as I walked over towards Windy. "What's the matter no sitter today?"

"No, I was wondering if you could watch her while I run to the store. She's so cranky I think she's getting a tooth."

I rubbed my finger along her gum line. "Yeah it feels like it."

"Do you mind? I'll just be a minute."

I looked up at her grinning. "Are you kidding, Win take all the time you need." I lifted Koko in the air. "What has it been, maybe nine hours since I seen her last, I'm starting to go through withdraws."

She laughed. "You're silly. Do you need anything while I'm out?"

"Don't think so. Oh yeah, could you drop this off for me?" I reached inside my briefcase and pulled out a videotape.

"Sure." She looked at it. "This is on my way."

"Thanks."

"Is it anything good?"

"Not unless you like blood and guts."

"You know I don't."

"Well then no, it's nothing good."

"Alright, I'll be right back."

"Win!" She turned around and I looked up. "Take your time, really." I hugged Koko tight in my arms.

She smiled at me. "Take care of my baby girl."

"Always." I smiled and winked at her.

She slowly walked out the door and I looked down at Koko. "Mommy's gone now how about some whiskey on that tooth to make it stop hurting."

The door burst open "Mel!"

"Kidding." I laughed.

She left and I held Koko until she fell asleep in my arms, and then tried to make another phone call.

Finally I hung the phone up just as she started to stir. I gave her a bottle and walked to the front of the gallery while I kissed her head and spoke softly to her. "Your auntie Mel just made your mommy and me a lot of money."

I saw Tara. "Tara, have you heard from Windy. I know I told her to take her time but..." just then I saw a police car pull in front of the gallery and I felt a sinking feeling in the pit of my stomach. "Tara, come here please." She ran over to me. "Here take her." I handed Koko over to her just as she started crying, and then went outside. I took no more than a couple of steps when one of the policemen came up to me.

"Are you the owner?"

"Yes, I'm Melissa Hadley, why?" I stepped closer.

"There's been an accident."

I felt panic set in throughout my whole body. "An accident?"

"Yes, a Windy Berrington has been in an accident."

I felt my knees wanting to give way. "What happened?"

"It was a car accident, she's at the hospital why don't you come with us." He stepped aside directing me to his car.

"One minute." I ran as fast as I could into the gallery and screamed at Tara. "Tara! Tara!"

"Mel I'm right here." She came walking up to me.

"Call Donna and tell her to come and get Koko. Then meet me at the hospital." I felt tears in my eyes. "It's Windy."

"Mel, no!"

"I have to go. Call her!" I ran out and jumped in the back of the police car. "Can you tell me what happened?"

One looked at the other then the driver spoke. "She was hit by a drunk driver while she crossed the street"

"She's okay though, right." My heart raced.

He looked at the other again and I screamed. "She's okay, right?"

"I don't know."

I sat back in the car with the most vividly horrible pictures going through my head. Then I saw myself holding Koko while Windy smiled at me just before she left the gallery. Tears were now rolling steadily down my face, and if we didn't get to the hospital soon I was going to become hysterical.

Finally we pulled in the hospital's emergency parking and the officers took me right to her.

I stood there frozen, looking at her. Then I slowly walked up to her and took her hand in mine. I didn't know what to think, my eyes were swollen and my mind stopped working, there were so many machines making so many different noises. I could only watch her lying there quiet and still with a tube running down her throat forcing her to breathe.

I heard the door and turned to see the doctor standing there. "You must be Melissa." He held his hand out and I stepped to take it.

"She's okay right?" I stared in his eyes searching for some answers, but he looked away.

"Melissa why don't we go outside and talk."

"No, just tell me. In plain English, is she going to be okay?" I stared, watching his eyes.

"No I'm afraid she's not. You see her brain is already dead, it's just that the rest of her body doesn't know it yet."

"What are you saying?" Tears rolled down my face and dripped off my chin landing on my blouse.

"In her wallet next to your name was the name of a lawyer. We called him and apparently Windy had made out a living will."

"What?"

"In case of something like this Melissa, where there really is no hope, she named someone to take care of everything."

"What exactly do you mean?" My eyes were squinting and I knew exactly what he meant.

"She has a Living Will." He stared at me. "It's in case of something like this she does not want do be kept alive by machines."

I screamed in anger. "I know what it means."

He looked at me. "Melissa…We're to that point."

"There's no hope, that can't be. There's got to be something you can do."

"There's not. There is one other thing though."

I watched his eyes and knew exactly what he was going to say.

"Melissa she named you as the person to shut her respirator off."

"Me…Why me?" I looked down at her laying there, machines pumping all around her.

"The lawyer is on his way with the paperwork. I'll let you be alone for a while, then I'll be back later."

He stood there for a minute, and then walked out the door. I couldn't move I just stared at her lying there. Finally I sat down in a chair next to her bed and held her hand, staring at her face. I couldn't stop the tears, I was thinking of nothing and everything at the same time. Then I felt a hand on my shoulder; I turned around to see Ivy standing there. I couldn't even talk; I just turned back to Windy.

She knelt down next to me. "Mel I just heard."

I still didn't say anything.

"Mel, did you call her mother?" She wouldn't look away from me. I shook my head no.

"Alright, I'll go and call then." She left the room.

I stared at Windy. "Oh Win, why? Why did this happen?" I laid my head on her arm. "I can't do this again Win, I can't go through this a second time. I can't bear the thought of living my life without you. God, I love you Win. You're my best friend; you're the one who replaced Sarah as my rock. What about Koko, she needs you as much as I do. How could I possibly go on without you? Please Win, give me a smile right now and I'll give you the world."

I couldn't stop crying. "Please Win, look at me. Give me your world famous smile." I continued to lie there rubbing her hand. Then the doctor came back in.

"Excuse me Melissa."

I looked up wiping my face. "Yes."

"The lawyer came with the papers."

"I have to wait for her mother, maybe in that time she'll improve."

He walked over and stood next to me. "Melissa believe me, if there were any hope, I wouldn't be here talking to you about this."

"What about her baby?" Tears just flowed over my cheeks and down my chin.

He stood there saying nothing. Then I laid my head back down on her hand.

As I lay there I heard Ivy in the room, then I heard silence. I looked up and I was alone again. This time I got up and sat on the edge of Windy's bed. I kept staring in her face, hoping and praying that she would open her eyes. "Win why would you pick me to do this? I don't know if I can, I don't think I'll have the strength...Win, how could I flip that switch and watch you die...Watch you struggle for breath...Win I'm not that strong."

I heard someone open the door and turned to see Ivy.

She walked up to me and put her hands on my shoulders. "Mel why don't we take a walk, Donna and Vicky are here."

I jumped up. "What!" I screamed. "Where's Koko they are suppose to be taking care of her!"

"Mel, calm down." She moved to stand in front of me. "Let's go for a walk and we'll see." She turned to catch my eyes.

"No." I rubbed Windy's hand and watched her face. "I'm not leaving her."

She shook me. "Mel!"

I turned around.

"She'll be alright alone for one minute."

"Ivy I can't. I just can't leave her, not right now." I stared at her, loving her with tears in my eyes.

I heard her sigh loudly behind me, and then she removed her hands and walked out. I turned my attentions back to Windy.

I took my hand and rubbed her hair, and then I lightly stroked her face with the back of my fingers. "Oh Windy, you don't know how many times I wonder if I made a mistake. Should I have chosen you? Would it have made a difference today? Every time that I look at you I see and feel nothing but true love. I hurt you so many times, I often wondered why you still wanted me around." I stared at her and wiped my tears. Then I turned my head when I heard someone at the door. I saw Donna come in, and then I turned back to Windy. "Donna where is Koko?"

"Mel." She grabbed my arms. "Don't worry she's fine. Tara's at my house right now with her." She squeezed my arms tightly. "Mel come on, let's go get some air." She pulled me up.

I stood up. "Donna I don't want to leave her alone." I threw my arms around her and hugged her tightly.

"You don't need to, Vicky will stay with her." Donna stepped back and stared in my eyes.

I let go of her and looked around. "Where is she?" My head snapped to the door when I heard it open.

I watched Donna walk and open the door. "She's right here Mel." She put her arm around me. "Now come on."

I moved to the door, and then looked back. I didn't want to leave, but I knew that I had to get my head together.

I finally stepped through the door. Walking out I saw the doctor standing talking to Ivy. When she saw me she came right over.

I immediately hugged her.

Then she looked at me. "Let's go get some coffee okay?"

"Yeah, alright, but then I'm coming right back."

"Sure." She had her arm around my shoulder as we walked down the hallway.

"Ivy." I stared straight ahead while we walked. "When is her mother going to get here?"

"Late tonight."

I shook my head and we kept walking.

We went downstairs to the cafeteria and sat down while Donna got everyone coffee.

While we sat there Ivy had her hand on mine and I stared down at her fingers tangled in mine. "Ivy is this true, is there no hope?" I looked at her with tears in my eyes.

She looked down, then back up, and stared deep into my eyes. "Mel." She patted my hand. "No, there is no hope. I'm sorry but everything Dr. Richards has told you is true."

I put both my hands over my face. "Ivy how could this be happening?"

Donna came and sat down with our coffee. I looked up at her. "Donna did you see the document? Is it real?"

"Yeah Mel, it is. She must have thought you would be the one with the strength to do what she wanted."

"Donna I don't know if I can. I don't think I have that kind of strength."

"Don't worry Mel, you'll do the right thing."

Ivy put her hand on mine. "Honey, sometimes the hardest thing to do is an act of kindness."

I looked at her then sat there sipping my coffee. "Did the police say what exactly happened?"

Donna put her coffee down following it with her eyes. "All they would tell me was that she got hit crossing the street. Apparently the guy who hit her was drunk and went through a red light." She looked up at me. "She still had her video tape in her hand."

My hand started shaking so bad I dropped my coffee. "Shit, I'm sorry." I tried to wipe it up.

Ivy grabbed my wrist. "Mel what's the matter?"

I turned to her barely able to talk. "Ivy, that was our tape." I wiped my face. "I asked her to take it back for me."

I placed my hand on the table as I stood up. Then I closed my eyes. "I killed her!" I felt Ivy's hand on my back.

"Mel! You did not!"

I looked at her. "I did! No matter what you say I did." I started walking away. I heard Donna yelling for me but I just kept walking.

Opening Windy's door I saw Vicky sitting in the chair next to her bed. I walked past her then sat on the edge of her bed grabbing her hand.

I stared in her face. "Windy I did this to you. It's because of me that you're here, yet I'm the one who's suppose to let you die. How in the hell am I suppose to live with this?" I looked up at the ceiling. "Sarah I don't think I've ever needed you more."

I turned my head when I heard a door. Vicky must have left. I pulled the chair next to her bed while I still held her hand. I sat down, staring at her till my eyes where tired, then I laid my head on her bed.

The next thing I heard was Sarah's voice whispering, Windy's going to need you Mel. With my eyes still closed I saw her face with a glow around it. I reached my hand out to her, then I heard a noise so loud I almost fell off her bed. I lifted my head to see Windy's mother in the room.

I didn't say anything; I just got up and walked over to her, and hugged her. Instead of putting her arms around me she began to beat me with her fists.

"Mel I know what happened." She started crying hysterically. "And don't think you are going to kill her. I've got my lawyer coming over here right now."

I just cried as I stood there, letting her hit me.

Then I heard Donna burst through the door. "Hey! What's going on here?" She pulled her off of me and I just stood there. I watched her fall to the chair, and then walked out the door.

I ran into the bathroom and let the cold water run over my hands and fingers before splashing it on my face. I raised my head to look in the mirror and I saw Ivy standing behind me.

"Mel, are you okay?"

"Yeah…I'm okay." I looked down into the sink with my hands resting on the edges, watching the water rush down the drain. Then I looked up in the mirror again at Ivy. "Ivy, I'm going to let her mother stay with her a while, then could you please bring the doctor in."

She stared at me in the mirror. "You sure?"

"I'm sure, I mean this is what she wanted. She must have felt I would do the right thing. From the looks of her mother she wouldn't, and I'm sure Windy knew that. It is the right thing, isn't it?" I looked in her eyes for some sort of reassurance, then I saw her nod her head.

"Yes Mel, it's the right thing. I'm going to go and talk to the doctor. You going to be okay?" She put her hands on my shoulders.

"I'm fine."

I stood there staring at myself in the mirror trying to convince myself I was doing the right thing. As I stood there I felt myself starting to get sick, I ran into one of the stalls.

When I came out I saw Donna standing there and she handed me a bunch of paper towels. "You okay?"

"Why does everyone keep asking me that? No I'm not!" I bent my head down in the sink and splashed my face with water and rinsed my mouth out. "Donna I'm sorry." I rested my head on my hands, and then lifted it and Donna gave me more paper towels.

"Don't worry about it. I understand."

"Thanks." I wiped my face and sat on the edge of the sink. I looked back at Donna. "How's Koko?"

"She's great, Tara's still at my house with her."

"Good." We both sat quietly not saying a word for what seemed like forever.

Finally I climbed off the sink. "I'm going back in there."

"Mel her mother's still in there."

"So." I walked out the door. Then I heard Donna running after me.

"Mel, wait!" She grabbed my shoulder. "Why don't you let me get her out of there first."

"Alright go ahead and try, but if you can't I'm still going in."

"Okay, but just give me five minutes."

"Alright, I'm going to go and call Tara then."

I walked over to the phone while I watched her go into Windy's room. Tara answered on the first ring. I really didn't need to tell her anything, Donna pretty much kept her up to date. I guess I just wanted to know for myself that Windy's baby was okay.

I hung up with her and sat down in a chair that was next to the phone. I stared at Windy's door waiting for her mother to leave, and then I just couldn't take waiting anymore. I started to get up, that's when her door opened. I saw Donna coming out with her arm around Windy's mother.

I sat back down until they were out of the way, then I walked to her room. Opening the door I looked at her, hoping there would be some kind of change. There wasn't. I sat down on the edge of her bed and held her hand. "Oh Win I still can't believe all of this is happening. I've decided to do what you want even though I don't think I'll ever be the same afterwards." I laid my head on her chest and listened to her heartbeat. The soothing sounds of her heart and the pure exhaustion that I felt, I fell immediately asleep.

Again I saw Sarah and my head bolted up. I looked around the room and nothing. I started rubbing my head. "Not now, I can't start to lose it now." I heard a knock at the door and I turned my head, I saw the doctor walking in.

"Melissa."

I looked back at Windy. "Is there any improvement?"

"No. There's not." He walked over to me and put his hand on my shoulder. I was told you're going to go through with her final wishes."

I shook my head. "That's right, I am."

"You just have to remember, it's what she wanted. She picked you because she must have known that you loved her enough to do this. Only a selfish person would let her lay there."

"I know." I looked up at him. "So now what?"

He spoke, and I listened but I had no idea what he said. All I knew was that he left and I turned back to Windy with tears rolling down my face. "Well honey this is it. I pray to God that I'm doing the right thing. I want you to know as long as I live and breathe I'll be there for your little girl. If it's up to me, she will never want for anything. Remember always that I love you, and I'm sorry for everything Win. Everything, and I mean that with all my heart. When you see Sarah and I know you will, give her a big kiss for me." I sat there holding her hand until I heard the door opening.

The doctor came back in. "Her mother chose not to be here."

I looked at her and whispered. "I love you Win, go peacefully."

I sat back in the chair and held her hand as my heart broke watching the life drain out of her. At that moment I had flash backs of the first time I ever-laid eyes on her. I thought she was so beautiful, I even remember what she was wearing. She just opened up the gallery and was inside cleaning, she had on a pair of old jeans and an old tattered red sweater. She was so beautiful.

I believe the day I first fell in love with her though was the day she helped me move out of my house and into the barn. Laying playing games with her in front of the fire until we both fell asleep. But the most love I felt for her was when I helped her with the birth of her baby. As long as I live I'll never forget that.

God Win, no one in my life will ever match what we had.

All of a sudden I felt a hand on my shoulder. I turned around wiping my eyes to look in the doctor's face.

"It was fast, she really must have been ready."

I turned back to her, I must have blacked everything that was happing out by remembering the past. I heard him leave the room after he said something I didn't hear. Looking up at the ceiling I closed my eyes and prayed for her. Only minutes went by before I heard the door open again. Without turning around I knew it was her mother. She grabbed me from behind pulling me away from her; I was so weak she threw me around like a rag doll.

I looked back at Windy with her mother lying on her chest and just felt empty. Standing there I watched as her mother screamed at me.

Then I turned to leave, but not before she came up to me and grabbed my arm.

"I'm taking my daughter and my granddaughter home with me, and I never want to see you again!"

I walked out and she was still screaming at me as I passed Ivy and Donna. Vicky ran up to me trying to grab my arm but I jerked it away from her.

I heard Donna yell to her. "Vic, let her go!"

Vicky stopped.

"Just let her go."

I kept walking, I had no idea where. I just knew that I had to leave. As I walked I felt like my head was in a cloud. Everything was fuzzy. I felt dizzy. I couldn't really think of anything all I did was have memories of Windy. Then Windy's face turned into Sarah's. I kept seeing Sarah's face surrounded by an orange glow, smiling at me. I could feel my self starting to panic so I turned to the nearest bar. I walked in not even looking around and ordered a beer and a shot of tequila. I sat down with my hands holding up my head when the bartender came over.

"Thanks. Don't go anywhere." I drank the shot and asked for another. He poured again and I held my hand up for him to stay.

He looked at me. "Are you alright? Do you want me to call anyone for you?" He stood with his hand resting on the neck of the bottle.

I shook my head no and motioned for him to pour another. He left after the third shot and I lifted my head to look at myself in the mirror behind the bar. I hated what I saw. I waved the bartender down and asked him if he could call me a cab. He shook his head yes, then walked away.

I sat there wondering what the rest of my life would be like without Windy in it, her, Sarah, Koko all of them gone. I could only wonder if Ivy was next. I finished my beer just in time for the cab driver to come walking inside.

I crawled in the back and told him to take me home.

It was a short ride, I walked most of the way, but it was long enough that I still couldn't get everything out of my head.

I walked around the house remembering all the times that Windy and the baby were here. I sat in the chair she sat in just looking around. Then I got up and went upstairs. I packed a bag, grabbed my car keys and walked out the door.

I sat in my car grasping the steering wheel wondering what I was doing or where I was going. I didn't know, but I did know that I had to leave. Before I put my jeep in reverse I pulled a piece of paper out of my glove box and a pen. I began to write.

Dearest Ivy,

I love you, that's for sure. I know that for a fact. Nothing else in my life is for sure though. It seems like everyone I love dies. I know that sounds like an excuse for what I'm doing but it's not really. My body and soul just can't go through one more tragedy like this.

What I'm trying to say is I need to get away. I don't know where. I'd stay to say goodbye, but I can't bear to have Koko ripped out of my life too. So I'm leaving before that can happen. Plus I can't bear to look in your incredible green eyes and see how much I'm hurting you.

Can you please leave word for Tara to close the gallery down until further notice. Thanks.

Ivy, please don't forget the love I feel for you. I will understand though if you feel you can't wait for me, and you have to leave. But where ever you go and what ever you do please carry the love I have for you in your heart. You will always be in mine.

I love you,

M.

I folded the paper and got out of my jeep.

After setting the letter on the kitchen table I opened the back door and picked a wildflower then laid it on top of the letter.

With tears rolling down my face I turned and walked out.

CHAPTER 33

❀

*A*fter driving for a few minutes I realized I was in no shape to drive for any kind of distance, so I went straight downtown to a hotel.

Once in my room I ordered a pitcher of martinis to be sent up. Then I ran a bath.

I poured a drink and climbed in the tub. While I lay there I wondered if Ivy came home from the hospital yet. Then I went over and over everything that's happened to me in the last couple of days...I still couldn't believe it.

Getting out of the tub I poured another drink, then laid on the bed. I tried to close my eyes but images of Windy kept fogging my head. I sat back up and got dressed. While I combed my hair, I stared at myself in the mirror, and then I leaned on the sink with my hands. I still couldn't stand what I saw.

I turned and left.

I sat down in the hotel bar and ordered a martini. Sitting there I ordered drink after drink, trying not to think of what happened today, but unable to forget.

My head fell to my drink, and then I pulled my hair back from my face and looked up in the mirror. "My God!" I turned around. "What are you doing here?"

"I heard about Windy, Mel I'm so sorry."

I got off the barstool and hugged her. "Lily, I'm really glad to see you."

"Come on let's go and sit down."

I grabbed my drink and Lily grabbed my arm to help steady me. We walked over to a small table in the corner of the bar.

"Mel what happened?" She put her hand in mine and stared into my eyes.

"Lily, could we please not talk about this right now. I just want to have a good time." I looked at her hand.

"Okay, well then let's go."

I looked up at her. "Go where?"

"Go some place where we could have a good time."

I picked up my drink and downed it, then grabbed her arm and we both walked out. I crawled into the back of her limo while she talked to the driver for a minute, then she came in.

I looked at her. "So where are we going?"

"I don't really know myself, but my driver knows where he's going. So we'll just leave ourselves in his capable hands."

She handed me a bottle of water.

I turned it around in my hand looking at it. "Don't you have something else?"

"No, right now I think that you need this more."

Where ever we were going it wasn't that far. Lily and I hardly had a chance to talk.

We walked inside and the combination of the drive, fresh air and water must have helped clear my head a little because I felt a lot steadier on my feet. I looked around the bar and I remembered being here one other time with Donna.

I turned to Lily. "Thanks. I feel a lot better."

"Good. You said you wanted to have fun, and the night's still young."

We went up to the bar, ordered ourselves a couple of drinks then walked around looking for a seat. There was one seat open at the bar.

I let Lily sit while I stood next to her with my arm around her chair. "So, how did you manage to get some time off?"

"I actually have a couple of weeks off. My character's in a coma so I get some time off for a change."

I laughed. "Great, so what do you have planned?"

"Not a damn thing."

As we sat there laughing, we didn't really talk about anything of importance. We had what I always had with Lily and that was fun. It seemed like for a couple of hours out of the day I actually thought about nothing.

I leaned forward close to her ear. "So Lily tell me, are you still married or are you available?"

She laughed. "Like it would matter. I know you're in love with someone." She pushed me. "So stop teasing."

I laughed at her while I stared in her eyes. "Who's teasing?"

She looked at me questionably. "Well, I did get a divorce about a month ago. I just couldn't live a lie anymore."

"Good for you. You're a wonderful person and you really deserve to be happy."

She stared into my eyes. "I was happy."

I looked at her and didn't know if it was the alcohol or everything that happened today but I found her irresistible. I placed my hand that I had on her chair around her neck and pulled her to me staring into her eyes.

I stopped just before I kissed her, and then pulled her to me.

I kissed her as if I haven't kissed someone in years, and then whispered. "Let's dance."

A slow song was playing. I don't know what it was and I didn't care. My hand fell down her waist and she hesitated as she looked at me, and then jumped down off the barstool.

I had my arm around her waist as we walked to the dance floor, then I pulled her to me.

My hands traveled her back then slowly made their way around her. She laid her head against my shoulder and my hand moved up her neck and played with her hair.

"Mel, what are you doing to me?"

"I don't know Lily. I don't know." I gripped her even tighter. "Do you want me to stop?"

"You know that I don't."

I leaned back to look in her eyes then touched her face, first with the front of my hand, then with the back. She laid her head on my hand and I pulled her to me. I didn't know what I was doing, all I knew was that right now I thought about nothing, and that's what I wanted.

I held her close. "Let's go."

She leaned back and looked at me.

I smiled at her and threw my head to the side. "Come on."

I was the first to crawl in the limo, and then pulled Lily in after me. She landed next to me and I immediately put my arms around her. "Come here."

She laid on me and I held her head in my hands. "Lily I had a great time tonight, thanks."

I started kissing her and instantly remembered how passionate our relationship used to be. My hands traveled from her face to her sides, then up her shirt.

She pulled back and looked at me. I stared at her as my hands lifted her shirt and unhooked her bra.

"Mel…"

"Shhh…"

She fell back on top of me.

We pulled up in front of the hotel and I helped Lily fix herself up, then I grabbed her face. "Stay with me." I looked straight in her eyes.

She said nothing and we both got out of the car.

CHAPTER 34

✿

Waking, I rolled over and held my head then realized I was alone. I got up, threw a t-shirt on and went into the bathroom.

When I came out I heard a knock at the door. I opened the door to Lily. "Come on in."

She stepped through the door. "How do you feel?"

I rubbed my head. "Better than I thought I would."

She came in and I shut the door behind her. "Lily I don't really remember much of what happened last night."

She put her fingers on my mouth. "Don't worry Mel nothing really happened. I put you to bed, and I left."

I don't know if I felt sad or relieved. "How about I buy you breakfast."

She smiled. "Alright."

When I went to change I felt good. It seems like when I'm with her my other life never existed.

I walked back to her and took her in my arms, when I did I thought of nothing but her, nothing. Windy, Sarah, Koko, Ivy nobody existed. I thought of nothing, and no one.

I looked in her eyes and wondered how I could do this. I knew I was in love with Ivy and the last thing I wanted to do was hurt her, but I was so confused. It was as if I was out to destroy everything in my life that was good, like I didn't deserve it. I pushed all of that out of my head and fell to the bed with Lily.

I pulled her hair back from her face with my hands. "Let's go. Let's hop on a plane and just go."

"Mel, you're crazy." She tried to push herself off me, but I held on tight.

"I'm not. You said yourself you have time off, and I don't want to be here. So let's go."

"What about Ivy? What about your family?"

"Let's face it Lily they would be better off without me."

"Mel! That's not true."

"It is true. They might not know it now, but they will. Come on what do you say?" She looked in my eyes like I was crazy. "You can come with me, or I'm just going to go alone."

She started laughing and rolled off me onto her side. "Okay! Okay, I'll go."

I jumped on top of her. "You will!"

"I will. Where are we going?"

"I don't know. Let's go to the airport and see what the next flight is."

"You're nuts!"

"That could very well be." I bent down and kissed her passionately on the mouth then rolled off of her on my side as my hands traveled her body. She stopped my hand just as it started to cross her stomach.

"Mel maybe we should wait."

"Wait, why?"

"Deep down I know you don't really want to do this. I know you and you'll hate yourself."

"See that's what no one understands Lily." I rolled off the bed and stood up. "I already hate myself. But if you want to wait, we'll wait." I walked into the bathroom, then back out. "Now come on let's pack up and go. I'll buy you that breakfast on the way."

I sat next to her on the plane thinking of everything that I was leaving behind. Then I looked at Lily and wondered what she was thinking. I turned away again looking out the window as the plane lifted off.

Well if I was going to turn back it's too late now. Now I'm on my way to Mexico. I laid my head back and wondered if anyone even cared that I was gone. I know for a fact that Windy's mother didn't. I wish I could have gone to Windy's funeral, but what's the point. I turned my head and watched as we climbed higher and higher into nothingness.

After all I said my goodbyes to Windy, the last thing that I would be able to handle would be a funeral.

I felt Lily's hand on mine. "Do you want to talk?"

I turned and looked at her with tears in my eyes. "Not yet." I gripped her hand then turned to face the window again.

CHAPTER 35

O nce we were finally settled in I grabbed Lily. "I'm starving let's eat."

We ran out of the hotel and found a great restaurant and ate and drank until we could barely move, then we went to the bar and we danced, and drank...and drank. Before we knew it, it was dark out and we were pretty drunk.

While we sat at our table I watched Lily, she was having so much fun. I was starting to hate myself all over again for dragging her down here. I felt like I was just using her to forget my problems, not worrying how this would affect her.

She turned to me and smiled. "Mel this is great. It's just what I needed. Thanks!"

I watched her for a little while longer then grabbed for her hand. "Come on let's go for a walk."

We walked the beach and looked at the stars, then I turned to her, standing there in the moonlight beneath billions of stars I wished it were Ivy.

"Mel, are you okay?"

"No Lily, I'm sorry for all of this. I'm going through such a rough time that I didn't even consider your feelings. I'm sorry."

She smiled. "Don't be. I'm having fun, and if I could help you through this then that would make me happy." She held on to my hand and stared in my eyes. "You know how much I care about you."

"It's just that I don't know what's going to happen from here." I looked out towards the ocean.

"Mel I'm here for you. I'll always be here for you. I'm here because I want to be here, believe me I know where your heart is." She turned my head with her hand to look in her eyes. "Maybe one day your heart will be mine again."

I smiled because I knew that she meant everything she said. "Come on let's sit down." We walked over to a table that was in the middle of nowhere.

"So." She rested her hand on top of mine as we sat there. "Are you finally ready to tell me what's going on with you yet?"

I turned and looked in her eyes. "Lily I missed you. We always had such a good time together."

"We did, we still do."

"Ever since you, my life has been so confusing." I rested my elbow on the table and ran my fingers through my hair. "Just when things seem to be going great for me, all hell breaks loose. First Windy being attacked then everything that went along with that."

"What do you mean?"

I sat there telling her everything, from beginning to end, starting with Windy and ending with Windy. She was so caring and understanding I'm happy I was finally able to talk to someone about this and I'm glad it was her. The whole time that I talked with her I couldn't stop my tears from flowing. People always say that tears cleanse the soul. Well not this soul, all they seemed to do was remind me of the guilt that's eating me alive.

While we sat there the bartenders constantly replenished our drinks. Hours went by while I bared my soul to Lily.

Lily got up to go to the bathroom and I turned my attention to the ocean surf.

Staring out into the ocean, I wondered what Sarah would say to me now. I know for a fact she would tell me I was being selfish for taking off like this, and I probably am. I thought about Ivy and how much I missed her, but I knew I was no good for her. She deserves someone who could give their full attention to her. I can't.

I felt Lily's hand on my shoulder. I turned around and looked at her. Then she touched my cheek. "So Mel." She knelt down beside me. "Ready for bed?"

I continued to look into her eyes. "Yeah." I smiled at her. "I am."

🍁   🍁   🍁

Opening my eyes it was near dawn and Lily had her arms wrapped tightly around me. I slowly crawled out from beneath her grip and put my robe on.

I walked out onto the balcony and sat down to watch the sunrise. As the sun started to crest above the ocean I remembered the sunrise I watched with Ivy in North Carolina. The rays that warmed my skin then matched the warmth in my heart now as I thought of her.

I looked down at my hand and touched the ring she gave me with my fingertips, and then pulled it off. I held it in my fingers and twirled it in the sun. It really was beautiful. I walked inside, addressed an envelope to Ivy and put the ring in it. Getting dressed I walked to the mailbox, and on my way back stopped to get coffee for Lily and myself.

I jumped in bed with Lily. "Get up sleepy head it's a gorgeous day and we're in paradise."

She moaned and tried to cover herself with the blanket.

"Oh no you don't." I pulled it away from her and started kissing her shoulder.

I rolled her over on her back and started to kiss her neck, while she grabbed my hair with both her hands. She moaned my name over and over and I threw her legs over my shoulders.

"Oh Mel!" She pulled my hair. "How I missed you." She shouted my name and pulled my hair as she shuddered beneath me.

I kissed her stomach and she hugged my head. "Let's go shopping."

I smiled up at her. "Great." I sweetly kissed her soft skin.

"So what kind of shopping did you have in mind?"

She giggled. "We both need bathing suits, and some more clothes."

I squeezed her with my legs. "Maybe bathing suits, but no more clothes."

"Agreed." She laughed.

We shopped around for hours and finally we were back at the hotel and Lily threw all of her bags on the bed. "I bought something for you while I was shopping." She pulled a tiny bathing suit out of her bag and handed it to me.

I grabbed it. "Lily do you expect me to actually wear this?" I fell back on the bed laughing.

"Yeah, try it on."

I sat up. "Okay, but you wait here."

She stood there while I went into the bathroom. I took my clothes off and put the bathing suit on. "Now Lily before I come out, tell me what possessed you to buy this suit?"

"I knew you'd look great in it. Now come on and let me see it."

I came walking out wrapped in a towel, then stood in front of her and dropped it. An instant smile came over her face and she started walking towards me. "Mel you look great, that suit is you?"

She put her arms around my waist and I fell back against the wall as she started kissing me, her hands were on the wall at either side of my head and her kisses were hard and passionate.

Then she stepped back and stared seductively in my eyes while a sheepish grin came over her face, and her fingers slowly pulled the string of my suit and my top fell down.

I laid my head back and pulled her hair, making her kiss and bite at my neck. Her kisses then traveled down my neck only to pay careful attention to each breast, and at the same time her hands pulled at the bottom of my suit.

My breathing became deeper and deeper as my heart pounded faster and faster, and Lily's hand lost itself in my bathing suit bottom.

I pulled her mouth up to mine and kissed her like nothing existed but our pure lust. I wanted her. My body wanted her. My soul ached for comfort, and she was always able to comfort me.

I bit her lip softly. "Oh Lily." I threw my head back while she bit my neck. Sucking, biting, driving me crazy. My head was dizzy and light and my hands were still tangled in her hair. With my head back and my eyes closed I totally lost myself in her as she kissed her way back down my chest.

I, for the first time felt nothing but passion and desire and down and dirty just plain lust. Her mouth was hungry and made its way slowly down my stomach.

My body threw itself against her while my hands held her head tight. My fingers ran their way through her hair loving the feel of it, and then they gripped tightly, gently pulling. Pulling her mouth tight to me.

Her tongue was soft and wet and hot, and I lost myself to her.

My knees became weak as my breathing became irregular and I lost focus of everything. It was the best I felt in weeks.

I pulled her head up to mine. "You're incredible." My eyes were half-mast and a smile fell across my face.

"How about I buy you a drink and we go for a swim." She stood in front of me with her arms around my neck giving me small and soft kisses.

I giggled. "I'll follow you anywhere. Now go and put that body in a tiny swimsuit."

"Mel…"

I held her face in my hands. "I mean that, you're beautiful."

392   Visions of Sarah

She smiled and went to change

We went downstairs, ordered some food, some margaritas and lay on the beach getting drunk all day. We talked and laughed and relaxed so much that when I happened to look over at Lily, she was sleeping in her lounge chair.

I smiled and looked out at the ocean. Then a woman walked by that made my head bolt up. "Ivy!" I screamed, sitting up.

But it wasn't her.

That's it I'm calling Donna, if Ivy's out of my life then she'll be out of my head. Or so I think anyway.

I woke Lily up and we went back to our room.

Lily crawled into bed, and I followed. I'll call Donna after a much needed nap.

I woke up to running water and after my arm fell across the bed and it was empty next to me, I assumed that Lily was in the shower.

I rubbed my head, and then decided to give Donna that call. "Donna?"

"Mel, is that you? Where the hell are you?"

"It doesn't mater." I sat up and held my head in my hand.

"Mel, Ivy has been going crazy. Did you call her?"

My elbows fell to my knees. "No."

"Why not?"

"That's why I was calling."

"Mel, I don't like the sound of this."

"Donna just listen, she doesn't need me. She deserves a lot better. How could I love her the way she deserves to be loved if I can't even stand the sight of myself?"

"Mel, so you're going through a lot. We all know that, but you have to come home sometime."

"No. Donna I don't." I laid back down on the bed. "I'll just go on with my life somewhere else. Right now I can't even face her."

"Mel…"

"Donna I'm not alone."

"Mel...No!"

"It's better this way." My hand fell to twirl my hair through my fingers.

"Mel, why are you doing this?"

"I love her too much." I covered my eyes, and then sat up.

"Then come home to her."

"I can't, with everything that's happened, it's only a matter of time before I freak out again. Donna I just don't deserve to be happy. I don't want to care for anyone again. I can't take that kind of loss again...I just can't." I started crying.

"Mel, just tell me where you are."

"Donna I have to go." I wiped my face with my hand. "Tell Ivy...I don't know. Don't even tell her I called. I'll have my attorney call her. I want her to have the house, after all I built it for her."

"Mel, you should really call her."

"Donna..."

"Yeah?"

"Tell her...tell her I really love her, that's why I'm doing this."

"Mel this is crazy." Her voice was stern and shaky at the same time.

"Yeah...well. Bye Donna."

I hung up and turned to see Lily standing behind me. "Mel you should really go to her."

"No I should really order us some drinks and take a shower, then make love to you all night." I grabbed her spinning her around.

She laughed loudly. "Go and get in the shower and I'll order drinks."

"You know, you could join me." My head leaned to the bathroom.

She pushed me. "Just go."

I went and jumped in the shower then stood there while the water ran down my body. Slowly I sat down and hugged my legs wondering if I was doing the right thing. I just wanted to take back the last week and start all over, but I knew that was impossible. Sitting there I watched the water rush it's way fighting to get down the drain and wondered if my life will ever be normal again.

I opened the bathroom door and saw Lily standing on the balcony in a little sundress holding a margarita. I quietly and slowly snuck up behind her and slipped my arms around her waist from behind. "You look and feel great."

She grabbed my hands. "Thanks." Then she went inside and turned the stereo on.

When she laid next to me I felt good being with her, comfortable. Turning my head I looked at her, when she was with me I almost forgot all about my life before now. I didn't think at all, all I did was feel. Everything with Lily was passion and fire. The time we spent in Mexico not a day went by that didn't involve one or the other.

Sex with Lily was amazing, although I knew it wasn't everything, and my thoughts often drifted to Ivy.

Again I looked at Lily and I put my hand on her forearm. I smiled then leaned in to kiss her. "I'm really glad you're here with me."

"Me too."

Days went by and the time that I spent with her was perfect I was hoping to talk her into staying longer with me. I walked out of the bathroom and saw her standing in the middle of the bedroom.

She looked at me. "Mel while you were in the shower I called the airlines and there's a flight leaving in the morning for New York, I think we should get on it."

I stared at her. "Lily I'm going to stay, but I understand if you have to leave."

"Mel I don't feel comfortable leaving and having you stay here all alone."

I moved towards her. "So don't leave." I grinned and grabbed her around the waist.

"Mel." Her hands landed on my shoulders. "I have to get back to work and you have to get back to life."

I pulled her hand and she sat down on the edge of the bed. "Don't worry about me. I have a lot of decisions to make." I looked away. "And maybe it's better if I'm alone. Besides I have nothing to go home to."

She smacked my arm. "Don't be silly, you have family and friends at home that I'm sure are worried about you?"

"If you're leaving in the morning, I certainly don't want to spend the time we have left talking about this." I grabbed her and pushed her down on the bed.

She kissed me, and then pushed me off of her. I laughed. "Why don't you go put your suit on and we'll lay by the pool."

She sat up. "Alright, if you promise me that you'll think about leaving with me."

I threw my hands over my head then I sat up next to her and kissed the back of her neck. "Lily I can't promise you that." My head landed on her shoulder.

She sighed and got up.

I fell back on the bed and wished I never had to go home, never had to face anyone or make any more decisions. Life would be so easy if I could just stay here forever and hide out.

I heard Lily yelling for me to get up. I laughed and chased her into the bathroom

We ordered drinks then laid by the pool.

I turned to Lily. "Don't be mad."

"I'm not. It's just that I worry about you."

"I know, and I appreciate it."

She stared at me. "Mel you should really call Ivy. I know if it were me I'd be going out of my mind with worry."

I turned away. "I talked to Donna, I'm sure she called her by now."

"But still."

I patted her arm. "So what are you going to do when you get back?"

She laughed and shook her head. "Boy you can really change the subject." Then she looked at me. "Maybe you should come home with me. I think we could really be happy together."

She lowered her head and looked at me from the top of her sunglasses.

I smiled. "I think we could too, but I'm going to stay. I need time to think." I laid my head back.

"Mel...could you ever love me?"

I looked at her and slowly took my sunglasses off.

She looked down then back at me. "I mean the way that you love Ivy. Could you ever love me that way?"

My eyes never lost hers. "Lily I do love you. I don't need to be ruining your life like I've ruined everyone else's and if I go to New York with you that's just what I'll be doing. You'll end up losing your career and blaming me for it. Trust me."

She didn't say anything; she just turned to look straight ahead. She knew I was right, even though she didn't want to admit it, she knew.

We sat quietly for a while then I pulled her by the hand. "Come on let's go for a swim."

It took a lot of pulling, but she finally gave in and we both jumped in the water. We grabbed a couple of floats and our drinks, and laid back.

❧   ❧   ❧

I woke up with Lily wrapped in my arms. I knew she was leaving today and I didn't want to be alone. I didn't want to think about my life or make any decisions. I laid my head on her pillow next to hers and squeezed her tightly.

"Mel, I can't breathe." She giggled and grabbed my hand.

"I'm going to miss you, are you sure you want to leave."

"You are making it hard. But I have to. I've got to get back to work." She rolled over to face me. "Besides if I stay here with you I'm going to fall harder then I already have." She started to kiss my neck.

"I'm really sorry Lily that I can't give you what you want right now." I laid my head on her neck then softly kissed her. "Maybe…" I looked up.

She put her fingers over my lips. "Shhh don't say anything that I'm going to hold you to."

I stopped and just stared at her. "Call me when you get home okay."

"Sure." She smiled her sweet smile.

"Promise me."

"I do. Now come on let's conserve water and go take a shower." Her hands ran over my legs and landed in mine.

I smiled as she pulled me by my hands. I stood up and took her in my arms. "I do love you Lily. I always will. Maybe one day it'll be right between us."

"That's the day I'm waiting for."

After we laid around all morning I put Lily in a taxi for the airport. Smiling, I winked at her and blew her a kiss as the taxi pulled away. I really felt sad to see her go, but I also knew that I haven't seen the last of her. She'll always be a part of my life, and who knows maybe once her career isn't so important to her, things might possibly be different.

I walked straight to the beach and ordered a drink, then lay in the sand. Alone.

I have a feeling I'm looking at my future.

The next few days I did nothing but drink and lay around thinking of everything and everyone in my life. When I leave here I had no idea where I was going. All I knew was that as long as I was alone, my life was simple, empty but simple.

I really did miss everyone in my life though. I missed Donna and Vicky. I do feel bad for deserting them, but I really feel like I'm doing the right thing.

I was beginning to miss Ivy more than I thought I could. Having this little fling with Lily I thought would make it easier to forget, but it just reminds me of what I lost.

I lay back in my chair and watched the sunset into the ocean, and what I wished for more than anything was that Ivy was here with me. Looking up in the sky I wondered which star was hers.

I didn't even care, I just wished upon all of them. I didn't wish for Ivy to be here, I wished that she was okay and wasn't worrying about me. I would hate for her to be sitting around thinking of me when she should be getting on with her life.

As I sat here thinking of Ivy my thoughts naturally drifted to Windy and looking up again at the sky I wondered if Sarah was taking care of her. I also wondered why she wasn't here helping me. If I ever needed her, it's now.

I set my drink down in the sand and steadied myself with the chair as I stood. I started walking to my hotel when I saw someone coming towards me, I stopped and stood still.

As the figure got closer and closer, I tried to focus my eyes. When I finally did, I thought I was going to fall over; I stood still because I couldn't move, and I just focused my attention straight ahead. I felt nervous and scared at the same time.

"I think this is yours." She held up my ring and stopped.

"Ivy, what are you doing here?"

"I came for you."

We still were standing about six feet apart. "You did." My heart was racing.

"Yes…I did."

"Ivy you don't know…"

"Yes I do. Lily is the one who told me where to find you."

"She did?" I wanted to run to her but couldn't. I couldn't move. I knew I didn't deserve her.

"Yeah she did, and I don't care. I just want you home. Mel I won't let you run away from me. I love you." She walked closer to me.

"But Ivy after all that happened, and I mean everything. How could you possibly want me?" I felt tears in my eyes. "I don't know that I could be that forgiving if you ran off and spent weeks with a former girlfriend."

"Well it's a good thing this isn't you then. Even though I don't believe you 'd give up that easy." She stared hard in my eyes.

"No. I probably wouldn't." I looked at the ground then back up into her eyes. "Ivy, I do love you. Whether you believe it or not, you never left my mind. The truth is I did all of this because of you. You don't need to settle down with someone like me. I'll only hurt you in the long run, look I already have."

"I think that's for me to decide." Then she took another step towards me and grabbed my hand. "Mel, this is for you." She put the ring in the palm of my hand and closed my fingers. "This ring is a constant reminder of my love. Now if you don't feel comfortable with that, then don't wear it. I still want you to come home though. I love you in spite of everything that's happened."

"You're sure?"

"Yes, I am."

"What about six months from now, are you going to look at me and hate me for what I've done?" Tears fell past my chin.

"Mel, all I know is that I love you. I know that under normal circumstances you would never have done this. I know you, and I know you love me. I accept what happened."

"Will it be different between us?" I stared at her.

"No...Never!"

"What about everything else Ivy. I still can't deal with what I did."

"I'll help you."

"You will?" She stepped to me and took me in her arms. I stared in her eyes "Ivy, do you think I did the right thing by Windy?"

"Mel, if it were me laying there, I would want you to do the same thing for me. So yes, I think you did the right thing. It's just going to take time for you to realize that it was for the best."

"Maybe." I looked away.

"So are you going to buy me a drink or what?"

I laughed as I wiped my tears away. "Of course."

We walked to the bar and got a couple of beers and shots then sat down. "Ivy." I looked in her eyes. "I'm sorry for everything. I'm really sorry for the note and the way I left. You deserved better than that."

"You had me scared to death Mel. I just wish that you would have called me."

"Didn't Donna talk to you?"

"She did, and what makes you think you could run away and hide from me forever?" She had a determined look on her face and her eyes never lost mine.

She put her hand on top of mine. "I love you, now take me to bed. I missed you."

I looked strangely in her eyes. "Really?"

She nodded her head yes.

"Ivy, I haven't stopped thinking about you since the last time I saw you."

"Let's go." She grinned and her eyes sparkled.

We went to her room. Once inside I threw my arms around her neck and pulled her to me. "Mmm babe, I missed your kisses."

She pulled me to the bed.

I laid on top of her and touched her cheek lightly as I stared in her eyes. "You're sure you want to do this here, right now."

"I do." Her hand ran through my hair. "I'm in paradise with the woman I love, why wouldn't I."

She kissed me and everything inside me came alive again. I lightly kissed each one of her lips, while I watched her face and unbuttoned her shirt.

I kissed her face lightly all over. "God, I missed you. I missed your body, your sweet kisses."

Waking up with Ivy in my arms I felt whole again. It didn't make me forget my pain, but it helped.

She moaned and threw her arms around me. "Good morning."

"It's a beautiful morning. Have I told you how glad I am to have you here with me."

"You not only told me, you showed me." She kissed my cheek tenderly. "Mel, I know you don't want to hear this but we really have to get back."

"Can't we stay here, I don't want to leave." I hugged her tighter.

"Mel, they're holding the reading of Windy's will until you come back."

I looked at her. "Ivy..."

"Mel, you have to."

"If I agree to go will you agree to stay for three more days?"

"Mel." She stared at me and grinned.

"Its only three days, come on. Please."

She threw her head back. "Alright."

"Great." I hugged her.

Three days with Ivy in paradise...that might be just what I needed to get myself back on track.

CHAPTER 36

❀

Sitting out in my backyard, it was as if nothing changed. My house was the same, Ivy was the same, everything was the same and I was glad. I watched her in the kitchen and smiled to myself.

My friends were the same, only better. Donna and Vicky finally brought their baby boy home from the hospital. They named him Jacob and he brought a whole new meaning into their lives.

As for me I felt the same on the outside, but my heart was torn between happiness and great loss. Losing Windy was still devastating for me, I guess it always will be, but the shocking reading of her will helped replace some of the loss I felt with great joy. It was no surprise that she left everything to her daughter, the surprise came when she left her daughter to me.

Both Ivy's life and my own has changed drastically for the better. We're a family and it's a dream I never thought I'd achieve.

It seems like all of us are entering the next part of our lives together, and it's comforting. It's good to know that we won't be struggling alone.

Turning around again I saw Ivy walking towards me carrying Koko. "Someone misses her mommy." She handed her to me as I sat staring out at the water. "Could you watch her while I run to the store?"

I reached up. "Sure."

"Donna and Vicky should be here soon."

"Alright, I'll keep an eye out for them."

"I'll be quick." She touched Koko's cheek and turned to walk away. "Ivy!"

She turned to me.

"Please be careful."

She looked at me smiling and placed her hand on my shoulder. "Always." Then kissed the top of my head.

She walked away and I turned my attention back to the water and Koko. As I sat, I lifted her up in the air. It's hard to believe she's a year old today. Windy must be so proud. Holding Koko I felt a smile come over my face and I looked into her eyes as she laughed at me.

At that moment my mind flashed back so strong I was afraid I was going to drop her.

"My God! I remember." I looked at Koko. "Koko, I remember!" Then I looked to the sky. "Sarah, I remember, I remember everything. I remember that missing day of mine." I looked around. "You're the one who brought me here, you told me that I would be needing a home. Sarah you were trying to warn me about Windy. You said that she would be needing me." I looked around. "And that wasn't sunset or sunrise around you when I saw you, that was the glow of a fire. The fire that we made love by." I started crying. "I remember holding you and kissing you, I remember it all Sarah." I felt tears running down my face and I looked down to see them falling on Koko's head.

She lay there smiling and laughing as she looked up at me, she had Windy's face. I dropped my head as tears rolled from my eyes.

I heard a noise and turned around to see that Ivy was back. I walked up to her with Koko in my arms.

"Mel what's wrong?" She rushed to me.

"I remember Ivy, that day that I freaked out and couldn't remember anything. Well it all just came back to me. I remember."

She stared at me like I was crazy. "Mel?"

I handed her Koko.

"Mel, where are you going?"

"Don't worry, I'll be back."

She stared at me. "Are you sure?"

I turned around and looked in her eyes. "I'm positive."

Then I ran to my car. I got in and drove away. I didn't know what I was thinking by just taking off, all I knew was that I needed to talk to Sarah.

I laid down on the grass just as the sun hit mid point in the sky.

I covered my face with my hands. "Oh Sarah is it happening all over again, or is what I'm remembering really what happened. Oh please don't let this be happening again, not now." I sat up and started picking at the grass. Feeling a cool breeze on the back of my neck I snapped my head around. "Sarah!"

"Hi Mel."

I went to touch her but I couldn't

"Mel, I'm here to explain. Everything that you're remembering happened."

"Sarah, how?"

She sat across from me. "Remember it was the one year anniversary of my death."

I grabbed for her hands, but mine went right through hers. "I remember."

"You don't know how bad I wanted to tell you about Windy, but I couldn't. You have to believe me Mel, I just couldn't. I tried to prepare you as best I could"

"By telling me about the property and that Windy was going to need me?"

"Yeah, and that was wrong of me. That's why you couldn't remember."

"What about us in front of the fire was that real?" My body felt cold and shaky.

"Very real. That's another thing I wasn't suppose to do. I was never supposed to make love to you. It was my entire fault Mel, everything was. I was being selfish. I saw you going on with your life and I didn't want you to forget about me and all the memories we shared."

I watched as she put her hands over her face, knowing that I couldn't console her.

"Sarah I could never forget about you, I walk with you everyday in my dreams, I carry you in my heart always." I tried to touch her again; this time I could feel her. She looked up, and then fell into my arms. "Oh Sarah I will love you until the day I draw my last breath and can finally join you."

I even felt her tears. With my finger I wiped one of her tears from her face then put my finger in my mouth tasting the salt from her body.

"Oh Mel I saw everything that you were going through because of Windy and you don't know how much I wanted to help guide you."

"I could have used it. I couldn't stand what I did and all I wanted to do was ruin my life the way I ruined everyone else's." I rubbed my eyes then pulled my hair back. "I mean running all the way to Mexico, I just lost it Sarah, the pressure got to me. My biggest regret is dragging Lily into all of this though, but all I wanted to do was forget. I should have known that it wouldn't be that easy."

"Mel, I still don't understand why you just didn't go home."

"I knew that Ivy would be her caring and understanding self and I felt like I didn't deserve that. I also thought I was going to start flipping out again and decided she'd be better off without me."

"She wouldn't have been."

I held her hand. "I'm really fortunate to have you and Ivy in my life, two people who love me so completely. Ivy really stuck with me through all of my craziness."

"You're lucky Mel, I can't believe you put her through all of that."

"She actually understood my running away, I'm not sure she understood why I took Lily with me though, but I didn't even understand that." I giggled and wiped my tears. "Lily did help me, and I think in a small way I might have helped her."

Sarah and I sat with our legs crossed facing each other while we held hands. "Sarah, you're taking care of Windy aren't you?"

"Just as well as you're taking care of her baby girl."

"She has made such a difference in my life." I looked down at the ground. "I just really hate the way things happened."

"Mel she doesn't blame you. You did exactly what she wanted. I'm just sorry it had to cause you so much heartache."

"Tell her I love her and I will do everything right by her baby. She can count on me."

"She knows. That's why she left her to you."

I smiled at her and squeezed her hand. "I think Ivy and I will be good parents."

"I think the two of you will be great parents."

I smiled. "You're amazing."

"I only want what's best for you, and Mel you can't get any better than Ivy. So don't screw it up." She laughed.

I laughed at her. "You're still so bossy."

"So tell me exactly how are Donna and Vicky? I miss them."

"They miss you, and they're great. They just adopted a baby boy and named him Jacob."

"Really?"

"Yeah, we're all becoming parents at the same time."

"Mel you have a great life ahead of you."

I looked at the ground. "Even though I'm so happy my heart aches for you Sarah."

"Don't worry about me. I'll always be here to guide you along, and as long as I can help it I'll never let you forget about me."

"I'm not worried, I could never forget my first true love. The last night that we shared together I'll carry in my heart forever."

She smiled. "I love you Mel."

"I love you Sarah."

She started to fade away. "I have to go."

"I know." I put my hand on my heart. "You'll always be with me honey."

She was gone and I was left standing, staring at her stone.

I kissed my fingers and rubbed her stone. "I love you." Then walked to my car.

On the drive home I felt like I had stepped from my past and into my future. Although I knew that Sarah would never leave my heart, or my memories, I knew that I had a new life waiting for me. Now I feel like I can totally immerse myself into that life completely. I finally feel like I came to terms with what happened to Windy and Sarah. For the first time in a long time I could honestly say I feel guilt free. I was looking forward to what was ahead of me. I wasn't forgetting about my past, I was just putting it behind me.

I walked into my backyard to see Ivy playing a wonderful hostess to Donna and Vicky as Jacob and Koko rolled around on a blanket together.

When Ivy saw me she came walking over with a beer in her hand. She handed it to me. "You okay?" She followed my eyes with hers.

"I'm better than okay." I put my arm around her waist and kissed her.

"What was that for?" She threw her arms around me.

"That was me letting you know that I am the luckiest woman on earth, and it's all because of you. Well and that little one over there." With my head I pointed to Koko, then turned back to Ivy. "I'm looking forward to spending the rest of my life with you."

She smiled. "Mel where did you go running off to?"

"It doesn't matter, all that matters is what's right here in front of us." I looked at her. "Ivy there's no more looking to the past for me, all I'm looking to is our future."

She grabbed my face gently and kissed me. "I love you."

"I love you more."

Donna and Vicky came walking over and we all threw our arms around each other and watched our children laugh and play on the blanket.

Standing there I looked up to the sky, knowing that Sarah and Windy would be taking every step into the future with us, leading us on the right path.

It was comforting.

The end

About the Author

Kelly A. Zarembski lives in Cleveland, Ohio. She is currently working on her second novel. If you enjoyed *Visions of Sarah* why not write the author and tell her so. You may e-mail her at: KAZ000@MSN.COM.

0-595-21962-4

Printed in the United States
902100005B